ONE WEEK

ONE WEEK

Zoey Derrick

First of all: Thank you to my loving and extremely supportive family! Without all of your help, doing what I love wouldn't be possible. So THANK YOU!!

Rachel - Girl, there are no where near enough words in the English language to express the undying thanks I have for you. You've been there EVERY Step of this wild and crazy journey and I cannot thank you enough!!

Mandy and the BEAUTIFUL ladies at RAW BOOKS! Mandy - thank you for putting up with me, for reading and for editing One Week. You've been an amazing inspiration! Ladies - thank you for being the first in line to read my books. Your love of my writing keeps me going every day!

Reggie, Gena, Kasi, and Eva - Thank you, from the bottom of my heart for helping me spread my wings!

Jenna and Sean - Your support, love and friendship mean the WORLD to me! Thank you for being there!!

Angel - You're seriously my angel of AWESOME! Thank you for being an amazing friend.

E. L. James, Thank you for being an amazing inspiration in all things! Sending Love

FANS! OMG I can't thank you all enough for reading my work, loving my stories and more than anything, you never ending love and support! Without you, I wouldn't be here writing, and doing what I Love!

XXOO!

For Laurie -

You haven't even begin to grasp how much you've helped my research, experience and explorations for this story, so this seems a minor thanks in comparison to the love and gratitude I feel towards you. All my Love! *HUGS**SMOOOOCHES*

1

You're Going...

"Cotah, what happens in Vegas, stays in Vegas." Rachel places her hands on my shoulders, like she is ready to shake some common sense into me.

"Rach, seriously? I can't."

"Why not? You have nothing holding you here. Nothing," she says with emphasis. "He's an idiot. He gave up a good, sure thing for some ho from the wrong side of the tracks. You need to get over it, and Vegas is a great place to do just that." Rachel knows what to say to crawl under my skin.

Jason and I broke up only a couple weeks ago. When I caught him in the bathroom, during our rehearsal dinner, with that bitch Jessica. I will never forget that night, and right now I feel as though I will never get over it.

Jason and I had been together since our junior year in high school. Twelve years together, and he wasted it sticking his dick in some chick two nights before our wedding.

"I am over it," I blurt out, but Rachel's face scrunches up at me and I know she can tell I'm lying.

"Don't give me that bullshit. When was the last time you even left the house?"

"Uh, this morning. I'm here aren't I?"

"Jesus, Cotah, your house is right next door. Nice try."

"I go to work, don't I?"

"Oh hell, so what? We all do that." She finally lets go of my arms and goes into the kitchen. She grabs a beer from the fridge, pops the top and slides it across the counter to me. She returns to the fridge to grab one for herself. I look at my watch; it's ten thirty in the morning. "Seriously. We're going. You, me and Mandy; no ifs, ands or buts about it." She takes a drink of her beer. "We leave tomorrow morning."

"What?" I freeze as the beer spews from my mouth. "Rach, I can't, I have to work tomorrow."

"Fuck that place, tell them you quit."

"Oh yeah, then what the hell am I going to do when we get back?" Rachel just shrugs and gives me a look that says who-gives-a-flying-fuck.

"Worry about it when we get back. Hell Cotah, you have no bills, you live in your grandmother's house which she left you free and clear. I know damn well you have money in the bank, otherwise you'd be working more than twenty-five hours a week at some lame pizza joint in the middle of Podunk fucking nowhere."

She's right, of course. My grandmother left me a small fortune when she died a little over a year ago. I have no family left anymore, and it is just me, myself and I. Lest we forget Mandy and Rachel; two of the only people in this world that mean anything to me.

"Dacotah, you've never done anything for yourself. You've always done everything for everyone else. It's time to give up on doing things for everyone, and take action for yourself. Now, let's go do this and have a great time."

She has a point. Up until my grandmother died, I'd spent the previous two years taking care of her and working when I could. Maybe it is my fault that Jason cheated on me; I was never around, we hardly ever went out and did anything. He was always so supportive, but in hindsight, I understand why.

By supporting me, he was able to hide the fact that he was cheating on me. After what happened, I'm certain Jessica wasn't the first woman he's cheated with.

"You're twenty-eight years old, you're single, and you have nothing to lose but the chance to have a great time."

"Rachel, I…"

"Stop thinking about it. Go home, pack up some clothes, and get ready to go. Mandy and I will be at your house tomorrow morning at seven; we'll drive into Minneapolis and hop a plane to Vegas. It'll be Friday and we will get there in plenty of time to start partying it up on the strip."

"Who's paying for all this?"

She gives me a half smile. "I paid for your airfare. We'll have to split the cost of the room, and each pay for our own expenses."

"What happens if I don't go?"

"Then I'm out three hundred bucks on your non-refundable ticket."

There it is, the guilt trip that Rachel is notorious for. "I'll pay for my ticket."

"I'd rather you just come with us." She takes a big long chug of her beer then crushes the can in her hand and throws it away. I roll my eyes.

Rachel is a beautiful girl, but redneck is the best word to describe her. She has long chocolate brown hair, brown eyes, and an amazing body. Years of throwing bales of hay around the barn have done her proud. She's skinny as a rail, looks great in anything she wears and has no problems getting laid. She is about five-seven and her waist looks tiny when she stands next to me.

I'm about five-eight, with long dirty blond hair, blue eyes, and hips that seem to go on for days and complete the hour glass figure that I have. I'm not entirely overweight, but I love my curves. I wasn't always like this, I used to be Rachel skinny, but over the years, my hips have gotten a little wider, my butt a little rounder and my boobs, well, let's just say that they are more than a good handful.

"Well?" Rachel interrupts my thoughts.

"Well, what?" I snap, unintentionally. Thinking about my weight and my own insecurities always makes me edgy. But Rachel doesn't flinch at my tone.

"You're still standing here."

"Did you want me to leave?" I ask her, deadpan.

"Only if you're going to go pack. Otherwise, you can stand here until I convince you to go."

Ugh! I finally realize what's the harm in going? I can call Pete and tell him that I need to take a few days off. In fact, I would've been doing just that anyway if I hadn't walked out on Jason. It's only a week. She can get it out of her system, and leave me alone about getting on with my life.

I put my beer down on the counter. I've taken maybe three sips of it. Beer is not my favorite, especially this early in the morning.

I turn on my heels and walk out the front door. Behind me Rachel squeals with delight and I can hear her jumping up and down as the screen door slams shut.

I've been trying for more than three hours to find clothes to take to Vegas, but I have nothing. Everything I own either looks frumpy or smells like a pizza joint, or they're old, faded, and in less desirable condition. I do have two decent pairs of jeans and a couple of tops, but that's it. I wonder if Rachel and Mandy wouldn't mind a shopping trip in Vegas. In fact, I know Mandy would be delighted. She's a shopaholic and I have no doubt that shopping is already on the agenda.

Around two, I call Pete, my boss. "Hey Pete, it's Dacotah."

"What's up?" Pete's a really nice guy; he's owned that restaurant since just out of high school when his dad retired.

"I need to take the next week off."

"Uh, Dacotah, you're not on the schedule for next week."

"What?" I can't hide the shock, Rachel.

"You were, um…" he hesitates long enough for me to realize what he is implying without saying it and it all makes sense now. I was supposed to be on my honeymoon this week.

"You don't need me to come in, do you?" I ask in vain as I know the answer to the question.

"Nope, we're all set here," he says back, avoiding the obvious.

"I get it, okay, thanks Pete."

"No problem." He hangs up.

"Well, I guess I won't be losing my job by running away to Vegas." There is a disappointed feeling that comes with the call and knowing that my last excuse has run out. I realize that I'd been hoping that Pete would need me this week so I could stay. What's the point in staying?

I pack up the few things that I have to take with me, get my bathroom stuff together, at least the stuff I won't need in the morning before we leave, and I'm about to head downstairs, with my suitcase in tow, when the doorbell rings. I pause. Rachel or Mandy would just walk right in; they both have keys, not that I lock the door often.

The suitcase clatters loudly behind me as it slides down each step. I'm thankful that I have a decent small, modern suitcase. Something I'd bought in preparation for going to Florida for our supposed honeymoon. When I reach the bottom of the steps, I pull the suitcase near the door and look through the window to see who is ringing my doorbell for the third time.

"Shit," I reach for the knob and swing the door wide open, nearly knocking my suitcase over. "What the fuck are you doing here?"

2

Life Sucks...

"Hi Dacotah, it's nice to see you again."

"Cut the bullshit Jessica, what the fuck do you want?" I lean into the jamb of the door and cross my arms. I look at her, trying hard to see what Jason could have possibly seen in her and I don't get it. She is not unattractive, but her clothes are all black, her make-up is dark, she has a nose and eyebrow ring and it is not at all unattractive on her. I remember her from our high school days and she was really pretty, then something happened, I don't know what, but the next year at school she showed up looking like this.

"I just came to talk."

"And what, you expected me to welcome you with open arms and doors? Forget it. Nothing you can say..."

"I'm pregnant."

Well fuck. "So what? What does that have to do with me?"

"He left me," she breathes and I can see tears welling in her eyes.

All I can do is shake my head. "I can't say that I'm surprised. It took him nearly six years to propose to me, then another four for us to actually start planning a wedding. The fact that he was fucking you, tells me the reason why he hesitated for so long."

"Dacotah, I didn't know. I didn't know you and him were still together." I roll my eyes. "He told me that you'd broken up."

There is a deep sincerity in her words and in her eyes, and for some strange reason, I believe her. "It doesn't matter. It's over now as far as I'm concerned."

She nods solemnly at me. "I just came to apologize to you. I'm sorry, if I'd known…"

I put my hand up to silence her. "What's done is done." But I don't let her apologize. I don't want to hear it, not from her. Jason maybe, but not her. I pull myself away from the door jamb and reach for the door. "Good luck, Jessica," I say and close the door. Falling against it then sliding down to the floor.

There is a sudden rush of relief that comes with the realization that Jason really is a douche. Then the feeling of stupidity for even thinking he was worth a damn. But then again, there were a lot of good years between us, years that I can't take back. Though I'm sure I don't want to take them back. I learned so much during our time together. Stuff that I don't want to unlearn. They're also years that I wasted on someone who didn't want me in the ways I needed him.

I don't know how long I sit there against the door, but all of a sudden the doorbell rings again. "What the fuck?" I growl.

"Cotah, open the door."

Jesus, what the hell is this? I stand up, throwing the door open.

"Get the hell away from my house," I shout.

"Don't be like that, sugar."

"Really? Are you kidding me right now, Jason? I told you I never wanted to see your face again. And I meant it."

"Please Cotah, I'm sorry. I came to apologize, to work this out."

The rage boils in my blood and I want so badly to hit something. "You gave up that chance a long time ago," I shout through gritted teeth.

"You're not exactly innocent in all this," he says, dead-pan.

"What the hell is that supposed to mean?" I'm dying to hear this one.

"Well, you know, you were never there for me, probably getting it from somewhere else too."

Shock. I scowl at him; I know the look isn't as angry as I feel right now. "Excuse me? What did you just say?" My teeth are clinched together, my hands balling into fists and I take a step closer to him. Now standing directly in the doorway, about two feet away from him, poised to knock his ass out. "I've never, in my life, slept with anyone but you. Regardless of how boring it was. You come to MY house to accuse ME of cheating on you? Let me tell you somethin', asshole. Your girlfriend was here tonight, apologizing to me because you broke up with me because of her. Said you lied to her about us being together, and now that she's pregnant, you leave her." I am shouting at this point. "If you think, for one goddamm second that I will come back to you like nothing happened, you need your head examined." I take two steps backwards, reaching for the door. "Get off my property, and never come back here again!" I slam the door in his face and quickly lock it.

"You stupid bitch. I was the best thing that ever happened to you. You're going to regret this." He's banging on the door as he says this and I don't care. I need to get out of here, away from Frederic, and away from Jason. More importantly, I need to figure out a way to change things in my own life. A week in Vegas is exactly what I need.

After a couple of minutes he finally stops screaming for my attention and I hear him get into his car and drive away. Thank god.

I peak through the curtains covering the window in the door, just to make sure he really is gone. When I don't see him or his car, I bolt out of the front door, straight for Rachel's house next door. I barge in, like always. She is standing in the kitchen making something on the stove. "Alright, I'll go."

She turns around to look at me. Pity on her face. Nothing happens in this town without everyone else finding out about it. "Are you alright?" She asks with real concern in her voice. I don't answer her question with more than a shake of my head. "Want to stay here tonight?" I nod. She walks around the counter and hugs me. I hug her back, I don't say anything and neither does she. She knows that I'm doing my best to get over him and that I don't need or want a pity party. "Mandy will be here soon. Should we pack up the car and leave tonight? We can stay in Minneapolis, near the airport."

I nod and she laughs a little. "Well alright then. Let's go get your stuff."

While we're getting my stuff and locking up the house, I don't say much to Rachel. She is content to let it be that way and I'm okay with that too. Rachel knows me better than anyone, maybe even myself, but Jason has crossed the line and I'm done. As we walk back toward her house I say, "You wanna know something, Rachel?"

"What's that?"

"Right now, I don't care if I ever come back here." She stops at my words and grabs my arm.

"Don't say that, I'd miss you like crazy."

I give her a half smile. "I'd miss you too, but after he showed up at my house tonight, it reminded me that no matter what I do, where I go, I will constantly be reminded that he's here. That he could show up anywhere I go, or I'll see him from a distance." I take a deep breath. "Or see her."

"Let's do this. Let's get away from here for a while and then see what happens. This is your home, Cotah; you have every right to be here." She looks at me, sadness in her eyes at the idea that I might not come back. But I can tell from her tone that she would be more understanding if it were really the case.

I shrug. "Who knows, it's just all so complicated and...stupid. I feel so stupid because I fell for it, because I was duped by him. Then she shows up at my door..."

"Wait, what? You didn't tell me that?"

I nod. "Sometime before he did. She came to apologize, said she didn't know and that he left her. Which is why, I'm sure, he showed up at my house trying to get me back, but what he didn't realize is that she'd been here and told me her secret." Rachel looks at me wide eyed and expectant. "She's pregnant."

It doesn't take long for Rachel's reply, "I knew he was a jackass." She tugs on my arm, pulling me towards her house. Just as we reach the front door, Mandy pulls up.

"Hey Bitches!" she shouts as she honks her horn.

"Change of plans," Rachel shouts back as Mandy turns off the car.

"What? No way, we're fucking going to Vegas, damn it." Mandy says as she climbs out of the car. She's a chubby girl with round cheeks, and bright red hair but she doesn't let her weight hold her back. She's absolutely gorgeous in her own way. Completely feminine when you compare her to me and Rachel. Not to mention the fact that she's extremely popular with the guys and can always be found at Wilson's, the local bar.

"Yes, Mandy, we're going to Vegas, we're just leaving right now."

I love Mandy for her free spirited ways. She can change plans at the drop of a dime and not think twice about it. "What the hell are we waiting for then, let's go?"

Within twenty minutes, we're locking up Rachel's house. I cleaned up her kitchen from the dinner she was making and never ate, while Mandy loaded up the bags into her Tahoe. Living in a small town hasn't hindered Mandy from making a career for herself. After she graduated from college, she started working at a tiny law firm on Main Street and does pretty well for herself. You wouldn't think this tiny town of about eleven hundred people in a county of about forty-four thousand, would need a law firm, but apparently there are a lot of divorces and drunks who need good attorneys.

On the drive to Minneapolis, we blast the tunes, go a little too fast, and enjoy the drive. When we get near the airport, it is about eight at night and we're all starving. We grab a bite to eat at the Mall of America and then get a hotel room.

Before I know it, we're boarding an airplane and headed to Vegas. As soon as we take off, for the first time in my life, I feel free and ready for anything.

3

Holy Crap...

I've never been to Vegas, or really anywhere for that matter. Minneapolis - of course, Milwaukee, Green Bay, Chicago and other places within a reasonable driving distance from Frederic, but Las Vegas is - wow. Las Vegas is huge. Bigger than anything I've ever seen in the movies. The buildings are massive and the amount of people wandering around is insane. It is the middle of May and it feels like a sauna outside compared to what we left back in Wisconsin, but it is nice to feel the warm air.

We pile, wide eyed, into a cab from the airport to our hotel, Planet Hollywood, where we will be right in the heart of Vegas. Mandy, being the crazy shopaholic that she is, quickly noticed my light packing and then my clothes this morning. After that she demanded that we go shopping first thing.

So, after a rather long line downstairs checking into our hotel, it is now one thirty in the afternoon and Vegas awaits.

We head downstairs to the Miracle Mile shops. It is a mall inside of the hotel with a wide variety of clothing stores, little souvenir boutiques and restaurants. But what quickly captures my attention are the massive drinks that people are walking around with. When I say massive, I saw a guy walking by with something that looked like a hookah and was nearly as tall as he was.

"We've got to get some of those," I blurt out. I'm ready to have a good time and to do that I need alcohol, and lots of it.

We finally find a kiosk that sells the massive drinks. Everything from an oversized martini and margarita glasses, to light-up twelve to thirty-six inch tall souvenir cups that can be filled with your choice of alcohol and flavoring; everything from strawberry to bubble gum. Mandy goes for the pink bubble gum because it matches her outfit. I roll my eyes. Rachel goes for the one shaped like a man wearing a speedo and while I originally wanted the guitar filled with eighty-eight ounces of a frozen alcoholic concoction, I settle instead for the light-up eighteen inch cup. It has a lid and a shoulder strap so I don't always have to carry it. I'm blown away by how cheap they are, considering their content. The best part of all- the refills are less than ten dollars. No matter, it will get me drunk eventually.

Once we have our drinks, we head into a restaurant in the mall. It actually looks pretty upscale; at least the black and chrome decor with ultra-low lighting gives off that vibe. Mandy goes to the hostess and gives her our name, and then we wait. I start to look around, people watching.

There are several groups of either all guys or all girls milling about. The girls are excited over the stores and the guys, well, they're watching the girls, making comments as they pass the groups of women.

There are a few couples, walking hand in hand, and my stomach turns. A feeling of emptiness washes over me as I remember the way Jason and I were together back in our prime. We were always hanging on each other and we were never more than six inches apart when we walked anywhere.

But my musings about being lonely and single are cut off when a very well dressed man comes into my line of sight. He's wearing a gunmetal grey suit, black shirt and silky black tie. His hair is dark brown, long and pulled back. His eyes are the same brown as his hair. He has a well-kept goatee, and a physique that makes my mouth water. I feel Rachel and Mandy nudge me, vying for my attention, but I can't seem to pull my eyes away from him. Then he looks at me. Square in the eyes and I'm transfixed further by what I see. He's not disgusted that I'm staring at him, actually there is a hint of intrigue in his eyes, but Rachel breaks it by pulling my arm. "Our table's ready."

I finally blink, breaking the trance and I know I blush as red as a cherry. I'm thankful for Rachel's distraction.

Once we sit down, Mandy is quick to point out my distraction. "What was that all about?" Her question makes me blush again and I find myself hiding behind my menu. "Cotah?" She says like a mother scolding a child.

"Nothing, it was just..." How can I even describe the Adonis that I just saw?

"Him?" I look out from behind my menu at Rachel, who is looking toward the bar. I follow her line of sight and sitting at the bar opposite of us is him and I want to run away.

"Can we go eat somewhere else?" I breathe.

"Hell no. Suck it up, buttercup. He's a damn fine looking man."

"Rachel," I scoff and she laughs. "Stop looking at him."

"Oh don't worry; he's not looking at me. He is looking right at you." Rachel isn't hindered by natural awkwardness, no, if she wants something, she goes after it and it doesn't matter if it is for herself or someone else. If I told her I wanted his phone number, she'd walk right over to him, tell him something that I didn't actually say, and come back with his phone number.

"Jesus, seriously?" I snap. "Don't even think about it, Rachel. You either, Mandy." I look at both of them, trying desperately to figure out a way to distract them. "Enough about him, so what's our plan, you know, after lunch?"

The prospect of either partying or shopping has Mandy's interest immediately and the two of them are off on their discussions. Steeling myself, I look in the direction of the man who has me stupid just looking at him. He is there, at the bar, talking with the bartender, but I watch as he keeps peeking in my direction, checking to see if I'm looking at him. He smiles very casually and I hide, once again, behind my menu.

Finally the waitress comes to the table, tells us about the special of the day and takes our drink orders. Despite the fact that we all have these overly large cups already in front of us, we all order a different drink. She leaves the table and I catch him looking at me again. He looks like a hunter, watching his prey, biding his time for that precise moment to strike.

Somewhere around our entrees, Orion, as I've named him, leaves the bar. I try to watch where he goes, but he disappears behind a wall and I can no longer see him. I feel a stab of disappointment and then relief. We eat, talk about going shopping and then hitting the strip tonight, wandering around with the crowds, maybe walking up to catch the pirate show or even the fountains. I'm distracted again as this group of girls comes into the restaurant and they're all carrying Eiffel Tower shaped glasses of alcohol, though theirs are mostly empty, and I make a vow to get one for myself, eventually.

When the waitress brings us our check she hands us an envelope, or rather me. "I was told to give this to you," she says and I take it from her. I know full well that it's from the bartender, compliments of Orion. The girls get all giddy about it and demand that I open it before the waitress leaves with our money.

"Seriously, you guys are like little kids in a candy store who don't know that too much candy will make you feel like shit." I give them a half assed smile and I tear into the envelope. Inside are three tickets. I pull them out and stamped across the top are the letters V.I.P. Below that, it says Marquee, Cosmopolitan. I flip over one of the tickets and read, "All inclusive cabana, all you can eat and drink included, up to 8 hours."

"Holy crap," I utter as I hand a ticket to each of them. They both inspect the ticket and look skeptical. I look in the envelope and find a small piece of paper inside. I pull it out. The handwriting is elegantly masculine and I have a pretty good feeling that the bartender didn't write this.

Bring your friends, have a good time, enjoy yourself, and don't forget to bring your swimsuits.

I show the note to Rachel, who then hands it to Mandy. "What are we waiting for?" Mandy says as her eyes light up. I blush again. "What?" she says, shrugging at me, wondering what my problem is.

"I don't have a suit."

"Oh for god's sake, let's get out of here then." Mandy stands just as the waitress comes back with our cards and change. We head straight for the shop down the hall that is full of swimsuits.

4

Alcohol and Vegas...

We spend so much time shopping that by the time we are done, it is nearly seven in the evening. Given the lateness and our willingness to take advantage of our V.I.P. Passes to Marquee, we decide to return to our room, change and spend the night on the strip. Tomorrow, sometime, we will head over to the Cosmopolitan and take advantage of our passes and the sunshine. Mandy did some research on her phone while she was busy forcing me to try on clothes, and she discovered that Marquee is a day and night club. Offering DJ's and sunshine during the day and a club atmosphere at night.

The hotel is connected directly to the Miracle Mile Shopping center by way of the casino. There are so many people milling about, sitting at tables or slot machines and the noise is insane, but exciting. I'd tried, futilely, to convince Mandy and Rachel to just hang out in the hotel, but there is so much to do and they told me no. So here we are on the strip. The sun is hanging low in the sky but the buildings make it seem like nighttime along the street and the party is hopping like nothing I've ever seen before. Even the State Fair has nothing on this crowd.

The people are milling about, drinking from their over-sized drink cups. I do the same realizing very quickly that I've managed to empty mine.

I stand along the railing and I can see a sea of heads bobbing up and down as they walk. To my right is the Eiffel Tower of Paris, across the street I can see the fountains spraying and dancing to music that I can't hear. You can barely make out the Bellagio Hotel from here because next to it is a sleekly designed Cosmopolitan Hotel. Following that line to the opposite side of the street, my eyes fixate on New York New York. It looks like the city skyline that you see in pictures, only there are tracks and a roller coaster running through it.

Deciding to forego my Eiffel Tower glass for now, I say, "Let's go to New York."

"What?" Rachel says and I point in the direction of the hotel. Rachel looks at Mandy and they both shrug and we set off, down the escalator and onto Las Vegas Boulevard. We walk south until we get to Tropicana Avenue and then cross Las Vegas Boulevard and into New York New York. As we step into the air conditioned monstrosity, I'm sweating so I pull my hair up into a messy bun, hoping to cool off faster.

No sooner than we enter do we find a stand offering more alcohol and Rachel and Mandy rush toward it, but I'm in awe of the bar we've come in near and I grab them and point.

"No way!" They both shout in excitement. "Let's go," Rachel says and we walk into Coyote Ugly.

The bar is hopping despite the early evening hour, and mostly contains men. I quickly see why when the song, 'Devil Went Down to Georgia' starts to play and everyone's attention is diverted to the bar. There are four girls dancing on it, much the way they did in the movie, and the crowd, including Rachel and myself, go nuts with excitement.

When you come from a small town that requires no less than a forty minute drive to a Walmart, seeing this is overwhelming and very exciting.

Once the ladies have finished their dancing, we head for the bar and order more alcohol. Rachel, I can tell, is bound and determined to get me as drunk as I can be, and I'm perfectly okay with that. We end up with three mixed drinks, six shots, and three beers. It doesn't take us long to dive in. The first round of shots is none other than tequila, complete with salt and limes. We all lick our hands, pour the salt and hold up our shot glasses and in unison we say, "Here's to you, here's to me, the best of friends we'll always be, and if we ever disagree, fuck you, and here's to me." I lick my hand and my face scrunches at the salty taste, but I down the shot and immediately place the lime in my mouth.

"Ugh, now I remember why I hate tequila," I say as my tongue and stomach process its new contents. To help wash it down, I drink some of my- whatever It Is- and it helps, but the drink is sweeter than I expect. No matter, it tastes good. We don't linger too much with the next set of shots which we figure out are jager bombs but the reddish brown hue of Red Bull and Jager being mixed together. This time we all just clink glasses. "To a great week in Vegas," I say and we down the shots and follow it with a reach for our beers.

The three of us start to dance to the music on the small dance floor in the back of the bar. David Guetta's Sexy Bitch starts to play and I close my eyes, dancing to the beat. I'm not a bad dancer, but I won't be winning any competitions any time soon. Lost in the music, I barely notice the crowd until suddenly I feel strong hands on my hips, swaying with me to the music. I peek through slits in my eyes, looking for confirmation from Rachel or Mandy that the person touching me isn't a total creep.

They've both stopped dancing and are staring blankly at the man behind me, and I know immediately who it is. It's Orion, from the restaurant this afternoon. So I continue moving, ignoring their faces. I work my hips back and forth and I can feel his fingers tighten against my hips as I inch closer to him and his crotch. After the shot of tequila, followed by the Jager bomb, the sickly sweet mixed drink, the beer and my monstrous frozen drink; I'm buzzed enough to no longer care. This man doesn't know me, or I him, but there is nothing wrong with a little fun.

The music quiets just as I make contact with his crotch and his fingers tighten against my hips at the same time his breath hisses through his teeth. I open my eyes and smile at Rachel and Mandy who seemed to have recovered from their dumbstruck moment. The music morphs into Toni Braxton's "You're Making Me High" and immediately my hips start to flick against him with the beat. His fingers tighten once again against my hips and now I can feel him moving with me. His hands move off my hips, one comes around to my stomach, splayed flat as he pushes me back against him and I can feel it now; he's enjoying this almost as much as I am. He is sporting an erection and feeling it against my ass spurs me on. I reach back, grabbing his hips to steady myself from the swimming feeling going on inside my mind, I'm not sure I can concentrate on staying upright anymore. His other hand is gliding along my arm toward my shoulder. The halter top I'm wearing leaves very little to the imagination and feeling his touch against my skin is like fire, leaving goose bumps in its wake.

I feel his hand come across my collar bone and gently press against my neck and jaw, possessing me, forcing me to put my head back onto his shoulder as we continue to sway to the music. His erection is pressed hard against my backside and I can't quite judge the size of it, but it is all I can think about until he whispers into my ear. "You're a bad girl." I feel a strong sense of authority in his voice and my knees weaken at the sexy raspiness of it. Strong, yet it's sweet.

The song winds down and I'm so caught up in his words, and our dance, that it takes a minute to realize we've stopped moving and that his hands are missing from my body. Realizing that I'm standing there all alone, I turn around, trying desperately to see him, but I can't, not over the crowd and I'm disappointed that he's left. Then immediately I realize that I've just had this extremely intimate dance with a man and I have no idea who he is.

Mandy and Rachel are on me in a nanosecond after he disappears. "Ohmigod Dacotah, what the hell was that?" Rachel asks, rather sharply.

I can hardly comprehend my thoughts long enough to even try and answer her.

Mandy helps, "Come on, let's get out of here."

I'm so dazed by what just happened that I barely realize that they're pulling me from the bar and into the hallway. Though it is quieter out here, you can hear the sounds of the casino and people shouting and having their own good time. Both Rachel and Mandy come and stand in front of me. "Are you alright?" Rachel asks.

"Yeah— I'm just, I don't know, that was just a really strange experience."

"What did he say to you?"

His words radiate shivers of promises across my skin; *you're a bad girl.* I'm not sure I want to share the specifics with these two, but their expectant looks tell me that I'm not going to get off that easily. "Something about being a bad girl."

I watch as confusion washes over their faces and they look at each other for a long couple of seconds then shrug and look back at me for more information.

"Jeez guys, all we did was dance." I can still feel him with his hand on my neck and stomach, holding my body to his.

"But damn it, he's fucking hot," Mandy spouts off as she takes my hand, pulling me towards the Big Chill, and another frozen drink. "Did he tell you his name?" I bite my lip and shake my head. "Well whatever he's after, go for it," Rachel offers.

"Rachel!" I scoff at her words.

She turns to me. "Think about it, Dacotah. What have you got to lose? You're here for a week, when it's done and over with you go back to Wisconsin like nothing ever happened. I say, if you run into him again, though unlikely," her brows knit together as she is no doubt thinking the same thing that I am, "Take him up on whatever he's offering."

"Rachel Lynn! You dirty whore." I bump my shoulder with hers and she laughs. "I'm not the type for casual sex."

"Sure you are, Cotah; you've just never tried it." I make a face at Mandy's words.

Both she and Rachel are far from the promiscuous type, but they're unafraid of what they want. For me, sex isn't anything spectacular. Which, again, is why I can't understand Jessica's appeal to Jason? I shiver at the memory of them in the bathroom together. Then I remember that aside from the mortification I felt at seeing her bent over the counter with him pounding in from behind her, the horror quickly turned to jealousy. He'd never done anything like that with me.

"Considering Jason is the only man I've ever been with, I'm sure you can see where my ability for casual sexual relationships is lacking." They both shrug at me and I roll my eyes.

"There is always a first time for everything." Rachel grabs her newly filled drink from the counter. Next comes mine and I grab it off the counter, forgetting to mix it up I take a big long pull on the straw and get a huge shot of tequila down my throat and my face scrunches up both at the alcohol and at the realization that I will likely never see him again.

"What's the point? I'm never gonna see him again."

"Okay, first of all, you don't know that. Second of all, I highly doubt he is the type to frequent Coyote Ugly of all places, and third, you've already seen him twice and we've been in Vegas all of—" she looks at her watch "— nine hours with over a week to go," Rachel says and we start walking back toward the door we came in.

"Don't hold your breath," I mumble.

"We still have the tickets that he gave us. Maybe there was a reason he sent you those," Mandy is quick to point out.

"So, just because we have them, doesn't mean we have to use them," I say back.

"Fuck that, we're using them, and we should use 'em right now."

"No way, not tonight. Let's use them tomorrow, hell Mandy, she bought a new suit." Rachel and Mandy both laugh and suddenly Mandy and Rachel's idea of a swimsuit makes me feel self-conscious.

"Alright, fine, but let's talk about it later. Let's find something else to do."

5

Extravagant Gestures...

We decide not to leave New York New York and we wander around for a while. We find the entrance to the roller coaster but the line is ridiculously long and the alcohol I've consumed is really starting to go to my head, so we skip it and eventually head back to Planet Hollywood. We're not ready to turn in so we head into the casino. It's packed, but we quickly find a spot at one of the craps tables. Somehow I managed to get pushed towards the head of the table where the roller stands and somehow, I manage to become his lucky charm. Blowing on his dice before he tosses it and even though I have no idea what's going on, the guy throwing the dice gets excited no matter what.

By about the tenth roll, I start to feel a strange tingling sensation across my skin. I shrug it off as effects of the alcohol. Since we have been standing around the table, there has been a constant free flow of alcohol going down my throat and my head is starting to swim.

Right before I feel a light touch on the small of my back, the hair along my arms starts to stand on end and as soon as the contact is made that electricity sparks and I know immediately that it's him. Orion. He's standing behind me, his hand on my back and when I try to turn around, he stops me. "Keep watching."

I look at Rachel, who is opposite me, for confirmation that he is really the one standing behind me and her wide eyes tell me that I'm right. When the guy goes to roll again, Orion shifts, arches around me and places what I can only assume to be a rather large bet on the table. "Mind if I roll?" I hear him ask the guy who looks from the table to him, to me, and back to the table. Reluctantly he hands over the dice and Orion steps to the head of the table. He places the dice in front of my face. "Blow." I obey, but I am lost in the deep dark chocolate of his eyes. He doesn't look away from me as he tosses the dice down the table.

I hear collective gasps and it is suddenly so quiet in the casino that I can hear the dice hit the table, and then the wall before they bounce back onto the table. All the while his eyes never leave mine and a connection is made between us. The warm tingling sensation I felt when he walked up spreads across my body and the table erupts into cheers. He is the first to break it and look along the table.

"Sir, how would you like your payout?" the dealer asks Orion who then looks at me.

"What room number are you staying in?"

"What— oh, um, seventeen seventeen." Why would he ask me that?

"Have it credited to the lady's room, plus the bet."

"Yes, Sir," the dealer says and the ominous man in the suit that's been walking between the tables all night makes a note of it.

"Why—?" All comprehensible speech is gone and I can't even think about what I was going to ask when he holds his hand out for me, and unthinking, I give him mine.

He turns my hand over and kisses my knuckles. He's looking at me, square in the eyes. "You really are a lucky charm." He smirks, and just like that, he's gone, just like in the restaurant and the bar, and the crowd that has surrounded the table makes it impossible for me to see where he went.

"Ma'am?"

"What?" I say, slightly irritated as I try and follow Orion's exit.

"Ma'am, here is your claim ticket. You'll need this when you check out, or cash out."

"Oh," I breathe, taking the slip from him. Rachel and Mandy pull me away from the table.

"Holy shit! That was intense. Do you have any idea how much his bet was?" Rachel asks me.

"Um, no. I wasn't paying attention."

"That's probably a damn good thing, otherwise you would've really been freaking out."

"I was freaking out. Just looking at him freaked me out," I say back to Rachel, but she doesn't falter.

"Look at the ticket he gave you," Mandy says and gives me an all knowing smile.

I look at it.

Bet: $100,000.00

Credit to Room #: 1717

Amount of Credit: $300,000.00

"HOLY SHIT!" I shout and damn near pass out.

6

Rebel, yeah right...

"I can't keep this," I tell both of them as we enter the bar off of the casino, and the one that stands in the way of our hotel room. At this point, I am most certainly going to drink until I'm stumbling drunk. We saddle up to the bar and I order another Jager bomb and a long island. I don't pay much attention to Rachel and Mandy as they're both chattering on about the money and what I should do with it. "I'm not going to do anything with it. Tomorrow morning, before you two go to Marquee, I'm going to have…"

"You don't even know his name," Rachel blurts before taking a sip of her own drink.

"So what? I didn't earn that money; it is his, not mine, or either one of yours." I down my Jager bomb and drink about half of my Long Island, then signal to the bartender for another round.

"At least get an explanation out of him. Find out why he did it before you go off halfcocked and give it back to him. It's probably best not to insult him," Mandy says and she has a point. Though I could probably just check out of the hotel without actually claiming the money and if he refuses it, I might have to do just that.

"Who bets a hundred grand?" I mumble.

"He does apparently." Rachel's eyebrows shoot up in a mock hubba hubba kind of way.

"If he has that kind of money, why is he chasing after me?" I say and both Mandy and Rachel look like they want to smack the shit out of me, but they don't argue with me because I can see it in their faces too. Not that there might not be anything special about me, but rather the fact that I'm not wealthy, I don't wear designer clothes and I certainly haven't done anything that would garner the attention of someone who has the means and ability to drop a hundred grand on a bet.

It doesn't take long before I become very light headed and tipsy. Mandy and Rachel help me up to the room and tuck me in. Neither one of them says anything about my binge drinking toward the end of the night and for that, I'm eternally grateful.

It takes all of two minutes in bed before I pass out with thoughts of Orion, our dancing and silent vows to give him back his money filling my mind.

7

Hangover Cure...

"You know what the best way to cure a hangover is?" Rachel says as we walk up to the entrance of the Marquee.

"Alcohol," Mandy and I say together.

Last night's casino escapade goes unmentioned throughout the morning and while I didn't throw up from my drinking binge, the sunglasses are a necessity, at least for right now. As we approach Marquee, there is a tall man, at least six five or six six with muscles so big you can see the blood vessels coming through his tight shirt standing at the door. Rachel lets out a whistle and the bouncer smiles at her. "Ladies?" he says in a very deep sexy voice.

"We were given these?" I tell him as I hand him the three tickets from the restaurant yesterday.

"Absolutely." He reaches for a button on the cord that stretches from his ear to his waist band. "Cabana one," he says and almost immediately someone is opening the door behind him.

"Ladies." A very attractive leggy blond comes through the door wearing a very short sequined black cocktail dress and matching pumps. "Follow me."

Bouncer dude unhooks the rope and the blond ushers us inside. The three of us follow behind her dutifully, none of us saying a word, but we exchange glances that are full of questions, unanswered questions that will likely remain unanswered.

We walk for what feels like forever until finally we come to a tent that is white with alternating red and blue stripes. As we come around the side of it, sitting inside the tent are two couches, a coffee table and tucked into the corners are stacks of towels, sunblock, various other lotions in one corner, and in the other corner there is a tin bucket, filled with ice and bottles of water. The three of us walk inside and turn back toward the blond who escorted us into the club.

"Welcome to Marquee, ladies," the blond says. "My name is America, and I will be your coordinator for the duration of your stay here at the Marquee. There are two pools, the one behind me." She points with her thumb. "Is a swimming pool, with normal pool depths up to eight feet. The one behind the tent." She points to the back of the tent. "Is a wading pool and there are two bars located in the pool and the DJ is on that side for dancing and partying." A gentleman enters the tent wearing nothing but swim trunks and his rather well kept physique quickly has Mandy and Rachel drooling. "This is Miguel, he will be your cabana boy, anything you want or need, you order through him. Anything additional or outside of his realm of approval will go through me. You're welcome to order anything on either the food or drink menu and Miguel is starting you off with a bottle of champagne."

Miguel sets down a golden ice bucket with a gold bottle of champagne in it and three glasses. He stands and waits for America to finish with her speech. "Menus are here." She reaches toward the coffee table rather awkwardly and I bite my lip to stifle a giggle from escaping as she opens a drawer and indicates the menus inside. "Lunch is served now until three and then after three the dinner menu is available. If food is ordered, we will make changes to your cabana to accommodate your meal. If you should choose to sit by the pool, please let Miguel know so he can find you." She smiles in an almost jealous way. "Everything is on the house," she says in such a way that I wonder if it is reluctantly on the house. But then I remember the outrageous bet last night and I have absolutely no doubt that Orion is footing the bill for our adventure today and I suddenly don't care. "Enjoy, ladies," America says as she leaves us with Miguel who is quick to pour us all a glass of champagne.

After our glasses are filled, he asks if we want anything to eat and I tell him to bring us something light and he scurries off.

"Holy hell," I breathe and I can see the look of wonder on both Rachel and Mandy's faces. "What have we gotten ourselves into?"

That doesn't even begin to describe the overwhelming anxiety I feel at being here. It was obvious last night that Orion has money. Throwing down a bet like that, and then just walking away from it, but this, this is over the top.

"It's Cristal," Mandy says. I look at her, dumbstruck, what the heck is that? I ask myself, but Mandy answers the unasked question written on my face. "Champagne, about four hundred dollars a bottle."

"Holy fuck," I breathe, but Rachel and Mandy don't seem to mind, taking a sip of their glasses. I watch as a sublime expression washes over their faces as they take in the taste. I look dubiously at my glass, can I really do this? Yes, yes, I can, because in a worst case scenario, if a bill shows up, hopefully with any luck, I can afford it after the money that ended up on our room across the street. Though, the cabana might be another story.

I put the glass to my lips and take a sip. It's crisp and light as it bubbles on my tongue. It tastes delicious and I take another sip. Deciding that this is probably better than anything I'll ever have again, I savor every drop in my glass and pour myself some more.

Between the three of us we finish off the bottle by the time we're done eating our modest lunches of sandwiches. Miguel offers us another bottle and I decline. Asking for something more my flavor, since we're hanging out in the sun, I order a June Bug made with Midori, Malibu, sweet and sour, banana and pineapple juice. The girls order the same; it is one of our favorites to drink together. When Miguel comes back with our drinks he has not only our three glasses but also a rather large pitcher with the same mix inside. If I didn't know any better, I'd think that someone was trying to get us drunk.

8

On the Prowl...

Eventually we all head toward the pool after we grab towels from the cabana and suntan lotion. Thankful that I brought my Kindle with me, I decide to lotion up and sit back and read for a while. Mandy and Rachel do practically the same, only they're having more fun looking at the man candy through their sunglasses. I prefer the sexy hero in the book I'm reading. I've always been one to get lost in a good book.

Eventually I turn over and am reading on my stomach as the early afternoon sun warms my back. It is really warm here in Las Vegas, at least compared to back home, but it is a welcome change.

After some time, I am just too warm so I leave the girls to their naps, and dive into the chilly water. The cold water feels great and sends shivers across my skin. There are not a whole lot of people in the pool, but looking around, toward our cabana and beyond, I can see that the other wading pool is starting to fill up and the party is really starting to take off. I have no idea what time it is, but I won't lie, I really don't care.

When Rachel mentioned going to Vegas, all I could think about was massive swarms of people and all the bright lights and loud noises of the strip, but being here, it's peaceful and relaxing.

I'm leaning up against the wall of the pool, looking toward the wading pool when I see him.

His hair is pulled back, much like yesterday. I'm surprised by how long it is, for one, and for two, how straight it looks, despite being pulled back. Instead of wearing a suit, he has on swim trunks, a rather tight t-shirt and he has a towel slung over his shoulder. The rather large watch on his right wrist captures my attention. Huh, he's a lefty.

Of all the things I can see of this man, I focus on the fact that he wears his watch on his right wrist. I shake my head. The man is practically naked and I can see every curve of every muscle in his chest, his biceps, and his stomach. I self-consciously wrap my arms around my midsection.

I've never been a super skinny girl, and I am far from it now, but I am thick in all the right places and my skin is smooth and my stomach is flat. I guess I'm a big girl, at least compared to Rachel I am, but I've always felt sexy and confident, but looking at him makes me feel that confidence slipping.

He disappears from my view, on the other side of the bar and I make my escape from the pool. I run over to my stuff, grab my towel and wrap up in it. "He's here," I say and both Rachel and Mandy come alive.

"What—Where?"

"Over there, by the bar." I wrap the towel around myself, covering myself as best as I can. "I'm going to go hide."

"No, stop. Has he seen you yet?" I shake my head. "Then put your sunglasses on and lay down. Your hair is wet and undone, he hasn't seen you in your sunglasses and there is very little chance that he will recognize you." Rachel tries to be comforting, and it's working a little bit. So I put on my sunglasses and sit down. "Without the towel. With it, you stand out like a sore thumb."

I unwrap the towel from my body and try to get comfortable. I look down my body, taking in the bright pink and green bikini I bought yesterday, then roll my eyes. The towel would've been less conspicuous but it's too late now. I grab my Kindle and try to read again, but I fail as I am hoping that my sunglasses are hiding the fact that I'm looking around for him again.

Miguel comes over and refills our glasses, replaces the pitcher of June Bugs and disappears, but when he stands up and moves, behind him on the opposite side of the pool is Orion. Looking at us, looking at me. "I knew I should have moved away from you two," I grumble as both Mandy and Rachel laugh and try to act casual as they've seen him now too. Except Rachel, being the brave one that she is, politely gestures for him to join us. "What are you doing?" I ask through gritted teeth.

"I'd rather have him here, talking to us, than staring at us from across the pool," she says while smiling and I want to melt into the chair. But he doesn't move for a few moments and when he does, I think he is going to come this way but instead he turns toward someone who is walking toward him. The kid hands him a phone and Orion puts up a finger, indicating one minute toward us and off he goes. He is far enough away that I can't hear what he's saying and he stays within viewing range until he disappears into the hotel.

"We should go," I say as soon as he is no longer in sight.

"Forget it. The least you can do is thank him for a wonderful afternoon," Mandy chides. "Besides, you're welcome to leave, but this is too much fun. I want to stay, and the party is only just getting started."

Leave it to Mandy to want to be the party animal. I roll my eyes.

"Look Cotah, like I said, what have you got to lose? It is one week, in Vegas, two thousand miles away from home. When the week is over, you go back to Wisconsin and he goes back to his life. Enjoy it; live it up a little bit. Besides, he's fucking gorgeous and if you're going to keep running away from him, I'm going after him."

"Rachel!" I scold and she laughs.

She has a point. Technically, I could give into him, give him what he wants so that he'll see I'm not worth all this trouble and in the morning I can walk away as if nothing happened. What's wrong with that? I'm a single twenty something with nothing to lose, except my dignity. And, it is Vegas and what better place to lose one's dignity, if only for a bit?

9

Captured Prey

I don't see anything more of Orion for the rest of the afternoon, but I begin to feel more hopeful as night dawns. The club begins filling with more and more people. Our cabana is changed around, from facing the pool to overlooking the club itself, and we now have a round table in the middle while we wait for our dinner to arrive. The alcohol combined with the sun has given me a feeling of euphoria unlike anything I've ever experienced before. It's almost like a high and I am completely mellow. Which is great, for now.

I'm looking forward to eating, hoping that will help level me out a little bit. We haven't eaten since lunch and I am nearly ravenous when our dinner arrives. As I watch Rachel and Mandy dive into their food too, I can tell I'm not the only one feeling this way.

Around seven, after we've eaten, we start to pack up just as Miguel comes in with more cocktails for us. "Leaving, ladies?"

"We, um, we were told we could only have the cabana for eight hours," I tell him, though we weren't actually told that, it was on the ticket.

"No, no. You ladies can stay as long as you like." He sets down our drinks in front of us. "I, on the other hand, am done for the night." Just then another man, similar in stature and build to Miguel enters the cabana carrying a tray of shot glasses, a salt shaker and some limes. "This is Michael; he will be serving you for the rest of the night." Miguel bows towards us. "Ladies, it has been a pleasure serving you today, enjoy your stay," he says and departs. I can tell immediately that Rachel is crushing on Michael as I watch her look him up and down. He is very attractive with tanned skin and blond hair. I smirk at the exchange they have and I can tell that Rachel is really tipsy.

Michael leaves us to our tequila shots and departs. As soon as he is gone, the three of us commence with our drinking and the next thing I know, we're all in the wading pool, dancing with drinks in our hands and having a great time.

Sometime later, I have no idea when, the crowd grows bigger until there is very little room inside the wading pool to even begin to move around and I am drunk, there is no doubt about that. I leave Rachel and Mandy to the guys they've claimed as theirs and the party. Only I don't go to the cabana, I walk right past it, right toward the other pool. While there are no less than a hundred people over here, it is much quieter and I take a seat along the side of the pool, just people watching, wondering what everyone is thinking.

At some point I climb into the pool and just hang out along the edge.

"Dacotah!" I hear and I turn in the direction of Mandy's voice.

"Right here," I answer and wave my arm. I prop myself up on the edge of the pool with my arms and Mandy comes to sit next to me with her feet in the water.

"You alright?" she asks as she sits down.

"I'm good, just needed a bit of a break. Too many people over there. What about you?" I ask her and she beams a bright smile at me.

"I'm having a great time. Chad and, oh hell I don't know his name, are trying to convince me and Rachel to go with them to their hotel." I raise an eyebrow at her. "Not gonna happen, but it is fun just the same."

"And here you were both trying to convince me that I should do exactly that with Orion."

"Orion? When did you learn his name?"

I blush, both at her question and at the fact that she dodged my jab back at her. "He looks like a hunter, so, Orion was a fitting name for him."

"As in the... Wow, you're good."

"Hardly. Now go get back to Chad. I'll be back over there in a bit."

She smiles wide and pulls her feet from the pool. "You sure you're okay?"

"Never better." I smile back at her and she turns on her heel and heads straight toward the party on the other side of the cabanas.

I don't move from my spot. I'm rather comfortable actually, as I watch the crowd from a distance. Everyone looks like they're having a ball and the music is bumping. If you'd have told me a couple of days ago that I'd be partying it up in Las Vegas, on someone else's dime, I'd have called you insane.

"Orion, huh?" I jump at the voice in my ear and try to spin around but he pins me to the side of the pool. I should fight to free myself, but the sound of his voice, the smell of his cologne, my drunkenness and the instant wetness between my legs has me paralyzed.

"You never told me your name," I breathe.

"Orion is fine, for now," he replies, but he doesn't ask me for my name, and I wonder idly if he already knows. Whether having heard Mandy say it a few minutes ago, or something else entirely. I feel him press into me a little harder and I can feel every inch of his warm, pool soaked body against my back. My toes reach down, seeking the bottom of the pool and I find it as I steady myself against him. I suddenly realize that I want this man, badly.

"Why the secrets?" I ask him.

"Why not? Isn't it more fun this way?" His mouth is right at my ear and I can feel the warmth of his breath caressing my face, along my cheek and down my neck. I shiver and feel my nipples harden. My desire for him is hot and I'm surprised because I've never in my life been so turned on by a voice.

"No," I answer his question. "Well, maybe it is for you, you have control."

"Just the way I like it." His hands begin to glide along my arms, to my shoulders, across my neck, but the contact of his front to my back never falters. "You, in my control, wanting and willing to do anything my heart desires."

My breathing hitches and fear spikes in my veins, but it is quickly cooled by his lips on my shoulder, right in the hollow of my neck. His kiss is hot and soft. I can feel the stubble of his tightly trimmed goatee prickling along my skin and goose bumps race across my body. I shiver. My breathing speeds and I bite my lip to stifle a moan. He knows exactly what he's doing, not missing a beat, he keeps going. His hands are tracing over my sides, light as feathers, and his lips continue their way along my shoulder, back to my neck.

Suddenly one of his hands disappears and I feel his fingers on the back of my neck, grabbing at my wet hair and gently moving it over my right shoulder.

"Well, aren't you just full of secrets," he says into my ear and then he kisses along my hairline, along the infinity tattoo on the back of my neck over to my other shoulder. His hands are gliding down past my hips, playing with the strings on my bikini and my heart rate spikes as I imagine him untying it, exposing me to the pool. But his hands slide past the strings, gliding down my thighs, only stopping when going further would push his face under the water. Emboldened by drink, I flick my hips, unable to sit still as his touch unravels me. His breath catches in his throat, and spurred by his reaction; I do it again.

His hands come quickly to my hips and he grips them, stilling me. "If you don't stop, I will take you in the pool. Right now. No matter who sees."

I am beginning to feel dizzy when I realize I'm holding my breath. I let it out in a rush trying to fight the urge to flick my hips. All dignity and self-preservation is completely gone as reality washes over me. I want this man and I don't even know his name.

10

Dignity Lost

Despite my best attempt to control my hips, they flick again as soon as I feel his fingers loosen on my hips. His breath hisses through his teeth and his hand comes around to the front of my bikini. He is pressing harder against me and his other hand has taken hold of my forearms, holding me in place and I squirm when his hand slides below the hem line of my bikini and his fingers come in contact with my mound. "Mmm. What I wouldn't give to taste you right now."

"Ah," I breathe as his finger slips deeps between the lips of my pussy, making contact with my wet slit.

"So wet," he growls. "Is this for me?" It's there, a hint of trepidation in his question, as if he's suddenly unsure of himself.

"Yes," I breathe. I feel his fingers slide down further, seeking entrance to my most private of places and I don't care. I want this man and I can't find it in myself to make him stop.

Just as his finger reaches the entrance of my cunt, he pulls back until the pad finds my clit and he begins to rub gently, gradually increasing his motion and my breathing grows heavy, labored and all the noise around us dissolves into nothing. It is just him and I. He continues for a few more minutes but I can sense his growing discomfort, maybe at my lack of response. It feels ah-fucking-mazing but I've never gotten off like this before. Though my unspoken realization causes his fingers to move, more determined to make me come unglued beneath his touch.

His hand comes away from my arms that he's been holding in place. It glides along my jaw, down my neck and further south. The pressure of his hand on my clit and the hand moving is possessive, holding me to him. His hand continues south, cupping my right breast. His thumb slides across my nipple and he nips at my ear, causing a silent hiss to escape my lips.

Then I feel it, his determination is paying off as he breaks through the barrier. My orgasm is building quickly. I moan softly and writhe against him. His erection is pressed against my ass and the subtle jump spurs my orgasm closer. His hand is more urgent against my clit. His right hand travels back up, gliding across my wet skin, cupping my neck, lifting my head so that it rests on his shoulder. My back is arched, my toes are beginning to tingle as my need to cum grows hotter.

His fingers are working tirelessly against my clit and I can feel it, my orgasm, growing with each rapid beat of my heart. My body begins to quiver against his and the increase in pressure against my most sensitive folds pushes me over the edge. My head held up, I'm forced to bite my tongue to stop from screaming my release. My breath comes in short quick bursts and he groans softly into my ear.

He flicks his finger once, twice and on the third, a warm sensation radiates across my skin, my whole body shakes. My eyes are closed, bright white starbursts exploding behind my lids. Reaching a height of ecstasy that has me melting back into him. His hand slows to sensual touching and flicking of his finger, milking my orgasm for everything it's worth. I tremble a few times more.

"Meet me in the lobby, tomorrow morning at ten."

"Huh" is all I can manage and just like that his hands come away. I shiver at the loss of his body against mine when the cold water replaces his embrace. I turn around, looking for him and just like that, and every other time, he's gone, nowhere to be seen. How does he do that?

As soon as I realize that he's gone, embarrassment washes over me and I start to look around the pool, no one is paying any attention to me at all, once I realize that no one has any idea what just happened, anger and frustration creeps in. How could I be so stupid?

Feeling dejected, I climb out of the pool, grab my towel and wrap it around myself. The feeling of insignificance and loneliness wash over me. My already fragile state of mind, still dealing with what Jason has done to me, and now this. I allowed myself to be used.

11

He Did What?

Used for what? He took no personal pleasure from me; he only gave me pleasure, amazing pleasure. I put my head in my hands, I want to cry, or drink myself stupid, either one works great for me right now.

"Dacotah?" I hear Rachel's voice, I look up and she is standing over me. "What's the matter?"

I instantly feel embarrassed all over again. I can tell Rachel anything and I know she will either understand or be really pissed off at me.

"Cotah, seriously, what's going on?"

"You don't want to know."

"Like hell I don't. What happened? You were fine when Mandy came over here." I can see the frustration with my lack of talking and I sigh heavily.

"That was before 'he' showed up."

I watch as shock crosses her face and she starts to look around for him. "Where is he?"

"Gone."

"Is that why you're upset?" She kneels down in front of me. I shake my head. "Then?"

"No." All conviction in my voice is gone and she looks at me, silently telling me to spill it. "He...god, this is so embarrassing Rachel."

"This is me we're talking about, you can tell me anything." She places her hand on my knees. "Talk to me."

"He um..." I blush, I know because I can feel the heat radiate across my skin.

"What...how...when...where?" she spouts off, and her line of questions tells me that she's concluded that we had sex.

"No, jeez, Rachel." I blush again.

"You're lying." She laughs a little at my words.

"Not entirely." My voice is hesitant.

"Cotah, you don't even know him."

"Great Rachel, thanks so much for reassurance. Weren't you the one telling me not too long ago that 'it's only a week' and now you're all, 'you don't even know him', which is it, Rachel?" I huff.

"Yes." She's hesitant. "But even casual sex has it's 'need to know'. Do you know his name?" I burst into a nervous laughing cry. "Oh hell, Dacotah."

"We didn't have sex, for crying out loud," I blurt, my brain to mouth filter is gone.

"Then, what?"

"He fingered me and then left."

"Oh," she breathes.

I bristle because of the look in her eyes. "Yeah, oh. Now do you get it?" I can't stop the sarcasm.

She ignores my tone, "Where?" and just like that curious Rachel has returned with over excited eyes.

"Curiosity killed the cat. You know that?"

She laughs, "Yes, but, dang girl, did he get you off?"

I blush again with embarrassment and bite my lip. I nod.

"EEK!" she squeals, stands, starts clapping and jumping up and down.

A refreshed sense of embarrassment comes over me and I stand up and walk away from her, back toward the cabana.

"Was it good?"

"Rachel!" I exclaim.

"What?" She tries to be innocent and fails.

"You know what, you... You can't be like this, so what, I got off, big deal."

She busts out laughing. "Did you return the favor?" I smack her on her shoulder. "What? It's only fair."

"No Rachel, I didn't return the favor. He walked away from me before I barely finished coming down from my orgasm."

"Whoa."

We step back into the cabana and Michael is there with a new pitcher of June bugs.

"We need shots," Mandy says as she comes into the tent. "A lot of them."

Michael nods and departs quickly.

While we wait for our shots, Rachel regales Mandy with my pool exploits, thankfully I hadn't gotten to the part about tomorrow. I'm not sure I can handle the scrutiny of Mandy and Rachel separately. When they are together, it is like their brains sync together and there is usually a common agreement from both of them. Mandy and Rachel have known each other longer and are closer to each other than I am to Mandy. Growing up, I had very few liberties to leave the house, let alone have the sleepovers that they had together in high school. While the initial jealousy was strong, I harbored those feelings and locked them away, deciding that they were good together, but that I still had a good relationship with both of them.

When Rachel stops telling the story, I decide it's time for the rest of the story.

"He wants me to meet him, in the lobby, here, at ten tomorrow morning."

"What?" they both practically shout as Michael comes back into the tent. Saved by the alcohol.

The three of us dive in. Last night I got completely wasted after my encounter with slick in a suit and now that is all I want to do again tonight. He makes me lose my head, hell, I'd lose my body to him too if I was given the chance.

"What are you going to do?" Mandy accosts me as soon as we're alone again.

"I don't know, but I get the impression that if I don't show up, he will find me somewhere in Vegas. He knows our room number at the hotel, and he found me easily enough yesterday after seeing me once, and then again tonight. So, I..."

"Meet him. Have a drink, maybe lunch, figure out what he wants, then—, "Rachel pauses briefly, her eyes glazing over in thought. "—then if you don't like what he has to say, walk away. You'd be closer to him, maybe at least know his name, and then you could tell him to leave you alone...if that's what you want?" I hate to admit it, but she makes a very good point.

"I don't know what I want. Or, what if I tell him I don't want him or anything to do with him and he doesn't take me seriously? The last thing I want is our entire trip being ruined by some creepy guy who pops up everywhere we go." I know my thoughts are irrational and I'm pretty sure that he wouldn't be that type of guy, at least I hope not. If he can afford this cabana, that bet, and everything else so far, I'd imagine that if I asked him to stay away or told him I wasn't interested, then he would actually leave me alone.

I'm reminded of his presence by the warm wet moisture between my legs. For some reason the idea brings about the thought of all the heroines in my favorite romance novels who fuck like monkeys then they get up, go about life as if nothing has happened and the authors always fail to mention the sticky wetness that seems to follow in real life. I want, no, I really need, to be able to clean up, or something, I feel like everyone can smell the aftermath of what he did to me. I squirm uncomfortably trying to wash out the sudden insecurity I feel about what *Orion* has just done to me and focus on what is happening in front of me.

"Cotah, I highly doubt that he would really do that." Rachel pulls me out of my romance novel analysis; trying to be reassuring, but I doubt at this point that he would really back off. He has given me no indication of that intention so far. At the idea of him backing off, I feel a sense of dread overcome me and I know my answer. I know that I will show up in the lobby tomorrow morning at ten, just to see him, to see what he wants, and what exactly he is after when it comes to me. There is obviously something about me that he finds intriguing and I'm overcome with the idea of finding out what it is. I smile.

"What are you grinning about?" Mandy blurts, then laughs, "You're going to do it, aren't you?"

I nod with enthusiasm and both of them squeal and bounce with excitement. "Then let's get out of here," Rachel says rather deadpan.

"No," I blurt. "What about the guys you met? Don't you want..." The look on Rachel's face tells me not to push the subject. "Alright then." I look at Mandy who is nodding too, though she has a lot less enthusiasm than Rachel does.

The three of us stand up from our table. I notice only now that the wading pool is very full, with very little room to move, which would be okay if the patios were not filling up, equally as full. I grab my bag and take a look at the watch attached to the handle and it's nearly eleven thirty. Whoa, where did the night go?

We all grab our bags and head to the door. The door man stops us. "Leaving so early, ladies?"

The three of us look at each other; we've been here for over thirteen hours. Mandy turns back to the good-looking bouncer and smiles. "We've been here since this morning."

"Ah, but the night is only just beginning," he says as he opens the door and I begin to wonder if he was tasked to try and stop us from leaving. We all step through the doors and begin walking toward the Strip when the guy stops us again. "Ladies, we have a ride for you." He whistles and as I turn around there is a guy dressed in livery who hops into a stretch limo, not just any limo, but a Hummer that could easily hold thirty people in it.

"We can walk," Rachel says to the man trying to usher us back toward the entrance and the curb as the car pulls up in front of us.

"Not tonight," he says as he walks toward the back door. It opens Lamborghini style, from the bottom upwards and there are two steps that lower automatically to the curb. "Ladies," he says as he swings his arm in the direction of the car. A look inside reveals that it is lit up in blue neon, with plenty of seating for at least twenty people. It is over the top, but I can't help wondering if Orion had something to do with this.

We all reluctantly climb in and take random seats. The driver turns to us. "Good evening ladies, where would you like to go?"

Once again we all have dumbfounded expressions on our faces. "Our hotel, Planet Hollywood," I tell him.

The driver looks disappointed. We didn't order this limo and the hotel is across the street from where we are now. "How about the long way around, down the strip?" he asks, as if keeping us in this limo for more than five minutes is his ultimate goal and I wonder why that is and the idea that Orion is behind this grows stronger in my gut.

"Sure," I say before the girls can protest and the driver turns around, the bouncer shuts the door, taps twice on the window and we're off.

"Help yourselves to any champagne or beverages in the fridge," the driver hollers back and then I watch as the privacy glass and screen go up between us.

Mandy is the first one to find this entertaining and reaches for the bottle of champagne in the bucket. Then she grabs three glasses from the shelf tucked into the side and starts to pour each of us a glass.

Once we all have our glasses in hand, she puts the bottle back and turns to Rachel and I. "To epic Vegas vacations." She's excited about this, but Rachel and I both have our apprehension, but regardless we both raise our glasses and drink. It's Cristal. I shake my head and I have no doubt that he's done this.

"I really hope we're not getting duped into paying for this because I sure as hell didn't ask for it," I blurt out. Frustration begins to overwhelm me over being shuttled and chauffeured around like this.

"We'll deal with it once we get back to the hotel, bottom line, we didn't ask for this, and I won't pay for it," Rachel says and I can't help but agree with her.

"What are you two so worried about? Stop worrying and have a great time." Mandy leans back against the divider and stretches out her legs. "It's not every day we get treated like royalty, soak it up. Besides, if we are stuck with the bill, you have over three hundred grand waiting for you at the hotel."

"Thanks for the reminder," I grumble. I'd nearly forgotten about the extravagant amount of money from last night's bet and I shake my head. "What the hell does he want from me?" I say aloud and both Mandy and Rachel look at me. "This is all too damn much and for what? A chance to sleep with me? I mean, what the fuck?" I slam back the rest of my champagne and slump against the seat, folding my arms around myself. "I'm nobody, I'm a girl from the middle of nowhere Wisconsin, who barely has a dime to her name, and I work in a pizza joint for crying out loud. I am way out of my league with this guy and I don't even know what I've done to garner this much attention from him." I take a deep breath and realize that Rachel has that are-you-stupid look on her face.

"Dacotah, you're fucking gorgeous, and what does it matter, you're going home in a week. Now is a chance to have the time of your life. Stop being a worrywart and enjoy it. Nothing has happened; nothing's going to happen unless you want it to." I blush, remembering what happened in the pool and I'm not so sure she's right. He holds a power over me that makes me putty in his hands, which was obvious. "Okay, apart from that, but still, what's the big deal? We walked out of the club without being stopped to pay for the cabana, odds are, we're not going to pay for this either. Just sit back, relax and try to enjoy it."

I peer out of the window and we've turned around, on our right is the MGM Grand and to our left is New York New York. There are literally thousands of people milling around Las Vegas Boulevard and many of them are watching our limo as we roll past them. Mandy and Rachel begin to enjoy themselves, pointing and laughing at the people on the street but I'm too caught up in all things Orion.

What does he want from me? Can I give him what he wants? Can I give him what he wants then just walk away next weekend like nothing happened? My own hesitation tells me that won't be an easy task to undertake and fear races through me. I don't even know this man, let alone his intentions, but all I can seem to think about is what happened in the pool and how much I want to experience that again.

Before long, we are pulling into the hotel's front entrance and the driver quickly climbs out and comes around to open our door. I look at Rachel and Mandy who look as exhausted as I feel and I glance at my watch, it is nearly one in the morning, we'd spent over an hour driving along the strip and other than the MGM and New York New York, I'd been so caught up in what's happening to me, to us, that I didn't even pay any attention until that point.

We climb down the two steps and head for the door. "Good evening, ladies," a gentleman says to us. "I have new room keys for you."

"What do you mean? We have our keys," Rachel asks, concern etched in her eyes.

"Ah, but your room, while you were out, needed to be changed."

"Whoa, what about our stuff?" I ask the man talking to us.

"We've taken the liberty of moving everything for you. Please follow me."

"What the fuck," Mandy exclaims and the man ignores us as he walks towards the door of the hotel. I turn back to tip our driver from this evening but he is long gone. Well shit, the tip was handled too. Fuck me, this is too damn much.

The three of us follow the man into the hotel, through the casino to a single elevator tucked off of the casino floor. There is a gentleman wearing the same get up as the man we're following standing guard at the door. Both gentlemen exchange nods and the elevator doors open immediately as we enter the alcove and the man places his hand along the wall to stop the doors. "After you, ladies," he says and as soon as we're all inside he removes his hand and steps back. "Enjoy your evening." The doors close and we are alone.

"What the fuck is going on here?" the three of us say, practically in unison and then the g-force of the elevator registers and my ears begin to pop as we climb. There are no buttons and no indication of where we are in relation to the floors until suddenly the elevator stops, beeps and the doors open. There is another gentleman waiting in the very tiny foyer.

"Good evening, ladies. My name is Alejandro and I will be your personal concierge during your stay here at Planet Hollywood."

"Uhm, what is going on? What happened to our old room?" I ask him.

"Your old room was needed for another reservation, ma'am, so we've relocated your items here and you may stay here for the rest of your stay in Vegas." He opens the French doors and beyond those all I can see is a brilliant panoramic view of the Las Vegas Strip beyond the windows. "We've laid out an assortment of sandwiches and snacks. The bar—"he gestures toward his left "— is fully stocked. If you need anything, dial one on the phone and I will be happy to assist you. Have a wonderful evening." He ducks back out of the door and we're left dumb struck staring out the window.

12

Sweet Dreams

After what feels like hours of arguing, questioning, and finally acceptance of what we've been given, we all find our stuff and set off for our own rooms. Mandy and Rachel determined that this has everything to do with the mysterious man that's been stalking me around Vegas and they give me the master suite. But don't feel too sorry for them, they both have their own bathrooms and their rooms are bigger than the one the three of us were sharing downstairs.

I climb into the shower, desperate to rid myself of the suntan lotion and pool gunk. As soon as I step into the warm shower, my eyes become heavy and my exhaustion sets in. One thing is certain about Vegas, I've forgotten all about the drama back in Wisconsin and my thoughts are filled with Mr. Mysterious and what he's done so far when it comes to me and can conclude only that he's wealthy, extremely so, and his desire for me is overwhelming any rational thoughts he may have once had.

I can't move my arms; they're pinned over my head. Panic rises as I realize why I can't move my arms, they're being held by something. I can feel a heavy weight across my body. "Shhh." The sound brings an immediate calm over my body and I feel desire flash hot across my skin. I try to open my eyes but there is nothing, I can't see anything.

I feel something warm and soft sliding along my thigh, up toward my hip and I arch my back. I feel my nipples harden and I shiver. I can feel the familiar need aching between my legs, growing moist and my breathing becomes ragged.

I feel something, someone, spreading my legs, my most inner parts being exposed but replaced by… Is that? He's between my legs, poised and I can feel the head of his erection pressing into me. "Please," I beg and the sensation disappears all together. "No," I moan and my back arches, reaching, trying to find what I lost and it's gone. All weight has been removed from my body.

Suddenly I feel my knees being lifted toward my chest, further exposing myself, and then without warning he slams into me, hard and hot.

My eyes fly open. I'm alone and daylight is pouring into the room. After a moment of disorientation I remember where I am, and then I panic about what time it is. I look at the bedside clock and it's five after seven. I flop back onto the pillow, breathing heavily and it takes me only a minute to realize that somehow I've managed to have an orgasm in my sleep and I throw my arm over my eyes.

What the hell was that all about? Why couldn't I move, or see?

I rub my eyes, trying desperately to figure out where all this is coming from. I know, deep down, that the man in the dream is Orion, but why? What's with the hands being bound, a blindfold or whatever caused the darkness in the dream? I've never been bound before, but thinking about the dream, that ache returns between my legs and I squirm thinking about having Orion naked and pressed against me and even more overwhelming is the fact that I'm turned on by the idea of being bound.

I shake my head and climb out of bed. I head for the bathroom and a shower, hoping that the warm water will help wash away the vision of Orion that is being painted in my mind without even knowing him.

The shower failed to wipe away the memory and mind-set that I woke up in. I fought the urge to take advantage of being alone and taking care of my own predicament, but decide against it. Instead I concentrated on showering and shaving. When I finish, I dry then straighten my hair. The make-up I put on is there, but subtle, like always with me. I don't have much experience with it, so I don't push any limits by doing something I'd feel self-conscious about later.

By the time I emerge from my room, Mandy is in the sitting room, drinking coffee and looking out the window. When she sees me, she smiles.

"You look fabulous." She smiles wider as she takes in my hunter green sundress and black wedge heels. I may be a fluffy girl, but I can rock a pair of heels when I want to, but it's rare.

"Thanks." I twirl around and she whistles. "Where's Rachel?" I ask, looking around the room.

"She's still sleeping. At least I'm assuming so. I've been up for a while and haven't seen her. There's coffee in the kitchen." Her eyes dart toward a small alcove. "There are also bagels and I put the cream cheese in the fridge." I turn toward the kitchenette and look at my watch. It's five minutes to nine and I decide to try and calm my growing anxiety about meeting Orion. I pour a cup of coffee and make half a bagel covered in cream cheese and scarf it down. I didn't realize how hungry I was until I started eating, but I know that my nerves are going to get the better of me here shortly.

I grab my coffee cup between both hands and walk toward the window. There is a balcony with chairs outside and I look along the windows, looking for a door to step out, but I don't see one and knowing me, I'd get so caught up sitting out there that I would be late to my meeting. I gingerly sip my coffee, but it's quite cool so I start to down it. Mandy hasn't said anything else and I look over my shoulder at her. She's sitting there, lost in thought. "Penny for your thoughts?" I ask her and she looks at me.

She shrugs. "Just thinking about home and how I'm not sure if I want to go back."

I cock my head at her. "What do you mean?"

"Oh you know, I've never been a small-town girl and I miss the big city. Being here reminds me how much I miss it."

"That's no reason to be sad, is it?" I ask her, trying to understand her mood.

"No, and I'm not really sad, just thoughtful. Thinking about what it would take to move." I take a sip of my coffee. "And—"she sighs "— I really liked that guy I met last night."

"Did you get his number?"

"I did, and gave him mine."

71

"So call him or text him."

She looks at me; I see something in her eyes. "He's already texted me."

"Oh, that was fast." I smile.

"I haven't texted him back. I'm not sure what to say or…" She blushes a little bit and it's kinda cute. Mandy is always so sure of herself and her confidence is admirable, so I don't completely understand her reaction and wonder if maybe this guy is bringing something out in her she may not have experienced before. "You should get going," she says and I look at my watch. It's nine twenty.

"Yeah," I say as I turn toward my room to grab my phone. When I come back out Mandy is still on the couch but her mood seems better. "How about I text or call when I'm done, and we'll meet up for lunch?"

She smirks. "Sure," she says and waves as I walk toward the door. When I open it Alejandro is standing in the foyer.

"Good morning," he says as he pushes the call button for the elevator. "Where are you off to this morning?" he asks as the door opens.

He ushers me into the elevator and then follows me inside. "Headed across the street, I have a meeting at ten." I smile politely at him, hoping he won't press me for more information.

"There is a car downstairs waiting for you," he says with a rather sheepish expression on his face.

"I was hoping to grab some coffee on my way out," I say, knowing that there is a Starbucks on the side of the casino that leads to the entrance to the Miracle Mile mall and the escalators down to the street level, across the street from the entrance to the Cosmopolitan.

"Certainly, miss. I'll let the driver know you'll be along shortly."

I try really hard to not sound exasperated toward him. "I'd really like to walk, please tell the driver that I won't need his services and that I appreciate the gesture."

The look in his eyes tells me that he's disappointed in my desire to walk. "As you wish," he finally says as the doors open to the casino and he holds the door open for me. I step out and turn immediately to my right. It is early and there are very few people in the casino and some of them look like they've been there all night.

After what feels like a mile, I finally reach Starbucks and while there is a line, it seems to be moving rather quickly. I feel my phone vibrate and look down, a text from Rachel.

> **Sorry I missed you this morning. Good luck. Here if you need me.**

I reply.

> **Don't worry, I'll be fine, see u soon.**

Last night they were both determined to come with me and watch from a distance, but neither one of them were up and ready this morning. For some unknown reason, I feel perfectly safe. At least as long as we stay in the lobby of the hotel I should be safe.

Coffee in hand, I'm ready, at least that is the confidence I am trying to portray. The sky has turned cloudy since I was upstairs, but the sun is still peeking through, it is actually quite nice out this morning, but still warmer than I'm used to.

Standing before the doors to the Cosmopolitan Hotel, I take a deep steadying breath. I have no clue what to expect from Mr. Mysterious, but I'm very excited to find out. I feel like it's Christmas morning and I'm going into the living room to see what Santa brought for me. Though it was never much, it was still exciting none the less. Well, most of the time.

I shake off the thoughts of Christmases long ago, or lack thereof, and focus on opening the door and stepping inside.

The Cosmopolitan is a grand hotel and well worth the price of admission. I see an overhead sign that says "Front Desk/Registration" and an arrow pointing up. I head in that direction, checking my watch. It is nine fifty and I'm right on time. I'd hoped to make it to the lobby before he showed up but when I round the corner, he's there. Sitting in a chair facing me. I'm not sure if he's seen me yet, but I take just a second to look at him.

He's lounging back, arm across the back of the chair next to him with his legs crossed. He is wearing a very sharp looking black suit, black shirt and a hunter green tie. Panic rises at the fact that obviously someone is feeding him inside information or that there is a camera in our suite and it is unsettling. What are the chances that he would be wearing a tie the same color as my dress?

I debate momentarily about turning around and leaving, but I know that he won't go away, at least not without me telling him to do so. Now is my chance to do just that.

13

Breakfast? Is He Serious?

Steeling myself, I take a step, then another and then he catches me. His eyes are like liquid milk chocolate as he takes in the sight of me walking toward him and he languidly stands. His arms and legs are longer than I remember or it is just his natural grace and overwhelming power that puts him into a higher regard. He doesn't take his eyes off of me and all I can do is pray that I don't trip and fall on my face.

I watch as his eyes slowly rake over my body, from my eyes down to my toes and I suddenly feel very self-conscious. I blush and look down just as I come to stand in front of him.

I feel his hand on my chin, lifting my face so that I will look at him. I do and his eyes are filled with his own desire for me and I know I blush redder. "You look beautiful," he says and his words send chills down my spine and that burning ache from this morning is back with a vengeance.

"Thank you," I breathe. Unable to speak as all my strong confidence I had about telling him to leave me alone, two seconds ago, vanishes.

"Have you eaten?" he asks. His voice is soft as silk and it washes over me, sending goose bumps across my skin and I can feel my nipples harden. Embarrassment rushes through my veins and I recover by remembering his question.

"Half a bagel," I say.

"That's hardly enough. Come," he says taking my hand in his and leading me toward a hallway at the far end of the reception area.

"I'm not hungry," I say but he isn't hearing me, not this time, because he keeps pulling me in the direction of the hallway that leads to where? I can't tell just yet but my nerves are on fire. The unknown scares the hell out of me, but to be honest, it is not fear. For reasons I can't even begin to explain I feel comfortable with him. I shouldn't feel this comfortable around someone I don't even know, but this just feels, I don't know, right?

We reach a door in the hallway and it opens automatically, well, there is a gentleman on the other side, holding it open and Orion ushers me inside.

I step inside and the room is good sized, decorated in browns and golds with strange looking paintings that I've come to expect at the Cosmopolitan. Everything here is a bit off the wall, but it all works. In the center of the room is a table, set for two, with two dome covered plates, water glasses, orange juice and just beyond that is a champagne stand that holds a bottle wrapped in a towel.

He leads me to the table and pulls out a chair, ushering for me to sit; I take his cue. Once I sit, he helps me slide in the chair and then takes the dome from my plate. Under the dome is the best comfort food ever. Eggs, bacon, sausage and hash browns. I'm not sure what I expected, but it certainly wasn't this. He takes his seat and removes his dome, placing them both on the floor next to the champagne stand.

"I ordered champagne because I wasn't sure what your hangover situation was going to be like."

I smile slightly. "I don't get hangovers." I watch as shock crosses his features. It's never been something that has gone over easy on anyone, but he seems genuinely surprised, or he thinks I'm full of shit. "Though, I didn't drink that much last night. A lot throughout the day. Speaking of which—"I look at him, steeling myself. "—thank you for the cabana yesterday." I smile.

His answering smile lights up the room. "You're most welcome. Did you enjoy yourself?"

Immediately the memory of the pool comes back, unwelcome right now and I shift in my chair slightly, remembering the feeling of his hands...*stop*! I tell myself. "Which part?" I blurt.

He smiles a wicked 'I have a secret' grin. "The entire day," he says, but his voice doesn't match the heat I can see in his eyes.

"The day was amazing, the whole day." I lower my head and I can feel the heat in my own eyes and he shifts slightly, uncomfortably as if I've just matched him at his own game.

"I'm glad you enjoyed yourself." He takes a sip of his orange juice.

"Didn't you?" I smile behind my own glass of juice as he tries to compose himself long enough to answer.

"I did. Tell me, how long are you staying in Vegas?"

Oh, he's getting right to it then. "I think our flight leaves Sunday morning."

"Good." He doesn't say anything else, but starts to eat his breakfast. I take that as my queue to start eating too, but the butterflies in my stomach have me feeling really full and I don't have a clue how I can eat right now. I have so many questions to ask him, but I can see from his expression while he eats that he's lost in thought and I decide to follow his lead. Mulling over all the questions I want to ask him when we're done.

It doesn't take me long before I feel full to the point of bursting and I set my silverware down. "You're done?" he asks me.

"I already ate, remember?"

"I hardly call half a bagel eating."

"Look, I'm nervous. I don't know you, or what it is that you want, why I'm here or even your name, so eating is far from what I want to be doing right now." He is just as surprised at my outburst as I am.

He swallows the food in his mouth, I watch as his long fingers are wrapped in a napkin and he wipes his lips, his gorgeous, full, slightly pink lips. I can't pull my eyes away as I watch him take a drink of water. He knows exactly what he's doing, determined to drive me insane so that he gets what he wants and right now, after watching that, I'm not sure I can deny him anything.

"What if I told you that I wanted to spend this week with you?" I gasp, but he doesn't give me a chance to say anything. "I'm in town on business until Sunday morning and I'd like you to spend the week with me."

14

The Question Comes Out...

"Why?" I breathe, trying to organize my scattered thoughts of why this man wants to spend a week with me.

"The details are unimportant," His voice deadpan.

"On the contrary, I think they are." He gives me a sharp look with his eyes, gaging me and my reaction, or my thought process and I am doing my best to hide the fact that I really want to say yes to this.

"Why?" he asks.

"Because I'm not sure I understand why, out of the thousands of women in Las Vegas at this very moment, you decide to choose me to stalk and make this kind of offer. Then the self-conscious part of me wonders how many women said no to you before you got to me."

"Women don't say no to me," he says very matter of fact.

"Is that so?"

"Most women know who I am and would jump at the opportunity I'm offering you. But, I offer it to you because you don't seem to know who I am, and I like that."

"I don't know who you are because you won't tell me," I mutter.

"You're right; I won't because I don't need you making your choice based on who I am. I want your honest answer, and then I will consider telling you who I am."

His brutal honesty is disarming, but it is also comforting. He is seeking a genuine attraction to him and not his money, which it's obvious he has by the lengths he's gone to thus far.

"What will this week entail?"

He perks up a little bit. "You, being at my beck and call, there when I return from work, ready and waiting for me. Your friends will be taken care of, they've already been provided a suite at Planet Hollywood, their bill is covered, regardless of what they choose to order, or bill to the room. Spending money is being delivered to them as we speak. At the end of the week you will be compensated for your time."

"I'm not a hooker," I say sharply. Irritation begins to boil.

He cocks his head at me. "I never said you were, nor would I treat you as such. I'm taking care of your friends because the three of you arrived here together. I'm trying to take you away from them and your little vacation, the least I can do is..."

"Money doesn't make up for friendship."

"No, it doesn't, but I have a pretty solid understanding about what makes the two of them happy. They love all the people and the party, you, on the other hand, are more reserved, held back, and enjoy being on your own with a good book." His eyes narrow and I can't help wringing my fingers at his words. He's been paying a lot more attention to me than I have to him and it is very nerve wracking. "Am I wrong?" I shake my head. "You see, you'd be able to do what you want during the day, when I'm not around, but when I'm there, you're mine, to do with as I please."

The dream comes into my mind and I begin to wonder what it is that he has in mind and my curiosity is peaked once again.

"This is not a contract, if at any time you feel uncomfortable; you're free to leave. *Anytime,*" he says more as a challenge, almost as if he is giving me an out right now.

"I want to stay," I say quietly.

"Then you're agreeing." He leans forward, expectant.

I look up at him through my lashes, biting my lip and wringing my hands nervously together. Rachel's words come back to me. *What have you got to lose?* I can leave at any time.

"If I stay with you, and I leave, what happens then?"

He is puzzled by my question. "Nothing, everything stays as it is, except you'll be with your friends. It is not my intention to make you so uncomfortable that you'd want to leave."

I think about his words. I think about what he's said, and then I think about Mandy and Rachel. They could do Vegas the way that they want to, partying every night, or whatever and I get what? I get *Orion* and a chance to truly forget my past, if only for a week. One week.

"Starting when?" I ask, stalling my answer.

"Right now." His words are soft and full of promise and I begin to melt a little more on the inside.

"I need to pack my stuff." He is shaking his head before I finish.

"If you choose to stay with me, I will provide you with clothes, food, and a chance to make your deepest fantasies come true."

For a brief moment, the dream thunders back into my mind, then I remember the clothes, "That doesn't help the whole whore factor, Orion."

He cocks his head at me with a smirk on his face, no doubt remembering when I called him that last night. "You're not a whore, nor would I treat you as such. When you leave next Sunday, the clothes and things that I give you are yours to keep, or you can leave them, the choice is yours."

What is so wrong with this idea? I can certainly think of a million and one reasons why this is a bad idea. Least of all being, I know, deep down inside, that when I'm forced to walk away a week from now it will be with a broken heart.

"Why do you call me Orion?" he asks, genuine curiosity in his voice and I can see that he's trying to turn an extremely tense situation into something more personal.

I swallow, "uhm…"

"I won't laugh," he says, his voice is soft, but I can see a light in his eyes that tells me that might not be the case.

I decide that I have nothing to lose at this point and go for it. "When I first saw you, in the mall, you reminded me of a hunter. Focused and driven to find its prey. Which you've only further proven by your actions since then." I give him a half smile.

"Okay, so where does *Orion* come from?"

"Orion, the star constellation is also known as The Hunter."

As I suspected, he starts to laugh, but there is a nervous energy ringing louder than his laugh. He sobers quickly and stares at me, intensity in his eyes, just like the hunter

I've deemed him to be. "You're right, I am a hunter, in many ways. I have my sight on my prey and I am so close to having her in my grasp."

His words and his stare send a shiver of fear and excitement through me at the idea of being in his grasp. I get the impression that Orion is a ruthless businessman who lets nothing stand in his way and right now, I am his latest business transaction. The choice is mine. Do I step into the fire and get burned in the end? Or do I back away slowly until I'm clear enough of his eyes to run? Do I run back to Wisconsin, stay in Vegas, or… So many choices and decisions, I don't know how I can even begin to decide how to go about this? I need a week just to analyze his words and his actions before I can consider his offer, but I know he won't afford me that and I'm forced to make a choice.

"What is your name?" I ask him, my voice is hesitant and he straightens to answer my question.

"What is your answer?"

"Not fair."

"I told you last night that Orion was fine and it should be fine with you if I tell you it is, so pressing me for my name is not the answer I want right now. Will you spend the week with me?"

"Will you tell me your name?" I counter.

"Depends."

"On what?"

"Your answer," he says as he steeples his long fingers and gently presses his lips against them. His eyes are intense and his posture is strong and determined, and unbelievably sexy.

"Yes," I blurt and immediately look down at my hands, afraid of what I've just said.

He gasps and I can see him through my lashes as he places his napkin on the table and stands. He offers his hand. "Come," he demands and I place my napkin on my plate and stand, taking his hand. I expect him to lead me from the room, whisk me off to wherever it is that he is staying or…before I can fully register, he's pulling me close to him, tight against his body.

The hand I gave him is twisted and pressed against my back. I place my other hand on his chest to steady myself before I feel his fingers wrapping around my wrist, and just like the other one, it is pinned behind my back and my front is pressed tight against his. He is looking down at me and I am lost in the chocolate of his eyes. He could take me, right here in this room and I wouldn't care. My sex heats and I can feel his erection pinned between us.

He leans forward, his lips are inches from mine and I feel like lightning is crackling through my veins at his closeness. My need for him is growing hotter, my breathing is sharp and uneven. His ability read me becomes clear when his lips spread into a warm gentle smile that causes the corners of his eyes to wrinkle. "You won't regret this," he breathes and his breath is sweet as it caresses my face and I shiver.

I open my mouth to say something, but his lips are on mine, hot, hard and insistent. I can barely breathe, my heart is pounding a million beats a minute and I am beginning to get dizzy as his lips are soft against mine. His hands pull me closer to him and I gasp at the onslaught of sensation with his body pressed to mine and my inability to move. He doesn't hesitate, his tongue is in my mouth, dancing and caressing my own. I can feel myself falling backwards as the dizziness is winning and I'm losing my balance, but his hands tighten further and I can feel his erection twitch between us. I want him inside me more than oxygen to fill my burning lungs.

I feel his entire body stiffen and he pulls back. Suddenly he turns his head toward the door and I understand why he stopped as my eyes lazily peel off of him toward the door. The gentleman that opened the door for us before has returned. Orion straightens himself and steadies me. "We're done," he tells the man, he appears unaffected by our kiss and I suddenly wonder if I made a mistake by saying yes. "Come," he demands pulling on my hand and I follow behind him, but his pace and these heels are making it nearly impossible to keep up with him.

"Slow down," I say when we reach the door. He stops completely and the momentum of his pace sends me slamming into him. "Oomph." I scramble, trying desperately to maintain my balance without falling over and just like that his arms are around me, holding me to him once again. The lightning is back with a vengeance and I don't understand the look in his eyes.

"Steady...are you good now?"

Unsure I have a voice, I nod. He grabs my hand and starts down the hall toward the lobby where we first met. As soon as we clear the hallway he turns left and crashes through a set of double doors. Inside is a man dressed like the one in the other room, and an elevator. As soon as we've come through the door the man jumps into action pressing the button, a chime follows, then the doors slide open immediately. Orion leads me in. As soon as we turn around, the doors close and the close proximity to him sends my heart racing again. I try looking around for a distraction and say, "I forgot my phone."

"Where?"

"On the table downstairs."

He looks at me, nods and then goes back to staring at the doors. He's gone cold and I don't like it. He's acting as though nothing happened a couple of minutes ago and I start to scratch at the elbow of the arm he's holding. A nervous, self-conscious habit I have and since his grip on my hand is so tight, it's not worth the fight to try and free it, though I'm desperate to put some distance between us.

15

And So It Begins...

Finally the doors on the elevator open and we are... Jesus, the view in front of me is breathtaking. We are at the top of the Cosmopolitan hotel and we are surrounded by a three hundred-sixty degree view of Las Vegas. I stop just beyond the elevator. Orion lets go of my hand and goes straight to the phone on the table.

I'm too distracted by the view that I'm paying him absolutely no attention what so ever. The room is wide open, with floor to ceiling windows, from this angle I can see Planet Hollywood, Paris, and the Bellagio, as well as all the way down the Strip.

Beyond the glass is a large patio, in the middle of which is a rooftop pool that is sparkling in the sunshine and I suddenly have a strong urge to go swimming.

Orion comes back to me, grabs me by the shoulder, turning me toward him. Our eyes meet. "Stunning isn't it?"

"It's absolutely gorgeous." A salacious grin forms on his lips as he catches the double meaning in my words.

"It pales compared to you," he whispers and I can't help the shocked gasp that escapes my lips. I look into his eyes and all that need and desire are back in his features once again. "Your phone will be up shortly."

I nod; unsure of what to say when I remember his icy demeanor in the elevator and how quickly that came on. Now all of sudden it is back to the heat of the room down-stairs and I don't understand. His willingness to hide his identity from me gives me the impression that he and I will not be having intimate chats about his feelings.

His mercurial mood shift solidifies my confidence in my ability to walk away at the end of the week unbroken. I can't be if he is already hiding things from me. This is a business transaction for him, so I decide it should be for me as well.

"Your name?" I ask.

"You're not going to let that go are you?" I see fear in his eyes over telling me his name and I don't understand why.

"No, Orion, I'm not, especially not if you want me to sleep with you while I'm here this week."

He takes a step back, appraising my seriousness and I try to stand a little taller, but I'm not fooling him.

"What makes you think I want to sleep with you?"

My toughness crumbles completely at his words. But I watch him closely, that smirk is playing at his lips. Pay-backs come to mind. "Well, I can't imagine why you'd go to all this trouble if you didn't expect something in return." That wasn't at all what I intended to have come out of my mouth, and 'whore' flashes in big bright Vegas style mar-quee letters in my mind. Then the reality of the fact that

I've only ever been with one man, sexually, and the sign flashes, pops and fizzles.

"Ah, well played. Tell me—"he steps back from me and starts walking backwards only he grabs my hand at the last second, pulling me along with him. "What is your name?"

"Nope, not going to happen. We more or less made a deal downstairs that you'd tell me your name if I gave you an answer."

"Oh, so you only answered me because you wanted to know my name." I can tell he's playing now; there is wild gleam of excitement in his eyes.

"No."

"Okay then. But I'm certain I can seduce you without telling you my name."

"Too late." I cover my mouth quickly with my free hand, praying like hell he really didn't hear that. But the Cheshire grin on his face tells me that I've been caught.

He comes to stand next to the bar and pulls out a chair. "Sit," he commands, and I do. Sitting on the counter in front of me is a folio. "First, business." I scowl up at him as he opens the folio and then pulls a pen from his jacket. "If you want to know my name, I need you to sign this." He points to the papers in front of us now. I can't make out what they are, but it looks legal and binding. "This is a non-disclosure agreement. It basically says that anything that is discussed between us, while in the company of any of my business associates, or anything that happens between us, cannot be discussed with anyone."

I'm shocked and my heart immediately begins to ache. I knew there were strings attached to this. "What happens if I do?"

"Then I can sue you for breach of contract."

"You do know and understand, Orion, that I don't have any money, let alone anything of value that would be worth suing over if I decided to talk, which I won't. What-ever happens between you and I is personal, and I won't allow my personal business to go public, regardless of who you are."

"Regardless."

He hands me the pen and I feel deflated, I hadn't ex-pected this. "If I sign this, will you tell me your name, who you are and why this is so important to you?"

"I will tell you anything you want to know, and I will answer any and all questions honestly, or as honestly as I can and it is not important to me, but rather my legal team."

Jesus. "How many times have you done this before?" I'm shaking, I can't help but start freaking out that this isn't his first rodeo with having a woman in his bed while on a business trip.

"Never."

My eyes dart to his and I can see that he's being honest with me. There is concern and fear in his eyes that this agreement will send me running out of the door.

I take his pen from him and scribble my signature next to the big X.

"You didn't read it," he says, seriousness in his voice.

"Look, I don't understand it, I don't see why it is neces-sary, but you can't seem to move on without it."

He softens his stance and I can feel his fingers pressing gently on my exposed shoulder.

"Derek. Derek Hunter."

I burst out laughing. I slide down from the stool he's set me on and back away, putting some distance between us. "Hunter? You're joking, right?"

He looks nervous. "No, should I be?" His eyebrows knit together and he cocks his head.

"Orion, the hunter… your last name is Hunter."

"Yes." There is skepticism in his voice.

I start laughing. "Now it all makes sense."

"So you do know who I am?"

I shake my head. "Not consciously, but I remember wondering why I'd dubbed you Orion and it is possible that I've seen you before, but I can't place it."

His posture softens a little. "Good, then I won't worry about it." There is still a hint of hesitation in his voice.

"Dacotah."

"What?" He looks puzzled.

"My name is Dacotah."

He smiles. "A beautiful name. Where are you from?"

"Are we playing twenty questions?"

He laughs and stalks toward me. "If you want to. But I had other things in mind."

"Oh." My expression matches my surprise. I think about asking him what that might be, but I think I'm afraid of the answer he will give me.

"Come, I want to show you something." He reaches for my hand and I don't hesitate to place my hand in his as he leads me down a hallway that runs between the elevator and one of the glass walls overlooking the strip below. He leads me straight through an open doorway, laying beyond the entrance is a room with plush, nearly white carpet. The bed in the middle of the room is white with a fluffy white duvet spread perfectly across it. There are bedside tables, a low dresser with a vanity mirror, along with another dresser. Toward the large floor to ceiling windows are two high back chairs divided by a small round table. The room lacks color, but the subtle dark wood colors of the chairs, tables and dressers pop. "You can stay in here while you're with me."

I cock my head at him, much like he does with me. "But *you* don't stay in this room?"

91

"No, my room is upstairs." The dreaded feeling comes over me again and I feel like I am suddenly stuck in one of my favorite books come to life, and after the dream last night it all starts to seem a little too real. "You don't like that idea?" I shake my head at his question. "You'd rather sleep with me?" he asks, there is innocence in his voice like he's never slept with a woman before, though I highly doubt that.

"Why does that surprise you?" He leans back against a vanity and stuffs his hands into his pockets. "I thought you've never done this before." His eyes dart to mine and I can see fear in his eyes. It all becomes clear when I can finally place it; there is something, a history with someone or something. "If you'd be more comfortable with me sleeping here, then I'll sleep here."

"Listen, Dacotah, I've never done this before, as in asked a woman to spend a week with me, but that doesn't mean that I haven't had my share of one night stands."

What he's just said shouldn't send a thrill of excitement through me, but it does. The fact that he's only ever had one night stands also saddens me for some unknown reason. That sadness is quickly replaced with knowing that there is a very good possibility that I'm the only woman he's ever planned on spending time with, in and out of the bedroom. And lastly, trepidation at the fact that I feel like he could get what he wants and then throw me back to the curb.

He continues, pulling my yo-yo thoughts back to the present. "Most women throw themselves at me, I take what I want and I walk away." He looks as though this upsets him. "You see, there are too many women in the world that will take any chance they can to sleep with a man of my power and authority and not even think twice about the morning after consequences. For years, I've preyed on that."

"How am I so different from them?" I can't help the question. I just don't understand it. "Is it because I didn't just throw myself at you? Because I kind of did, in a way." Thinking about the bar, when he was dancing with me, then last night in the pool. "Then again, each time you walked away from me, why?"

He looks down at the floor, seeming to be lost in thought, but the tension in his shoulders says something a whole lot different, as if he is debating on telling me something. "Because I knew, just by the way you reacted to me, that neither you, nor your friends, know who I am and I took a lot of satisfaction from that."

"Is that the only reason?"

"No." His tone is clipped, shutting me down from further questions along those lines. Reinforcing my earlier fears about him not talking about his feelings with me.

Disappointment wracks my brain, both in the shut down and his answer. Telling me I was hoping for something with more depth. "Does whether I know who you are or not really matter?"

He shakes his head. "No, it doesn't, because..."

He stops as he's interrupted when the elevator chimes. He pushes away from the dresser and I think he's going straight for the door, but instead he stops next to me, leaning down close to my ear, "To be honest with you, I could care less if you know who I am. You're here and you're mine for a week. That will be your phone coming up." He steps back, once again revving me up and walking away.

I'm too distracted by his nearness and overwhelming scent that my body reacts to like he's a walking, talking aphrodisiac. His warm breath caressing my neck and shoulder causes goose bumps to rise everywhere and my nipples harden under my dress. The moisture between my legs refreshes with a warm gush of need that had gone cold back in the elevator.

He knows exactly what he's done when he comes storming back into the room with two glasses and a bottle of champagne in his hands. He stops briefly, his eyes widen and I can hear his deep inhalation at the air around me. I blush because the only thought I have is of him sliding off my panties and sniffing them. I shiver as he steps away from me, leaning back on the dresser once again. Though he shoves his hands back in his pockets, he is very relaxed. I, on the other hand, want to melt into a puddle on the floor.

I decide to show my support of his decision to have me sleep in this room by sitting down on the bed to remove my shoes. My feet are starting to hurt.

I'm just about to take off the second one when he shifts against the dresser, the glasses clink as the dresser shakes.

"Champagne?" he asks and that husky tone in his voice is back. Bent over to undo my shoe, I look up at him, he's watching me remove my shoes and hunger is radiating off of him. My eyes don't make it any further north than his crotch. I'm breathless and frozen as my mouth begins to water hungrily to have him in my mouth.

Watching me, he stands up from his relaxed pose to one that screams caution flags. I suddenly feel smaller under his gaze, but rather than scare me, it thrills me. His hand reaches for his jacket. I watch as it slips from his shoulders and he hangs it from the mirror over the dresser. He catches me watching him and he smirks. I watch as he loosens his tie and begins to unbutton his shirt. My mouth goes dry as I start to see the skin of his chest appear between the buttons.

His long fingers work quickly to finish off the buttons until he reaches the button of his pants. I can't see what he's doing but I hear the unmistakable sound of a zipper going down and his shirt comes out.

The next thing I know, his tie is laying across the dresser and he is slowly sliding his shirt down his shoulders. It's like watching the most beautiful strip tease in the world. His shoulders are defined by muscle and I watch as his shirt slips down his back, further exposing him to me and I'm no longer breathing.

I'm shocked to see, on his left shoulder, is a tattoo. I can't quite make it out from here, but it appears to be letters and some type of wing design. Not at all something I'd expect to see on this man. Slowly he turns around and I see that the tattoo on his shoulder is not his only one. Over his left peck, extending onto his shoulder and down to his elbow is a broad tribal design that just accents the muscles on display for me now.

"Breathe, Dacotah," he says and I feel my eyes, heavy with desire slowly slide up to look him in the eye. They are milk chocolate again and I want to run my hands through his brown hair.

I watch as he stalks toward me, he kicks off one of his shoes, followed by the other along his path to me. Then, just like that, he is on his knees in front of me. His hands are sliding down my right leg, the one that is still wearing the shoe I hadn't gotten off.

His hands are soft and warm, leaving goose bumps in their wake. He takes my foot in his hand and works on untying the canvas from my leg. I shiver as he slides the shoe from my foot.

With gentle caresses back up my leg, my eyes roll up into my head and I want to plop back on the bed, just to break the crazy eye contact we have going on, but I can't.

I'm frozen with anticipation at what he's going to do next. I feel his hands as they reach the hem of my sundress and I don't stop him when his hands slide underneath it. When I feel his fingers tickle against my labia, I groan.

"So beautiful," he sighs and his hands search out the waist of my panties, then his fingers slip in underneath and his eyes are begging for my permission to remove them. I lift my hips in silent invitation. He smiles as he begins to slide them down my thighs, to my calves then, finally, off. I half expect him to take them and sniff them, but he doesn't, he's too much of a gentleman for that.

16

Let's get to it...

His hands glide back up along my legs on their sensual journey back to where they were mere moments ago. My arms begin to tremble from holding myself up. I watch as he stands up between my legs and he leans down, bracing himself on his knuckles, bringing our noses within millimeters of touching. His scent is intoxicating, my body quivers and I slowly fall back onto the bed as he follows me, keeping our noses so close. His eyes are hypnotic and I'm going to give this man whatever he wants.

Finally after what seems like eternity, his lips are on mine, hungry and needy and I'm kissing him back with as much passion as I can manage. The desire to run my hands through his hair is far too strong to resist. Without hesitation or the realization, my hand is pressed against his cheek. He is warm, a light stubble tickling along my palm as he leans into my touch. His reaction spurs me on, driving my fingers into his hair. It's so soft, almost like silk and my rustling it has caused it to fall over his face, creating a blanket of protection around our deep kiss. There is a rumbling growl in his throat as my hands fist in his hair, pulling him closer, deepening our kiss.

With his growl came a twitch of his cock, right across my now aching mound. I grind my hips, causing his growl to turn to a hiss and he backs away. The loss sends chills from my scalp down to my toes.

I can barely breathe as he slides back onto his knees on the floor between my legs. His hands are on my thighs, pushing my dress up, exposing my pussy to him and I watch as his eyes grow dark with lust. He gently lifts my legs so that my feet are flat on the edge of the bed. Then suddenly he is lifting my hips and pulling me to the end of the bed. I lift up onto my elbows to better see him. And nothing could have prepared me for the lust in his eyes, the sexual heat that flares in my pussy just as his tongue makes searing contact with my clit. I mewl. His back shakes as his breath quickens in a silent chuckle.

His hands are caressing my thighs, making their way higher, to my hips. He doesn't stop his gentle glide until his fingers brush the bottom swell of my breasts. I moan again. Gusto comes to mind when he starts sucking, licking and nipping at my clit. My need to cum, my need for him drives to a fevered pitch. My hips begin to undulate against his mouth. He groans and his hands seek my nipples. I shiver as soon as he reaches his mark and begins rolling them into tight pebbles between his fingers. The pinching mix of pleasure and pain has my body locking down, my moans turning to screams. Teeth graze along my clit and I explode. Falling over the edge of a cliff higher than I've ever been in my life. My body shakes with aftershocks and my muscles give out, and I fall against the bed as he languidly licks along my slick folds.

His gentle caresses along my pussy and the warmth of his hands slowly glide me back down from the overpowering orgasm he's just given me with his tongue and hands. Something I've never experienced before.

He pulls back from me, no longer being encased in his warmth causes a chill to run through me at the loss of contact. I want him to come back to me, but I quickly understand that I've unraveled him. He's pushing his pants and underwear down his thighs urgently and I can't help the spike in my heart rate knowing that I did that. I watch through heavy eyelids as his erection springs free. It's huge and I can't pull my eyes away from it as it bounces with his movements.

My mouth waters, desire drives me to sit up. I can't help my hungry need to take him into my mouth and before his pants are completely off I wrap my hand around him, pulling him to me. The shock is evident on his face, but I don't care.

He takes a hesitant step forward, then another. His erection is in my face and my tongue slips free of my mouth to lick the string of pre-cum, catching it before it falls. He groans at my touch. The sound is so feral, but I can't stop now. I continue to lick along his thick shaft, making it easier to move my hand up and down. I look up at him, his eyes are hooded, lust and desperate want etched across his features. I open my mouth and slowly suck the purple bulging head into my mouth. I watch him through my eyelashes as he's turning to putty in my hand. I keep sliding my mouth up and down, taking a little more in each time and each stroke of my mouth is matched by the stroke of my hand and his eyes close.

"Dacotah." His teeth are grinding together.

"Hmm," I hum and he shivers.

"Dacotah, stop, please?" It is evident in his voice that it is taking all of his will power to force me to stop. But I do as he's asked. Despite my desperation to continue, there is an underlying command in his voice that has me weak in the knees and I do as he's asked. The command in his voice that has me weak in the knees; I can't explain why, but the walls of my pussy throb.

Despite stopping, I can't hide the sadness in my eyes. "There will be plenty of opportunities for you to take my seed, sweet girl, but not now. Take that dress off." He pulls back out of my reach and I stand up, reaching for the bottom of my dress. I pull it up over my head. He gasps at my willingness or my nakedness; I can't look at him to be sure. The order to strip for him has me wanting to drop to my knees and bow my head. *What is that all about?*

Before my dress even hits the floor he has me in his arms, pressing me to him, his erection hard between us and my need for him fires anew. He gently presses me backward. I take a tiny step, then another until I feel the bed against my legs and his lips are on mine. Needy and wanting. I can't breathe anymore. When he realizes I'm holding my breath, he pulls back. "Lay down," he growls and just like that he produces a foil packet, placing it between his teeth, he rips it open and then removes the round, rubber disk from its sleeve.

I slide back on the bed, sliding toward the headboard. As I lay back, I open for him, fighting the urge to rub my fingers along my flaming sex. Need and desperation grows hot, my nipples pebble against the cool of the room. Their tightness is almost painful.

I watch as his long fingers pull the condom onto his hard-on. My mouth waters some more as he climbs in between my legs. With his eyes, he is silently asking me if we're still good and I spread my legs a little farther, inviting him inside.

He takes my invitation. Running the head of his cock against my slippery slit, I groan. And arch my back, pressing my hips further into the mattress. Begging him to slide himself inside.

Finally I feel him, poised at the entrance to my now soaking wet, overheated sex. After what feels like hours, he starts to slide inside me at an achingly slow pace.

He's huge and I immediately understand his slow motions but it is driving me insane. "Please," I beg him and he slides in a little faster, but still not fast enough. "I'm not going to break," I say between gritted teeth. I can't take his slow torture anymore but finally I feel him pressed inside as far as he can go, but he stops moving and I squirm. "Please, Derek," I beg again. I watch as his breathing falters, his eyes close in ecstasy and then I feel the twitch of his cock inside me.

"You're so—," he groans "—tight." His patience seems to disappear altogether.

After another heartbeat he starts to slide out, a little faster, but still slower than I want. Then without warning he falls in on top of me, holding himself up, as he slams inside me, coaxing a moan of beautiful pleasure to slide past my lips. He doesn't stop his pounding inside me. I can't stop the desperation that spreads like wild fire through my veins. I begin to match him thrust for thrust, urging him on.

My eyelids are so heavy that they close. I fight to open them because I want to see, really look at him as he comes undone inside me. When I finally peel them open, he's looking down at me.

Having him inside me sends a new flash of lightning through my veins and all my resolve earlier today about walking away at the end of this melts away into a lost puddle. I am going to get burned and I don't care.

He lowers his head and I think he is going to kiss me, but instead his hair falls into my face as he looks down between our bodies. He's watching himself disappear inside me. Without warning, he sucks one of my nipples into his mouth. His tongue is scorching hot against my hard nipples and I can't stop the overwhelming rush to cum. It is overcoming me, harder and faster.

My breathing is sharp, jagged, and my moans become more pronounced with each thrust. With my nipple still in his mouth, his eyes meet mine. His teeth bite down on my nipple, sending a ripple of sweet pain deep down. "Mine," he roars as my sex clamps down around his cock. With one final carnal thrust and an animalistic growl, he explodes.

17

Shopping...

"Come-on, sleepyhead," I hear him say to me. "I need you to wake up." I fell asleep shortly after we'd finished with a promise from him that he'd wake me up in a bit.

Slowly I open my eyes to him standing over me. Only now he's fully dressed in his suit and hunter green tie. "Where are we going?" I mumble as I start to rub the sleep from my eyes.

He smiles. "I have a meeting that I need to attend. You get to go shopping."

I groan. I hate shopping. "Don't you have someone that can do that for you?"

He laughs. "I do, but you're not shopping for me. Well, not directly for me." He hands me a black credit card. "I've made arrangements for you to be taken to Neiman Marcus, where you will meet a woman named Alice who will help you shop."

"What exactly am I shopping for?" I've never heard of this store before, but I'm hoping I don't lead him to that same conclusion.

"Clothes, for you, for this week."

Oh. "I'm not sure that's the best place for me to buy clothes." He cocks his head at me. "I wear a size fourteen, not a common size in the skinny girl stores."

He scowls at me. "Trust me, you'll find what you need." His tone tells me that he is unhappy with what I said, not that I said anything wrong, but let's face it, I'm no skinny mini. "Come on." He smiles. His unhappiness is washed away when I throw back the covers. The heated look in his eyes reminds me that I'm still naked. He wraps an arm around me in an awkward half hug. Looking down and blushing because I'm naked, I can see why. Apparently my nap was just long enough for him to get worked back up again.

He kisses the top of my head. "You're beautiful, never doubt that," he whispers. I know I blush, thankful that he is so much taller than I am, with my head down, he can't see my face.

"Can I bring the girls with me?" He stiffens slightly, something I'm guessing has made him nervous all of a sudden. "It's fine, I can go alone."

"No, it's alright, if you want to bring them, that's fine. I'll be done with my meeting around six. Please try and be back by then." I look up at him, puzzled. "I'm going to take you to Top of The World." My eyebrows don't unknit themselves and he smirks. "It's a restaurant in the Stratosphere tower."

"Oh." I'm surprised, both by the restaurant and by the fact that he wants to take me out.

"Disappointed?"

I smile at him. "No. Sounds like fun."

He kisses the top of my head once more. "Have fun shopping." He pulls back and starts walking backwards toward the door. I remember again that I'm still naked, fighting the urge to cover myself, I blush bright red. "Oh, I almost forgot." Sure you did, Orion. You forgot nothing. He takes a few steps back toward me and I meet him in the middle. He hands me my phone. "I programmed my phone numbers into your phone. I hope you don't mind, just call if you need anything."

I take the phone from him and he backs away again. "You're incorrigible, Orion." He laughs as he leaves my room. My dress is hanging on the mirror where his suit was earlier and sitting in front of the dresser are my wedges.

Thank god, I can bring the girls. I need better shoes.

I look at my phone, press the button and slide to unlock it. I press the call log and sure enough, the last number I dialed is labeled "Orion" and I smile.

I also notice three missed calls. Two are from Rachel and one is from Mandy, the one from Mandy came about ten minutes ago.

I call her back.

18

mmm Showers...

It is five when I return back to the hotel after dropping Mandy and Rachel off at theirs.

They gushed as soon as they were in the limo about what Orion offered them by way of one of his men. What he threw at them was nothing to sneeze at. Neither one of them is bothered by the arrangement, but of course they pressed for more details. I refused to give any, using the excuse that I didn't know much. Mandy was quick to try and probe me for information about whether or not I'd seen him naked. I never answered, but she took my blush as enough, for now.

I was surprised, maybe even a little disappointed, at the fact that they were both going along with the charade that had been offered to them. Sure, they are easily persuaded by money and all the trouble they can get into with it, but I figured they'd both be trying to change my mind about the arrangement. When I'd given them crap about choosing money over friendship, they both laughed, and then there was a little bit of hurt. A little while after that, Mandy took it upon herself to tell me that Rachel had been horrified, at first, and it really took a lot of persuasion by the guy, but Mandy later concluded that it was probably because he was hotter than hell.

"We even tried to tell him to forget the money if we could just have him," Mandy chortled. I had scoffed and she laughed it off like they'd been kidding. Somehow, I doubt it.

Of course they'd pressed me for all the details of what Orion wanted from me. I managed to dodge the questions with shopping and later told them that once it was all over, and we were on the plane, I'd spill the beans.

After we arrived at the store, I had to force myself to stop looking at price tags. By the time I'd gotten to the third outfit, I knew I was going to have a panic attack if I kept looking.

All in all I came away with at least two outfits for each day I was going to be with him, at his request of course. I also picked up two new bathing suits, like I didn't just buy a couple on Friday, and Alice was kind enough to inform me that I had to pick evening attire. Which I did, and a lot of it I'm actually really excited to wear.

I hadn't realized how much fun shopping could be, but then again, back in Wisconsin, shopping meant traveling to Minneapolis, and I never had that kind of money. With the exception of my cowboy boots, the most expensive article of clothing I wear on a regular basis are my bras. The curse of being bigger than most in the chest department.

Once everything is dropped off in my room, Arnold, Orion's personal concierge, hung everything up, and put things away for me. After he left, I shut my bedroom door and headed into the shower.

Despite the nap, the shopping wore me out and I was hoping the shower would help wake me up. I was so glad the girls had come along with me. They provided a distraction from my thoughts about what I'd gotten myself into with Orion and they were a necessary asset in helping me pick out clothes. I'm a jeans and t-shirt, small town girl, where Mandy is a little more versed in the finer clothes than I am. Their help was invaluable when it came to picking and choosing, mainly because Alice thought that everything I tried on was amazing. Mandy and Rachel knew me better, and could help me decide on the things they knew I'd be comfortable in. Needless to say, I have a ton of new sundresses to wear.

Somewhere between shampooing my hair and lathering with body wash, I feel the hairs on the back of my neck stand at attention. You'd think I would freak out, but I know immediately that he's here. I turn around. My breath sucks through my teeth as I take in his beautiful, sculpted, sexy nakedness not but a few steps away from me. Watching me like the hunter I know he is.

"Hi." I breathe then watch as a hungry smile spread on his lips. His eyes are heavy and hooded and I know that this shower is about to get a whole lot longer.

He charges into the shower with purpose and I think he is going to slam into me so I put my hands up defensively. There is a tiny rush of fear that slices through me, but then he grins a wicked hungry grin as he grabs my wrists. Lifting them over my head and effectively pinning me against the wall of the shower. With my arms tight above my head, I'm helpless to escape, I whimper. His mouth swallows my cries in a possessive kiss. My mind wants to scream, but my body betrays any ounce of fear I may have had by softening and pressing into him.

My breath leaves my body in a warm rush of pleasure when that now familiar lightning crackles across my skin, heightened further by the fact that he's holding me down. He makes an adjustment with my hands. In blinding speed, and with a painful grip, my breast is now in his hand. I moan again, and this time I tremble and slickness slides free of my labia and onto my thighs. I try in vein to rub them together.

He's being rough with me and I'm enjoying it a little too much. His leg slides in-between mine, parting them and stopping the friction.

His hand kneads my breast, rolling my nipple between his fingers and I tremble with desire. With his leg between mine, I try in vain to grind against him, needing relief as the orgasm builds in record time. I open my eyes to meet his. There is a hunger, a carnal need in his eyes. It drives me wild to see it, knowing that I'm doing this to him is beyond anything I could've imagined. He slows his kisses on my lips but I can feel him moving against me.

Then I feel it, his cock replaces his leg, pushing against me, begging for entrance into the warmth. He slowly rocks his hips against me, gently pushing into that space. The tension I didn't know I was feeling falls away, a foggy cloud settles in, my body going lax against his. "That's right, sweetness, let me in." His words are both commanding and soothing at the same time. I relax enough to let his erection slide along my clit. The probing forces the fire to pool right behind my clit. With his lips on mine, his hand holding mine hostage and his other wreaking havoc on my nipples, my body starts to lock down.

He pulls back his lips, his hand and his cock, forcing me to cool and groan, "Please, Derek."

He growls at me, the fire in his eyes rages. With his hand now free to guide himself inside me, he lines himself up, but the angle is wrong. Driving me wild, he stops there. He buries his face into my neck, finding that spot right behind my ear and my nipples burn as they tighten further, solid as granite, now pressed against his chest.

His hand, the one still holding my wrists to the wall, loosens a fraction. "Do not move your hands," he orders and his hand comes away. Holding my hands up is going to be hard. I interlock my fingers, hoping that will help.

Both his hands are now kneading at my breasts and my nipples, my knees begin to shake and I feel my orgasm building again. Knowing that I will fall to the ground if I cum, I focus on that. "Derek," I mewl, desperately.

Sensing my desperation, his hands come away from my painfully sensitive nipples. Soothing the ache, he slides his hot wet tongue along one, then the other. I begin to shake. I can't stop it, can't stop the orgasm anymore.

"Put your arms around my neck, keep your fingers interlocked," He says against my breast and his breath causes another shiver, but I do what he says.

At the same time my arms meet his shoulders, his hands reach for my thighs and he stands up straighter, bringing me with him. "Hold tight," He grunts and I do.

The next few seconds are a blur because the next thing I know my legs are wrapped around him and he is slamming inside me, unleashing an orgasm that has lightning flying through my veins. My body begins convulsing uncontrollably and the strangest sounds fill my ears. "Shh," He breathes and I try to bite my lip, but his mouth is back on mine, soaking up my cries with his tongue on mine. His tongue begins dancing in rhythm to his hips as they slam into me. Each thrust sends new waves of pleasure from my head to my toes, and with no reprieve from shattering moments ago, I'm brought back to him by another rapidly building orgasm.

Somehow he's managed to hold onto me and slam into me at the same time. I can feel every inch of his cock sliding into me, deep and bare. Damn it, that means he's going to pull out. I concentrate hard on what he's doing, ignoring the burning ache in my arms and the rubbing of the tiles against my back. He's now kissing my neck and my shoulder and I can tell he's fighting the urge to go lower and to slow down, but he can't.

Being a double D has its disadvantages in this moment. *Damn it Cotah, turn off your brain.*

"Stop thinking," I hear him say. "Feel it." Just then he slams harder into me and he has my undivided attention. I feel it building and my legs start to tremble. "Don't hold out on me." He grunts then bites into my neck. The overwhelming pain and pleasure tips me over the edge and I explode, clamping hard on his cock buried deep inside me and he groans. I scream his name and in an instant his hands loosen and I am slipping down his body. Surprisingly, I understand immediately what he's done. Without a thought, I drop to my knees and pull him into my mouth. With two hard strokes of my hand, he pushes himself against my throat. With a growl of appreciation, he lets loose inside my mouth. Grunts and flinches of his cock are sending salty sweet cum sliding down my throat. I open my eyes just in time to see his face relax and his body convulse with pleasure. Pleasure that he's just taken from me, like an animal, and I loved every minute of it.

He falls forward, bracing himself against the wall overhead. The water his body had been holding back from me comes crashing down around him, forcing me to look away.

"So Dacotah," his sultry, sated voice comes from above me, "you like a little pain with your sex?" I blush.

"I guess so, not something I've experienced before."

I catch his proffered hand in my peripheral vision and I take it. He helps me stand up and I look him in the eyes. "Just how many men have you been with?"

Oh dear. I'd hoped he would never ask me that dreaded question. Though I'm obviously not a virgin, my sexual history reads like a pamphlet on what not to do during sex-short and boring. But he's waiting for an answer and I realize I've looked away from him when his hand comes to my chin. Our eyes meet and I can't hide anything from him. "One," I breathe, embarrassed. "Well, two now."

"That's nothing to be ashamed of, Dacotah. In fact, it's nearly admirable."

I look at him then; do I want to know how many women he's been with? No, I don't. "When you're twenty-eight and only been with one man, it's kind of pathetic really."

"No, not really." He smiles and I shiver at the coldness in the shower. "Were you done in here?" he asks as I wrap my arms around myself.

"Uhm, no, I need a minute." He smirks, knowing exactly why I want a minute.

"I'll go get dressed. How long before you're ready to go?" he asks me.

"Forty-five minutes, an hour maybe."

There is a little bit of shock on his face. "You can have more time if you need it."

I shake my head. "I'm not one of those girls that spend three hours getting ready, Hunter." I try and smile sweetly at him, he narrows his eyes.

"That's because you don't need it," he huffs and steps from the shower. If that is as mad as he ever gets with me, I'll take it. It was quite cute.

19

Showing off...

Fifty minutes later, my hair is dried, curled slightly and pulled up on one side by a small pink flower that matches the bottom of my dress. I'm wearing a halter-top maxi dress that is deep purple up top, embellished with a few rhinestones to accent the bodice. The dress has an empire waist created by a belt, which makes it easier to go without a bra. Though the neckline is quite low and leaves little to the imagination. Not that Orion needs any. The dress fades from deep purple to nearly black and then into pink along the bottom. It has to be my favorite purchase of the day.

The ensemble is completed by matching purple peep-toe pumps and I'm thankful that they feel so great, and aren't very high. They're really comfortable.

I text a picture to Mandy and Rachel who are quick to reply with praise for my dress choice. Mandy is even impressed with my make-up skills. This says a lot because wearing make-up is not something I do often.

When you come from a small town, wearing make-up 'just because' usually gets people talking about what kind of person you are. Though mascara and eyeliner are always in my arsenal; the rest, not so much.

I take one last look in the mirror and I'm grateful for the double sided tape Rachel suggested because I'm afraid that my boobs are going to cause a slip and I don't want that.

I take a deep breath as I reach for the door handle on my bedroom, leaving my phone, purse and all other essentials here, I don't feel that they're truly necessary for whatever Orion has planned for me tonight.

I walk down the hallway, trying to step lightly because I want to surprise him, and as I come around the corner, I think I have. He's standing in front of the window. His legs are spread shoulder width apart and his hands are clasped behind his back. The stance sends a shiver through me, and once again I feel like falling to my knees. Is it possible that he's...? Of course it's possible; look at all he's done so far.

He is wearing a dark grey suit and I can see the shimmer of pinstripes in the light. I can tell he's irritated by the tenseness in his shoulders.

"No, I am unavailable tonight." Short pause. "Starting now. We can deal..." He turns toward me and my heart rate increases dramatically as I brace myself for his reaction. "With it tomorrow," he says harshly into the phone, pulling it away from his ear, pressing a button and tossing it on the couch. All while his eyes remain on me.

I know I blush, but it is becoming something I'm going to have to get used to. He makes no secret of his approval of anything I'm doing or wearing and I like it. But I also have no doubt that he'd be the first to make any dislike known as well.

"Turn around," he says and I do as he's said and I can hear his shoes cross the tile, walking toward me. When I come back around to face him, he is but a few inches away from me. He lifts his hand and gently runs the backs of his fingers along my cheek, down my jaw, to my neck, then he follows the line of my dress to the point right between my breasts and I shiver. Goose bumps rise across my now heated skin. His hands have left a trail of fire in their wake and my nipples harden. His breathing is ragged. "You're so beautiful," he whispers. "You look amazing."

"So do you," I manage. While he was staring at me, I took in his dark grey with white pinstriped pants, black shirt and a vest that matches. He is sans tie and after this morning, I wonder if he was waiting to see what I would wearing before he chose a tie for tonight.

He takes my hand and leads me toward the bar, where I signed my non-disclosure agreement this morning. The bar isn't empty this time either. But rather than a folio, there is a really nice looking black box sitting atop it. Something close to panic begins to rise in my chest as I take it in. It is too big for something small like earrings, rings or even a bracelet.

"This is only on loan." My heart rate decreases dramatically as he picks up the box to show me.

"Do I even want to know how much they cost?"

He chuckles. "No, probably not." He opens the box and I gasp.

Inside the box, nestled in satin, is a beautiful pink stone necklace. Each pink stone is surrounded by smaller pink stones. There are also matching teardrop shaped earrings and a bracelet. I smile. They're beautiful. "Would you wear these tonight?" I look at him, I know the fear I feel is radiated in my eyes. "What's wrong? They're insured, if anything happens…"

"That's not it." I start to play with the necklace around my neck.

"You don't take that one off?" He is quick to understand and I shake my head. "Well, what about the bracelet and the earrings?"

I smile. "That, I can live with."

"Good." He removes the bracelet from the box, unclasps it and holds it open for me. I give him my right wrist and he clasps it in place. It's a little snug, but when he's done it sits nicely against my skin. He smiles his approval.

I start to take out my bottom earrings. I have three holes in each ear. The bottom ones are just little hoops that fit against my ear, and the top two are just little silver balls. Nothing fancy. "Do you want me to take out the other four?" I ask, not wanting to, but out of respect for these beautiful earrings, I feel compelled to ask.

"No, they'll match the silver in the earrings."

I go about putting them in and when I'm done I look at him and his face lights up. "They're perfect." He kisses my forehead.

When his lips meet my forehead I feel that zing that fires between us. It is obvious that there is major chemistry between us, but this seems like so much more than just chemistry. I get the sense, that while he's being sweet, he too is hiding something from me. Or maybe it is just reservations about knowing that a week from now we will part ways. My heart sinks a little at the idea already and we've barely concluded our first day together.

"I'm going to go finish getting ready," he says as he heads toward the stairs on the opposite side of the elevator. I want to follow him upstairs, just to see what his room looks like, but I don't. I have no doubt that I will have plenty of alone time this week to go exploring.

20

Fuck!...

He isn't gone for even ten minutes when he comes back down, and his ensemble is complete with a deep purple tie. "Is there a color of tie that you don't own?" I ask and he looks surprised at my question.

"No."

I laugh. "Tell me, how did you know to wear the green one earlier?"

He looks petrified at my question. "I'm not sure you want me to answer that."

I stand and walk toward him. "I already know you're a hunter, which means you keep eyes on your prey until they are in your talons. So, I can guess that either Alejandro called you when I refused the offered ride or..."

"Come here," he smirks then takes my hand, pulling me past the stairs leading to his room. There is a door in front of us that looks like it is next to mine, but there is no direct path to my room from here. He stops in front of the door and I can hear a series of beeps but I don't see where they're coming from. With a turn of his wrist, the door opens.

The room beyond the door is dark, but there are flickers of light coming from behind the door. He leads me inside then turns to close the door.

Along one wall of the room, though it's not large when compared to mine, are no less than fifteen monitors. Each monitor is displaying something going on, but where, I can't quite tell.

"On the left, you have various camera feeds from the Bellagio. Next to that, various feeds from Planet Hollywood, and on the right, the Cosmopolitan," he says matter of fact, but there is a fear in his voice that I can't quite place.

"Why do you have all this?"

I hear him take a deep breath. "Because I own, or have a controlling interest, in all three of these hotels."

My breath catches and I take a step back. I'm mesmerized by what I see on the screens and am transfixed by what he's said. I look at him, his eyes are glowing in the light of the monitors and they're weary and afraid.

"Say something," he says.

"I... I had no idea," is all I can manage to say. I imagine that just these three casinos earn him more than enough money, but he said he was here on business, so I imagine there is more.

"I also have interest in six other hotels in Las Vegas."

I put my hand up to stop him. The reality of what I'm facing with the man before me is simple. He's absolutely loaded. Damn it. I knew, earlier, when he was so reticent about telling me his name, that there were a lot of layers to Orion and I wasn't oblivious to his financial standing, but seeing it here, flashing across monitors in a room, inside his penthouse, it all becomes clear. "What are you so afraid of?" I ask him.

He sighs. "That I'm going to say something, or show you something that will send you running from this..." I step toward him, placing my finger over his lips.

"Derek, what you do, or what you own means nothing to me. Yes, I won't lie, your wealth is overwhelming to me, but I'm not here because of your money. Though it explains that outrageous bet Friday night and how you so easily parted with three hundred grand. But it doesn't explain why they didn't seem to have a clue about who you are?"

"I can explain that," he says behind my finger. I remove it quickly.

I shake my head. "I don't need explanations. You were so unwilling to give me your name earlier; I can imagine that there are very few people in these casinos that know who you are." I'm shaken by the fact that this just proves how different our worlds are and how easily he can offer me a week long proposal like I'm Vivian in Pretty Woman, minus the hooker status. It also explains why he'll be able to walk away from this a week from now, unaffected and unchanged by anything that happens between us.

"Dacotah, I'm sorry. I really thought you knew." I look him square in the eye. "But your reaction right now tells me that you truly have no idea who I am." He takes a step toward me and I step back, trying to keep some distance between us and he stops.

"No, I have no idea. I can conclude that you're here on business, and that a week from now you're leaving town, so I can put two and two together and determine that this isn't all you own and to be honest, Orion, I don't care." I try to stay strong to show my determination at keeping some level of anonymity between us. "Derek, do you understand that I am a waitress at a pizza parlor in a small town in Wisconsin? That nothing about me screams money? I did not have an affluent upbringing and could better be described as lower middle class."

"Dacotah, I don't care," he says through gritted teeth. He's angry and I'm not sure I understand why. He takes a deep breath, calming himself down. "I knew, before I found you in Coyote Ugly Friday night that our 'worlds' are opposite, but it didn't stop me. I also have a pretty good idea that the only reason you went to the club yesterday was because of the voucher you were given, though I suspect that the fact that you had three hundred grand in an account at Planet Hollywood made it a little easier for you to accept that voucher because you figured that money would cover whatever tab you could run up."

I can barely breathe and I back myself against the wall for balance.

"Dacotah?" I look up at him with extreme hesitation. "Do you want to leave?"

I quickly weigh my options. Cut my ties now and walk away before things really get out of hand between us, or stay and suffer the consequences a week from now? Either way, it's going to hurt. "Not if we're going to dinner and we stop talking about money," I say boldly. My words are like a litany to him as I watch him sag with relief.

He takes a hesitant step toward me and I don't stop him, so he takes another and then finally the last step to reach me. He takes my hand in his and he kisses the back of it. "Deal," he says and we leave the room with all the creepy monitors. "I didn't mean to upset you," he says as we stand at the elevator, waiting for it to arrive.

I lean into him and rest my head on his shoulder, my silent acceptance of his apology. I try to shake it all off. I knew he was wealthy, but my vision pales to the reality of the situation and it is clear to me now as I lift my head and look around the room. It's not that it's a penthouse rental, but the kitchen, furniture and the drabness of my room tells me immediately that this is his personal condo and I didn't see it earlier. Then reality that he's brought me into his home warms my heart a little to the idea of what stands between us like a ten ton anvil.

The elevator arrives and he ushers me in.

21

Modes of Transportation...

Once we leave his suite, we don't say anything to each other. While we walk toward the limo that's parked in the valet area, he doesn't even hold my hand. But rather than be insulted by the gesture, I realize that there is a rather thick line between Derek Hunter, the businessman, and Orion, the man I get behind closed doors.

I'm suddenly thankful that I'm not like most girls that would be riddled with jealousy or hurt because he didn't hold my hand. I've known the man for all of a few hours and even though we've seen each other naked, that's hardly cause for public displays of affection.

I am, however, having a hard time processing the overall tenderness I feel from him when we're together. Forehead kisses and nicknames like sweet girl and sweetness only add to that confusion. I decide that I am not going to allow the mixed signals to consume me; instead I swallow them down so that we can have a good night together.

I watch him carefully as we walk through the lobby. I realize that he's also watching me. Despite the physical distance between us, I can tell we're closer than I thought we were as soon as I feel the air charge between us. I can feel that magnetic pull that he has on me. The same one that lets me know he's near me, whether I can see him or not.

I feel the energy like I'm a kid who's just rubbed her stocking feet all over the carpet to make her hair stand up. I'm a live wire, coming to life, being filled with electricity. I wonder idly, with a smirk, if my hair is standing on end.

I see his eyes light up when he takes in my grin as we step through the doors. The limo driver is nowhere to be seen, but that doesn't bother Orion as he stands next to the Lamborghini style door, with his arm out, gesturing me inside. He offers me his other hand as assistance to step into the limo. As soon as my fingers grace his palm, all that charging is pinpointed to this one small point of contact. The following zing is like lightning crackling in a dry desert sky. Though there isn't a physical shock, it shoots straight to my heart.

His grin widens when I take his hand, lifting my skirt to allow me to ascend the stairs. I'm watching him as I step into the limo and then that smirk changes into a wide, panty-melting-all-knowing smile. My sex clinches in a very delectable way, making me needy for him. All from a smile.

I step into the limo, dropping my dress back to the floor; I take a seat on the far side, waiting for Orion to join me. I'm looking out of the window closest to me when I feel the air charge once again and I know he's returned. The charge in the air and Orion in the car sends shivers across my skin. I can't quite comprehend why there is this deep attraction to a man I barely know, but just watching him fold his tall, well-built frame into the seat next to me has me all hot and bothered again. Regardless, I squirm in my seat, watching him out of the corner of my eye; he's watching me too.

I hear a strange whirling sound and I don't have to look to know that it's the privacy glass going up between the driver and us. As soon as the noise stops, he's on me, hot and hard with a deep, fervent kiss. He wastes no time sliding his tongue between my lips as I gasp at the sudden contact of his body with mine.

I hate that my body's reaction is so primal to him. I wrap my arms around his neck and pull myself into him. His breath hitches when my chest comes into contact with his and our hips connect. I moan low and desperate into his mouth. He responds to the noises I make by reaching up and gripping on to my left breast with strong, skilled fingers. His fingertips graze along my nipple and I feel my pussy clench tight, soaking me.

His other arm snakes its way around my waste, pulling me tighter against him. The heat in his hand sears through my dress and I'm filled with lusty need. Desire runs like fire through my veins, there is no holding back with him. I reach for the skirt of my dress, pulling it up. I watch as his eyes follow the motion, and releasing my breast, his hand finds mine, helping me slide the dress up higher.

His hand is sliding along my leg, higher, towards my hip and my sex. "Dacotah," he growls as his hand caresses the exposed skin between the top of my thigh highs and my panties. He breaks our kiss completely, pulling back to look. I feel his fingers pull at the belt holding up the thin nylon then the sharp snap against my skin.

His reaction has ignited the lust in me and I can't stop myself from hitching my free leg over both of his. Using my grip around his neck, I pull myself on top of him. He stiffens as my need becomes clearer to him. I slant my lips over his, kissing him. Desperation to soften his posture takes over. I grind my hips against the erection trapped between our bodies. As my hips glide slowly over his erection, my tongue slows into tasteful strokes. His mouth goes slack in a rush of hot breath that covers my face in humidity.

I feel his hands lifting my dress higher up my legs, and then he pulls back when he's satisfied. I let out a groan of disapproval that he's stopped. Then his hands are gently caressing the swell of my breasts, along the deep V neckline of my halter top. He starts to tug on the material to expose me, but he finds resistance. He tugs harder and I yelp as the tape comes away from skin. He breaks our kiss, looking down at my now exposed chest.

His lips twitch as his eyes morph into melted dark chocolate spheres. I follow his gaze. "Oops," he breathes. Where the tape was holding my halter top together, there are two thick red lines. "Sorry," he says, but I don't feel the conviction, he's enjoying this too much. To soften the sting that still lingers on my skin his hands begin to slide gently along my sternum. With his warm hands between my breasts, and the promise of more, I arch my back, thrusting my breasts toward him. He tugs on the fabric, pulling it away, exposing my breasts and my nipples immediately harden. "You're so beautiful," he breathes as he cups both my breasts in his hands, kneading the sensitive flesh, then his tongue sears against my cool nipple, causing me to tremble. I flick my hips again, reminding him that I am right there.

My hands fall between us and somehow I manage to slide my hips back, his legs come up to support my weight, and my hands find the button, then the zipper of his pants. "I want this," I breathe against his temple. "I need this." His mouth slides from my nipple, licking, biting and sucking to the other one.

I pull down the zipper right as he takes my other nipple into his mouth and I can't stop the flick of my hips. I'm so hot and ready for him, I need him inside me to soothe the heavy ache pooling there.

I place my hands on his hips to steady myself, straightening my legs so that I can get some leverage to remove his pants. He senses what I'm doing and I watch as his cheeks hollow completely, pulling hard and tight on my nipple, letting it go with a very audible pop and a twinge of pain as I begin to shake.

His hand comes up under my dress, sliding along the inside of my thigh, his breathing spikes the closer he gets to my hot, dripping center. I stop breathing all together. So ready for his touch. He draws out the anticipation which is killing me. When I finally feel him touch me down there, he is grabbing the crotch of my boy shorts, hard. Followed by the sound of ripping fabric and a hard tug. My pussy trembles as a cool rush of air slides its way through my labia. My panties are in his hand. "Breathe."

I obey, letting out a rush of air then quickly sucking air back in. Clearing my head, I put the tips of my fingers in the waist band of his pants, but I can't seem...he's commando and I'm instantly turned on even more knowing that only this small piece of material separates us. I pull his pants down to his knees and his cock flops down then instantly back up, lying hard and thick against his stomach. "That's far enough," he says, stopping me. "Come here." I climb up his body, desperate to touch him, but when my hands go up under his shirt he stops me, grabbing me by the wrists. I pout at him, he smirks. Pulling my hands up to his neck I try to kneel back but my dress is in my way.

"I can't move." There is a glint of something in his eye and he smiles as he lets go of my hands and pulls up my skirt, exposing me. My most intimate parts are now on full display for him. Resting on my knees, I'm straddling him. Trying to reach around the bunch of my skirt to stroke him, his hand is already there, blocking my touch. With the head of his cock, he lines up perfectly with the entrance of my sobbing pussy.

I hiss through my teeth as I start to slide down. "Slow," he orders and I slow slightly. His hand drops my skirt, covering both of us up. If I didn't know better, I'd look like I was just sitting on his lap, but then I feel his cock twitch in anticipation, so I keep sliding down, sucking him into me. When I feel some resistance within me, I slide back up, then right back down, this time hungrier and faster than before. My juices coating his naked cock. I can't take anymore.

His hands come to my hips, helping me to adjust to take in just a little bit more of him. I am stuffed full. I give myself a second or three to adjust to the fullness and then, spurred by the look in his eyes, I start to slide effortlessly up and down. His eyes roll up and close, his breathing quickens the faster I move.

The orgasm I know I need starts to build and my sex tightens around him. He responds by gripping my hips and helping me move up and down. He's pushing up and pulling down, forcing me to take every inch of him. With each thrust inside, I take a big step closer to exploding.

My sex spasms hard, hanging on to his cock, milking him and he grunts and moans. Suddenly his eyes open and I know my face is contorted with need and the building orgasm I'm feeling. He knows it too. I can feel his hands tighten and then loosen and come away, but I can't keep up the rhythm so his hands come back to me. Guiding me. "Grab your tits, Dacotah. I want to watch you play with them while you cum."

I don't hesitate. My nipples are my hot button and my desire explodes as soon as my hands cup and caress. "Your nipples," he says between breaths that are forced out with each downward thrust of my body. I begin rolling my nipples between my thumb and forefinger. He is watching me play, licking his lips. I can see he wants them so I lean forward slightly, rubbing my nipples along his now moist lips and I'm lost the moment his mouth grabs hold, baring his teeth so they graze my nipple and I shatter into a million pieces.

I'm so lost in my own orgasm until the moment I feel him twitch and explode inside me. His seed is scorching. His release causes his jaw to flex as he thrusts into me. I can feel the hot stickiness of his cum being slammed inside me, filling me full as my pussy clenches around him, sucking every ounce of his seed into me. My heart is racing, blood rushing through my ears, and my breathing is short and quick.

Something changes between us. The charge between us ignites anew as his arms wrap around my back, holding me to him. It isn't until I feel his cock swelling again that I remember he's still inside me.

22

Dinner Date...

Top of The World is a beautiful sight to behold. Derek and I are greeted by a waitress dressed in all black, simple black slacks and a black button up dress shirt, but there is something elegant about it. Or maybe it's her. I watch as she looks Derek up and down, eye fucking him while he gives her our reservation information. She pulls up something on the screen and she stiffens, stops eye fucking him and returns to her business self. "Right this way, Mr. Hunter."

I understand it more now why not knowing who he is was so important to him in the beginning. Reading his name was like a lightning bolt that told her to knock her shit off. Either that or realizing who he is, she panicked. I relax almost immediately, though I hadn't realized I'd gotten worked up over the fact that someone else was looking at him until she was no longer doing it.

We follow her dutifully until we come to an area of the round restaurant that is mostly secluded, as it is some distance away from the next table. Derek pulls back a chair for me and I take a seat, after helping me slide in, he takes his own.

"Your waiter will be right with you," the hostess says as she walks away a bit flushed and flustered and I completely understand why. Derek, especially in this light, is gorgeous. So much so that looking at him steals my breath right out of my lungs. It takes me a moment and a sip of water before I'm able to fully recover myself. I start to look around, trying to gather the lost thoughts and I realize that we're moving.

"Are we spinning?" I ask.

His smile is big and bright and I know we are. The speed at which we're moving is steady and slow. "In about an hour, we will have made a full three-sixty rotation." I look out of the window and I can see the lights of Las Vegas itself. Not the strip, but the city. The sun is setting and there is a beautiful orange and red hue that fills the restaurant.

My stomach flutters knowing that we will watch the sunset as we eat, and from the few clouds in the sky, I can tell it is going to be gorgeous. "What are you thinking about?" he asks me, but my answer is interrupted by our server.

"Good evening, my name is Andrew and I'll be your server for the evening. What can I get you to drink?"

I leave all the ordering to Derek, and I have no clue what he orders, but his confidence in whatever he orders is comforting. When the waiter went over the menu options many of them were more or less French and I barely understood most of them.

Derek doesn't say a whole lot, in fact he hasn't said much since we were in the limo, but I don't get a cold vibe from him, he seems contemplative about something, though I haven't a clue what, nor do I even know what to ask him to try and uncover it.

Once Andrew returns with our drinks, wine, a white one at that, Derek holds his glass up to me. "To one week together." His toast is sweet, and we clink our glasses together. The wine is great, sweet, but not too much so. But his toast also manages to bring me right back to what I was trying to avoid, the reminder that this is only temporary. "So, I have a question for you." I look at him, hoping to convey my best 'go ahead' look and it works. "Your necklace, why don't you take it off?"

Oh dear, that's really personal and I can't stop the uncomfortable squirm that follows. But despite the personal question, I feel an overwhelming need to tell him. At least I hope that the shortened version will pacify him. "It was my grandmother's. Well, the pendant anyway."

"I'm sorry," he says, but I can see it in his eyes, he's curious and he is going to give me the inquisition. "When did she pass away?"

"A little over a year ago." I feel my heart pound at the memory. No one has asked me in months how I'm doing since she passed. I guess everyone assumed I'd gotten over it.

"Were you close?"

"Yes," I whisper, fighting back the tears of the memories of her last day on earth.

He cocks his head at me. Trying desperately to read me and I can tell that he's seeing something there. "You took care of her, before she died, didn't you?" My eyes grow wide. How on earth did he know that? "You're fidgeting with your necklace, your face is covered in emotions and your eyes are glassy. It was a guess."

"This isn't something that's easy for me to talk about, Derek. I'm not sure I've gotten over it yet," I say, then take several gulps of my wine before returning the glass to the table.

"I understand, but I'm curious about something." I nod and he continues, "You talk about your grandma and this happens, what about your mom?"

I know what he's doing and it works. Bringing my mom up is a perfect counter balance to the sadness I feel about losing my grandma. My mother makes me so angry that the two cancel each other out enough to balance me out. Two completely opposite ends of the emotional spectrum at least that is what I like to call it. "What exactly do you want to know?" I ask, my tone is clipped. Though I know he's read my emotions regarding his questions about my mom, but I can also see a ghost of a smile playing on his lips as he realizes that he's brought me right back to him. "Talking about my mom is easy, Derek, I didn't have one, at least not until it was too late and my grandmother was already taking care of me," I say before actually thinking about it. "When she finally came around, it was a ploy and a game."

"What kind of game?"

I raise an eyebrow at his question. "She waited until my grandmother was dying. Hoping that she would be out of it just enough so that my mother could con her out of her money." I drink the last of the wine in my glass, wishing I had something stronger.

"For what?"

I let out an audible huff and I can see he's enjoying my reactions for reasons that I can't quite understand. "Drugs, alcohol, sex, whatever it was she was into at that moment.

Once she realized she wasn't going to get what she wanted from my grandmother, she bailed and I haven't seen or heard from her since. I doubt that she even knows her own mother is dead."

Thankfully Andrew arrives with more wine and I can't resist the urge for something stronger so I ask him for a Disaronno on the rocks. Derek cocks his eyebrow at me and the look is so...so, gah! There really are no words for it.

Derek and I spend the rest of the meal talking, mostly about me, and I get the impression that he's determined to get to know me, but I also get the sinking feeling that getting to know me is okay, but getting to know him is going to be a lot harder.

We leave the restaurant and head back to the Cosmopolitan. This time I behave myself, but I wouldn't be disappointed if Derek tried something. I can't take my eyes off of him. I couldn't do it during dinner either. And while I'm glad he asked some of the questions he did, I'm happy about the ones he asked that I didn't want to answer. They forced me to talk, to bend my own rules and walls. He knew just enough to push me for more, but knew exactly when to stop. It made the conversation that much more enjoyable.

When it came to my family, my grandma was it. I am an only child, my grandmother raised me, and there really isn't a lot more to it than that. He asked about where I lived, though told me he didn't want to know exactly where. That puzzled me more than anything about the evening and I wondered why, of all the things he didn't want to know, where I lived in Wisconsin was one of them. Him not asking or not knowing solidified the fact that this really was only going to last for this week and I try to tramp down any ideas that I might have had about where we go after this week.

When we get back to the hotel he tells me that he has some work to do and that I can make myself at home. I go into my room, find a pair of my flannel pajama pants and a tank top before stepping into the bathroom to brush through my hair and wash my face. I debate on a shower, but decide that I don't want to. After I change, hang up my dress, and clean up my strewn towels from earlier, I go back into the living room and turn on the TV. I barely see five minutes of a rerun of one of my favorite crime dramas before my eyes start closing. Each time they drop, it takes longer for them to open. I keep telling myself to get up and go to bed, but finally my eyelids close and I fall asleep.

At some point in the night, I wake up to Orion carrying me, where I don't know and I want to protest, but he smells too good and feels too comfortable for me to care. I snuggle into him as he carries me into my room.

I wake up again when the cool bed sheets touch my skin as he lays me out on the bed. "Don't leave," I whisper. "Stay with me." I'm conscious enough to catch the sharp intake of breath he pulls through his teeth and then I feel him disappear.

I know I frown when I realize he left and I try to get comfortable again, but the bed is too stiff and too cold. It's nearly impossible.

Then, I feel the comforter move with a tug and the bed dip as Orion climbs into my bed. I finally start to feel warm once his arms are wrapped tightly around me and his chest is pressed against my back. I can tell, through my tank top, that he is shirtless and I can feel his rock hard cock sliding against my backside. When I try to twist in his arms he stops me, holding me in place. "Just feel it," he breathes into my ear, and I feel it alright.

It is after four in the morning before we both finally fall into a deep sleep.

23

Monday...

When Monday dawns, I am left on my own for most of the day. Derek had a lot of business to attend to and he left me right after eating breakfast. He asked me to stay here all day, when I asked him why, he gave me his wolfish grin that told me to expect him around lunch time for a nooner. I can't help the butterflies that form thinking about him coming back; just to fuck me before going back to work. It seems so wrong, but yet with him, it is equally right.

In anticipation of his arrival, I start making lunch, this way he can eat before, or after. Just thinking about a nooner with Orion has my heart racing. At exactly twelve the elevator dings. When I step out of the kitchen, he looks agitated about something, but I distract him with lunch. I made a light lunch of grilled salmon Caesar salad. "You can cook?" he asks me, but the shock in his eyes is real.

For some reason, his surprise is a comfort to me and I smile.

I nod in answer to his question. "Don't get too excited, at least not until you've tried it." He takes a seat at the head of the table, where he sat this morning and digs in. I watch him take one bite, then another, and then another. Finally, after the third bite, he looks at me. His eyes are filled with overwhelming approval and I smile at him as I take my own seat, folding one leg underneath me and pulling my knee up. "So you like it?"

"It's fantastic. But where is yours?" He's eyeballing my empty place setting.

I put my elbow on the table, with my chin in my hand, appraising him, doing my best to give him the best seductive look I could manage. "I'm not hungry for food, Hunter."

My words put him in motion. He stands with his plate in hand, walking briskly into the kitchen. The view of his backside clad in a tailor made black suit is the most beautiful sight I've ever seen. His posture is stiff as he disappears; I straighten in my chair, excitement and panic coursing hotly through my body. I'm unsure of what he's doing or if he's actually mad at me.

I can see the light of the refrigerator through the breakfast bar and then the clink of glass as it closes. Everything starts moving in slow motion as I watch him come back around the corner. That wild, hungry for my body look is back in his eyes and it's primal, animalistic, making me want to get up and run, but I will fail because he will catch me, especially considering I'd have to scoot past him to get to my room.

He comes to stand next to me, so close that I can feel the heat radiating off of him. His cock is right there, just beyond the covering of his pants. I know he's not wearing any underwear just by the way his cock is laying- loose, off to his left and falling down his thigh.

My mouth waters. I can't pull my eyes away from the chunk of manhood in front of me. I reach for it. Just as my hand is about to make contact, he captures my wrist. I pout prettily at him and he grins at me. His eyes grow narrow and hooded. There is a dark depth to them that causes my pussy to clench and weep. My need for him blossoms to nearly unmanageable levels in only a matter of seconds.

He doesn't let go of my wrist. Deciding to test the waters, I reach for him again with my free hand. Immediately he captures that wrist and both his hands squeeze. It doesn't hurt, but I'm no longer able to fight and pull them away. Being captured by him, with that look in his eyes, is highly erotic. I can feel my nipples harden to the point of pain at the restraint he's placed me in. My sex clenches and I can't help the rapid breathing that follows.

"Do you have a safe word, Dacotah?" I blink up at him, lost as to what he means. "A safe word is a word that you choose, whatever the word is, if you say it, everything stops, no matter what is happening."

"Are you talking about BDSM?" His eyebrows shoot up at the anagram, more in surprise that I'm familiar with the term. He doesn't answer exactly, but he nods. "I've never needed one," I admit in a quiet voice.

"Pick one," he commands and apprehension rips through me. I can feel myself start to shake. He bends down, looking up at me. "Breathe, Dacotah. I will not hurt you, in fact, right now, all I want to do is strip you out of that pretty little sundress you're wearing, get naked and crawl on this table. For now, all you have to do is say stop, and I'll stop, without hesitation, if I do something that is uncomfortable for you."

Instinct dies out and excitement takes over. I know that I'm not wearing anything under this dress right now, so I'm a little too eager when I stand up. He backs away slightly, watching me. With his eyes on me, watching and waiting, I quickly grab my dress and whip it up over my head. The hunter can no longer contain himself when my body is exposed to him. Before I even have the chance to look into his eyes, he is on me, hard, hot and greedy. He's captured his prey and now he's starved, half crazed with his lust for me. My heart swells.

His hands roam, with no real purpose, all over my body, from my knees, to my ass, my back, my breasts, my neck. Touching, exploring, kneading my skin and leaving a firestorm of goose bumps in his wake. All while his mouth hasn't moved from mine, stroking my tongue, nipping at my lips. He's hungry.

I place my hands against his chest in a moment, a very small one, of clarity. I need to feed the hunter before he devours me in one bite. I push back. His body goes, but his mouth remains on mine. I push a little harder and he pulls back. Without hesitation, I climb up onto the table, laying myself out like a buffet to be eaten.

His eyes never leave mine as he comes to stand closer to me; my skin prickles and my back arches in anticipation of his touch. Unable to pull my eyes from his, I don't see, but rather hear his zipper, then a whisper as his pants slide down his legs. There is a clink then a thud when his belt and something heavy hits the tile floor.

I can feel a tickle along my toes as he brushes against them. "Grab the other side, do not let go." The authority in his voice is too much. An unexpected feeling of desperation washes over me. I'm desperate for him, so I do what he's commanded.

Raising my arms above my head, I close my eyes, my fingers go in search of the edge of the table. When I find it, I curl my fingers around the lip. My arms, like my knees, are bent. Suddenly his hands are wrapping around my thighs and I feel him lift. "Do not let go. I mean it," he growls. I grip a little tighter and I'm certain my knuckles have turned white at the force I'm placing on the table's edge.

Just like that, he lifts and pulls. My shoulders bouncing almost violently across the smooth surface of the wooden table. The motion is so quick that there is no lingering sting. My arms are now stretched as far as they can go. "Good girl." He appraises my ability to hang on causing me to shiver at his words. Then, I feel one of his hands rubbing lightly across the underside of my breasts, the most sensitive part —aside from my nipples— and I can't stop a moan and the bowing my back does. I can hear him smile. "So receptive, Dacotah, so…" He doesn't finish his sentence.

Two things happen at once. Without any warning, he slams into me, hard, with his hand, fingers gliding in effortlessly from my slickness and my right breast is slapped hard.

My pussy immediately explodes, my body milking his fingers to the point that I can feel him pulling, but not moving. All I can see is white, and while the pain isn't blinding, the orgasm is. I whimper and beg. "Again."

"So eager," he says against my breast. "But next time, it won't be my fingers."

I shiver and another small moan escapes my lips. "Please," I beg. His fingers slide out of me in a rush and even the now familiar prickles of awareness have disappeared completely. I try to open my eyes, but it is too bright and I am too boneless from the explosion of the best orgasm I've ever had.

24

The Best Ever...

When he returns I'm too lost in my own thoughts to notice. He makes his presence known by a light tapping against the top of my toes. First the left, then moving over to the right. It doesn't hurt, but it feels- strange. It's hard and soft at the same time. Then, suddenly, it begins to move, taping lightly against the inside of my left leg. As it climbs higher, so does the pressure behind the tapping until it reaches painful. The pain is sharp but fizzles outward quickly, subsiding, driving me higher. The pain turns pleasurable the higher up my legs he goes.

I'm lost to the sensation. The ache for him becoming too much, but reality seeps into my mind at how fucked-up it is that I'm enjoying this. I have no idea what he's doing to me, and I'm doing nothing to stop it. He never told me to close my eyes, I made that choice. Unable to take back that choice, I feel a shiver of fear. What is he doing? Why the hell am I responding like this?

There is a sharp smack across my left breast. I grit my teeth, my back bowing off the table. I don't explode, but the air that hisses through my teeth is audible. "Ow," I groan. "That really hurt."

"I know. Get out of your head."

"Wha…" I try to say something but he cuts me off.

"Stop thinking, whatever you're thinking about, stop. Feel it. Don't think it." He soothes away the sting of the smack, whatever it was, with something cool and soft. But it doesn't stop there. The softness slides along my body, from my breasts to my neck and back down, down toward my now dripping pussy and my legs pull together in antici-pation of a touch that I'm sure is coming, but instead, my legs are pushed outward, separated by his hips.

The softness continues to glide along my body, down my thigh, to my calf, over my toes which wiggle in re-sponse to the tickling sensations. Just as the softness starts up the other side, I feel him slide into me. Not hard, but gently. Matching the sentiment of the softness running along my body, making its way back toward my breasts. I expect to feel the soft, feather light touches caress my breast, but it disappears as Derek stills inside me. My posi-tion on the table prevents me from moving; from sliding along his erection that now sits hard as stone and perfectly still. I'm locked down by his earlier command to hold on, no matter what.

Then, his hands are on me, cupping my now swollen aching breasts and pinching my nipples between his thumb and forefinger. My back bows once again just as he pulls out of me and slams back in. I explode. Fireworks, light-ning, everything flashes before my eyes and I shatter help-lessly into a thousand pieces. Quivering and shaking uncontrollably. It barely registers that he is pouring himself into me, grunting and calling my name.

Derek collapses on top of me, careful to maintain the majority of his own weight. "Let go, Cotah." I shiver at my nickname, it's the first time he's used it. I groan as my hands come away from the table, but I was holding on so tight, they're all cramped up.

I groan as I try to straighten them. Derek notices my stress, pulling back from me. I feel him lift off of me a little, only to shift. I hear his elbows hit the table and feel more of his weight on me. "Give me one of your hands, please," he says, not a command but a request. "Can you open your eyes?" he asks and my head rolls back and forth and I can feel him shaking with silent laughter.

"Too bright. Too tired," I groan.

"You're shattered," he says as his fingers go to work on one of my hands, gently massaging them until my fingers relax. When he's done, he places my hand on his shoulder and takes my other one, doing the same thing, though I'd managed to get that one worked out. He works his way down my hands and arms to my shoulders where he lightly massages both of them and I instantly start to feel better.

"What was that?"

He pulls off of me completely and I force my eyes to open. My eyelids are heavy and the light streaming in through the floor to ceiling windows is way too much. All of sudden, the room falls into darkness, silently. "Try again," he says, but from much further away than I thought. So I do, I try, and succeed this time in opening my eyes.

He's done something to the windows and I look up to where my hands were on the table and there are handprints that are still wet from my sweat. I shiver knowing what caused that. Beyond that, I can still see outside into the daylight, but I can't make anything out. The windows have drawn darker, much darker, and Derek turns on a lamp near the kitchen, far enough away to not be blinding, but close enough to see. "Can you sit up?" he asks and I shake my head no. But not because I don't want to, but because my hips seem to be stuck right where they are.

He comes back to me, massaging my feet, then working his way up to my calf then finally my thigh and hip. He repeats the process on the other leg. I'm ready to sit up. He holds out his hand to help me and I take it.

Coming up off of the table is like ripping off a band aid and he knew it. I can see the gleam in his eye at my displeasure because the highly polished table and my bare backside do not mix well together.

"This," he says as he holds up a green riding crop, "is what I smacked you with when you were in your own head. It is what I was using on you at the time. Then," he holds up what looks like a car washing mitten that is no doubt what he used that was soft. "This is what was soft."

"Why the switch?" I ask, though I don't expect an answer.

He smiles and provides me with one. "I know that pain is something you enjoy with your orgasm, Dacotah, I wanted to see if pleasure was too."

I raise an eyebrow at him. "Did I pass?"

"With flying colors." He comes over to the table and scoops me up off of it, cradling me against him, he walks us toward the...

"We're going up?"

"Shh, yes," he says, offering no explanation for why we're going upstairs. Despite my curiosity yesterday, I didn't go running upstairs the minute he walked out the door. I suspected that the camera room was one of the many things that stopped me from making that adventure.

He climbs the stairs, carrying me with little to no effort. Either he is really strong, or very highly determined. I expect him to set me down as soon as we are upstairs, but he doesn't. He keeps walking until he steps through a door, straight into a bathroom.

The coloring is not what I thought it would be. The walls are painted blue, accented in white, and all the fixtures are polished silver. It's gorgeous when you put it all together. He sets me down on the side of the tub and begins running the water. He lets it run, checking and adjusting the temperature. It doesn't take long for the air to grow thick with humidity from the water and I don't mind. In fact, it feels inviting.

I can smell something that reminds me of home, lilacs. I turn to see him pouring lilac scented bath oil into my bath.

"Thank you," I say then lean into his shoulder. I can't help noticing that he too is completely naked and I'm thoroughly enjoying the view.

25

Everything Shifts...

I all but begged Derek to join me in the tub, but he refused saying that I needed some alone time after that.
Though he did sit with me for quite a while, still completely naked mind you, and we chatted a little bit. When he
left he said that he was going to get dressed and finish the
rest of his salad that I'd interrupted with my honesty about
what I wanted for lunch.

Though I got what I wanted, I was completely starving. I
wanted to climb out of the tub, but I stayed, enjoying the
warmth just a little longer. He was gone when I finally
came downstairs after my bath. And he didn't come home
until well after midnight and I only know this because he
was nowhere to be found when I woke up and he wasn't
there. Though I didn't get up to look for him.

When he did finally wake me, I looked at the clock, it was two in the morning and I had an uneasy feeling in the pit of my stomach. "You okay?" I asked.

"Shh, I'm fine. Go back to sleep."

"Stay?"

"I have some more work to finish up." He kissed my temple then left the room. I fell back to sleep without a problem.

I wake up Tuesday morning to Derek sucking my clit into his mouth, like his life depends on it. My fingers snake their way into his hair so I can hold him to me tighter. He never complains.

We round out Tuesday morning with a fuck in bed, then one in the shower before he leaves for work.

I spend all of Tuesday, well a good portion of it anyway, by his private pool. I call Mandy and Rachel and they are both having a blast. When I tell them that this makes me happy, they are concerned that I'm not having a good enough time on my vacation.

"If it makes you feel any better, I haven't thought about Jason once."

"Sure you have, you just said his name," Rachel chides me.

"True, but I'm still not thinking about him." She laughs at me.

"What are you doing?" she asks.

"Lounging by the pool, hoping I don't burn."

"You never burn," I hear Mandy shout from a distance and realize that Rachel has me on speaker phone.

"You're both really okay?"

"Absolutely, we miss you like crazy, but we're really glad you seem to be having a good time too. Can we get together? Tomorrow, maybe?"

Rachel sounds so innocent when she asks the question and I can tell that she really does miss me. "Absolutely. Let me figure out what time works best and I'll let you know. Okay?"

I can practically hear her smiling and jumping up and down in silence on the other end of the phone. "I can't wait." The excitement in her voice confirms my suspicions.

Derek returns around three on Tuesday afternoon. He looks flustered and very irritable when he comes into the suite. I stand, taking him in, trying to read what's on his mind, but if I've learned anything over the last three days with him, it's that he's unreadable.

"Orion?" I say softly and he stops, his eyes meet mine and there is something that passes between us, something deeper than what I've seen in him. Suddenly the rigidness is gone and his shoulders relax. Not in a way that he's trying to hide something, but rather he's taking comfort in me. I watch him carefully, silent communication between us. Seeing him in his black suit, black shirt and vest, accented only by the crimson red tie he's wearing, I feel my sex heat at the sight and my mouth parts as I begin pulling in quick breaths. My nipples harden and I can't take it anymore, he needs me and I need him.

He walks quickly toward me. Hunger and need in his eyes as he all but slams into me with his body, his hands instantly in my hair. He's holding me tight to his body when his lips slam into mine. His kiss is rough, the two days of growth on his goatee around his lips begins rubbing my lips raw. His hand twists into my hair, pulling my head back further, but his mouth comes with me, harder and hungrier. Abruptly he stops kissing me, but his hands never leave my hair, and his lips move to my neck as he kisses, sucks and licks his way lower.

One of his hands loosens in my hair and begins sliding down my back, searching for something. He finds what he's after and in one swift move, the zipper is down and my dress falls away, sliding off my shoulders, down my body and into a pool at my feet.

He growls as he takes my nipple into his mouth, sucking and licking me like he needs it to breathe. My legs begin to shake at the onslaught of pure raw need in his actions. I'm weak to him. Everything he does drives me insane and makes it impossible to breathe.

His hand lets loose from my hair and glides down my sweat damp body. My head falls back, unable to hold it up anymore. His eyes meet mine and it's there, something I didn't expect to ever see in this man, something I can only describe as love.

I lift my hands into his hair, holding him to me and his mouth continues its starving suction and then suddenly his hand is there, stroking along the lips of my pussy, teasing my clit and I moan, fighting my heavy eyelids. His mouth comes away and I can see that my nipple is cherry red from his suction and it spurs my desire for him higher. "I need you," I whisper.

"You're disarming me," he breathes against that spot on my neck, right behind my ear, and I tremble at his words. There really is something different between him and me. There is honestly so much more than lust crackling the air between us. The relief I feel at his words is overwhelming.

My need for him peaks and I reach for the lapels of his jacket, sliding it down his shoulders as he begins to nibble at my ear. He's not fighting me, not taking control the way he usually does and I realize that whatever is bothering him is enough to make him let go, to let me take the lead with him. I go for his tie as soon as I throw his jacket across the couch. Pulling it free, I begin working on the buttons of his shirt while he plants light kisses along my neck and shoulder. Finally I reach the button of his pants and I undo it, knowing full well that just beyond the confines of his zipper is my prize.

I slowly slide the zipper of his pants down and he groans. I can feel the hunger of my hunter, he needs me. I pull his shirt free and try to free his cufflinks, but I can't because his mouth takes mine. His lips are passionate, softer than before and I know what's changing between us. All the blind lust between us is gone, replaced by an unwavering desire for more. He wraps his arms around me, pulling me off of my feet, but his lips never leave mine.

He begins to walk, but not toward the couch, or my bedroom. I realize he's taking me to the stairs. I squirm and he pulls back. Through heavy eyelids he asks, "What's wrong?"

"Where are you taking me?"

"My bed," he replies, scooping me up. "I need you, in my bed."

My heart starts pounding. I have a feeling that I know what this means to him. What it means to have a woman in his bed. I snuggle into him and he carries me away to his part of Castle de Hunter.

26

Our World Turns...

While desire spikes higher for him as he carries me away, I can't help but ask him. "Are you sure?" He pauses his climbing and looks at me with the same intensity he had in his eyes a few moments ago.

"Sweetheart, I don't know if I've ever been more sure of anything before in my life." His lips come to my forehead and he starts climbing again. The endearment of sweetheart is overwhelming and I feel that tightness in the back of my throat, the one that makes me want to cry.

Thankfully we reach the door to his bedroom and I'm instantly distracted. "Turn the knob." I do as he commands; noting absently that it wasn't a command this time, but a request. His tone is soft, reverent, causing my adrenaline to spike as my hand touches the door knob and I turn it.

The room beyond the door is nothing like I expected, though at this stage in this strange turn of events, I half expected something close to eccentric.

The room is bright, lit up by the same floor to ceiling windows that encase the rest of the apartment. Straight ahead of us is a dark, cherry wood dresser that is similar to the one downstairs, only taller. Above that is a very vivid picture, and in the short seconds that my eyes focus on it, it changes, but what it changes to steals my breath away. It's me. "When..." I look at it a little closer. "The club?"

I look at him and he looks rather sheepish. I wrap my arms around his neck, and he sets me down, but wraps his own arms around me as his face dips into the hollow between my neck and shoulder enjoying my embrace. I hear him take a deep breath before he asks, "What's this for? I thought you'd be mad."

I pull back, forcing him to standup again and our eyes meet. "Just knowing that there is a good possibility that Saturday night you went to bed with me on your wall, it's really..."

"Creepy?" He smiles then.

I can't help but laugh. "Maybe a little, but it's very flattering, Orion."

He comes toward me again, the intensity from earlier is back in his eyes and I expect him to slam into me again with a rough, passion fueled kiss. But he doesn't. The kiss I get this time is warm and very sensual. For the first time since I met this man, I want him to make sweet gentle love to me.

Cuddling with Derek isn't something I expected to be doing this week, but after what I just experienced, I'm so glad he pulled me into his arms. It was like he was in my head, doing everything that I needed and wanted him to do

to me. Hands exploring and roaming blindly, mouths licking and sucking sweetly. It's all very heady and I shiver.

"Are you cold?" he asks, he sounds groggy.

"No," I whisper, hoping to hide the crazy emotions rolling through me. I feel him shift and look in my direction,
but I can't bring myself to look up at him. I don't know
why I feel like hiding, but after what I just experienced
with him, I know without a doubt that this week is going to
destroy me emotionally and... I feel the tears I was fighting
earlier. I begin to nibble on my lip, but it is useless as I try
to get them under control. "Bathroom," I whisper, desperate to get away before he sees them, but the idea of pulling
away from our embrace is making the tears harder to maintain.

I climb off of the bed and head straight for the open
door in his room. I close it behind me and I let the silent
tears fall.

You agreed to this, Dacotah, why are you so... so....
Ugh, I can't even berate myself properly anymore. Though
my anger at myself does halt the trickle of tears. I take a
minute, trying desperately to regain control. Looking into
the mirror, I pray that I don't look like I've been crying. I
need to go back out there, go back to him, and face him.
Can I do that without letting my emotions get the better of
me? Who the hell falls in love with a man after three damn
days? No one. I barely know him, at least not beyond the
intimacy that we share and it's stupid. I finish calming myself down by telling myself that it is lust and not love. I take
a deep long breath, flush the toilet so he doesn't suspect
anything, rinse off my hands and face with cool water and
leave the bathroom after drying off.

When I open the door, he's there. Sex hair, tossed
sheets, and Derek freakin' Hunter sprawled out on the bed,
naked, with his eyes closed. I stop breathing as I look at

him. His shoulder length dark brown hair is everywhere, including a few stray strands falling into his eyes. One hand rests on his stomach, the other one is reaching out toward where I'd left him a few minutes ago, like he is searching for me.

Finally I pull myself together and start breathing again. Instead of standing here staring like a fool, I could be snuggled up to this glorious sex-god. I start walking toward him and it seems as though he's honestly fallen asleep. Knowing how late he was up, and how early he woke me, I hesitate climbing into bed, not wanting to wake him.

Then his beautiful eyes meet mine, as I stand next to the side of the bed and his hand reaches out toward me. I smile, climbing back into bed with him. He pulls me close and I nestle into the crook of his shoulder and my hand goes to his stomach, landing on top of his. When I go to move it he stops me by linking our fingers together. He brings his other hand up and he starts to play with a chunk of my hair.

"You okay?" he asks. I nod my head, not trusting my voice not to betray me and cause more questions. "The bathroom isn't soundproof you know."

Shit. My skin flushes; thank god he can't see me. I didn't think I made that much noise, let alone cried loud enough for him to hear me.

"You know you can talk to me, about anything," he says as a way of coaxing me to talk to him.

"I'm not ready," I tell him and thankfully it is enough to stop him from pressing further into why I'm so upset. Truth is, I'm mad at myself for letting myself feel like this, feel what I'm starting to feel for him and there isn't anything he can do about that.

"I respect that, but I will be asking you again, soon." he says, a little bit of a warning in his tone and I secretly hope that he forgets about it before Sunday comes.

"Rachel and Mandy would like to see me tomorrow, have lunch or something," I say, but it's not really a question. I'm hoping to change the subject.

His hand stills in my hair. "Listen, I came up here to talk to you about something." My heart rate increases at the tone in his voice, whatever it is seems extremely personal.

"Oh," is all I can manage. "So, not a nooner?" I tease. Then his chest starts to shake in silent laughter. With that comment, our mood lightens by a ton of bricks. The thick aftermath of 'what the hell just happened' shifts to a more fun, playful mood and I rather like it.

"Well, there is always that."

"But you were upset, pacing, when you came in the room, you didn't even notice me."

"I hope that is the last time this week that you will have to see me that way. I got a phone call right as I got on the elevator that I didn't need to hear. I'm sorry you had to see that." I can hear some resentment at the fact that I saw him that way.

"I'm not."

He hugs me closer to him and confusion washes over me again, but he doesn't talk about his phone call anymore. "Tomorrow might not be the best day to see your friends," he says and I can't stop looking at him. "I came up here to ask you if you'd be my date to a charity gala tomorrow night."

I sit up, looking at him and his hand falls to my hip, and his thumb starts running gentle circles on my skin. I watch as my hunter returns with hungry eyes that rake across my nakedness. He doesn't disappoint my reading abilities when he languidly draws the hand at my hip up my body.

The touch is so light that I fight the urge to laugh and squirm, it tickles. When his fingers slide over my nipple feather light all coherent thought is gone. There was a reason..."gah," I moan and he smiles.

"Will you, Dacotah, be my date for the charity gala tomorrow night?"

My eyes roll back in my head as he rolls one of my nipples between his fingers and my sex ignites with desire like we haven't touched in months verses minutes. "What's, ah, the charity?" His hand continues its assault on one of my nipples, pinching and pulling.

"That doesn't matter. What matters is that I want you there."

"Jesus," I moan as his hand switches nipples followed quickly by a sharp pinch and I feel like I could come undone from nipple play alone with him. I've always loved my nipples, aside from the fact that they are much darker than my skin tone would suggest and they're bigger than most I've seen. But what I love most is that they're hypersensitive and Derek knows exactly how to get me warmed up.

"Do you trust me?" His voice is sensual and seductive. I look into his eyes.

Without a conscious thought I answer his question, "Yes."

He sits up, his hand coming away from me causing me to shiver, needing his touch to help keep me calm. The look in his eyes tells me that he knows exactly that. "Lay down," he orders. "On your back, arms up." The commanding tone is back and my sex clenches, twitching with the promise of something that will test me beyond my limits.

Yesterday on the dining room table, he commanded me in a way I never thought I could possibly enjoy, but I took so much pleasure in it and I get excited any time I think about the next time he has me open and submitting to him.

27

Trapped...

I get so lost in my own thoughts staring up at the ceiling that I don't know what he is doing, at least not until I felt the bed dip up by my hands. I look up in his direction and there in his hands are purple suede cuffs with silver buckles on them. They hang from his finger by tiny silver links. "Have you picked your safe ward, Dacotah?" There is a devilish grin playing at his lips, matched by hooded eyes.

"Chasseur," I throw out without even thinking. I hadn't thought about it because I didn't think he was serious.

"Hunter? In French."

I can't stop my eyes from darting up to his. "You speak French?" Something I didn't know, though with all his businesses, it would make sense.

"Occupational hazard," he smirks at me. "I like it, but if you scream 'hunter' in English, I won't stop." I know my eyes go wide. "I rather enjoy when you call me hunter, so I won't allow you to stop saying it." I nod my agreement.

His fingers glide gently along my arm from the inside of my elbow to my palm and down my fingers. "Give me your wrist," he commands, though softer than earlier. I dutifully lift my arm and he slides the cuff on. The material is soft against my heated skin and my nipples harden. I watch him as his eyes drift down my body. My hunter is back. Watching his prey.

The chain makes an ominous sound against the iron of his bed as he strings the loose cuff through. The sound sends shivers of excitement across my skin and I try to rub my legs together, seeking relief from the flood of arousal I feel.

"Look at me." I do and I can see him staring at me, his eyes narrow. I can barely make out the fact that his own hand is sliding along his now rock hard erection. "Keep it up and I will tie your legs to the bed and force you to watch me stroke myself until I come all over your delicious body." My mouth goes dry, my lips part and I start panting. He smiles then, knowing exactly what watching him stroke himself is doing to me, whether I can touch him or not, it would be one hell of a hot scene to watch. "Or perhaps I shall reward you with it." I lick my lips as he reluctantly takes his hand off of his cock. He quickly cuffs my other wrist.

I tug and they are certainly secure and I feel my eyes roll up into my head, getting lost back there; lost to the idea of what he is capable of doing in this position, with me trussed up, unable to move. "Lift your head." I try in vain to open my eyes as he slides something over my head. It doesn't take me but a second to realize it's a blindfold. "Yesterday you kept your eyes closed by choice. Today, you don't have one." My skin heats and I am hyper aware of the coolness of the air and the warmth of the sheets against my back. "If this gets to be too much, use your safe word, Dacotah. What is your safe word?"

My brain scrambles momentarily as I realize that the table downstairs was nothing compared to what he's about to do to me. "Chasseur," I say before he can ask me again. I realize immediately that my lack of response could result in this not happening and I want this, need it.

"Good girl." I feel his hand stroke along my hair. The comforting gesture takes me by surprise when suddenly I feel completely and totally relaxed by his touch. I hear him hum softly; no doubt he can tell what effect he's had on me by that simple touch. I feel him shift off of the bed, the blindfold over my eyes has brought everything else in to clearer focus. The smell of the room changes, my skin prickles at the cool air from the fan above me. I can no longer sense where he is in the room, but the blindfold has made me more aware that I can hear the shuffling of his feet. I remember that he is still gloriously naked and the idea of him walking around, looking at me makes me shiver and my nipples harden into tight peaks.

I flinch slightly when his hand begins to softly caress my right ankle. His hands are gentle and then something soft, like what's around my wrists, wraps around my ankle and goose bumps creep from my ankle to all points north. The cuff wraps tight effectively stretching me out across his bed. The same happens with my left ankle and just like that, I am bound to his bed, unable to move and fully exposed. My heart rate skyrockets in anticipation of what he plans to do.

After the crop yesterday, I'm expecting something similar or even harder, so I am surprised when I feel something very soft, like fur, gliding lightly over my leg, from my ankle, up to my knee and then finally my thigh. I feel the bed shift and the softness continues its path across my lower belly. It tickles and my stomach muscles jump as he continues to my other hip. Then he slides down my thigh to my knee and beyond.

He continues his path back up, but he doesn't stop at my hip, this time he goes up my side, to the softness of the lower swell of my breast and I shiver again. The softness has created a slow sensual massage and I feel slightly lightheaded as he continues along my breast to my shoulder, across my collarbone and around my neck, then he repeats the process in reverse. I writhe. The longer he runs the softness over my skin, the warmer and wetter I get.

"So beautiful," he breathes.

I can't stop the moan that parts my lips. I try to fight my restraints, arching my back, seeking his touch, begging him to continue what he's doing but the fur comes away from my body. I know he's paying close attention and my pout registers on him because I can hear his soft chuckle. It's breathy and the sound brings every nerve in my body to life.

I decide, right here and now, that no matter what he does to me now, it is never going to be enough. The way my body responds to him is something I can't deny. I try not to think about what my heart is thinking, or feeling, because right now, I want to be here, with him, anyway I can have him.

That's when I feel it, tickling my palm, and my hand closes on instinct and all I can feel are soft leather strips. My eyebrows shoot up and I can tell from the shift in the atmosphere between us that he's smiling at my expression, but he says nothing. He slowly glides the tips of the leather down my arm, along the inside of my elbow. I can't stop the giggle that passes my lips as it tickles then disappears.

There is a whooshing sound that is followed by a short burst of silence, and then the crack comes as the leather hits my skin. As it slides away from my body, it leaves goose bumps rushing across my skin. There is a twinge of arousal forming in my nipples; they begin to throb, painfully. There is no pain and I realize that the sound is much more intense than the pain it produces. I writhe in anticipation of being hit again. I expect him to hit my arm, but when the whoosh sounds again, the sensation is on my thigh, and again the quivers continue, this time I can't stop the moan of desperation for more. I fight my leg cuffs because my need to rub my legs together is too much.

The whoosh and smack happen again, in the same spot, this time it's harder and my skin prickles with the slight sting of the leather and my breathing falters. "Slow, deep breaths," he murmurs and I comply with a deep breath through my nose and an exhale out my mouth. "Good girl," he praises. I fight my lips from forming into a smile. Then suddenly the sound picks up again, there is a whooshing noise. I can't stop the flinch of my muscles in anticipation of the contact with my skin, but there is nothing. The air hissing continues but now I can feel the cool caress of the wind he's generating across my ankle. Then it hits, lightly across my ankle, then again and again, each pass getting harder and begins to sting as he continues. Suddenly the sensation starts to move higher up my leg. "Ahh." I can't fight the squirm, concentrating hard on my breathing, but unable to ignore the wonderful sensations I'm starting to feel all over my body.

My body relaxes into the bed. My skin tingles from head to toe. My body turns to melted caramel as he continues up my leg to my stomach and then he works his way across, down my other leg, just like the fur. I shiver again, realizing the path he intends to follow is the same as before. My breathing hitches and my mind becomes cloudy, unable to focus on anything but the raw sensations the leather is generating across my skin.

He doesn't disappoint and his motions climb up my body, along my stomach to the soft under swell of my breasts and I can feel the leather inching closer to my hardened nipples. Unable to control my breathing any longer, I start breathing in a near pant. My sex is so wet and warm, I can feel it dripping from the opening of my pussy, down the crack of my ass and settling in a pool on the bed. Embarrassment over my arousal washes over me and I can feel my skin heat at the moment the leather makes contact on my chest. Without warning, my head goes completely blank; I'm flying in sheer bliss. Nothing matters, I don't care about anything. But I feel my body stiffen and an orgasm I didn't know was building, explodes. My whole body is shaking and my eyes are screwed shut. I vaguely register that the whooshing air noises have stopped and I feel disappointed.

His hand is suddenly gliding along my shin, down toward my ankle and I can feel him messing with something and just like that my ankle is free of its restraint and his hands begin massaging from my ankle, up my calf, to my thigh and my hip. The feeling loosens the tight muscles I didn't realize I had in my hips. The gesture is repeated with my left ankle.

Now that my legs are free to move, I don't have the strength to move, to even try to rub out the rest of my orgasm. Then I feel his hands under my knees, pulling them up, further exposing my sex to him. The bed dips between my legs. His breath caresses along my sex. "You're beautiful," he breathes, gliding his fingers along my cleft. Oversensitivity forces me to try closing my legs. He stops me, "Don't." His command has me frozen in place and I clench my hands into tight fists. The sharp pain of my nails into my palms keeps me grounded and suddenly his mouth, wet and hot, presses hard into my cleft, stroking from my clit to my entrance and back again. My back arches off the bed as I fight the need to close my legs tight-ly around his head. His tongue is sending me back into that blissful orbit. Soon my moans start stringing together as it becomes too much. The urgency on my cleft increases, he knows what he's done to me. Driving me higher.

His finger slides inside me, probing, while his tongue continues to circle my clit and drive me insane. Just when I think I'm about to explode, he stops. All contact from him is gone. I begin whining in an incoherent protest that he's left me, driving me wild. The bed shifts again, and he rears up, taking my legs with him, lifting my hips off of the bed and that's when I feel him, he's rock hard and heavy lying across my sex. Using the new leverage, I flick my hips, hoping I can get him just right so that he will slide inside. But he holds me tighter by my legs, squeezing his hands in a silent warning. I melt back into the bed, giving him com-plete control and it is by far the hardest thing I've ever had to do. I'm going crazy with need, lust and anticipation of what is going to happen next.

I feel his fingers tracing lightly across my skin, across my body, from my thighs, up my hips, to my stomach and then I feel his nails scrape across my chest from the base of my neck, between my breasts and down to my stomach. I flinch and shiver. "Please," I beg.

He stills. "Please, what?" His tone is nearly a growl and my sex heats more, if that is even possible, and I groan.

"Please, I need you," I whimper and his hands grip onto my thighs, the sensation carrying with it a warning that what I said was wrong. "Please Sir, please fuck me." I'm surprised by my own words and he doesn't hesitate. Sliding hard and thick, deep into my pussy and I explode around him.

"Jesus, Dacotah," he growls as he starts sliding in and out of me, pumping me, moving me. My hands wrap around the chains holding my wrists to the bed. The sudden intrusion and the soreness of my sex has me trying to pull away from him, but his arms are wrapped around my legs holding me to him.

It doesn't take him but a moment; I can feel his erection harden further, swelling inside of me, needing me as much as I need him. I stiffen again, unsure of how I've come to this point so fast, but I fight it. I'm holding back so that I can enjoy a shared orgasm with this magnificent lover of mine. "Come, Dacotah, NOW!" he bellows harshly. I explode once again, my own juices mixing with his and I can't stop the shakes and trembles as reality of our inevitable end dawns on me. I don't know how I will move on from this, from him. I don't know how I will ever be able to walk away, let alone find a lover who makes me feel as he does.

Derek quickly unties my wrists, slowly, like my ankles, he massages my wrists. He moves down my arms and finally into my shoulders. While I was restrained, I hadn't realized how tight my shoulders were until I couldn't move after he untied me. I didn't want to move, and I am thankful that he hasn't taken the blindfold off just yet. I need a moment to compose myself; I don't need to have him see me crying. He surprises me further by rolling me onto my right side, then sliding his hand under my head, his other arm around my waist without removing the blindfold. I realize that he's sensed my need to stay hidden for a few moments.

He spoons in behind me, holding me tight and having been shattered into a million pieces more than a few times this afternoon, I'm completely content to lay here. I fall asleep in his arms.

28

Moodiness Amplified...

When I wake, sometime later, the blindfold is gone from my eyes and the blinds have been opened. Outside, beyond the glass castle walls is the Strip, lit up in the low sunset. The view is breathtaking and it takes me a moment to realize that I'm in his room. Then the afternoon comes flooding back to me. First our sensual lovemaking, followed by something that I can't even begin to describe as reality.

I lay there, staring at the hypnotic lights of the Las Vegas strip. The lights are something else to watch, never faltering, never changing pace, or pattern. I remember before I'd fallen asleep that I realized the gravity of the emotional situation I've gotten myself into and it scares me. I barely know this man, but in the three days we've been together, I've never been treated the way that he's been treating me, and I know that I will never be able to find another man who is capable of the things that Orion has shown me. There is a sensitivity to him that I don't know if I can live without.

Sure, I've read the books, read about finding a new partner, someone who knows me, who I am and what I need. It will not be an easy task because Derek seems to have an acute understanding of that and he does it with very little effort, which of course makes it that much harder to be able to think about letting him go. Today is Tuesday and I only have a few more days left with him.

Knowing that my time with him is severely limited, I climb out of bed quickly and search for my clothes. Then I remember that I left them downstairs. Jeez. Looking around the room, through the outside lights shining through the window, I can see a small table, upon which lies a glove of some sort. I walk toward it. Running my hand along the soft fur, I realize that this is what he used on me first. Then, sitting next to it, I now notice the flogger and it's beautifully braided handle and dozens of leather strips hanging from it. I shiver, remembering what it felt like across my skin. I run my fingers through the fall and decide that I like this toy and secretly pray that he will use it on me again, soon.

I pad quietly to the door. Opening it, I can hear shouting coming from downstairs and I freeze. I don't want to go downstairs if someone else is here because I'm in my birthday suit. For god's sake, I could be stuck up here all night. I step lightly toward the top of the stairs to listen further. I can hear him, but no one seems to be responding.

"No, you need to deal with it. I have time sensitive responsibilities here in Vegas; I cannot and will not go running off to Paris until the week is over. Deal with it now, or we will not be able to continue our arrangement..."

"Paris," I whisper, my heart sinks into my stomach at the fact that he needs to leave, and go take care of business. But then what he said registers and I feel slightly hopeful, that maybe his business in Vegas will keep him here, at least for a few more days.

"Damn it all to hell, Jack, deal with it. I won't leave, not now. I will be there sometime on Monday."

I let out a breath I didn't realize I was holding as I realize that when he leaves me, it won't be until Sunday, and then the sadness comes. When he leaves me, he will be leaving the country and I start to fidget with my hands.

Finally his voice calms down and I can barely make out what he's saying and the reality that he really is on the phone propels me down the stairs. I need to see him, but as I draw closer to the bottom step, my heart begins to race and desire washes through me at seeing him again. When I finally reach the bottom step, I look out across the open living area of the apartment and I can see him, dressed in a suit. This one is dark blue. His hands are behind his back, his legs spread wide. I watch as the muscles in his back tighten and roll with agitation and I start to step really lightly toward the couch, hoping to grab my dress and put it on before he turns around, but I'm mesmerized by his slight reflection in the glass. Despite his earlier irritation with whoever he's talking to, there is a smug smile playing on his lips. Can he see me?

I look toward the glass and the only thing that reflects back into the room are the things closest to it. There is his face, he is only inches from the glass, and I can see a couple of decorative pieces that are on tables up against the glass, but other than that, there is no reflection and I take comfort in knowing that if his back is turned to me, he can't see me. But it doesn't stop me from watching his reflection.

"We're done." I hear him say, but I'm the one who falters her steps and fights to silently regain my balance. When I look at him, I can see the same smile across his lips, but his eyes are a little wider, searching for something. "Good-bye," he says into whatever he's talking into, I can't see anything, but it doesn't matter. Now that he's done he is going to turn around. I take those last few steps toward the couch and look on the floor. It's gone.

"What?" I breathe.

"Looking for your dress?" My eyes shoot to him and that smug 'I have a secret' smile is playing on his lips. He looks so young and carefree, at least in this moment. I fight to straighten myself, then realize that I'm naked and instead curl in, trying to cover myself. "It is for that exact reason that I've put your dress away."

"What? Why?" I groan and fall onto the couch.

"Several reasons." Is all I get and I scowl at him. "One being the fact that you're so self-conscious about your body, I want to show you that your body is beautiful, and sexy and sensual."

"How does me being naked do that?" I huff.

"Stand up." The authority is back in his command and I can't stop myself from obeying him. I do so, hesitantly, still covering my breasts. "Hands down." The barked command sends shivers across my skin, hardening my nipples into stiff, tight peaks and I lower my hand, but I can't seem to move the one that is covering the mound between my thighs. I look at him with all the horror and fear I feel inside me and he takes a few steps in my direction. "The other one," he says. Though the command is there, it lacks finality and is filled with a sensual promise. My body begins to tremble, both in fear and from the need that's growing for him between my legs.

My hand slowly slides out of the way, exposing my entire body to his scrutiny and I do my best to try and gauge his reaction. I notice that he stops moving, but his mouth falls slack and I can hear his breathing take on a more carnal tone, and my hunter is back. His eyes are sharp, seeking me, surveying his territory once again and I'm instantly hungry for him. Needy and desperate for his touch. He's ready to pounce and I can't help the fact that I start to shake with anticipation at what he might do to me when he comes closer to me. But the look in his eyes, the lust and desire, has me trying to cover myself again. Being the hunter that he is, he is sharp and his eyes harden, giving me a look that dares me to continue trying to cover myself. A look that I can't conceivably cross, no matter what. The hunter becomes the dominant male and I'm weak in the knees. Something about the look in his eyes tells me that this is a lesson for me and then his mouth twitches into a smile.

"Go get dressed," he orders. "Something casual. We're staying in tonight." I don't move for several moments, disappointed that whatever was building between us stopped like someone poured ice water in my veins and I shiver. "We have all night," he breathes and instantly the ice turns to smoldering desire and I feel sweat forming on my lip and brow. Desperate to get away from the look in his eyes, I head toward my bedroom and clothes. "Dacotah," he calls and I stop, turning to look at him. "No bra, no panties." I let out a rush of hot air at his request, lower my head, looking at the carpet; I turn back toward my bedroom.

With the request of no underwear, I can only assume he has plans of seduction and getting me to bed. The thought excites me as I seek out one of the many sundresses that now fill the closet of my room downstairs. I find one that is a soft pink with spaghetti straps and an empire waist that helps hold my breasts in place. Though I second guess the choice when I realize that it barely covers my sex, but decide that this is his choice and if he doesn't like it, he will request that I change.

I head into the bathroom to try and run a brush through my crazy hair, and I apply just little bit of makeup to my too wild eyes. Derek has proven, on more than one occasion, to be a gentleman, but the request for tonight's attire reminds me that he is not only a gentleman, but a sex fiend and I'm excited by that idea, at least until I'm reminded that this will all come to an end in just a few days' time. The thought grounds me and I vow to rebuild the walls around my heart for protection.

29

And We Shift Again...

When I finally emerge from the bedroom, he is standing at the window once again. Now he is in a pair of grey flannel pants and nothing else. They are hung low on his hips showing off two very sexy dimples just above his hip bones. The sight of him standing there takes my breath away. He's gorgeous and I can't help the self-conscious thoughts about why he's chosen me. I've never thought of myself as ugly, but my body type tends to lend itself to low self-esteem whether I want it or not. I lower my eyes to the floor, trying to bring my own issues under control. I can't understand why a man as gorgeous and rich as he is would want something, anything to do with a poor, chubby girl from middle of nowhere Wisconsin.

"If you keep thinking like that, Dacotah, you will never be able to see you the way that I see you."

My eyes snap up and he's looking at me. The familiar hunger is back in his eyes and his flannel pants don't hide much. I can see his hard, heavy cock lying across his pelvis and I shiver. "How'd you know?"

He takes a couple of steps toward me. "I can tell, by your body language mostly, that you're wondering why I chose you, why I wanted you." I blush, unable to hide the insecurity and the realization that he's read me perfectly, like he's read my mind. "I will tell you why I chose you." He pauses momentarily and the elevator dings, signaling someone's arrival and I stiffen. "Over dinner," he adds, walking toward the dining room table.

I watch him as he interacts with the concierge delivering two carts worth of items. In the center of one of the carts is a vase that contains no less than two dozen bright red roses. I slowly walk toward the table as the gentlemen discuss where to put things and the table, bare moments ago, is now filled with plates covered in silver domes with the roses as the centerpiece.

After a few more moments, Derek hands him something, the concierge bows and turns, leaving through the elevator. As soon as the doors close, Derek stands next to a chair to the right of the head of the table, gesturing for me to join him. I reconnect my brain and my feet start walking toward him. The romance laid out on the table is confusing to say the least. Sure, we've eaten together, but this; this is very romantic and confusing. I try hard to stifle my thoughts as he takes my hand, assisting me into my chair. He helps push the chair in before kissing each of the knuckles on my hand.

As he takes his seat, I can't stop myself from looking at his naked torso. He is muscled and sexy. Each muscle is accented by the soft light of the room. I watch as he moves and his chest muscles roll and contract with each motion.

He reaches over to my dome and pulls back the lid. My eyes lazily follow the lines of his forearms up to his biceps, which are pulling the skin tightly, further accenting the muscles beneath. My eyes lazily move to his shoulder then finally our eyes meet. I can't stop my tongue from darting out to wet my lips, then I capture my lower lip in my teeth and I can feel the heat blossoming in my core, my need for him growing hotter with each passing nanosecond.

He lets out a breathy laugh, but says nothing as I break my stare. I look to my plate and it is covered in pasta with a white sauce and chicken. I expected something far more elaborate than fettuccine alfredo, but I'm comforted by the food in front of me. He too removes his dome and to reveal the same underneath. He continues releasing the lids on the remaining plates. There is a Caesar salad and several breadsticks and my mouth waters and my stomach rumbles. He chuckles again. "Enjoy," he says and I don't hesitate in picking up my fork.

We eat in companionable silence until I've polished off all of my salad, a few breadsticks and about half of my bowl of pasta. It dawns on me around my last few bites why we're having this type of dinner tonight. One of the things I know that bothers Derek is the fact that he is wealthy and a well-known businessman and it too bothers me. It adds to our already massive differences, not to mention the physical differences. But tonight is about me. The fettuccine, while I'm certain isn't cheap, it's simple and grounded and I can't help the smile that spreads across my face as I set down my fork and wipe my hands and mouth on the napkin.

"A penny for your thoughts," he says. His voice takes on a sultry tone and I look at him. His eyes are alight with curiosity and I smile again.

"I was just thinking about our meal."

"Oh." His eyes grow puzzled.

"How simple it is." The puzzled look remains in place and he cocks his head, begging me to continue. "You could have ordered steak, duck, filet mignon, or anything far more extravagant and expensive, but you choose fettuccine alfredo, why?"

He gives me a crooked smile and his eyes light up. "Nothing wrong with comfort food."

I can't help my answering smile. "No, there is nothing wrong with comfort food. I find it comforting that you would think of it that way."

His crooked grin turns into a full blown smile. "Dacotah, would you believe me if I told you that even I enjoy good old macaroni and cheese." My eyes grow wide with shock and my mouth falls open. He laughs. "Why is that hard to believe?"

I sober and wave my hand around, "Why would you eat macaroni and cheese when you can afford to have some overpriced, famous chef prepare it for you, from scratch?"

"Because I can," he says simply, but the look in my eyes tells him that I need more than that and he doesn't disappoint me. "There is far more to me than expensive penthouses, fancy suits and an overly extravagant lifestyle, Dacotah."

The tone in his voice tells me that he's offended. "I'm sorry; I didn't mean it that way."

I look down and begin fidgeting, desperate to disappear into the chair or the carpet. "I didn't say you did. But there is a lot about me that you don't know. Yes, I have money, a lot of it. Yes, I can spend it however I want, and yes, I can spend it on the little things in life like a box of macaroni and cheese. I enjoy it because it reminds me of growing up. It reminds me of my mother and the things she would always do for me." His eyes grow sad and unfocused, as if he's disappeared somewhere else, sometime else.

I don't know how to respond to him, so I don't and we lapse back into silence. After another sip of my delicious wine I look at him, he's looking at me, searching for something. "I'm sorry, Derek, I had no idea."

He smiles slightly. "Of course you didn't, I didn't tell you. I haven't always been rich, Dacotah."

Once again I have the breath stolen from my body as I realize what he's saying. He's fought for everything he has and everything he's earned, my respect for him grows. "Tell me," I breathe, desperate to know more about this man, but for reasons that I know will hurt a lot more later.

"What would you like to know?"

"How old are you?" I'd measured a guess a few days ago, placing him in his early thirties.

"Twenty-nine." I baulk at him.

"You've amassed an empire in eleven years, that..." words fail me. "Wow."

He smiles. "I'm a very hard working man, Dacotah. Despite my ability to be here, with you all afternoon, I've neglected a lot of responsibilities, a lot of things that I needed to get done today so that I can leave on time Sunday morning, which means that I will likely be working late into the early morning hours."

"I'm sorry if I kept you from..."

"Stop. I stayed because I wanted to, because..." He doesn't continue and I stare at him, silently begging him to continue. "I stayed because I needed you."

I pull in a sharp audible breath at his words. He needed me.

"Still do, which is why I am here and not in the office. I can't be in Vegas twenty-four-seven. I have other responsibilities to other portions of my business so I am forced to entrust the men who work for me to do their jobs. Which is exactly what they're doing right now. Rest assured I will not be leaving tonight." Just then he reaches under the table to take my hand in his. The gesture is sweet and I don't resist as our fingers intertwine.

"Why me?" I bring up the subject from earlier and he gives me a hard scowl. My shoulders slump under his gaze.

I hear him take a deep breath, steadying himself for something. I want to look at him, but I can't seem to lift my eyes. "Look at me, please." he says, though his voice is soft, the command is there. I slowly lift my eyes to look at him. When our eyes meet, he smiles. "Why not you?" I open my mouth to say all the reasons why not me, but he places a finger against my lips. "You're beautiful. Every inch of your body begs to be touched, to be kissed, and to be honored. Dacotah, you're a beautiful woman with soft, supple curves. Despite what you may think of yourself, you have everything a real man should want in a woman." He stands and I watch his long body flex and relax. The movement sends shivers through me. I want to reach out and touch him, afraid it's all a dream and I'll wake up back in Wisconsin in my bed, alone.

"I've never enjoyed skinny girls, Dacotah. They hold nothing for me." He comes to stand behind me, placing his hands gently on my shoulders. His fingers begin to move lightly and the shivers return. "You're beauty is something that can't be replicated and it is nearly impossible to explain." His hands begin to move slightly across my shoulders and I feel his fingers wrap up in the spaghetti straps of my dress, tugging, trying to get them to fall down my arms.

"Your skin is soft and warm. It begs to be caressed." He succeeds in sliding my straps down my arms. The heavy weight of my breasts push the dress down further. His hands glide gently down my collar bone toward my chest, his fingers pushing at the thin fabric covering me.

My head falls back against his stomach as his hands begin to move further south, then one hand glides lightly toward my throat. The sensation is intense and I push my chest forward, an invitation for him to continue to expose me. My skin is heated and every nerve is coming alive. His hand wraps gently around my neck.

"When I saw you dancing at Coyote Ugly…," he continues as he moves his warm hands along the upper swell of my breasts and along my neck and shoulders. Seducing me with the softness of his hands. "I saw a confidence in you, a confidence that you can't find in women who are vain about their looks. The way you moved turned me on more than anything. It didn't matter to you who saw and I admired that." His hands continue moving, making it harder to concentrate on his words. "When I came up behind you, something about the connection between us spurred me on. You knew who I was without even turning around."

I vaguely remember that night. "I knew you were there before I felt you pressed against my body."

"How?" he asks. His voice is growing huskier and his breathing is becoming shorter and sharper.

"I don't know how to describe it. Something charged in the air when you came closer to me."

"Then it wasn't just me," he mumbles as if trying to convince himself that our connection is deeper than looks and money. Which I know it is, but I don't know how to tell him that.

His hands continue along my shoulders and down my arms. His nails begin scratching lightly along my now sensitive flesh. "Why all the toys and bondage?" I couldn't stop the question from being asked. His hands still.

"Do you not like it?"

"Would it make a difference if I did or didn't like it?" His hands come away and he gently raises the straps of my dress. I shiver at the lack of contact.

"No," he finally answers.

"So, if I told you that I wanted vanilla, and not all the toys and being tied up, what would you say?" He sits in the chair next to me.

"I'd put them away, or get rid of them."

My heart sinks and judging from the look on his face, he knows full well that I would never ask him to do that. "I don't want you to put them away."

He smiles at me then. "Good, because I rather enjoy you at my mercy."

"But this afternoon, before you cuffed me to the bed…"

He blushes slightly. The action makes him appear vulnerable and he looks years younger. "That…was me making love to you."

"Oh." My heart flutters. It was exactly what I felt it to be. He put away all of his desires for bondage and toys to just be with me. My heart swells at the idea that Sunday morning will be equally hard on both of us. "Did you enjoy making love?" My voice trails off toward the end and suddenly I feel embarrassed that I asked the question. I lower my eyes back to my lap.

His hand comes to my chin, bringing my face up to his. Our eyes meet and the air is charged with a new wave of energy between us. The energy is so strong that I can't stop from squeezing my legs together and my nipples harden painfully. I'm desperate for his warm touch. "Immensely so." His finger strokes along my cheek, then down along my jawline. I shiver in anticipation of what he will do next but his hand falls away.

We sit there in silence for a few moments. I watch him and he seems to be warring with himself about something. "Whatever you have to say, you can tell me, or ask me." I prompt and he looks at me.

"That obvious?"

I smile. "A little."

We're interrupted by the shrill of his cell phone. He goes to it, picks it up and barks his name into it. After a few heartbeats he covers the mouth piece, "I'm going to be a few minutes." He turns and heads toward his room, the one with all of the monitors. I shrug, assuming it has something to do with one of the casinos.

30

Busted....

Orion is gone so long, and I am tired and a little weary after everything that happened this afternoon. Since I was given access upstairs yesterday, I decide to head up there and maybe take a soak in the massive tub I enjoyed. I realized, after being in his room that I'd been in his bathroom yesterday. There is just an additional access door from the hallway. When I reach the top of the stairs, something catches my eye. There's a door at the end of the hallway that's open. It wasn't open before and I just assumed it's his office. The room beyond the door is completely dark.

Curious, I walk toward it. I'm not a snooper, so as I draw closer to the door, I slow. I can't help the internal monologue that this is wrong and that I shouldn't be looking in here.

"Go ahead, open it." I yelp and turn toward him.

"Jesus, Orion, I'm sorry...I..."

"Shh, it's okay, I wanted to show it to you anyway." He steps past me, reaching up, he pushes open the door. Beyond the door is complete and total darkness. Blacker than black darkness, despite the light from the hallway. It's like all light in the room is absorbed. Curiosity spikes. His hand reaches in and then finally the lights come on. I stop breathing.

The floor is a dark, heavily polished, cherry wood. Beyond the floor, the walls up to the high ceiling are painted black. The room is very dark and not what I expected it to be. At least the literary books I've read led me to believe that all rooms like this were blood red and womb-like, but this is different. Also, the room is rather bare.

On the wall opposite me is an "X" made of wood similar to that of the floor. At the four points of the cross there are metal hooks and my body quivers at the idea of being tied to that, much like the bed this afternoon. My eyes slowly move away from the cross. To the left there is a chest of drawers and I can only imagine what secrets lay within.

To my left is a floor to ceiling mirror that is as wide as the wall. The entire room is reflected back. Including my wide and excited eyes. Beyond me, along the wall to the right, there are several hooks that showcase a number of floggers, similar to the ones in his room. There also appears to be a number of crops and paddles. All in varying sizes and colors.

Imagining the feel of the flogger this afternoon across my skin has goose bumps rising across my flesh.

In the former behind the door there are two additional pieces of furniture. A black leather couch, and then something that looks like a small version of a pommel horse. The top is coated with brown leather, or maybe even suede of some kind and I walk toward it.

When I reach it, I let my hand glide across it and it is soft like suede, but it is harder than it appears beneath the softness of its covering.

"Say something. Please Dacotah, I can't read your mind."

"You could have fooled me; you seem to read me pretty well." I turn back to look at him and his eyes are wary and he's frightened and I want to go to him and embrace him, but I don't. "Is this about pain, inflicting it on me?" I ask and my heart starts pounding harder.

He shakes his head. "It is about pleasure. Like what we've experienced before. You seem pretty well versed in what's in this room, you care to explain that? Have you been a submissive before, Dacotah?"

I shake my head. "I like to read, and I read a lot, Derek. This is the first time I've ever stepped into a room like this, and you're the first person with whom I've experienced any form of pleasure through bondage and toys, but I'm not an idiot."

"Dacotah, I didn't mean..."

I put my hand up to stop him. "I know what you meant. The crop yesterday and the flogger this afternoon, along with being cuffed is the most adventurous I've ever been when it comes to sex."

"Jesus, I... fuck," he growls. "Dacotah, I'm sorry, when I had you on the table yesterday, the way you took to it, it was, well, it seemed so natural to you, and I just assumed you'd done it before. Why didn't you stop me?"

I smile, I can't help it. His hands are in his hair in frustration and I'm rather enjoying the view of his naked torso. The raging erection in his pants and his overly sexy bare feet, and being in this room, I realize that I want this. Whatever he has to offer, I want it more than anything else in my entire life. "Orion..." His breath hitches and his eyes

186

dart to me at my nickname for him. "First of all, you gave me a safe word, a word I would have used if at any time I wanted you to stop. I also know that we didn't lay down any ground rules, so my trust in you was certainly earned by me allowing you to do the things that you did to me and finally…" I take a deep breath, "It's been the best experience of my life. I never knew what real submission felt like until you had me on that table. Then again today, when those cuffs were wrapped around my wrists, all else washed out of me. I was in your hands and in your control and deep down, because the safe word was so important to you, I knew that you wouldn't push me to the point of using a safe word."

"You're right. It is never my intention to push you to that point." His voice is soft and his hands finally come away from his hair. "Look, I didn't bring you in here to freak you out, but I wanted you to understand that I enjoy these things, and I am enjoying them with you." His eyes are wary and I can see the fear in his body. He's afraid that I'm going to tell him no. Though I know deep down inside that I should, but I can't, not now.

"What's in the dresser?" I ask, honestly curious, and wanting to convey my decision without spelling it out right to him.

He doesn't disappoint me. He smiles, satisfied, for now. "Toys, mostly different things that can't be hung on a wall." I watch as his eyes dart to the wall behind us. I can see it in the mirror, so I don't need to turn around.

I nod at his reply, still unsure of what to make of this room, and unsure of what to make of the situation and while I know that over the course of the next few days, something could happen in here, I'm not sure I'm ready for what he has to offer from this room. I start to walk toward him and toward the door.

"Dacotah, please say something." His voice is husky and unsure.

"Like what?" I look at him square in the eye and he doesn't miss a beat.

"What are you thinking?"

"I'm honestly thinking that this is all so overwhelming. I'm also thinking that while I like your kind of kinky, I'm not sure I'm ready for all of this." I wave my hand around the room. "I've only ever had two experiences with anything remotely related to BDSM, and they've both happened in the last two days. I hardly think that I'm ready to be brought into this room and cuffed to your cross." I give him a hard look and he takes a step back.

"And I respect your choice."

"Why show me the room at all? Come Sunday morning, I'm headed back to Wisconsin and from your conversation earlier; you're on your way to Paris. So..." I trail off, losing steam for whatever argument I was trying to muster up. "I'm okay with the things that we've done so far. Though I'd prefer to not be blindsided, like this afternoon."

He looks at me, confusion mars his features. "I thought you enjoyed this afternoon."

"I did," I say, ignoring the hurtful tone in his voice. "It was just a lot to take on all at once." He nods his understanding. "Look, Derek, I have spent the majority of my teenage years and my adult life, up until a couple of weeks ago, with one man. One man whom I obviously bored in the bedroom so much that he had to seek fun and adventure between the legs of the town door knob. So, I'm sorry that I can't jump in, feet first toward the bottom of the ocean, of your kinkiness. It is something I need to fully build up to." I take a deep breath, playing with the hem of my dress. "Yes, I thoroughly enjoyed this afternoon, both aspects of what happened between us, and I appreciate the introduction into your lifestyle, but it is all a lot to take on for someone who is a few fucks shy of virginal status."

He smiles, and then his smile quickly turns to a laugh. My skin heats and anger flares. My vision turns red and blurry and I want to run screaming from this room. As soon as I start for the door, he sidesteps in front of me, blocking my path. All signs of laughter gone. His face is hard and his eyes are calculating my reaction. I push against him and it does no good. "Stop," he orders and I'm too upset to fight him, and even more upset to listen to him. I try in vain to move around him, but he is with me every step.

"Derek, move."

"No. What's wrong?" Though the command colored his no, his voice softened immediately.

"You're laughing at me."

He stops moving, the motion is so abrupt that I stumble and he catches me in his arms. "Dear sweet girl," he says as his hand moves into my hair. He starts stroking lightly, playing with the errant strands. "Cotah, look at me."

Tears of frustration well in my eyes and my anger flares again when I realize what he's called me. "Don't call me that." I grumble, trying to be fierce and failing horribly.

I feel his chest shake with silent laughter. "You're a damn tiger, aren't you? Now will you please let me explain?"

"Ugh," I growl. "Fine," I snap at him.

"I laughed because you are far from being a virgin, for one thing. The other thing being the fact that you're truly not seeing yourself clearly." He moves to straighten me out, with his hands on my shoulders, he steadies me. Then with a gentle nudge he pushes me in the direction of the mirror, turning me so that I can face it. "Open your eyes," he breathes against my neck.

I obey, of course, and do as he's asked. I see him stand-ing behind me. His chin resting on top of my head, his hands on my shoulders. "Now, what do you see?"

"You, you're beautiful and confident."

He smiles at my words then shakes his head. "What do you see of yourself?"

I try to take him seriously, looking at my too wild eyes, my hair is falling down my back, and my shoulders are slumped slightly under all the stress and emotion of the day. "I see me."

He shakes his head again. "What about you?" I shrug. His hands move slightly and the straps of my dress are in between his fingers and the next thing I know, they've fall-en to my arms. His hands disappear and I can feel him be-hind me, grazing his knuckles along my back, between my shoulder blades and I shiver. The vision before me chang-es. I now see a woman whose eyes are heavy with lust and desire. Her face is flushed and her mouth is parted slightly. "Do not close your eyes," he says, the command back in his voice and I know that I will obey him.

31

What the EFF was that...

I feel the top of my dress stretch as he pushes it down in the back. His warm hands glide south toward the small of my back and the swell of my ass. The pressure on my dress in the back is pulling down the front and in a few more seconds my breasts are going to fall free of the thin confines.

My breathing spikes when his hands reach the bottom of my ass, seeking something, when suddenly the front of my dress slides past my breasts and with nothing to hold it up, it falls softly to the floor at me feet. His breathing spikes as he takes in my nakedness and I see it now, in his eyes, the hunger, the need, the hunter seeking out what he wants, seeking the woman who he needs to be satisfied and I shiver at the heaviness of his eyes.

That melted milk chocolate has returned and he presses himself against me. His bare chest pressed against my back and his erection against the crack of my ass. I flick my hips and desire spikes a new. The couple in the mirror now is absolutely beautiful. Eyes alight with excitement and anticipation. "Don't move," he breathes against my neck and I freeze. He steps back from my body and I shiver, suddenly cold without his warmth close to me. I can't stop watching him.

He steps back another step, then another until he disappears into the corner of the room. There is the sound of old metal wheels and I see he is pushing the horse thing out. My heartbeat intensifies, and fear runs wild through my veins at what he intends to do to me. But he brings it to a stop in front of me. The height is perfect for me to lean forward and rest my elbows on.

He stands between me and the mirror, blocking my view of myself and I can't help but try and see around him. "Lean onto your elbows, spread your legs," he says and I comply without hesitation. "Good girl." He comforts me with a caress along my cheek and I can't stop myself from leaning into his touch, but all too soon he pulls away, walking around me until he is standing directly behind me. I can see his taut chest; the tattoo along his shoulder and down his arm and fire ignites within my heart and my core. I need him and I realize that my pussy is wet and I'm beyond ready for him.

Looking in the mirror at myself, spread eagle, leaning on this contraption, I can see the lust in my eyes and in the color of my skin. It is red and warm, just like the fire that is licking its way through my veins. His hands begin to rub along my back in sure strokes, my eyes roll up and I drop my head. Letting out a moan of satisfaction that he's touching me. "Look in the mirror." I feel his hands grip my hips hard, and I lift my head.

Now my eyes are slits, half open with my need for him.

Without any warning he slams into me, all the way to the hilt and our bodies crash together in a loud smack, the momentum of his thrust forces my eyes closed and stars to appear as his balls smack against my clit, and my legs tremble. "Open your eyes," he grunts. "Do not close them again." The threat in his voice is real and my eyes drift to the line of floggers and paddles along the opposite wall. "Exactly. Now watch yourself."

I notice only now that he is not completely naked. His pants are still up, but he's freed himself. He pulls back out completely and then slams into me again and I watch as my eyes blink and they're very heavy with bliss. He repeats the process, each thrust and pull is drawing me closer to an orgasm. I can feel the tightness in my belly and my legs begin to stiffen. "Do not come," he barks as he continues his thrusting. I can see him in the mirror as well. I focus my attention on his beautiful face, strained with pure pleasure as his body rocks back and forth against mine.

Then finally his eyes screw shut and his grip on my hips tightens, pulling me back into him. His thrusts are more urgent and needy and I'm ready to explode. "Please, Derek."

"Please, what?" he grunts. His eyes open lazily and it's there, all the lust, need and devotion I feel for him is reflected back into my own eyes.

"Please, I need you, I need to cum."

He thrusts into me a couple of more times, not answering my question, but I can see his own orgasm is building hotter and he's fighting it. "Damn it! Cum Dacotah, NOW!" he growls and I come unglued, watching both of us in the mirror, my eyes are heavy and I feel shattered, but he grunts again, growling my name as we both come undone.

He falls forward onto my back, his cock still buried deep inside, but my legs are trembling so bad that I can barely hold us both up. The look on his face when he exploded inside me is a face I will never forget. All his own vulnerabilities and insecurities showed, if only briefly, but all the while that was displaying in his eyes, they never left mine in the mirror and I know that the purpose of this whole exercise was not about me and my insecurities, it was about seeing his own vulnerabilities, bringing us to the same level. But more than that, it was to show me exactly what I look like in his eyes.

He slips his semi hard cock from me and I can't help the cold shiver as he leaves my body, but he doesn't go far, though I can hear the zipper of his pants slide up, our conversation isn't yet over.

"Now do you understand?" His voice is soft and comforting. I nod, looking at him in the mirror. "You see, Dacotah, that no matter what you think about yourself, you're absolutely beautiful to me." He kisses my shoulder and strides out of the room. Leaving me in a whirlwind of his scent.

32

Safe word...

Derek never returned to his mystery room. After I realized he wasn't returning, a sense of loneliness set in and I
managed to disentangle myself from the horse I was
propped up against and ran from the room as fast as I
could and shame washed over me.

I ran to my room, found some comfortable yoga pants
and an overly large t-shirt in the drawers and climbed into
bed. Desperate to escape him and his cruelty. I wanted to
pack up my things and leave, but the grief of what I'd just
experienced consumed me and I crawled under the sheets
and curled into a ball. Thankful for the darkness and the
distance, the tears washed over my eyes and poured like a
faucet down my cheeks.

It wasn't until some point later that I realize I'd fallen
asleep, then awareness hits me at what woke me up. The

bed dips and shifts behind me and then Derek's arms are wrapping around me. I want to fight, to push him away, but I shiver into his warmth and realize I am freezing. His warmth against my back, spooning against me settles me and I fall back to sleep.

I wake to gentle hands caressing my breasts and thumbs stroking along my nipples. I squirm and try in vain to open my eyes. My back arches, pressing my breasts into his hands and I rub my legs together in an attempt to put out the fire raging between them. "Good morning, gorgeous." I hear him breathe, the heat of his breath caressing one of my nipples. The coldness that follows hardens my nipples further and an involuntary moan escapes my lips.

"I'm mad at you," I groan as his weight hovers over me.

"I know." His hands move along my ribs, seeking something, then the next thing I know his warm hands are caressing along my stomach, working higher toward my breasts.

"If you know I'm mad, then what are you doing?" My breath hitches as the warmth of his hands find my too sensitive breasts. My back arches and I feel a tear streak down my temple. "Stop, Derek," I say but he doesn't stop. My body and my need for him betray me and I try and buck him off, but I fail as my heels can find no purchase against the soft sheets, so I flop back into the bed.

His mouth begins trailing kisses along my abdomen, around my navel. "If you want me to stop, you know what to say," he whispers.

I can't bring myself to utter my safe word. My heart and my mind are at war with themselves and I can't decide which to follow. My brain screams 'chasseur' but my heart is breaking because I can't tell him, I can't say it.

Just then his tongue dips into my navel and I tremble as the sensation radiates to every single part of my body. I try to move my hands in order to push him down, to encourage him to move further south to take my cleft into his mouth, but I can't move my arms.

My eyes fly open and I struggle against my bonds. I turn my head to see my hands cuffed to the headboard of the bed. Panic rises at the same time he tweaks my nipples, hard. "Chasseur!" I shout. Sobs wracking my body, his breath pulls sharply between his teeth. He is off of me lightning fast and just like that my bindings are gone. I pull my hands over my face and the sobs overcome me as I curl into a ball on my side.

"Jesus, Dacotah." His voice is gruff, but his emotions can be heard clearly. "Fuck," he spats and I hear his feet shifting along the floor, the thought that he's leaving me, that this is it, we're done. I've safe worded him and he's going to kick me out. I sob harder.

I'm so lost in the fact that I've ruined this that it isn't until his arms wrap around me, tightly pulling me into him that I realize he's not leaving and I snuggle into his arms, his chest against my back. "I..." I shudder, sobs stopping me from uttering my apology.

"Shh, please Dacotah," he breathes and his hand is gently stroking along my hair, comforting me. The comfort is far from sexual and I melt into his arms. "Please, Dacotah, I'm sorry." He breathes as he buries his face in my hair and his arms are tighter around me.

I don't know at what point I fell asleep, but when I wake again, the room is much brighter than it was this morning and the sun is pouring through my floor to ceiling window. I uncurl myself and stretch, reaching for Derek, but the bed is empty and cold. There isn't even the faintest hint of him in the room. I open my eyes, rolling onto my side and on the nightstand the clock says 11:58, but I'm distracted by the fact that there is a card leaning against a glass of something that is a pale red color and bubbles are dancing and clinging to the side of the glass.

The side of the note that I can see says:

Drink Me

In an elegant script. I sit up, swing my legs over the side of the bed, and pick up the card and glass which is still slightly cool to the touch. I put the glass to my lips and drink down more than half of the glass before I realize that it is cherry soda. I take a few more long drinks, draining about three fourths before I set it back down. I look at the card and see it is folded in half.

I lift the top to find the same script and a rather long note.

Dearest Dacotah,

Words cannot express how sorry I am, both for last night and this morning. I hope that you can find it in yourself to forgive my Neanderthal actions.

I wanted to be here when you woke, but work is very pressing today, and for that I'm sorry.

I've made some arrangements and Arnold, my concierge, will be along around 12:15 to explain.

Please don't leave, allow me to explain, and to apologize in person, when I'm done, if you still want to leave, I won't stop you, but please, wait for me.

X

Orion.

A tear drops to the paper, right on his signature. I didn't realize until now that sometime between this morning and waking up, that I was going to leave him. I knew it was the right thing to do, I knew that my emotions were far too much for me right now and to stay four more days is going to kill me and I need to cut the ties.

But his words cut me deep, bringing me back to the fact that I really do want to stay and I believe that he truly is sorry. I read the note four more times before I look at the clock, realizing that it is now 12:13. I scurry from the bed, into the bathroom.

33

Plans...

When I come out a couple of minutes later, I've changed into my swimsuit, determined to enjoy the sunshine in the pool with a book.

I walk into the living room and a man is standing near the table, setting down dome covered plates, dressed in full livery and I can see that it is the same man from our food yesterday and assume this is Arnold.

"Good afternoon, ma'am."

"Please, Arnold, call me Dacotah." His face falls slightly. "Okay, if not Dacotah, then Ms. Miller will be fine. You say ma'am and I start looking for my grandmother." My heart clinches at the memory of my grandmother.

"Yes, Ms. Miller." He walks away from the table to come stand before me at a comfortable distance. "Mr. Hunter has asked me to arrange lunch. Your friends, Ms. Jorgensen and Ms. Smith will be here momentarily." My mouth falls open. "Mr. Hunter has arranged for you to spend a few hours with your friends, then around four, you will be treated to a massage and a make-over. Mr. Hunter is asking you to attend a charity gala this evening and he is making all the arrangements for you to be pampered and prepared for this evening."

My heart sinks, so we're not going to talk then. "I don't have anything to wear."

"Nonsense, miss. Mr. Hunter has arranged for in-suite shopping. You needn't worry about a thing."

Just then the elevator doors chime and I can hear Mandy and Rachel's voices as the doors open. They let out squeals of delight as soon as they step into the penthouse and I roll my eyes, trying hard to not have a Cheshire grin on my face when they see me and come running over, practically tackling me to the ground. Their enthusiasm is infectious and I can't help but feel lighter and freer.

I turn to Arnold. "Could you please move lunch to the patio?"

"It is quite warm outside." I give him a look that tells him that it doesn't matter, "Yes, Ms. Miller." He bows graciously and sets about returning the plates to his cart.

"Jeez girl, you've got him wrapped around your finger." Mandy fans herself. "He's right though, it is quite hot." I look out the windows and I see Arnold raising the umbrella on the table closest to the pool that is already half in shadow from the building, no doubt it will be fully covered shortly.

"There's a pool." I wink at her and she squeals, grabbing Rachel's arm.

"Where can we change?" Rachel asks and I point to the hallway that leads to my room and off they go.

I was content to sit by the side of the pool, soaking up rays and reading, but this is going to be much better.

"I'll meet you outside," I shout and I hear one of them scream back "Okay" but the voice is muffled and I can't tell which one it was. I subconsciously tighten the belt of my robe and head toward the door to the patio.

I step outside and Arnold was right, it is very warm out here and I quickly shed my robe, laying it over one of the chairs where Arnold is finishing up. He turns to me. I take a look at the table and I can see different juices, but no alcohol. "Champagne?" I ask.

I can see his hesitation. "It's very warm."

"I promise we will drink all our juice like good little girls." I can't stop the sarcasm but it is lost on Arnold.

"Yes ma'am." He bows and heads back into the penthouse, returning a few moments later with three champagne flutes and a bottle of something. Before uncorking it, he holds it out to me so that I can read the label. Bollinger Grande Année Rosé 2004. I nod, no doubt this is an expensive bottle of champagne and my stomach tightens and I regret my decision.

Just as Arnold pops the cork and fills the three glasses, Mandy and Rachel come out onto the patio in their suits with their sarongs wrapped around their waists. Taking in the view, they both wear the same awestruck expressions and I smile. Though it is not my place, a small swell of pride occurs as their faces light up. That pride is quickly squashed and my smile fades.

Before either of them looks at me again, I manage to put it back into place. I'm not sure I'm willing or wanting to discuss what it is that is driving a wedge between Derek and me. I'd rather explain it when I walk back into the hotel later tonight.

"Lunch is served," Arnold announces and the girls come toward us. Arnold takes a bow and leaves us alone.

"My GAWD," Rachel and Mandy squeal in unison as soon as Arnold is back inside.

"I know, right?"

The girls both take their seats and we dive into delicious sandwiches and chips. Devouring our food, our juice and nearly half the bottle of champagne as we chat about the things they've been doing over the last few days. Regaling me with tales of their days sleeping and their nights hitting the town, though I find it interesting when they mention their bodyguards.

"What are you talking about?"

Both the girls shrug. "We got used to it and got over it. Though it is hampering both of us from getting laid while we're here."

"Rachel!" I scold and she snorts.

"What? It is. They don't hover over us, but they are ever present, though their presence has gotten us into some pretty high end clubs. I suppose the hummer limo is helping that status."

"Jeez," I mutter. Derek really is taking care of them, and I can't help the little bit of jealousy that stems from their having a great time while I'm beginning to feel miserable about what's transpired since last night. I do my best to show them my best smiles, but neither one of them are fooled.

"What's wrong?" Mandy finally broaches the elephant in the room and I remember something as I'm about to open my mouth and spill all.

"I'm not at liberty to discuss it," I say and she scowls at me. I suppose the effect of teasing I was going for would've been better played if I laughed about it. "No really, I'm not. I can't even tell you his name." Sadness colors my tone as I realize that I want nothing more than to discuss what it is that is going on and talk to my girlfriends about it.

Just then, before Mandy can press me, Arnold comes out of the penthouse. "Ms. Miller?" I look at him; he has his hand over the mouthpiece of the cordless phone. "Telephone, for you."

He reaches out the phone to me. "Who is it?" I ask him puzzled. He doesn't answer, just gestures for me to take the phone. I do, bringing it to my ear. "Hello?"

"You're wearing my favorite bikini," he growls into the phone. My heart rate spikes and I walk away from the girls.

"Why are you calling me?" I say, a little bit of irritation coloring my tone.

"Please don't be cross with me, Dacotah, as promised in my letter, we will talk."

"When? Because I've been told by Arnold that we're going out tonight."

"We are, but I assure you, we will talk, but I'd like to take you out first, then we can talk."

"That's not fair, Orion." I can hear his smile on the other end of phone. He knows that if I'd called him by either one of his names that it would express my being mad at him, but the nickname served its purpose.

"I know, and I'm sorry." Jeez, two apologies in one day. "Listen, I realized, rather belatedly, that your girlfriends are going to ask you questions and while you've signed your non-disclosure agreement, I don't mind if you talk to your girlfriends. What I do mind however..."

"Is the mention of your predilections?"

He snorts. "Yes, I'd also prefer it if you refer to me as Orion to them."

"What you've done for them this week, it's amazing. Thank you," I say before I can acknowledge what he's said.

"It's my pleasure. Are we in agreement, Dacotah?" The way his husky voice caresses my name makes my heart swell and I know that our conversation is going to lead to me staying here with him.

"Yes," I breathe.

"Yes, what?" His voice is a growl, but there is a hint of playfulness behind it and my insides warm.

"Yes, sir," I whisper.

"Good girl. Now, run along to your friends, enjoy your afternoon, and Dacotah?"

"Yes, sir?"

He lets out a small breathy laugh. "I promise to make it up to you."

My breath hitches and before I can respond or say anything further, the line goes dead. I stand there, staring at the phone at his clipped cut off and I scowl. Then look to the rooftop of the penthouse and sure enough, there is a camera pointing in my direction. In a very uncharacteristic move, I lift my bikini and flash the camera and smile wickedly as I replace my bikini and the girls burst into fits of giggles.

The phone in my hand starts ringing. I look at it like it's on fire and against my better judgment, I press the talk button.

"I'm going to spank you for that," he growls.

"Promise?" I whisper.

"You have no idea." And just like that, he's gone again.

With my mood visibly lighter as I return to the table, I begin telling Mandy and Rachel all about my week so far and what we're supposed to be doing tonight. Of course I leave out all the juicy sex details, like crops, floggers, cuffs and his own personal heaven- the dungeon.

34

Lavish Delights...

By the time we're done chatting, we're so warm that we all take a dip in the pool. Eventually we end up playing volleyball, or some semblance of it, with a large beach ball.

Around three-thirty, Arnold comes to collect me and the three of us dry off and hug before they leave. They assure me that they're having an amazing time, though they miss me and wish I could come along, but I tell them that I too am happy and that I'm enjoying myself. They're pacified, for now, and they leave.

I find Arnold cleaning up our mess on the patio. "I'm going to go rinse off, I'll be out shortly."

"Yes, Ms. Miller. I will have them set up for you for when you're ready."

"Thank you," I say and turn toward the bedroom.

Once in the shower, it feels so good that I end up washing my hair in preparation for tonight.

When I exit my room, I can hear several voices coming in from the other room, a couple of females and one male, though not Arnold. When I round the corner it is like most of the living room furniture has disappeared completely. In its place are a massage table, a salon chair, one desk vanity combination, and one additional table, both of which are covered with all the things you could imagine for a makeover. To their left are three different, very tall, racks of clothing. On these racks there are the most elegant looking evening gowns and I'm drawn toward them.

"Ms. Miller?" the gentleman says.

I look at him. "Dacotah, please." I all but beg and he smiles, fanning his hand.

"Fine then, Dacotah," he says, his voice is sweet, too sweet and I take in his too tight attire and really fancy shoes and I smile. "I'm Michael, this is Cherry." He points to the smaller of the two women. "And this is Monica. Massage first, then shopping, then pampering." He comes to lead me by the elbow and I can tell, just from our brief encounter that he and I could very easily be friends.

"What are you wearing under your robe?" The tinier of the two women ask me.

"Uhm, panties."

She smiles. "Good. Lay down on your stomach and I will get to work."

I purse my lips and stare dubiously at the table, trying to mull it over how I am going to lay down and shed my robe and then I decide I really don't care and secretly hope that Derek is watching me. I walk to the table, climb up, while on my knees atop the table, I loosen the belt of my robe and let it slip from my shoulders.

Suddenly a whistle sounds from behind me and I blush. "Oh honey, you're gorgeous," Michael says a little too proudly and I blush a little more. Lowering myself onto the table, placing my face against the padded hole and do my best to relax as Cherry begins spreading warming massage oil across my back.

Despite Cherry's tiny frame and small hands, the woman has skills. I nearly fall asleep on more than one occasion as she works out all the knots and tensions I didn't know I had.

After a long time she finally covers me up with my robe. "You're all done. How do you feel?" she asks.

"Amazing, thank you."

"Absolutely. Go ahead and put your robe on; it's Monica's turn."

Somehow, while lying face down, I manage to get my arms into my robe with a little help from Monica. Once I do, I sit up, wrapping the robe around myself. My eyes blink rapidly in the bright light of the room. I gather my balance for a minute. Swinging my legs over the side of the massage table, which was surprisingly comfortable. "Hop down, I'll adjust the table and you can sit back down."

I blink at her and she helps me step down. I turn around and watch as she pulls a couple of levers and the table morphs into a lounger. "Have a seat," she says and I comply.

The back of my head rests nicely in the padded hole, thank goodness, because the massage has me weak and my limbs are like jelly. She wraps a towel tightly around my hair and then begins placing something on my face. When I look at it, it looks like mashed up avocados and I scowl at her. "Trust me," she says and I smile. Leaning my head back, enjoying the warm sensation, followed by the tingly cleaning feeling the mask is creating. When she's done covering me in goop, she covers my eyes with something cool and I guess they are cucumbers or something. Embarrassment floods through me at the thought that Derek will come in while I'm like this, but then decide not to worry about it. He's paying for this after all.

Michael and Monica crack jokes while I relax and feel the mask start to harden against my face. Before long, I can feel someone messing with my feet, it tickles and I squirm. "We have a squirmer." I hear Michael say and I try to calm myself down and then one of my hands is being worked on. My hands and feet are pampered and I can't help but relax back into the chair with the thought that I could get use to this. But I quickly let the thought diminish because it will never be like that. I'll never be able to be pampered like this again, but rather than let my melancholy mood overshadow the beauty that is happening to me, I sigh and relax a little bit further.

"We'll color your nails once we decide on your dress." I hear Monica's voice as she pulls the cucumbers from my eyes and I look at her. She smiles warmly at me and then begins to remove her mask with a hot, wet towel.

Once I'm free of all things avocado or whatever that stuff was, I'm helped out of my chair and the limp noodle legs I had before are gone and I feel slightly energized now that we're moving on. "Go ahead, pick a dress."

I look at Michael, pleading with my eyes at the concern I have about the dresses being big enough to fit me. "Oh no, girlfriend. These are all for you if you want them and believe me, they will fit. I even picked about five that I think will be beyond fabulous for you." He leads me to the racks and I notice that one of them isn't dresses but rather undergarments and nightwear and I blush. Then realize that depending on the color and cut of the dress, these might be important.

"I'm going to guess that your favorite colors are either black or purple or blue," Michael muses and I blush. "Ha!" he shouts and I jump. "I knew it." He starts laughing as he holds up the first dress. I scrunch my nose and shake my head. There are far too many ruffles on the black, old-fashioned long sleeve number he's holding up. "That's what I thought," he says and then goes back to looking at some of the numbers behind it. Though there are a couple that I like in the black variety, I'm not impressed.

Twenty minutes or so pass and he smirks at me. "You know I'm messing with you right?"

"Huh?" is all I can manage and he turns around, pulling a dress from the rack and turning around with it.

My mouth falls open and Michael's face lights up like Christmas. "I knew it!"

"He did, that was the first one he picked." Monica helps defend her friend.

"Then why all the fuss, we could have been done with this half an hour ago," I chide him and his face falls. "Relax, I'm kidding. I love it, and it's perfect."

"Yay!" He squeals, "Now sit! It is time for hair and make-up."

I dutifully take my seat and he goes to work immediately on my hair and Monica starts to paint my nails to match.

"Oh my god, girlfriend, you look amazing." Michael claps his hands flamboyantly and his excitement is infectious. Once he was done with my hair, he decided to stick around and help me dress, making sure that I didn't screw anything up.

He was a bit crestfallen when I refused to look in the mirror when they were done. I cheered him up when I told him that I wanted the whole effect at once. He clapped and promptly took away the mirror. Monica called a few people from her staff downstairs to help clear out and Arnold was there to put everything back in its place when Michael and I ducked into the bedroom to finish getting ready. He left me in the room long enough for me to replace my panties with the deep purple laced boy shorts, the garter belt, thigh highs and a bra that could be worn beneath my dress without showing. Though the garter, panties and bra were all deep purple, the thigh highs, much to my dismay are black. I didn't want to wear them, but he kept telling me that the deep purple velvet Louboutin open toe pumps will look better in nylon clad legs.

Michael had shown me the shoes and I balked at him. "Stop that, they are not as high as they seem. Have you ever worn Louboutin before?" I shook my head. "Girl, these things are like walking on a cloud." Monica quickly agreed with him, and though I was skeptical, I agreed. The pumps had a slightly raised platform with an even higher heel.

He helps me climb my way into them and he was absolutely right. They fit my foot perfectly and I begin to strut around the room, though I am still in only my undergarments. He whistles and claps his approval. "Ready for the dress."

I take a deep breath. My nerves are getting the better of me. I don't know what Derek is going to think and the fact that he is taking me some place public, my self consciousness starts to rear her nasty little head.

"Stop that," Michael says.

"Stop, what?"

"Come on Dacotah, you're a freakin' knock-out and you ain't even seen yourself yet. So stop. We can still make changes if it is too much."

I frown at him and he shrugs. I use his shoulders to steady myself as I step into the circle of deep purple fabric on the floor. After making sure that I'm not stepping on any part of the dress, he begins sliding the material up my legs.

The soft satin of the dress sends shivers across my flushed skin and I blush. Here is this man I only met a few hours ago, helping me dress, though the fact that he is gay is helping tremendously and he makes no qualms about that fact. He even started whining about his boyfriend to Monica while he was doing my hair.

He stands to his full height and his arms wrap around my neck, hooking the halter top of the dress into place. Then his hands are between my breasts as he clasps the silver buckle that holds the two sides of the very low V of the halter together. The bottom of the V-neck ends just above my navel. Spending so much time in the sun has given my skin a sun-kissed glow that both Monica and Michael were admiring as they worked me over earlier.

Also it is nice to know that I shouldn't have visible tan lines due to the halter of my bikini.

He moves himself around me, zipping up the back, which only stops just above the line of my garter. The only reason that the bra works is because there is a thick strap of silver, matching the front that hooks in the back. When Michael tugs on it, I can see the tightness in the material as it stretches across my chest. Though the zipper went up easily enough.

"Oh the joys of being well endowed," I mutter and Michael laughs.

Once he was done hooking the strap in the back, the material relaxed a little bit and the tightness disappeared altogether. I felt him doing a couple things back there and I wasn't sure what it was. I tried to look over my shoulder, but I failed. He laughed. "Double sided tape. This is to make sure it stays with your bra."

"Oh."

"Alright, gorgeous, let me see."

I blush but turn around, feeling the silky satin brush along my legs and I understand the necessity of the pumps and why he insisted. There is quite literally a thigh high slit on my right side that comes together just below the elastic line of my nylons, I look down, satisfied that it will stay below that line.

Michael whistles again. "Now. Close your eyes," he says and I flush, embarrassment and excitement clashing within me and I can't help but let the excitement win out.

He leads me gently until I know I am standing in front of the full length mirror on the wall next to the dresser.

"Stop," he commands, then begins fussing with the material a minute. "Ready?"

I nod my head. Unsure I can actually say yes. I feel him shift away from me.

"Good. Open your eyes."

I take a deep breath, steeling myself and then I slowly open my eyes.

35

Can I Possibly...

The woman standing before me, isn't me. Her hair is piled into a beautiful up-do with small tendrils of curled hair falling away. Atop her head, surrounding the loose bun is a small, though subtle, silver tiara that is accented with a few purple stones. My hair has changed color, though it is still blonde, there are several different shades of blonde that are highlighted in the way my hair is done.

My eyes travel to the woman's face and there, her skin is glowing with a beautiful tan and beautifully subtle make up. Including blush, which I never wear, and lipstick that is a pale pink. In her ears a pair of teardrop earrings with similar purple stones. The earrings look like the ones from our first night at dinner. Panic sets in when I realize that my necklace has been replaced by one that has five purple stones surrounded by diamonds.

"Where's my necklace?" I can't stop the rising panic in my voice.

"Hey," he says as he comes to stand behind me. I look at the woman in the mirror whose eyes are terrified. "It is hanging on a stand, in the bathroom." I go to walk to it. "Listen to me, Dacotah. Please?"

I look back at him, panic subsiding slightly. "I just need to see that it's there."

He ushers me toward the bathroom with his hand and I go quickly.

There, in the center of the counter is a t-stand that has my necklace hanging from it. My fingers brush across it and the need to replace the one around my neck is so strong, but I fight it. I know where it is, and I know it's safe in this penthouse. I take a deep breath, swallowing my panic and go back into the bedroom.

"Better?" Michael asks me. I nod. "I'm sorry, Dacotah, I didn't know."

I look at him and guilt runs through me. "I'm sorry. It was my grandmother's."

"Understood. I should have asked."

"No, it's okay, if you'd have asked, I would have told you to go to hell." I smile and he laughs.

"Now, where were we? Oh yes, the beauty in the mirror." He comes over grabbing my arm, leading me to the mirror again. Again, the woman is unfamiliar.

The purple dress with the small silver accent in the front is gorgeous and my sun-kissed skin does it amazing justice. There is a lot of purple going on, but it turns out that Monica went with a French manicure on my nails instead of the purple, at least after Michael had convinced her that it would be more elegant.

"Thank you," I breathe.

"Of course. You look amazing."

"Do I have to be in before midnight?" I ask trying to shake off my panic over the necklace.

He laughs. "No, silly girl. Though you're like Cinderella, you're far more beautiful." He squeezes my arm and then suddenly his phone chimes. He goes to the dresser to look at it.

He turns to me and smiles. "That's my cue to go. Your date awaits you. Though give me a minute to leave before you come out. I'll tell him you're coming, yes?"

I nod. "Thank you for all your hard work."

"It was a pleasure. Be sure to stop by the salon downstairs to say good-bye before you leave on Sunday."

"I will."

With that he air kisses my cheeks, not wanting to tarnish his masterpiece and he leaves.

I take a deep breath, examining the beauty in the mirror once again and I can't help the spread of confidence that washes through me. Steeling myself to face Mr. Hunter, I take one last look and exit the room, hitting the light switch as I leave.

As soon as my pumps hit the tile of the hallway, they sound ten times louder than I know they are, but the penthouse is silent and it brings back the nerves I thought I shook off. With each step away from my necklace, I grow more concerned. It is such a silly thing to be attached to, but it was hers and now it is mine, and aside from the house, it is all I have left of her.

Thoughts of the fact that I know Derek is waiting for me holds back my tears.

When I round the corner into the living room, the hunter is standing, his back to me, facing the window. Beyond him a gorgeous sunset is throwing reds and oranges across the slightly clouded Las Vegas sky.

His hands are in his pockets and his legs are spread apart in a stance of power and sophistication making my insides warm. His tux is black and from the back, the tux itself is rather unremarkable, but the man wearing it is a symbol of sex and power. His hair is pulled back into a ponytail that ends between his shoulder blades and I have an itch in my palm to walk up and grab it.

I take a few more steps, my heels clicking along the floor and he puts his hand up, I stop and after a few nervous heartbeats he slowly begins to turn.

His body turns, but he refuses to turn his head in my direction and I can tell that his intention is for both of us to get the effect of one another at the same time. I steel myself and he turns to face me.

His black tux is accented with an equally dark black shirt, vest and a deep purple tie.

Our eyes finally meet and it's there, that emotion from last night. There is awe and reverence on his face and I watch as he hooks a finger into the collar of his shirt, making a show of being warm and wanting desperately to loosen his tie.

"You take my breath away," he whispers, but the room is so quiet, his words sear into me as if he were standing right behind me.

I blush, my eyes darting to the floor and I feel like a little girl who's just been told she's adorable by someone. I start to fidget with my hands, concentrating on the bracelet around my left wrist.

My hair begins to stand on end and his pointy black shoes come into view, then his hand is on my chin. "Gorgeous," he breathes, but his hand prevents me from hiding again. "I'm honored to bring you with me tonight."

"Where are we going?"

"The Wynn."

"For?" I try pressing him for more, but he doesn't answer me.

"I have something for you."

"Derek, please, I don't..."

His finger is on my lips and I can't stop the kiss that I give him against the pad of his finger. "I won't hear you out. This is a gift from me to you, an apology of sorts."

"Another loaner."

He smirks. "No, this is for you, this you will keep."

"Derek I ca..."

"Please, let me do this, do not deny me my chance to give you something special." I look into his eyes; the severity I always feel from him is there in his eyes. They are intense dark chocolate, speaking all the words he can't say to me.

He reaches into his pocket and produces a long rectangular box. My breath hitches and I reach for it. He pulls it back slightly. "Nope, I'll open it." He smiles very warmly at me, then I pull my hand away and he begins to open the box. He does, only I can't see what's inside. He looks at it and smiles. Then very slowly turns the box around.

My hand goes to my mouth. "Derek, I can't."

"Shh, you can and you will." Nestled in the ice blue satin is a beautiful silver watch. The face is a light purple with no numbers, only an amethyst to mark the twelve. Under the hands, in an elegant script is the word Rolex.

"No, Derek, it's too much."

"You wound me, Dacotah, please. Accept it as my apology for being an asshole last night, for pulling you away from your friends, and for forcing you to use your safe word this morning." His hand comes to my cheek and I can't stop from leaning into it.

"I'm sorry I said my safe word this morning."

"Dacotah, never, ever apologize for using a safe word. I cornered you this morning and I didn't realize the implications that might have and for that I am deeply sorry."

It was my turn to silence him with my finger and I do, though he kisses it, then his tongue slides out to lick it and it is almost as if he's licked me, down there. My head starts to swim. "I accept."

His face lights up and I smile, trying to hide my discomfort at such a lavish gift. He begins to disentangle its confines and I hold out my right wrist. "You're left handed?" He raises an eyebrow at me and I shake my head, holding up my other wrist. He smirks and begins to add the watch to the bracelet already adorning my left wrist. Once the watch is in place, he unclasps the bracelet and holds it out for my other wrist and I give it to him willingly. He clasps it around my wrist, but his fingers linger a little longer on my arm than necessary and the goose bumps return.

"Are you ready to go?" he asks, and I nod. He offers me his elbow and I take it. He escorts me to the elevator, presses the button and it opens immediately. He ushers me inside and we begin our descent.

I begin to reach for my necklace, a fidgeting habit I've hand for as long as I've worn it, but it isn't there. "Where's your necklace?" he asks me, his voice is soft, slightly concerned as he turns toward me.

"Uhm, in the bathroom."

"Why aren't you wearing it?"

I try hard and succeed in smiling at him. "And spoil this gorgeous dress."

He smiles. "Nothing could spoil the dress, for it isn't the dress but the beautiful woman wearing it."

He gives me a sweet, chaste kiss as the doors open on the bottom floor. He gestures for me to step out first and I nod, stepping over the gap and onto the soft carpet, catching a glimpse of the giant man standing guard at the elevator. His eyes are on me, rather approvingly and I smile.

"It seems I'm going to be fending off the suitors all evening."

"Be serious," I say and his eyes dart to mine, though he can't help the fact that his eyes wander down the line of my dress.

"Deadly serious," he says and offers me his elbow once again.

In a move no doubt to build my confidence, rather than go out the door in front of reception, he escorts me through the casino and, to prove his point, every single person we pass is staring at us. The room even falls a few octaves quieter as we progress. The women make a show of mock drooling and fanning themselves as Derek draws near. But the men, they just stare.

"You've made your point," I whisper to him. And I am thankful that the Louboutin pumps have made me even taller, though still shorter than Derek and that gives me even more confidence.

We finally reach the doors that I came in Sunday, they open for us and we step out into the warm Las Vegas air.

The streets are quieter tonight, either it is really early or it is the midweek blues that Vegas goes through in between departures and arrivals.

Sitting at the corner is a sleek black limousine and two gentlemen dressed in suits. One immediately scrambles for the door once he gets past looking me up and down. Derek takes my arm from his elbow, raising my hand to kiss my knuckles before taking my hand in his. He escorts me to the other side of the limo and my eyebrows come together. The men scramble to beat him there. "I don't want you to have to slide across," he says and I lower myself into the seat of the car, pulling my legs and my dress inside. He smiles at me and I can't help but smile back.

The door closes and in a couple of heartbeats he is sliding in next to me from the other side.

36

Confessions...

Once the doors are closed and the limo moves out into traffic, Orion turns to me, taking my hand in his. "I need to tell you a couple of things about tonight." I look at him quizzically, but he takes that as my acceptance of whatever he has to say and goes on. "There will be a red carpet. Your photo is going to be taken." The blood begins rushing in my ears. "Is that going to be a problem?"

I feel the blood drain from my face. "You want to have your picture taken with me?"

I can tell instantly that I've offended him. "Of course, Dacotah. I would have come alone if I didn't want to show you off."

"I'm sorry. It's just..."

"Just, what?" he snaps. I look at him, fear in my face and he calms.

"It's just that…" I'm having a hard time saying the words. "People are going to talk if you have your picture taken with a woman, and well, on Sunday we're going to part ways and…"

"And nothing. Let them talk. Dacotah, I don't care. You're gorgeous and sexy and I'm honored to bring you to this event." His voice is sincere and my heart lurches and speeds up.

"That is probably the nicest thing anyone has ever said to me." I try to blink back the tears that threaten, and though one escapes, I manage the rest. He gently wipes it away.

"Well, they should be said far more often." His voice is gruff and his hands around mine are soft as he tries to soothe me.

"Am I going to run into any of your old flings?"

His eyes widen in shock at my question. "You read too many romance novels, Dacotah." Then he laughs. "Despite what you think, I'm not an animal, and I don't go around bedding every woman I meet."

"Derek, I know, it's just, well, damn it, I'm insecure as it is. I don't want to be cornered by anyone who's slept with you, or whatever; that's not fair to me."

"You're absolutely right, it's not, and while I can't promise that no one will be here, I have no intention of letting you go long enough for them to approach and talk to you."

I sigh. "Is there anything else I need to know?"

I see relief wash over his face. "Yes, there will be celebrities at this event. While I know it's easy to get excited, I…"

"I won't get all giddy fan girl, if that's what you're worried about." My tone is sharper then I wanted it to be and I regret it instantly. "There isn't anyone that could be at this event that will make me so stupid that I'll make a fool of myself."

I see defeat wash over his face, then he is slightly angry. "That is not at all what I meant. I just meant that there will be a lot of cameras, a lot of buzz, and tons of excitement surrounding some of them, this is a very high end event."

I close my eyes. "Maybe you should go by yourself," I say, playing with my dress absently.

"Why do you say that?"

"Because Derek, first you freak out that I'm going to make a fool of you by being a bumbling idiot around celebrities, then you point out the fact that we are as far as we can be from each other financially, which doesn't help you any. If you're embarrassed by me, why bring me?" I pull my hand out of his and slide as close to the door as I can manage.

I hear his sharp intake at my sudden coldness. "Alex, drive around the block." I can see the Wynn up ahead on the right. "Keep driving until I tell you otherwise." Suddenly the black carpeted barrier goes up between us. Though the glass was up, now we are absolutely alone.

He reaches into the bar, grabs a glass and pulls the top off of a crystal decanter, pouring two fingers of the amber liquid into his snifter, though it only stays there a moment before he pours it all down his throat.

"I am trying very hard to not rip off your panties and punish you for your comments. Do you understand me?" His hard voice and the threat send a thrill through me.

"Call a spade a spade, Hunter. I am not rich, these are not my people, and for all I know the people here tonight that know you are going to assume I'm a well-paid hooker or escort. I've seen your Google profile. You've NEVER brought a woman to a function before, now all of sudden you want to bring…"

"Shut up Dacotah!" he growls and the tone in his voice has me reaching for the handle of the door, I don't care if the car is moving, I want out of here.

"Let me out."

"No!" he growls again.

"You're scaring me," I blurt and start to sob.

"Shit." He comes to me and I can't get any closer to the door. "Fuck, Dacotah. I'm sorry."

"You keep saying that."

"Fuck." His hand goes to his hair and then he remembers that it is tied back and he stops. "Damn it, you are not a whore, you are not a mistress, or a well-paid call girl. I don't take women to these things because I've never met anyone remotely worthy of being seen with me in public. Every woman I've ever slept with has been a one night stand or they've been married and I've been a convenient escape from their husbands."

My heart sinks. I try to look at him and all I see is panic in his eyes. He deflates into the seat of the limo and guilt washes over me.

"Derek, I am a small town girl, from the middle of Podunk Wisconsin who, until recently, had never heard of the likes of Louboutin, Prada, or anything else you've thrown at me. You came at me with this outrageous opportunity and you've, damn it, you've made this the best damn week of my life but it is all so damn much to take in and take on. The penthouse, the watch, the pampering, whatever, it is so damn much; I'm not used to this. You're rich, you're ridiculously handsome and there are so many debutantes out there that are no doubt better for you than I am, and for whatever reason you chose me."

"Because you're gorgeous, because you're, fuck. Dacotah, you're challenging and exciting and no matter what I do, you seem to enjoy it, and there is nothing hotter than

225

that. I…" his voice trails off. "I don't want a debutante that is only involved because of my wallet. I want a woman, like you, who sees me for exactly who I am, not because of the penthouse, the suit, the private jet, it doesn't matter. I would gladly give up everything I have for the right woman, and that woman is you."

His voice softens and falls to a whisper at the end. "Say that again."

Our eyes meet and the intensity is gone and the melted milk chocolate is back, his features are soft. "You're the only woman I have ever brought into my bed. You're the only woman who has ever made me want to throw all of this…" He waves his hand, "away."

I don't know how I manage it, but I do, I pull up my skirt and fling myself at him. Pain and fear in his eyes. I know he's not used to being overpowered, but I don't care. My hands are on his neck and I look into his eyes. "Then prove it," I breathe and I crush my lips to his. Immediately his soften and our lips and tongues begin to dance a slow sensual assault against one another. My head immediately begins to swim, the scent of Armani and Derek clouding any cognitive thought I might have had before this.

His hands begin sliding along my hips and to my ribs, I shiver in delight and feel my nipples harden and his hands come up to cup my breasts. "Damn it," He growls against my lips. "You're wearing a bra."

I smile against his lips. "So take it off."

He shakes his head. "Not here." I feel deflated again. This roller coaster of emotions is going to wear me out. "I want to make love to you, Dacotah, but a limo is hardly the right place to do that." His hands slide along my ribs, down to my hips and onto my thighs. "You're unraveling me and damn it, you're wearing stockings."

I can't help the smile at what I know lies underneath my clothing. "Please," I beg and watch as his resolve fades and he shakes his head. "Not fair," I mutter and he smiles.

"I know, but it's hardly the right place." He kisses me again, a little more chastely, but with no less passion than what we had a few moments ago. "Alex, we're ready."

I pout at him. "Let's do this, then I can take you home and unwrap you." He kisses the tip of my nose.

"Why can't we just go now?" I'm still pouting.

"Because of two reasons. One." He kisses me again. "I want to show you off, you look amazing tonight. And two, I am one of the major benefactors of this charity, my presence is required."

"Tell them you're sick."

He laughs. "I can't, not tonight, but I promise you, as soon as we can leave, we will." I nod. "Thank you."

"I don't like fighting."

"Neither do I, but..." He takes a deep breath. "It was necessary. We've both been hiding something and it was better to get it out."

"Am I still going to get a spanking?" I raise a hopeful eyebrow at him.

His breath hitches and his eyes bore into mine. "Do you want one?"

"No, but I might need one."

He groans and engulfs me in his arms and gives me one more amazing kiss. The limo slows. "Showtime," he says and I slide off of him. Messing with my hair and straightening my dress. "Gorgeous," he breathes and then the door opens.

Derek is met by a mountain of flash bulbs snapping his picture. But Derek doesn't miss a beat, he is in business mode, as if nothing just happened in the limo a few moments ago. "Mr. Hunter...Mr. Hunter..." Is all I can hear, but then his hand is back in the limo after buttoning his double breasted jacket, waiting for me to take it. I slide my hand into his, take a deep breath, and I pull myself from the car.

Immediately his hand is on my back, right above the top of my dress. His fingers are splayed wide, and I no longer care about the fact that there are no less than three times the amount of flashbulbs capturing my exit from the car.

Questions start flying, everything from who's your date? to questions regarding his business, but the bulbs don't stop flashing. "If you look toward the ground, it makes it easier to not be blinded," he whispers in my ear and I try and comply, keeping my eyes down, while looking toward all the men, women and their cameras. "Smile, beautiful," he says and his words make my face light up in a warm smile.

37

New Friends...

During our entire time on the red carpet his hand never leaves my back, a gesture that is both erotic and comforting. He pauses to talk to a few of the reporters and we spend no more than ten minutes on the carpet, until all the attention drifts from us to the newest arrivals. "Mr. Michaels...Mrs. Michaels..." I feel my heart rate increase and excitement flutters through my veins like a wild butterfly. Is it possible?

Once we cross the threshold, I can't help but blink more than a few times to dispel the crazy flashes from my eyes.

"Remember what I said about being a fan girl?"

"Yes." His tone is soft but still a growl.

"I lied. At least if those that arrived after us are who I think they are."

He smiles at me. "Are you referring to Tristan?"

I slump. "How did you...?"

Before I can finish, Derek gestures around the room. It is wide, the ballroom is massive and there are no less than eighty tables spread around the room with chairs and fancy place settings, but what captures my attention is what's on the walls. Massive posters with the charities slogan, "We Are One" emblazoned over various shots of both Tristan and his wife Cameron.

"Tristan and Cami are founders of 'We Are One' an equal rights charity organization." My heart melts at the fact that Derek is using their first names and that he is a major benefactor of this charity. "They will be dining with us, so I will do my best to introduce you so you can take a deep breath. Believe me when I tell you, they are both amazing people, and very kind, and they will do anything they can to make you feel welcome."

"Have you told them about me?"

He doesn't answer, but there is a playful smirk on his lips and my heart is turning into butter; he talks about me.

"Remember to breathe," he whispers.

"Derek." I follow his line of sight and coming straight toward us are none other than Tristan Michaels and his wife Cameron.

"Tristan," he greets him and they shake hands. It feels like I've walked into a dream. "How are you, Cami?" I watch as Derek leans down, kissing Cami on the cheek.

"I'm fabulous, you?" Cami is gorgeous, though I've seen her pictures; they've never done her justice. Or Tristan for that matter.

"Wonderful. Tristan, Cami, I'd like you to meet Dacotah." What, no.

"Hi." I extend my hand, and Tristan takes it. "It's an honor to meet you."

"Same to you." He cocks his head, similarly to what Derek does when he's trying to read me. "Dacotah, this is my wife Cami." He places his hand on the small of Cami's back, similarly to the way Derek is holding me. I extend my hand and we shake.

"It's a pleasure to meet you." She gives an all-knowing wink to Derek. "We've heard a lot about you." I elbow Derek and both Tristan and Cami laugh. My fan girl moment is effectively broken.

"Hey now," Derek teases but I can see the faint flush of red in his cheeks at knowing he's caught.

"Well, I hope it was all good things." I smile and Cami returns my smile.

"Of course."

"Tristan." A male voice from somewhere behind them calls.

"Please excuse us. We'll see you at dinner." He nods and gently takes Cami off toward the gentleman who'd called for Tristan.

"That could have gone better," I mutter.

"You did great. The one thing that drives Tristan nuts is girls who swoon and make mention of his movies. Believe it or not, he's a very shy person."

"Whoa, really?" I look at Derek and he smiles.

"Yes, really. A lot of actors are."

"When you said there would be celebrities here tonight, I didn't expect him."

"I know. But he is here, he's a nice guy and we've become friends in dealing with We Are One. So I don't think of him as a celebrity, though I never pegged you for a celebrity crush." He grins at me and I nudge his shoulder with mine. He laughs. "Come on, the bar is over here."

"Thank God," I say exasperated and he chuckles.

38

Can I do this?...

Derek stays true to his word; he doesn't leave my side throughout the entire reception, at least until my second glass of champagne works its way to my bladder. "Gentlemen, if you'll excuse me." I start to turn away.

"Where are you going?" Derek whispers in my ear.

"The ladies room."

"Oh, sorry."

I le lets me go and I head toward the bathroom. When I cross the threshold, there isn't anyone but the attendant in the room, which is surprising but I'll take it. While I'm sitting there, I hear the noise from the ballroom filter into the room as the door opens. "Did you see that dumb blonde with Derek tonight?"

My heart sinks. I bite my tongue to stop myself from lashing out through the stalls. I do not want to start a fight here.

"What the hell does he see in her?"

The noise filters back into the room again. "Who the fuck cares, she's blonde and she's awkward, no doubt she's the charity case of the night."

"She's not even pretty and that purple dress, what the fuck is that about, who wears purple to a charity gala?"

There is laughter from at least three girls and I can see two sets of shoes underneath the wall of the stall.

"Derek deserves better than her. I'm going to go work my magic on him and take him upstairs and…"

"Did you see that Tristan Michaels is here?" One of the girls says.

"Oh my god, I know. Now that is a fine specimen of a man I'd like to…"

"You're going to do what exactly?"

There is a lot of shifting and I see two pairs of feet turn around in the direction of the voice. "Who are you?"

"Does it matter?" the other female says.

"Hell yes, it does."

"Well, let me enlighten the three of you, if I catch you in this bathroom, talking shit about someone else, I will throw you out, along with your dates. Judging from your own attire, I imagine your dates are pretty important to this event. Now with that being said, if I see you near Derek tonight or any other night, I will have you thrown out. Do I make myself clear?"

There is some muffling and rumbling "You think you're going to claim Derek, do you? News flash, sweetheart, he prefers girls with stature and poise, which you lack. So I'm pretty sure one of us would have better luck."

There is a snort that comes from a female. I finish my business, fastening back up and I step out of the door and lean against it. "Hi Cami," I say with far more confidence that I feel.

"Hi darlin'. These girls bothering you?"

I shake my head. "Nah, though I'm pretty sure they didn't realize I was in the bathroom before they started running their mouths."

"No, they didn't, which is exactly why Derek is here with you tonight and not one of these three..." I watch as Cami gestures in their direction. "Nope, sorry, I ain't got nothin'."

I can't help but laugh at the three women's faces. "Me either. Hey, how's your husband?" I ask her and she smirks at me.

"Tristan is great, I'm sure he'd have a fabulous time throwing these girls out of his gala."

All three of the girls' faces pale instantly and I take two confident steps toward them. "Scram," I bark and all three of them jump into action, pushing toward the door, fighting each other to get out. As soon as they are out of the door, Cami and I exchange glances and burst into a full on fit of laughter.

After a moment we both settle down. "Thank you for that."

Our eyes meet in the mirror. "You're welcome. I used to be the bathroom gossip, probably still am, but..." She just shrugs. "I know Tristan, and I know my own confidence. Tristan and I have been through a lot, and you can't be with a public man without having the skin to take the backlash."

"I'm gathering that. I wasn't gonna say anything, but your attitude gave me some confidence. Thank you for that."

She smiles at me then. "It gets a little easier as time progresses."

We both finish what we came into the bathroom to do, I wash my hands and check my make-up, thankful that

Cami came when she did and stopped my tears from overcoming me.

"Listen," Cami says as we're both drying our hands. "I hope you don't mind, but Tristan and I are flying back to Phoenix late tomorrow afternoon, I'm wondering if you and Derek could join us for lunch tomorrow?"

I smile at her. "I'd love to, but..."

"I'll ask him, but even if he can't, will you join us?"

"Absolutely, thank you."

She pulls on the door to open it. We step out of the bathroom and the washroom idiots are nowhere to be seen, thank god. "Hello ladies."

I look over Cami's shoulder to see Derek and Tristan walking toward us. My heart flutters at the sight of Derek and all my nervousness regarding Tristan is gone.

"What took you so long?"

Cami snorts. "Let's just say that those three ladies over there," she nods her head toward the right, "Got caught with their mouths hanging open.

"Cami, you didn't." Tristan laughs then wraps his arm around his wife.

"Believe me, she did. Though she was coming to my defense more than her own." I look at Derek. "They we're um...talking trash about me. Then they brought up what they were going to do to garner your attention, or Tristan's, whichever worked better."

Both men burst out laughing. "Well alrighty then," Tristan says.

Derek wraps his arm around me. "I'm sorry," he whispers in my ear.

"No harm done."

"Dance with me." He doesn't exactly ask, and Tristan gives him an approving look then looks at his wife.

The four of us set off toward the dance floor where there are only a few couples taking their turn on the make-shift hardwood. But to get there, the four of us have to walk past the bathroom sluts, I take great pride in the fact that both men have their arms on the backs of their women and it causes some murderous glares from the three women.

"Don't." I hear Cami tell Tristan. "They're not worth it. Okay, maybe a little, but Dacotah and I handled them, and now we're stuffing it in their faces. Just let it go."

I watch as Tristan nods at her and then we all walk in companionable silence until we reach the floor.

Dancing has never been a strong suit for me, and after the bathroom fiasco, I don't want to fall on my face. But Derek is a beautiful dancer and I find myself swaying to the soft beautiful lyrics of Mary Lambert's 'She Keeps Me Warm'.

I notice that around the room and even on the dance floor that there are a lot of same sex couples milling about and it warms my heart to see them so open. I mentally make a note to thank Tristan for the wonderful charity.

"Are you enjoying yourself?" Derek asks me.

"I am, when I'm not being cornered in the bathroom." I smile sweetly at him.

"I'm sorry."

"Stop apologizing, Derek, please. It's not your fault and they would have done it whether or not I was in there. I just happened to be there and heard it."

"What did they say?" he asks as he spins me around.

"One of them said something about me being a dumb blonde; the other said something about my dress. Then one of them said that they were going to seduce you and bring you up to their room upstairs." I shrug. I hear him growl, but not what he says. "It's over. Cami was there to defend me, though, had they not mentioned Tristan, I'm not sure she would have said anything."

"Oh she would have."

"She asked us to lunch tomorrow. When I told her I wasn't sure, she said that I should join them, whether or not you could." His smile is warm.

"That's very nice of them, would you be comfortable going alone."

I pout and he smiles. "I would be, if you absolutely can't make it."

"Well, I'd intended to bust my ass tomorrow. I was originally supposed to leave early tomorrow afternoon. But after taking half a day yesterday, I'd like to finish up tomorrow so that I can spend Friday and Saturday with you."

The song comes to an end and the lights flicker. I look up. "I'd like to spend all day Friday and Saturday with you, but if it means you have to work a little on Friday so you could join us for lunch, I'd like that very much."

"Dinner is ready," he says as he leads us off of the dance floor. "I will see what I can do. Why don't we invite them to the penthouse, this way, if I can make it, I don't have to spend travel time?"

I smile at his thoughtfulness. "I think that would work. Can you make it then?"

"Yes," he says as we reach our table at the front of the room, right in front of the stage.

I smile wider at him and stand in front of my chair, he helps me sit, then slides in my chair. I notice that Tristan does the same for Cami and that she and I are right next to each other. Both men have their hands on our shoulders as they wait. For what, I'm not sure.

"Derek suggested we have lunch at his penthouse tomorrow. That way he can make it."

"Oh, that would be awesome. What time?"

I shrug and Derek leans down. "What time is your flight?"

"We have the jet, scheduled to leave around four." Cami looks up at Derek.

"How about noon?"

"Perfect. Then I can get home to the little one."

My mind drifts back to something, about a year ago. "Oh, how is he?"

"Perfect." Cami beams and then digs out her iPhone. She starts showing me an entire roll of pictures of their son and he truly is adorable. "I miss him, but it is so hard to travel with him. We just flew in today, and we're headed back out tomorrow. "

I smile at her. "He's about a year now, isn't he?"

She smiles and her shoulders shake in silent laughter. "I guess no one missed that announcement."

"Oh Cami, I'm sorry."

"Shh, it's alright. Yes, he'll be one at the end of the month. We're throwing an overly extravagant birthday party, you and Derek should come."

I feel Derek's hands tighten on my shoulder. "I..."

"It's alright, decide closer to." She winks at me as if she knows a little more about our relationship than what Derek has led me to believe and I flush.

An emcee stands at the microphone, breaking up my embarrassment regarding her request for Derek and I to attend their son's birthday party, and I'm grateful for it.

Derek and Tristan both take their seats and there are two other couples at our table, both of which Tristan and Derek begin making small talk with that is interrupted by our dinner's arrival.

I am comforted by Derek when his hand slides along my leg, the slit in my skirt exposing a good portion and I'm thankful he discovered the garters in the limo. I flush again remembering our heated moment.

Maybe with what was said in the limo, maybe Sunday really won't be the end of us. Maybe…I squash the thought. I can't bring myself to hope. He's made it clear…

The memory of what he said floods back…

I would gladly give up everything I have for the right woman, and that woman is you.

Damn it. Sunday morning is going to hurt like hell.

While we start to eat our dinner, I quietly plot how best to make my escape before things get way too out of hand with Orion.

39

There's always more...

"Dinner was delicious and your speech was amazing. Thank you, Tristan."

"Don't thank me." He hitches his thumb in Derek's direction. "He brought you, and I am most grateful that he did." He leans over and kisses my cheek. I don't need to mention to Derek that the action nearly gives me a heart attack, at least until I look at him. For some reason, no matter how hot and sexy Tristan is, he doesn't compare to Derek.

"Dacotah, it was a pleasure," Cami says then puts her hands on my arms. "If he" her head jerks in Derek's direction "gives you any hell at all, call me." She smiles and I can't help but smile in return and she gives me a hug. "We will see you both tomorrow."

"Absolutely," Derek declares and we finish our good-byes with handshakes and hugs.

As we turn away, headed for the door. "How are your feet?" he asks me.

I look at him. "A little sore, but they're okay."

He smirks. "Comeon, we're going to walk back to the hotel."

"Oh no, not in this dress or these shoes."

"Oh yes, though you can dump the shoes." We reach the limo then and he gestures for me to climb in.

There is a small bag sitting on the seat. I unzip it and inside are a pair of flats. I quickly rid myself of the gorgeous Louboutins and trade them for the simple black ballerina flats and his hand is waiting for me to climb back out. "Derek, this dress is going to drag on the ground."

"I don't care." He shrugs.

"I do, it's a gorgeous dress."

He leans in, whispering in my ear. "I'll buy you another one."

I shake my head but drop my protest and we head back toward the Cosmopolitan. I can see it in the distance, but between us are Paris and the Bellagio, and probably a few other hotels, but I don't really care. The evening has cooled off and the streets are relatively quiet.

"Thank you for a beautiful evening," I say as I grab onto his arm and allow him to escort me down Las Vegas Boulevard.

"You're absolutely welcome, Dacotah. I'm not sure I said it enough, but you look amazing." He leans over and kisses my cheek, but I turn quickly and our lips meet. The sparks begin to fly in my veins and his hands are quickly caressing along my jaw and cupping my cheeks.

All too soon, however, he pulls back. "I've wanted to do that all night."

"Why didn't you?"

He shrugs. "Inappropriate maybe."

"What's that supposed…" His finger is over my lips before I can finish.

"Did you see Cami and Tristan kissing?" I shake my head. "He gave her a chaste kiss on the cheek before his speech, and that was all. That is all I meant by it being inappropriate. Though after the bathroom wenches, I was tempted to walk over to them and plant a big sloppy one on you just to watch them squirm."

I laugh at his idea, though I could totally see him doing it. "Another time, perhaps."

"Perhaps." His mood is somber and I can't quite grasp why.

We continue walking, rather slowly down the strip in companionable silence.

"What would you say if I asked you to come with me on Sunday, instead of going to Wisconsin?"

I stop walking and he pauses too, looking back at me, a thousand questions pouring out my eyes, and I try to grasp onto one of them. "Are you serious?" It's all I can come up with.

"Deadly."

"There's that word again, Mr. Hunter."

He smirks.

"Derek, I can't just drop everything in my life." What the hell am I saying?

He catches my second guessing of myself and he quirks an eyebrow at me. The look is surprisingly cute and I let out a small laugh. "What do you have in your life better than me?"

"You so don't play fair."

"Well…"

"I don't know about better than you, Mr. Hunter, because I think that is impossible. But my best friends, they'd miss me and I'd miss them."

"Is that all?" I think for a moment and then nod. "Well, do you really think I would keep you from your friends?"

"You have this week." I regret the words as soon as I've said them. "I'm sorry, that's not true, and you haven't done that."

"No, I haven't, in fact you saw them today, and if you wanted to see them tomorrow or Friday, I would have no objections whatsoever. Though, if you go back to Wisconsin, you will get to see them whenever you wanted, so I hope that Friday and Saturday you will give me as mine."

"Of course, Derek. I didn't mean what I said."

"Shh, it's alright. In a way, I have. I understand that your friends have been soaking up the Las Vegas nightlife."

"Yes, so they told me, though your bodyguards are helping with that."

"Well, whether you stayed with me this week or not, they would have been there."

"Why?" I ask.

"Because you're all so young, you're women, and you're in Vegas, land of the pigs."

I snort, involuntarily of course. "Well then I thank you for that. I understand that the limo and their presence has granted them some serious all access passes."

"Money helps," he says. "The girls only go to clubs that I approve of, or that I own. Though I doubt they told you that part." I shake my head. "While I don't mind paying for them to party it up while they're here, I wanted them to do it safely."

"Mandy said something about your men being good at cockblocking." He laughs. "Though I can't say I agree, I'm glad they are. Especially with Mandy."

"Why Mandy?"

I roll my eyes. "Because Mandy thinks that any man who pays attention to her is the one, or at least until the next morning when either she bails out on them, or they sneak out in the middle of the night. Or she sobers and realizes what an idiot she is."

"I'm sorry to hear that."

"Mandy has a confidence about her, but it is easily crushed when it comes to men. She takes sex any way she can get it, from anyone she can get it from." I roll my eyes at myself. "Jeez, that sounds so bad. She's not a nympho or anything like that. Mandy, as far as I know, has really only slept with a few men. Blowjobs however..." I trail off, embarrassed because I am telling someone else's life story.

"What about you?"

I look at him. "What about me?"

"What's your story, Dacotah Miller?" I stare at him.

"How'd... damn Arnold." I scratch my head, "you have no scruples do you?"

He laughs. "He let it slip, don't blame him, you're the one who told him to call you Ms. Miller."

"I don't like ma'am, it reminds me of my grandmother." My hand goes to my neck for my missing necklace and he sees. He grabs my wrist and begins to gently kiss my fingers, pushing me backwards until I am pressed against a low wall.

"Thank you for not wearing it tonight." He leans in, kissing along my neck, along the necklace I'm wearing and my head falls back and every nerve in my body comes alive.

"Michael convinced me that this looked better."

"I have to agree." He keeps kissing along my collar bone and over to my shoulder. I shudder at his soft lips and molten hot kisses.

"I can tell," I say breathless.

"You didn't answer my question." His voice is muffled against my neck.

"Which one?"

I feel him snort against my neck. "Come with me to Paris."

"That's not a question."

He growls in frustration against my neck and I can feel his teeth nipping along the soft skin. "Paris is right over there," I tease him.

"You're maddening."

"Well, it is."

The next thing I know, he's grabbing my hand and pulling me toward Paris Hotel.

40

Eiffel Tower...

We finally reach the steps that lead to the small Eiffel Tower that stands in front of Paris hotel. The doors to the stairway are closed, but he swipes a card in the lock. "Jeez, is there anything in this town you don't own?" I snort and he looks at me.

"Not much." Then he pulls me around the stairs to the elevator, pushing the call button and then pressing me against the wall. His lips are on mine, hot and needy. I'm breathless in a matter of moments, the combination of his cologne and him and then his kisses on top of that have me thankful I'm no longer in my heels.

His hands come to my cheeks, cupping my face in his hands and I can't stop the shiver of anticipation that courses through me. Suddenly the elevator chimes and without any break in his kiss, he guides me into the elevator and I'm immediately pushed against the wall.

His fingers intertwine in mine and my arms are slowly sliding along the cool wood paneling of the elevator. The doors close and we're shuffled to the top. It doesn't take but a few moments as this version is far smaller than the real one in Paris, but still.

When the elevator opens, he breaks our heated kiss, dragging me from the elevator. "Close your eyes." His voice is a soft command and I do, trusting him to lead me.

It takes about ten steps and a turn to the right and we stop. He is standing behind me, his arms running slowly and gently up and down my arms. I shiver and goose bumps form across every inch of my skin. His voice is right next to my ear. "Open your eyes." Then he pulls my ear-lobe into his mouth, sucking and nibbling gently. I have to force my eyes open.

I gasp.

Before us is the Bellagio and the fountains are spouting their water high into the air. Water and colors are dancing along the surface and from here I can see other couples standing before the fountain. Some are kissing and embrac-ing, some are just watching, but the sidewalks are quiet. "It's beautiful," I breathe.

His lips continue along my neck, down to my shoulder. I feel his hands working to open the strap across my back. When he can't get it, he gives up in a huff, but his hands are around my hips, pressing flat against my stomach, pushing me back into him.

His erection is evident and he's purposefully pressing it into me. "I'd rather do this in Paris, overlooking the city."

My breath catches and I feel his hand slide into my skirt at the slit and I hear his breath catch again when he feels the top of my stockings and the catches to the garter. "So beautiful." He says against my neck and my heart swells.

His hand continues along my thigh, toward my lace clad mound. His fingers slide below the material and before I know it, his fingers are dancing along my clit, stroking small rhythmic circles and my legs begin to tremble. My hands fall slack at my sides and I reach for his hips, something to hold onto, something to steady me, but when I find them, I pull him tighter against me.

His other hand is brushing gently along my collar bone to my neck. Gently pressing, holding me to him and the fire ignites. "I need you," I groan and his fingers against my slit increase their pace and I feel the fire burning, ready to erupt. "I'm going to cum," I breathe and his hand stills.

"No," he growls. And I groan. "I want you to come on my cock."

I feel his fingers twist in my panties, tugging and pulling and in the silence of the room around us, I can hear, as well as feel, the rip of the boy shorts I'm wearing and just like that, they're gone, along with his hand. I feel him stuff my now destroyed panties into his pocket and I'm wetter for him.

His hand comes back around to the slit in my dress and he pulls it back, lifting it up, exposing me. "Unzip me," he breathes as his hand tightens, only slightly against my neck. I push my hand between us and I find the zipper of his fly, I quickly slide it down. "Now, free me." I reach inside his pants to find nothing but his erection. No boxers, no nothing. I pull him gently from his confines and as I do, I start stroking along his shaft.

His breathing hitches, intensifying the ache I feel for him and then just like that, he's spreading my legs, pushing me forward. "Grab it," he says and I pull my hands away from him to grab the railing along the glass.

Then he is slamming into me. No preamble and my breathing stops, I hiss through my teeth, both at the sudden intrusion and the dryness of his erection. But he stops himself, allowing me a moment to get use to the fullness and for my own juices to coat his cock. I feel my walls tighten and a flood of more warm wetness and he groans.

Immediately he slides out, then slams into me. His hands are on my shoulders, steadying me, and pulling me back into him with each powerful thrust into my body. I moan.

"Let me hear you."

"Yes," I breathe and he pounds out his rhythm against my cervix. There is a mix of pleasure and pain and delectable fullness. I need him to cum. I need him to fill me up. "Harder," I nearly scream and he pounds me harder, pulling me back into him and I'm there, balancing on the edge of a major orgasm and he knows it. His strokes increase in speed and decrease in length and I know he's close. "Fill me. Let me feel you," I moan, ready to explode. I open my eyes as my orgasm rocks through me, shattering me, my legs trembling and the fountains across the street reach their own peak and shoot high into the air before falling black and quiet against the night.

"You have a very dirty mouth." His hand comes around my neck, pulling me to stand up. There is no pressure and no loss of breathing ability, but the sensation sends a nervous shiver through my body. I stand up and he slips out of me. In the silence, I can hear two drops, then a third as they hit the floor. "Holy shit." I hear him say as he lets my dress fall. I can feel what he heard dripping out of me.

I can barely walk, but I need to clean up, if my dress isn't ruined from walking, our Eiffel Tower sex didn't help. He knows what I'm thinking. "I'm sorry, but that is fucking hot." He breathes against my neck and I shiver at the warmth. "Let's clean you up."

He leads me around the elevator where there are restrooms and he guides me into the women's. I roll my eyes. "I can do this."

He doesn't answer, but his hand on my shoulder tightens as he leads me into the bathroom. He lets me go and reaches for some towels, wetting them in the sink and then kneeling before me, he slides my dress out of the way. Embarrassment washes over me at the fact that he is cleaning me up, but I know better than to argue. He's already threatened me with a spanking. I bite my lip as the warm towel makes contact with my still very sensitive cleft, but he's gentle and there is nothing sexual about it.

Once he's done he stands up and guides me back out of the restroom. "What about you?" I ask.

"Oh no, I like having you on me." I flush.

"You say I talk dirty."

"Oh, you do, but in a good way." His lips find mine in a very warm, passionate promising kiss. Then all too soon, he withdraws. "Shall we go home?"

"Yes, please." I suddenly feel spent and I'm not sure how I'm going to make it to the hotel.

We get back into the elevator and ride back to the first floor and exit the tower just as quickly as we entered it. "What about cameras?"

He laughs. "That's the nice thing about being an owner." He winks at me.

"Will you save the video?" I ask him, suddenly nervous.

"There is no video. My swipe of the card turned off the cameras, they will come back on in a few minutes."

"Jeez."

He smiles and we continue our strides back toward the Cosmopolitan.

We didn't talk much the rest of the way back to his penthouse, which was okay. I was very nervous about him asking me again. I know deep down that I want to say yes, if for no reason other than his declaration earlier. But in all honesty, I'm not ready to make that choice.

41

Lighter than Air...

When we enter his penthouse, he leads me straight upstairs to his bedroom. I don't argue, mainly because I know he slept in my room last night. Taking his time, he helps me out of my dress and when he takes in the nearly full effect of my undergarments, sans the ruined panties in his pocket, he takes me again, this time slower, gentler, and very passionately, until we are both shattered and fall asleep in each other's arms.

Thursday brings me waking up to an empty bed, something I'd expected based on his intentions for the day, but it still brings a twinge of sadness to my heart that he's had to go off to work. When I roll over, I see that it's nine thirty and I groan. I'd wanted to get up earlier, and am surprised because, in doing the math, it is nearly noon in Wisconsin and I never sleep that long. Then again, it was well after five this morning when we finally passed out.

I feel guilty because he stayed up so late and now he is off doing what he does best, working. I stretch and sit up. On the nightstand is another glass of pinkish liquid and another note. I smile because he took the time to do this before he set off on his super busy day. I drink down the sparkling cranberry and pick up the note.

Good Morning Gorgeous,
Thank you for an amazing night. I've never enjoyed an event as much as I did last night.
You're an angel, especially after the bathroom incident, so thank you again for putting up with my baggage.
I will be back around 1. I hope you don't mind entertaining T & C until I arrive.
Thank you for hosting. Arnold has instructions on how to handle lunch, see you around 1.
Have a good day.
X
Orion

I smile at the letter thinking it will smile back at me. I finish my drink and slide from the bed, taking the note with me into the bathroom.

Sitting on the counter is another note.

Feel free to use my shower, I took the liberty of moving your stuff in here. There are clothes in my closet. I'd like you to stay in my room for the rest of your stay.

If it's possible to have your heart warm and sink all at the same time, that's ultimately what happens. I want to spend as much time with Orion as possible, but I'm taken aback by his sudden need to have me closer to him.

What would you do if I asked you to come with me?

That is the million dollar question, isn't it? What would I do? Would I go with him? What would it mean to my friends, what would it mean for my life?

I slump down on the toilet and put my head in my hands. Too many decisions to make, too much pressure to decide.

My life in Wisconsin is boring, to say the least. I have very few friends and since my grandmother's passing, the people in town only seem to have sympathy for me. Damn it, I'm not a child, but that's all they seem to see, an orphaned child. I haven't been out since the disastrous breakup, all I do is work and go home, and most days, going to work is a challenge. But maybe it's time for a change.

The idea of change and maybe moving to Minneapolis has plagued me since I caught *him* with her. It felt like running away at the time. So I stuck around. But for what?

I take a deep sigh as I realize the answer to that question. Nothing.

After my shower, I'm surprised to find, in his closet, that he's cleared a spot for my stuff. While he didn't bring everything up, there are a couple of dresses, including the one I wore last night, a few pairs of shoes and hanging on the back of his door is my bathing suit. I decide to throw that on underneath one of the light blue sundresses hanging in the closet with a pair of flip flops.

When I go downstairs, I decide that I need to finally check my phone. I head to the breakfast bar where it has been sitting and it's dead. I go in search of a charger. Finding one in my old bedroom, I take it back to the kitchen and plug it in. While that charges a little bit, I find myself a bagel and cream cheese, making that up. Just when I'm putting the stuff away, my phone begins to chirp and chime and go nuts. "Jeez," I mutter and pick it up.

8 missed calls

15 text messages

And countless emails.

I start with the missed calls. I take a seat at the bar when I see Jason's name with (4) next to it. "What the fuck do you want?" The other are two from numbers I don't recognize, one from the pizza restaurant and lastly one from Mandy, this morning. Odd.

I go into voicemail and there are eight messages to correspond with the calls. I listen to Mandy's first.

"Hey chick, wanted to remind you that you have a massive credit over here, you need to take care of it. Oh and girlfriend, you're in the paper!" The call ends.

"The paper... damn it, the gala."

I flip back over to the calls from Jason; thankfully all of them occurred prior to this morning. Good, maybe he hasn't seen it.

I listen to the voicemails; the one from the restaurant is Katie, wanting to know if I can switch shifts with her next week.

One of the numbers I don't recognize, I pull it up.

"Hey baby..." I immediately pull the phone away from my ear and hit delete as soon as I hear Jason's voice. I shake my head. The next one peaks my interest.

"Hi Dacotah, it's Jessica." I roll my eyes. "Listen, I just wanted to apologize for (sigh) well you know what for. I realize what a mistake I made, and I'm (deep breath) sorry. Can you call me (leaves her number) I'd like to apologize, not on voicemail. Um, thanks." The call ends and I delete it, not wanting to go there, and realizing that my return to Wisconsin is going to be met with both Jason and Jessica and I feel sick.

The messages from Jason I delete without listening to them. I don't care what he has to say, it doesn't matter, nothing he can do or say will make up for what he's done.

I move on to the text messages. All of them, thank god, are from Rachel and Mandy. I browse through them and they're just random, except one that Mandy sent this morning with a link. I click it, unsure of what to expect.

When the page loads on the web browser my jaw falls open.

Is Billionaire Bachelor Derek Hunter off the Market?

Billionaire Tycoon Derek Hunter arrived to tonight's We Are One Gala at the Wynn Hotel with a lovely beauty on his arm. Sources close to the billionaire claim to know nothing about the woman on his arm, but state that things seem pretty serious between the two lovebirds. This morning, hearts are breaking around the world. Similar to the way they broke a year and half ago when Hollywood Star Tristan Michaels announced that he'd married the CEO of Bold International, Inc. during a private ceremony a couple weeks prior.

The happy couple of Derek and his guest were spotted throughout the night talking with Mr. and Mrs. Michaels, including sitting with them during dinner. We understand that Tristan and Derek are quite close friends.

But what about the beautiful woman on Derek's arm? When will we see her again?

I scroll a little further down to a gallery of pictures from the evening, beginning with our arrival at the Wynn, our mingling, our dancing and then finally one of Tristan, Cami, Derek and myself as we waited for the other guests to take their seats. There is a Cheshire grin on Derek's face as he looks down at me. "Pictures really do say a thousand words," I mutter. I quickly press and hold the picture to save it, along with the other pictures in the roll. At least I'll have something to remember him by. I shake my head. Maybe that's not such a good idea, but I decide not to worry about it too much right now.

I text Mandy back; thanking her for the link, and the reminder about the money. Then I go to Yellow Pages and look for a number to Planet Hollywood.

After being passed around, I finally end up in the right place. I ask the accountant to issue a check and have it delivered to the front desk at the Cosmopolitan. She tells me that it will be there within the hour. I look at my watch, ten thirty. Good, it will be here before Cami and Tristan show up for lunch and I can get it.

Then I immediately regret the check, but it doesn't matter, not anymore, it is better at this point to cut and run.

42

Lunch Guests...

Half an hour later, I receive a call from the front desk, surprised because they knew I was here, the gentleman lets me know that there is something at the front desk for me. Thanking him, I hang up and head for the elevator. The door opens before I arrive and Arnold steps out. "Good Morning, Ms. Miller."

"Hello, Arnold."

"Where are you going?"

"There is something at the front desk for me."

He pulls an envelope out of his pocket and hands it to me. It has the Planet Hollywood logo on it. "I grabbed it on my way up."

"But they just called...," I trail off, shaking my head. No doubt they called Arnold first. "Thank you," I say, taking the envelope from his hand. "Am I allowed to leave this penthouse?" I ask him, more irritated sounding than I wanted to be, but still it pisses me off.

"It is not advised that you do."

"Excuse me?"

"Mr. Hunter asked me to make sure you stayed put today."

"Why?"

"Something about the reporters hanging out downstairs."

"Shit," I sputter then cover my mouth, apology in my eyes and Arnold chuckles, moving off to do whatever he came to do before lunch.

I decide to deal with Derek tonight, hopefully, if I can manage to see him before I pass out. He reiterated to me that he would be working late tonight and that the likelihood that I would be seeing him tonight was slim and it was disappointing. Though I'm glad he's coming up for lunch. I decide to kill the next hour and half waiting for Tristan and Cami by grabbing my Kindle and heading outside to the pool. I rid myself of my sundress and sandals, laying out after covering myself in sunscreen.

It's very warm out here today, but I don't mind and Arnold keeps me fully stocked with water and juice during my laying out. Around noon, I decide on a quick dip into the pool to cool off. But I slide in slowly, not wanting to get my hair wet. Though it is nothing fancy this morning, I don't want wet hair when they show up.

When I climb out, grab my towel and look up, Derek is standing but a few feet away from me, looking sexy with his hair down, but pulled back, his eyes are milk chocolate, radiating intensity and I gasp, surprised he's here. "What are you doing here... I thought you were coming up at one?"

He smirks, "I finished a meeting early, so I came up, hoping to help you entertain before food arrives."

I give him a half smile. "While I'm glad you're here, I would have been fine."

He stalks toward me and I wrap the towel around myself. "I know, but I missed you."

I look up into his eyes. "Really?"

He chuckles, "Yes, really. It drives me nuts when I leave you alone in the morning."

"Speaking of, thank you for um...moving my stuff."

"Sorry I didn't ask you first, but then again, I had no intention of giving you a choice." I scowl at him and he begins to rub his hands along my arms. I instantly melt to his touch and stop myself from embracing him. His suit looks very expensive and I... he crushes me to him.

"Derek, you'll ruin your suit."

"Fuck the suit."

His hands slide up my arms, over my shoulders and along my neck, sending goose bumps racing across my skin and my nipples harden. His hands cup my face and then his lips are on mine. This kiss is different, but no less passionate than the others. It is just softer and I melt into his body.

Someone clears their throat, my skin heats, and Derek growls. He kisses me a couple more times, quickly, before turning to who interrupted us. My heart goes a million miles a minute as I realize we've been busted by Tristan and Cami who are fighting their own laughter.

"Hi guys." I finally manage to get my mouth and brain connected.

"Hello Dacotah, Derek." All the stuffed shirt pomp is broken when Derek and Tristan burst out laughing; both Cami and I look at each other, she rolls her eyes and smiles wide and inviting.

"Did you bring your suits?" I ask Cami and she nods enthusiastically. She's really cute, if you want the truth of it. Today she is wearing a dark blue halter top that bunches at the waist with white skinny jeans and matching heels. Her hair is pulled up off her shoulders, but the black and blue of her hair stands out. Her tattoos on her shoulders are gorgeous, and she wears them well.

"Lunch will arrive around one," Derek says. "But how about a drink?"

Both Tristan and Cami agree and Derek ushers them to the table, the same one the girls and I sat at yesterday.

"Ditch the suit, would you, Derek?" Tristan chides him. I watch as Derek rolls his eyes rather uncharacteristically.

"I have to go back to the office by about two, so I'll keep the suit, but I'll be right back," he says, turning to me and kissing me on the head before he disappears into the penthouse.

Deciding that I'm dry enough for my sundress, I go over to the lounger I left it on and pull it over my head and slip into my flip flops, pulling my hair free of the claw I put it in earlier and join them at the table.

"How are you?" Tristan asks me.

I smile, "I'm great, a little tired." Cami giggles and I can't help but smile too. "How about you?" I ask them.

"Can't complain, but I am ready to go home. I miss Jaden." He smiles reverently as he talks about his son and Cami looks at him with those happy-in-love eyes.

"I can't imagine being away from him," I say sympathetically.

"You think it would get easier, but it never does." Arnold arrives with a bottle of wine and glasses, pouring each of us a glass. Once he departs, Tristan continues. "I'm thankful that Cami has the type of job where she can come with me, wherever I am, and bring him with. I can't imagine spending weeks away from him." I regard Tristan, and the happy father look in his eyes as he pictures his son, and realize that there are not a lot of men in this world like him and my heart swells.

"That's great." I turn to Cami. "How's business?"

She smiles and sighs at the same time. "Business is good, but busy. Between the charity and Bold, I feel like I am constantly coming and going. But it is good, it keeps me busy. What about you Dacotah, what do you do?"

Oh crap. "I live in Wisconsin and work for a pizza restaurant." I suddenly feel embarrassed by the job I've had since high school.

"Where in Wisconsin?" Tristan asks.

His question washes away my embarrassment as I realize that neither one of these two people sitting in front of me are going to look down their nose at me or my job. "A small town called Frederic; it is about an hour and half north and east of Minneapolis."

He smiles at me. "I miss small town life."

I take a sip of my wine. "Really?"

He smiles. "I grew up in a small town, but even if I wanted to now, I couldn't return to living there. The whole 'everyone knows everyone' thing is really kind of annoying."

I laugh. "You have no idea. You can't do anything without everyone hearing about it." Another reason why the idea of running away with Derek is so appealing.

"Then again, Hollywood is like small town life, just on a much bigger scale."

Cami and I both laugh a little bit. "You can say that again," Cami says. "Speaking of which, have you...?" she trails off.

"You mean the pictures?" She nods. "Yeah, one of my girlfriends texted me a link. At least the one she sent me was favorable. I'm sure there are several that aren't." I try and smile at the realization that more than likely there are dozens of articles that bash either me or Derek and his choice of woman. But I realize that I don't care.

"Well, my advice." Cami leans forward, taking a sip of her wine. "Ignore them. Believe me, they will lead to more frustration and heartache than you want to face. Speaking from experience, of course."

"You read them?" I ask her.

"I have no choice. I'm his PR Rep, same with Derek. I have to read them, at least the less favorable ones, for damage control mostly. It's been a long time since they've printed anything about Tristan that I've had to handle a backlash from." I watch as she squeezes Tristan's hand and he smiles sweetly at her. "But believe me, they've certainly tried to."

Tristan snorts. "That's an understatement. But believe me Dacotah, nothing good can come from reading articles about either yourself or Derek for that matter. People are highly opinionated and they don't care who they tear down in the process. Especially reporters." He smiles at me reassuringly and I decide then and there that I will do my best to stay away from articles pertaining to myself or Derek.

"Sorry about that." Derek comes to stand behind me, placing his hand on my shoulder. "I had to take a phone call."

"Such is the life," Cami says, smiling at him, then raising her glass. "A toast. To new" she looks at me "and old friends."

We all clink glasses. "Speak for yourself, missy, I'm not that old," Derek chides her and the four of us start laughing.

Lunch flows seamlessly as the four of us discuss anything from life, to business, to the charity and I realize that Derek is rather philanthropic when it comes to the various charities that he's involved with. He joined We Are One because two of his best friends are gay and have been together for over fifteen years and he wants to see their rights equalized among the heterosexual and my heart grows a little more fondly for his charity and drive.

As lunch progresses, I realize that, because of that article, while I knew Derek was rich, I didn't realize that his net worth was in the billions and watching the man sitting next to me smiling and laughing, having a good, carefree time, he seems like his age. I noticed last night that he was far more the stick-up-his-ass type than he is right now and again, I find myself awed by him.

A little after two, Derek takes his leave, leaving me with Tristan and Cami and I find that, compliments of another shared meal together, that the conversation flows, becomes less strained. Cami starts asking me about school, job experiences and the like, and I get the feeling that I'm getting a job interview, poolside, clad in skimpy bikinis while Tristan swims a few laps in the pool.

I nearly lose my mind when he took off his shirt. Yes, Derek is far more than sexy, but Tristan, is well, damn it, he's Tristan freakin' Michaels and there is hardly anything sexier than that. But what surprised me the most were the tattoos that covered his skin. There was a dragon's head, wings and spine, then part of the tail was wrapped around his leg. Cami too had more tattoos than I'd seen last night, including a very nicely placed corset running down her spine.

She teased me when she realized I was staring and I apologized profusely. She laughed it off, telling me she was used to it. I still felt bad, but she was very reassuring.

She asked me about how Derek and I met and she seemed surprised, then she also said that Derek is a very determined individual and that he always gets what he wants. I couldn't help but laugh and agree with her.

I was sad to see them leave, but they were both very quick to give me phone numbers and an open invitation to visit them in Phoenix or Los Angeles anytime, with or without Derek. At least that's what Tristan whispered in my ear before they left to catch their flight back to Phoenix.

43

What Now...

After they left, a part of me starts to regret having the check from Planet Hollywood written to Derek. I decide that it is best to give it back to the source, but I know there is going to be a fight when I give it back to him. Though I am prepared for it. At least I hope I am.

I spend the rest of the afternoon lounging around, feeling helpless and bored, if you want the truth of it. After Arnold delivers dinner for one, and I get over my disappointment that he wasn't just going to show up, I settle into the couch to read, reflecting back on the day with Tristan and Cami. I don't know if I've ever been happier, aside from being bored to death. But when compared to my life in Wisconsin, it's not much different. Though I am missing my friends.

I text Mandy and Rachel out of nostalgia and they tell me that they are also staying in tonight, resting and gearing up for two more nights of partying before we leave on Sunday.

Then I get a text I wasn't expecting.

If you decide to stay with him, and not come home, I will miss you terribly, but I have never seen you happier and I hate to see you come home and be miserable.

The text is from Rachel, and while I can sense the sadness in her message, I know that she speaks the truth. I text her back.

He's asked, but it came out more playful than serious. It's a big decision to make, and I don't know if I can sit as arm candy and a bored housewife with nothing to do all day. We're spending all day tomorrow and Saturday together, I guess we'll see. Hugs.

Her reply is quick.

I love you like crazy girl, but you've been dying for an excuse to leave Frederic, don't let it pass you by. Hugs back.

Rachel's texts give me a new confidence that I didn't have before, but I'm still not certain. My emotions when it comes to Derek are a mess, and I'm having a hard time giving up the life I know for something so completely unknown. That is the crux of the whole situation. I have no doubt that he would take care of me, but could I honestly sit in a house all day, waiting for him to come home? As I yawn and recognize the boredom I am feeling right now, that answer is no.

Although, if I had things to do, like cooking and cleaning or whatever, it wouldn't be that bad...would it? I know the answer, it's yes. I love to cook, though I'm not sure I'm very good at it. And cleaning - ugh, forget it.

I brush the thoughts away and dive back into my book, deciding that I will let sleeping dogs lie, for now. We still have two more days together and it is possible that I could be swayed either direction, to stay or to go.

"Come on, sleepy head, wake up." I hear his voice, soft and comforting. Then I feel his hand brushing along my forehead, pushing hair off of my face.

I groan.

He laughs. "This couch can't be comfortable. Come on, let's go to bed."

"Huh?" I open my eyes rather sleepily and have a harder time because the light on the table is on. "Too bright." He laughs again and turns off the light. "Not helping," I grumble.

He laughs. "You're so cute when you're sleepy, but come on. I want you in my bed."

My eyes open quickly, seeking his. Thanks to a light behind me somewhere, his eyes are alight, but there are dark circles under his eyes. "What time is it?" I try looking for my watch but I can't see it.

"It's just after three."

My eyes widen. "In the morning?" I rub my face. "No wonder you look so tired." Knowing that he's been running for nearly twenty-four hours without much sleep spurs me to get up. He steadies me as I stand up and we go upstairs.

Once we're in his room, he turns on a lamp on his side of the bed and brings me around to the other side where he pulls the covers back. "Climb in." I look down at my sundress and remember I'm still wearing my bikini underneath. I start to slide the dress down my shoulders and his breathing spikes, causing my insides to clench with anticipation.

I continue with my little strip tease and his eyes are watching me intently. The dress slips down my bust to my hips, with a little encouragement it slides all the way down. It doesn't take but a flick of my fingers to pull the ties along my hips and my back. Though my posture is such that the front and back fall away, my sex remains covered.

My favorite look comes over his face and the hunter is back, gazing hungrily at the junction of my thighs, begging me to reveal its secrets. I smile, a little smug, and widen my stance.

The material falls away and my hunter pounces, knocking me onto the bed, his mouth on mine as soon as he settles in on top of me. He's still dressed, though his tie is hanging loose and a couple buttons are undone. His vest and jacket are nowhere in sight.

His lips are hot and hungry on mine and I can't help the moan that escapes when his fingers intertwine with mine and he slides them up over my head. I feel disappointment wash through me. Touching him seems to be something I can't do and I groan against his lips at the pressure of being exposed to him. "Let me touch you." He freezes. "Derek?"

He doesn't move, simply breathes in and out, his breath caressing my neck. Then he rears up, trying to stand, releasing my hands. "Oh no," I breathe, I grab a hold of his tie, pulling him back to me and our eyes meet. There is a fear there that I can't quite understand. "I need you," I breathe against his lips and I kiss him.

After a beat he relaxes, I release his tie and then bring my hands up above my head of my own accord. He seems confident that I'm not going to try anything.

His lips move from mine to my jaw and points further south. His hand slides in under my back, reaching for the tie of my top. To help, I unclasp the halter top and bring the top down, freeing my breasts and his eyes grow needy and hungry. His lips are on my nipple, warm and wet, searing me and coaxing a moan from my lips as he pays homage to my nipple. He doesn't stop there; he trails hot wet kisses from one nipple to the other.

As soon as he's satisfied that he's undone me from the last of my confines, he pulls the bikini away, both of his hands slide under my back, lifting my chest to his hungry mouth. Being wrapped in his arms while he continues licking and sucking is nearly my undoing. His body is warm, but there are too many clothes separating us.

I don't want to risk upsetting him, "Please, Orion, I need you, now." I half growl at him and he nips at the nipple in his mouth and it shoots straight to my clit. I can feel it harden with arousal and my need for him becomes a raging fire, desperate to be put out by him sliding home inside me.

He pulls his tie and his shirt undone and tosses them on the floor as I watch through heavily hooded eyelids. Lust and everything else bubbles to the surface and I know, if he asks me that question right now, I will say yes.

Pushing it aside, I watch with hungry eyes, my hands roaming across my chest, down my stomach, making their way further south. I can't stop myself and his eyes are watching me, watching his prey. I freeze, afraid of his eyes. "No, don't stop. I need to watch you pleasure yourself," he breathes and the hunger in his eyes and the subtle stroke of his tongue across his lips pushes me on.

Slow but steady my hands slide down between my legs. The feel of my fingers along my hypersensitive sex causes me to moan and my back to arch. He continues with his clothes, until he is standing before me, between my legs. My tongue darts out across my own lips; I'm hungry for him. I need him and I want to touch him but he stares at me in awe as I begin the slow leisurely strokes around my clit with two fingers.

I watch him as he takes the long, thick, hard length of his cock into his own hands. Starting at the base of his shaft, his hand encircles himself, and I watch as he begins sliding his hand up his rigid length. I stop what I'm doing to watch, his hand stills. "You stop, I stop. Got it?" His voice is raspy with desire and I immediately begin stroking my clit again. "I want you to come; I will not take you until you cum for me, Dacotah."

"Ahh," I moan and my hand picks up its pace from slow torture to determined. Each flick of my fingers causes him to stroke his own erection faster. I watch as his eyes roll back into his head at the pleasure that radiates from his own ministrations against his erection.

The fire is building and I begin squirming, my free hand sliding along my stomach, seeking my breast and a nipple, desperate to help bring my orgasm to the forefront of everything. His hand continues along his shaft and he brings his other hand down to play with his balls. I watch as his legs spread a little wider, strengthening his stance. At the right moment, our eyes meet "Cum," he orders and I explode.

My fingers are instantly soaked, and then I am being pulled to the edge of the bed in one motion, and in the next he is slamming into me, pushing my orgasm to a new height as he grunts my name at the peak of his own orgasm. He starts to move, groaning and grinding out the rest of his release. I am so close to cumming again and my legs tremble. His thumb is on my clit, causing my legs to twitch with the sensitivity and I can feel his erection inside, it grows harder by the second and he continues sliding in and out of me, pounding harder and harder with each thrust.

I reach out to touch him, determined not to stop, determined to feel his muscles under my fingers. His eyes screw shut, but there is a subtle nod. I reach out, placing my hand over his heart. His mouth goes slack, his breathing spikes and his eyes open. There is no fear and no pain, only adoration and pure raw emotion similar to what I saw last night.

The look in his eyes is too much, my eyes roll up into my head at the building knots of warmth, ready to unravel me. I bring my other hand to his chest and he hisses, but continues sliding in and out of me. I run my hands across his chest and up to his shoulders, though out of reach, he leans forward slightly, changing the angle of his thrust and I'm right there and he knows it. I wrap my hands behind his neck, pulling the rubber band from his hair and he growls, leaning closer to me. Once his hair is free, I bring my hands around to his forehead and slide all ten fingers into his soft, silky hair. My nails scraping lightly across his scalp and he leans down so that we're nose to nose. Our eyes look deeply into each other's. "Come for me, Dacotah," he says so softly, I shiver, and shatter into a thousand pieces with an orgasm so fierce that I start to cry. I hold him to me, refusing to let him go, as his own orgasm takes him.

Once we both have recovered from our orgasms and the roll in the hay, he helps me snuggle into bed, then kisses my forehead with a silent promise to return in a moment.

When he comes back, I'm on my side, facing his side of the bed. I'm hoping that we can reverse our snuggling positions, but rather than crawl in on his side, he snakes his way in behind me, wrapping his arms around me. I sigh and close my eyes, desperate to ask him why it is that he didn't want me to touch him, but rather than argue with him about it, or further prevent him from sleeping, I keep my mouth shut and fall asleep in his arms.

44

Understanding...

When I wake in the morning it's light in the room and there are no arms around me. I sigh, then I hear his soft snoring coming from behind me. I smile, he's still in bed, and according to his clock, it is nearly ten.

I turn over slowly, but my breath hitches when I capture the full effect of Derek sleeping next to me. His mouth is slack, and his eyes are relaxed, he looks every bit the twenty-nine year old that he is. All the worry lines I didn't know I was seeing around his eyes and mouth are gone. His hair is a mess, but some of it falls softly onto his shoulders.

I shiver when I remember the way it felt, and I fight the urge to reach out and touch him, afraid to ruin this rare moment of raw Orion. The arm closest to me is up over his head, giving me the perfect spot to snuggle into, just to hold him, or at least feel held by him. The urge to cuddle is too much and I slide against his side. Afraid of his rebuff, but instead, the arm that was up comes to wrap around me, his hand resting on the small of my back and he pulls me closer to him.

I can't help but stare across the bumpy lines of his abs, down lower to the rising erection that's appearing since I snuggled into him. The smile that spread across my face radiates through my entire body. He knows I'm here and…

"Good morning, gorgeous," he breathes and I snuggle into him a little tighter. His other hand comes to rub along my arm in slow, lazy caresses. I know that I blush at his words.

"You're awfully excited this morning."

"Wha…" I feel him shift and lift his head up. "What can I say, there is a gorgeous woman in my bed."

I blush and duck my head. His free hand comes to my chin, lifting my head so that I'm looking at him.

"Why does that make you blush?"

My smile from watching his morning erection form beneath the thin cotton sheet fades away. "Honestly?"

He gives me a stern look. "Always."

I give him a half smile. "Because no one has ever called me gorgeous."

He pulls back slightly to take a better look. "Well get used to it, please, because it is true. We've already had this discussion."

My skin heats as I remember his room down the hall, and what he made me do that night. Then I remember how he left the room, never to return, at least not until he finally decided to join me in my bed. "I know we have, but you left the room like a tornado."

He sighs. "That was not my finest hour."

"No it wasn't, and we've yet to talk about it."

"You're right, we haven't, but is it a conversation that we really need to have? I thought we hashed out most of it in the limo."

His words come flooding back, the words about how I'm the woman that he would give everything up for. "We did, which is why I haven't brought it up. Though you never told me what happened that had you running from the room."

He kisses the top of my head. "I'm not sure I'm ready to fully discuss that."

I shrug and decide that when it's time, he will tell me. "Why didn't you want me to touch you?"

He stiffens at my question and doesn't answer. But his hands go back to their gentle motions across my skin, causing goose bumps.

"I know that I did touch you last night, but you seemed petrified. I don't mean to pry, but if touching is something you can't handle, I need to know."

He sighs. "I don't know how to explain it without coming across as a douche."

"I'm not sure that's possible right now, Derek. I wouldn't have asked that question if I didn't need or want the answer." I prop myself up on my elbow and the hand that was stroking my arm goes up to cover his eyes. "Believe me, I understand if it is something personal, but..." I frown, more at myself than him, "I really liked being able to touch you. But I also understand that my lack of touching allows you the sense of control you like..."

He peeks out from under his arm. "Go on."

"Does my touch do something to you that makes you lose control?"

That look is there, the go on, you're on to something... I shrug, not knowing what to say next.

"Dacotah, until you, no one has ever touched me during sex. It is the exact reason why I had you cuffed the other morning. It's not something I'm used to."

"Do you not enjoy it?"

"Until last night, I never knew if I did. I've never let anyone touch me before."

"And when I was touching you…"

"When you were touching me, I didn't need control."

I sit up fully. Looking at him, but he can't stop his eyes from wandering south to my fully exposed breasts.

"The way you touched me last night, it…" he swallows hard "it was like nothing I've ever felt before, it was exactly what I needed to feel."

"Is that a bad thing?"

Looking at me, he shakes his head.

I smile, and throw the covers off of him. His erection is standing at full attention, begging to be touched, to be licked, to be sucked, and my own arousal blossoms deep down.

I move to straddle his legs down closer to his knees and he is watching me like a hawk, wondering what I'm going to do.

With my hands, I slowly slide them up along his thighs, toward his hips. Avoiding his erection, and all those sensitive spots. I stop at his hips and move back down. I can't pull my eyes away from his. I'm lost to them and emboldened by the newfound information regarding what my touch does to him, I continue back up his thighs with my hands. This time I keep going, allowing my hands to slide along his stomach, towards his pecks that are bouncing slightly with his now ragged breathing.

I continue gliding north until I am stretching to reach his shoulders and his erection is in my face, right where I wanted him to be. My tongue darts out of my mouth and I lick that flat spot, where the head meets his shaft and his arms fall slack, with his thumbs stroking along my knees, I bring my hands back down while my tongue teases the head of his erection.

When my hands come to his hips again, I bring them in closer to his erection, driving that anticipation in him that he loves to build within me. Though I hope he thinks I'm going to go for his cock, I decide to play with my own pre-dictability bringing my hands to within mere centimeters away from taking a hold of his shaft I glide them north along his abs and wrap my lips around the soft head of his erection, and suck, hard. His hips buck, but I don't stop.

His breathing has stopped all together, and I swallow, pulling him deeply into my mouth and he moans, the sound heats my sex to a fevered pitch and I am suddenly envious of his self-control, because all I want to do is climb up his body and sink myself onto his raging hard on.

I continue sucking and sliding my hands along his body, savoring the feel of him under my fingers, a feeling that I know I will never forget.

When my hands reach his chest, I let them slide down his ribs, placing them on either side of his chest and I lift myself up, bringing my mouth higher along his shaft.

With his cock still in my mouth, I begin to slide myself up his body, along his legs, his breathing is uneven and the groans he is letting out cause a pulse inside of me. My hunger for him grows further and I have no doubt that I'm leaving my own trail of juices along his legs and I don't care.

Once I'm too close and can no longer hold him in my mouth, he pops out and hisses as my pussy comes into contact with his erection. I begin kissing, licking and nip-ping along his stomach, up his sternum, up to his neck where I continue until I feel the sharp stubble of his jaw along my tongue. The sensation sends shivers across my skin.

The moment our lips meet, his hands are in my hair, holding me to him, deepening our kiss, my lips bruise with the ferocity of his lips on mine. I moan when I feel his hips flick below me, rubbing his shaft along my clit causing a breathy moan.

"I need you," I breathe against his lips and one of his hands comes away from my hair. I can feel him snaking it between our bodies, going for his cock. I lift my hips and he lines us up expertly. The moment I feel his thick head begging entrance to my pussy, I start to slide down, slowly, soaking his cock as I go. I'm lost to him, having him buried deep inside me is the happiest place I know and it is the only place I want to be.

45

Back to it...

Boneless and spent, I collapse on top of him. His arms are around me instantly and he is still deep inside. I can't stop the warmth that spreads from my heart to my fingers and toes as he holds me tight to his chest. His heart is pounding, matching the rushing blood in my own ears, and his breathing is short and erratic.

I did this to him. I alone made him come unglued and I take pride in that fact. My hands slide under his shoulders, trying to hold him tighter to me. I am filled with so much overwhelming emotion, it takes me biting my lip, hard, to stop the tears from flowing. This is going to kill me.

"Do you trust me?"

The vibrations in his chest tickle against my ear. "Yes."

He lets out a rushed breath. "Will you allow me to do something to you?"

"You're asking for permission?"

I feel rather than hear his chuckle. "Yes, I guess I am, because what I want to do is different than anything we've done so far, and the last time..." He trails off.

"I safe worded you."

"Yeah."

"Is that why we haven't?"

"Yes."

"Does that bother you?"

He sighs. "Honestly?"

"Always." I throw his word back at him.

"No, it doesn't. I rather enjoy vanilla sex." I giggle at his term. "So long as it's with you."

Now it's my turn to stop breathing. He doesn't say anything for a few heartbeats, "Breathe, Cotah." The commanding tone is back and I shiver, kick starting my breathing again. "Good girl. Now, I want you to go to the bathroom, clean yourself up, put on a pair of panties, then go down the hall, open the door, and kneel in the middle of the room."

My head pops up, the fear I feel is played out in my eyes.

"Cotah, I will not harm you, as you saw the other morning, if you call out your safe word, I will stop, no matter what. But I've determined that while you like some pain, or slightly painful things, you prefer the pleasure and I want to give you all the pleasure you can handle and maybe more than you think you're capable of." His voice is soft, and sincere, but the commanding tone hasn't disappeared. Not yet, and the excitement radiates and it takes all I have not to jump up right this second.

His cock twitches inside me and I groan. Ready to go again. "Go, do as you've been told."

"Yes."

Smack, his hand meets my ass and my nipples harden.

"Yes, what?" The soft menace is back and my insides clench along his cock and I can see its effect in his eyes.

"Yes, sir." I look deep into his eyes and he pulls himself away from me, all contact is gone. Silently telling me that now it's time to go and do what he's asked of me. I resist the urge to start sliding along his shaft to suck him back in. Before I can gather my nerve he pops out, both our eyes close at the sensation and the loss sucks.

I go into the bathroom, grab a super-fast shower, not wanting to take too long, I don't wash my hair. When I'm done, I dry off, put on a pair of white boy shorts and pull my hair back into a pony tail. I grab a soft terry bathrobe off of the back of the door and exit the bathroom. Derek is nowhere to be found when I pad my way down the hallway to the door.

Standing outside the door, my hand on the doorknob, I take a deep breath, turn the knob and step inside. There are no lights on, only several large and small candles throughout, lit and glowing around the room. With the black walls and dark wood, the appearance at first is ominous, but the more I look at it, the more inviting it is.

I step across the hardwood, finding the middle of the room and I kneel down, sitting back on my feet to wait.

46

Shibari what...

"Spread your legs," he commands as he breezes into the room. I can feel him standing behind me, despite the fact that I can't see him. I spread my knees. "Wider." I go a little wider and his hand is running through the loose strands of my pony tail. "Good girl."

He walks away from me, over to the chest of drawers near the cross on the wall. I can see him clearly and all he is wearing is a pair of grey pants, they look soft like flannel and nothing else. His feet are bare, his back is rippling with his movements, his ass is, well, it's damn fine, and his hair is pulled back, fanning out between his shoulder blades. Watching him move is making me aroused, and after the night in the Eiffel Tower across the street, our juices dripping to the floor, I'm overly thankful for my panty choice.

Derek continues doing things at the dresser, though I can't see what. "Dacotah?"

"Yes, sir." His head comes up, almost reverently at the fact that I responded with his preferred title.

"Today is all about pleasure, do you understand?"

I fight the squirm. "Yes, sir."

"What is your safe word, Dacotah?"

"Chasseur. Sir."

"Good girl. Now, because today is about pleasure, I am going to do two things to you before I begin. First, I am going to put headphones in your ears, blocking out all noise, except the music you will hear. Secondly, and this I am giving you an option for because what I am going to do will be intense enough, but I would like to blindfold you."

"Yes, sir." I don't hesitate in my response.

"You want to be blindfolded?" he asks, turning toward me.

"Please, sir."

"Very well. Close your eyes."

I don't hesitate at his command, lowering my head and closing my eyes. As soon as he comes near me, my skin prickles as I know he draws closer. "Chin up," he says softly and I raise my head, keeping my eyes closed as I feel a headband of sorts and earbuds sliding into my ears. His hands slide down my neck lightly, and I shiver, absorbing his touch. Desperate for more.

There is no music in the headphones, not yet, but I also don't feel any cords falling along my body, only his hands as they slide slowly down my chest to my exposed breasts, and my nipples harden as the trail of goose bumps draw nearer to them. Then, without warning, he pinches my nipples, hard, and my legs slide wider apart across the hardwood, and there is a strange tingling sensation that radiates down my arms. I'm his.

"Stand up," he commands, though his voice is slightly muffled by the earbuds, I can still hear him clearly. I do as

I'm asked, standing up. "Open your eyes, Dacotah." I do, and we are face to face. His eyes are wild and alight. Gone is the milk chocolate, replaced by a lighter, warmer caramel, and the fierceness in his face has my breath spiking. "You're so beautiful." He caresses my cheek and I lean into his touch. Distracted by his hand on my face I don't notice immediately when something starts tickling along my leg. I fight the urge to move, lost in his eyes.

Whatever he's doing is rising higher up my leg. It is soft as it tickles along my knee and my thigh until finally his other hands comes into my line of sight.

In his hand is a bundle of red rope and I can't help the squirm and the heating of my sex. My eyes widen. "Touch it," he says and I reach out. It is softer than it looks, almost silky to the touch. It's strange because I suddenly want to be bound by this, by him, at his mercy. My knees tremble and he smiles. Then his hand comes away. The warmth of his hand isn't felt until it is gone and suddenly I feel cold without his touch, but when his hand comes back to me, he is holding a white blindfold. He drops the rope to the floor and stretches the blindfold and bring it over my head, though he rests it on my forehead and not over my eyes.

I enjoy the last few moments of sight and then out of nowhere, his lips are crashing into mine. Whatever resistance I may have had, washes away, the tingling in my arms grows far more intense and I realize that I am going to wholeheartedly submit to this man. I want to touch him too, but I don't, his kiss is tender and I can feel his need mixing with mine and all too soon, he pulls back. "Close your eyes." His voice is breathy, husky and desperate. I lower my eyelids and right before they close, I catch a glimpse of his hard on, trapped by the pants he's wearing and a moan escapes my mouth just as the blindfold comes down.

"Spread your legs, steady yourself." His shoulders are on mine helping me. Being blindfolded alters my equilibrium a bit. "Good girl." His fingers slide across my already sensitive skin as he moves behind me. Then I can hear the rope as it lightly thuds to the floor and my entire body comes alive in a rush of tingling and desire. I can feel the soft wisps of air as he manipulates the rope into its desired position. "Hands behind your back, bend your elbows and grab your wrists." I bring my hands behind my back and he helps position them together behind my back. My breasts feel very exposed this way, open to him to do as he pleases.

The music starts in my ears. It is soft, an opera of sorts, the tones are on the higher octave and the sounds send chills across my body at the same time Derek moves my hands out, just enough, then suddenly the softness of the rope is running between my hands and my back. I can't stop the involuntary arc my back forms and his hand comes around to steady me. His hand is warm and spread wide across my stomach and my head begins to feel foggy and I let out a rushed breath.

Once he's satisfied that I'm steady, his hand comes away and it goes back to work, binding my hands and wrists together behind my back. Then, he begins bringing the rope around me. The softness and the slight burn of the rope heating my nerves and my skin, the fogginess in my head grows thicker. The music reaches its peak and I shudder. The next song that begins sounds familiar but I can't place it. It is a jazzy number with trumpets and soft drum beats. I wait for lyrics but they never come. Or if they do, I don't hear them as what Derek does next puts me in a deeper fog, new sensations as the rope slides up between my breasts and I can't stop the whimper that escapes my lips.

His hand comes to my cheek, reminding me that he's there, then his hand slides down my throat, almost scratching but not unpleasant. Then his mouth is on my ear, hot and wet and I tremble. The fog is getting deeper and I feel like I'm floating. All weight and pressure on my legs seems to just disappear and I moan.

Derek continues to bind me with the rope, always soft and sensual, but he pulls the rope along my skin and I can't help my body's reaction to the sensations. It is overwhelming, yet calming at the same time. I can think of nothing but what it is that he is doing to me. His warm hands caressing and touching me, his wet lips taking away any control I could possibly have. Nothing matters, but him and me.

The music continues on, taking me deeper and deeper into the fog of a warm fuzzy feeling.

The process of tying me up takes some time, but he never rushes, never increases his pace and certainly never stops making me shiver with anticipation of what is going to come next.

When he finishes, I feel him messing with something between my shoulders and then he is tugging, lifting me slightly, though I am still firmly on the ground. Almost as if the music has disappeared completely I can feel and hear the tightening of something like a screw and when he's done, both of his hands slide down my arms, but I am still being tugged upward and I know that I can no longer move from this spot. Completely at his mercy to do as he pleases to me and I can't stop the shiver and moan as it escapes my lips. I need more, I want more.

My panties are soaked with my juices and my clit is throbbing with the burning need to be touched and stroked. The need to orgasm is overwhelming me. I feel his body pull back from mine and I whimper, then he is back, pressing every inch of his body against the front of mine. His fingers are trailing up my arms, I can feel minor bites of his nails as he goes up, reaching my shoulders, I can feel each bump and tug of the rope as his hands pass over it. Then his hands are sliding down my chest, pushing closer to my nipples and my back arches, begging him to run his fingers down my breasts and my nipples. When they do finally reach that point, I shiver and shudder so much that I nearly lose my balance, but I am held steady by the rope holding me up, and he doesn't stop his hands.

They move past my breasts and nipples, making their way down to my stomach and the lace of my panties. I am desperate to have him remove them, to find the wetness between my legs and exploit it. But he doesn't. His hands begin sliding back up toward my breasts and my clit is throbbing so much that it hurts.

"Please, sir," I whisper.

"Please what?" I hear over the music in my ears.

"I...I'm going to cum."

There is a loud audible hiss that escapes his mouth and his hands continue their assault on my body, bringing me higher than I ever thought I could reach, just on the brink of an explosive orgasm, but he won't let me, he isn't touching me there. The fog is heavier now, every inch of my skin burning to be touched, every ounce of me needing this man more than I need air to breathe. I can no longer hold my head up, the weight of the fog and the flying sensation I feel is too much and my head rolls forward. My breathing is spiking into short raspy breaths. His hands never stop moving.

Between the music, the comfortable tightness of the rope around my chest, the slight sting as I breathe in deeper, and last but not least, my desire for him reaches peaks I never imagined I could feel. My heart is pounding, my mind stops thinking, the heavy weightlessness becoming an addiction. Everything in my life ceases to exist as I am laid open for him, for everything this man has to offer me.

I can feel the shift in his hands as he moves around my body, then suddenly the tension in my back is gone and I feel him press between my shoulders, pushing me to bend. I do, and the tension returns, I am still connected to something in the ceiling, but now I am bearing forward, baring my panty covered sex to him. His hands begin moving along my back, across to my ass, kneading and teasing. His motions continue down, around the curve of my ass, past my panties and onto my thighs and I wobble, unable to handle the overwhelming sensations he is providing for me.

My legs begin to tremble; my sex is on fire with need and desire for Derek, for Orion, my hunter. Then he is gone. All sense of him disappears and I want to scream in frustration because he is no longer touching me. Then, out of nowhere his mouth, wet and hot, is on my nipple, sucking and pulling like his life depends on it. "Sir, I'm going to cum," I moan and he doesn't stop, but he doesn't grant me permission. No, not yet. His lips come off my breast, the inaudible pop rattling my core. Then without warning, he takes the other nipple in his mouth, only this time his hand begins pulling and tugging the other nipple and I can't. "Sir, please."

His mouth stops, his breath is cool across my soaked nipple. "Please, what?"

I shiver again at his voice. "Please sir, may I cum?"

His mouth is back, his fingers pinch and pull the other. "Yes," he growls against my breast and I explode.

The orgasm sends me flying, over the cliff of my lust for him. Bright white stars flash in my eyes, and I moan, writhing against his mouth on my nipple. I am floating on a cliff above the clouds, unable to see the ground. Then he is gone for a heartbeat. When he returns to me, a moment later, my panties are sliding down. My nerves are on edge, my body still trembling on the waves of the biggest orgasm I've ever had. Then Derek is slamming into me. Rocketing me higher and straight into another orgasm, my whole body is limp, my knees are no longer able to support me, but that doesn't stop his pounding into me. His hands are on my hips, his nails digging into the soft flesh, holding my hips up to his thrusts and pounding.

His groans are carnal and animalistic as he takes me. Without warning, there is a wet finger playing around the tight pucker of my ass and my whole body falls slack. He's pushed a limit I've never tested and then his wet finger slides inside and the strength in my knees returns and I start pushing back into him. Another orgasm on the verge of peaking, my sex clenching and releasing around his cock, and I hear him grunting, his cock twitching, he's fighting his own orgasm. "Please sir, I need you," I scream and he explodes inside me, the hot jets of his cum sending me over that cliff one more time.

47

Finding Me...

Before my orgasm has stopped ripping through me, he is undoing whatever is holding me up. His arm is wrapped tightly around my abdomen, holding me in place. His breathing is still ragged and he is still buried inside me. My pussy is clenched tightly around him, pulsing with the beats of my heart. Though the action could bring me to a climax again, I know it is not his intention. As soon as the binding holding me up is gone, all his strength kicks in, holding me up, then bringing me to stand back against his sweat covered chest and I melt into his embrace as his cock falls out of my body, limp from his own exertions.

I feel the blindfold come off, followed by the head-phones but I can't open my eyes. His arms are around me tightly, then without any warning, his hand is in my hair, pulling the pony tail free as my hair falls in waves, tickling down my shoulders and my back. Then his nose is in my hair, his face pressed into the nook between my neck and shoulder. Unspoken emotion courses between us. "Come," he whispers and he slowly starts to back up, bringing me with him.

I take a deep breath and the ropes bite lightly into my skin and I moan again. They're still there and they will have the power to undo me, but the fog isn't lifting either. We walk more than the room is wide and I realize when the light changes that we've gone into his room. He backs me up and then brings me down to sit on him, to sit on his lap. His arms have yet to leave my body and I snuggle into him. His hands are soft against my skin and I am boneless and shattered.

He begins to undo my bindings, holding me as much as he can in between passes. The sliding of the rope makes me shiver and while it seemed to take hours to tie me up, it takes a matter of moments to undo me. There is no wild array of sensations, though my being snuggled into him forces the rope to slide between us and each pass brings the fog back, but it disappears and then the fuzzy begins to retreat slowly.

Once he is done unbinding me, his hands begin to work my shoulders then one disappears and I hear something that sounds like a wrapper. "Open your mouth." I obey and he begins rubbing something along my lips so I stick my tongue out, but he pulls it back, teasing me. I groan as the chocolate registers on my tongue. He brings it back up, teasing a little longer until I hear his quiet chuckle then finally he lets me have it. I chew on it; it tastes like heaven.

"Lay down, on your stomach." It's not a request or a command, his voice is soft and tender. I manage to open my eyes enough to see where the bed is and I reluctantly slide off of him to slide onto the bed, face down. Then I grab a pillow, pulling it under my head and snuggle into it. Then his hands are on my back, soft kneading begins as he works my muscles, but I can feel the sensitive skin where the rope had been and each time he passes over a new spot, goose bumps race along my skin. He continues to massage me gently until I more or less melt into the pillow. I'm still flying high and I just want to lay here and close my eyes. Sensing the need I have to relax, Derek comes off of me and I can feel him shifting on the bed until he lies down next to me, on his back. I can't resist the urge to snuggle into him, desperate for the contact, so I do.

Nestling my head into the crook of his shoulder, I wrap my arm around his stomach, sliding my hand across the taut muscles and I note how he visibly relaxes into my touch. His arm comes around me and finds the small of my back again. My eyes are heavy with fog and a desperate need for sleep. It doesn't take long and I'm sleeping in his arms once again.

Everything about my body is freezing. My feet are ice cold along with my hands and I shiver awake. "You alright?" Derek asks me, his voice is soft, a whisper almost.

"I'm so cold."

I feel rather than hear his soft laugh, then suddenly the duvet is on top of me and his hands are rubbing along my back and arms. It doesn't help and my teeth begin to chatter. "You're coming down, just take a few deep breaths and relax."

I breathe in deep and let it out slowly, trying to think of anything other than the coldness I feel. It works and I quickly fall back to sleep.

"Cotah, come on, baby, wake up."

"Go away," I groan and he laughs.

"Not a chance. Come on, sleeping beauty. You need to eat."

Just the mention of food has my tummy growling, much to his amusement. I open my eyes and fight their heaviness and realize that all the fog is gone, I can think clearly but my body still feels like jello. His hands are soft and warm as they stroke along my back. I look up, our eyes meeting. "There's those baby blues," he says with a smile. His posture is relaxed and I can see the same blissful happiness that's roaming through my body reflected in his own features.

"What happened?" I ask without clarification but he seems to know what I'm referring to.

"I can only assume that you reached something called sub-space. It's where your mind goes when you give yourself over to someone completely. Like you did to me." He smiles warmly at me, the smile reaches his eyes and they crinkle at the corners. The effect is breathtaking as he looks so much younger and so relaxed. Then I realize that he's dressed and I'm disappointed. "We're not going anywhere today, so why don't you clean yourself up, find some comfortable clothes and meet me downstairs for lunch." He leans down, kissing my forehead. I want to turn and kiss him, but the massive orgasms earlier have left me sore and sated and I want to just enjoy him.

"Okay," I breathe and he backs off, climbing off of the bed and he leaves me to get dressed. Good idea.

48

Exasperated...

After I shower and dress in a t-shirt and a pair of rather skimpy shorts with my bikini underneath, I climb down the steps slowly. Still not trusting my limbs. My muscles are weaker than any other time I've ever had sex, but I feel amazing.

As I reach the bottom of the steps, I hear Derek talking to someone on the phone, but I notice on the table that there are a couple of empty plates, a large bowl of salad and some other stuff spread across it. I go over, taking my seat next to the head of the table, to his right. There is soft music playing, it is the gentle melodies of Bach by the sounds of it. I'm no music buff and I'm still trying to figure out the song I heard earlier without lyrics. It is a song I know, but I can't place it.

I notice there are three glasses in front of me. One looks like normal water, the other is the soft pink of cranberry and soda, and the other is an empty wine glass. There is a bottle of white wine sitting on the table. My thirst overcomes me and I pick up the cranberry and soda, drinking it down quickly. I hear him chuckle and I look up to see him standing a few feet away. "Thirsty?"

I nod as I take the last couple swallows of the cranberry concoction. It is light and refreshing, but I'm still thirsty and suddenly understand the reason for the water. I take a few sips as he takes his seat.

"How was your nap?" I smile then frown.

"You didn't sleep with me?"

He gives me a sheepish smile. "No, I laid there for some time, and then shortly after you woke up with the shivers, I got up. I had a couple of little things I needed to take care of."

"So that's why you wore me out." A smile plays on his lips, but not in a I've-been-caught kind of way, but more in a why-didn't-I-think-of-that kind of way and I smile. "Were you able to finish?" I ask as I pick up my water for another sip.

"I was, I'm all yours." His eyes light up at his own words.

"Good." I stand up, walking toward my bedroom, headed for the envelope, desperate to get this part over with. I can feel his eyes burning into my back as I disappear down the hall.

I grab the envelope and return to him, holding it in my hands. "I have something of yours," I say, handing him the envelope, preparing myself for the onslaught of whatever his wrath is going to be.

He looks at the envelope and without even opening it he hands it back to me. "No. I will not accept it. You won that money fair and square."

"Derek, don't be ridiculous. I would have never bet more than what I could afford, so I would have never won this kind of money, from one bet. So please, it's yours, take it."

I sit down in my chair again, steeling myself for the argument that he is going to make with me. I knew it was coming. "I don't want to fight with you; we don't have much time left together."

"Good, then accept it graciously and we can move on."

He glares at me and I feel my insides quiver and the feeling of submission washes over me again. Damn it. He's going to use his dominance over me to make me accept his money. "Please don't," I whisper and I can feel his irritation wash out of him. "Can you please listen to me, if only for a moment?"

"Of course." His voice is soft.

"Last Sunday, you propositioned me with a week in your presence, and I accepted, not because of the clothes or the money you were spending on my friends to help keep them happy. I accepted because it meant a chance to spend time with you. Get to know you, and..." I take a deep breath, steadying my nerves. "This has been the best week of my life."

His hand comes to me under the table; I can feel his warmth on my leg. "Mine too," he says so quietly that I'm not sure I was meant to hear it, but I look up, our eyes meeting, my resolve washing away.

"I can't accept the money, Derek, it's too much."

"Please Dacotah, let me give this to you, let me do this for you. I can't..." Words fail him too, "I can't let you walk away..." A pregnant pause. "Without knowing you'll be able to take care of yourself." He slides the envelope across the table to me.

"What happened to you asking me to go to Paris with you?" I breathe.

He stiffens and his hand slides away from my leg and those words, the ones from the limo, the ones from Wednesday night now feel like they were empty, said in the moment, said at a time that it was easier to say them, to shut me up, to avoid whatever the real issue was at the time. My appetite vanishes. "Excuse me," I breathe and dart for my room. I lock the door behind me and race into the shower, desperate to bury myself beneath the scalding hot water, desperate to rid myself of the dirty whore feeling that is crawling all over my skin.

I climb into the shower, clothes and all, not caring nor needing or wanting to be naked, not being able to stand the sight of myself. I knew when we started this on Sunday that come this Sunday morning, I would be walking away, and I would be forced to step away from him with the pieces of myself that I could hold onto. This was the reason why I didn't want to do this. Knowing that at the end of the week, he would reject me. But he… god, Tristan and Cami, he took me out, he pampered me and showed me off, his motivations could have only been one of a few things. One, he really did feel for me and that by taking me to the gala, he was saying to the world that I was his and he was taken. Or two, to humiliate me, to take me there, introduce me to friends, let the reporters dig their way into my life, dig up my own humiliation surrounding being left at the altar, or my mother's past, or…

The tears and sobs are too much, too overwhelming. I can't even begin to think rationally and I am just making up the worst case scenario in order to make myself feel better, but what if it's true? What if he invited Tristan and Cami here because he needed to talk to Tristan, which he did, several times, and the bond that formed between Cami and I is just collateral damage?

Suddenly the water cuts off. "Get up." He is standing over me.

"Fuck you," I growl.

He stumbles backward at my tone and the forcefulness in my voice like I've slapped him. "Dacotah," he breathes.

"Don't. So were those words Wednesday night empty? Were you placating me?"

"God, no," he growls back, taking a step toward me. I crouch back into the corner when I take in the anger in his eyes. When he's angry, he is truly terrifying and sensing my fear, he stops, his eyes soften a little, but his features are still hard. I shiver because of the coldness I now feel in the bathroom, with my clothes soaking wet and dripping onto the tile below me, but he is blocking my exit.

I look at him, my eyes blurry with unshed tears. "Then what, Derek?"

"Damn it, I don't know, I don't know what you want me to say, Dacotah."

I stare at him. "Then let me go," I whisper, trying to straighten and stand, trying to be able to make my exit.

He's on me in a flash, my sobs race like fire in my veins and I'm shaking, his hands are on my cheeks and his mouth is inches from mine. "I can't," he protests and his lips engulf mine, soft, warm; filled with lust, passion and promises. My body arcs into his, letting myself feel every inch, ever sinew of strength behind his clothes. "I won't," he breathes against my lips, breaking our kiss momentarily before he continues his assault on my mouth. No tongues, no touching, just kissing. I can't breathe, my mind is blank, my heart is racing and I feel the anger wash out of me. The control he demonstrated this afternoon is making me comply with his lips, to his touch; all thoughts of my argument and my anger are gone.

I let my hands roam up his body, he doesn't flinch and he doesn't stop.

A few more heartbeats and he pulls away from me and I collapse against the wall of the shower, shaking and shivering. "Let's get you dried off." His voice is soft.

I don't fight him. He takes my wrist, pulling me from the wall and he starts to undress me, starting with my shorts, unbuttoning them. There is absolutely nothing sexual about the look in his eyes and the loss of hunger, of my hunter, causes my skin to grow colder. He realizes that I'm wearing my suit, and there is a small sigh of relief. He pulls my shirt up over my head and then grabs one of the big white towels hanging outside the shower, wrapping me up in it. The dry warmth is comforting, but he helps by running his hands along my arms, creating friction, then once my shivers subside some, he pulls me into his arms, wrapping them around me, rubbing my back. His lips come to my hair, then my forehead. I'd hug him back, but I am trapped in the confines of the towel, and right now, remembering what he said about my touch, I'm grateful.

We need some distance. "I need to get dressed," I say and he sighs, but steps back, allowing me the freedom to pass him in the shower. I leave the bathroom and go to the closet, walking into it. I close the door, wishing I could lock it, but it's a closet and there is no lock. I slump against the back wall, falling to the floor. I let the tears overcome me.

You love him.

The voice doesn't surprise me and I want to shout back, no shit Sherlock, but I don't need him thinking I'm crazier than I am. I am completely insane. I've fallen in love with a man I barely know, a man who is keeping secrets from me and more than anything, a man who I can't be with. Yes, the sex is amazing, more importantly he makes me feel things I never knew existed, or even that I needed. He's like a drug, once you've had a taste, you can't stop. I'm addicted to the way he makes me feel and I hate it. I hate that I've wasted this time with him being irrational, but damn it, I'm scared.

49

Forgiveness...

Realizing that I've been in here way too long, I fight my own body to stand up, and I fail. I feel safe from him in here, safe from the emotions, but if I don't get up, he's going to come in here, and I don't know that I want that. Or maybe I do and that's why I can't get up. I don't know, nor do I really care.

As predicted, the door opens. He is standing on the other side, his eyes cautious and wary. He doesn't need this, he doesn't need some week long fling weighing him down. He has enough on his plate, but the look in his eyes says more than his mouth is saying. He surprises me further by coming to stand against the wall next to me. He's watching me carefully as he slides down the wall to sit next to me. With his knees up, his back pressed against the wall, he brings his arm around me, coaxing me closer to him, and I lean into him, unable to forego the chance to be closer to him. His hand starts a slow comforting circle along my hip.

Neither one of us say a word. Content just to be and I relish the moment, desperate not to sour it with my mouth. If I hadn't chosen now as the time to bring up the fucking money from the hotel, this wouldn't have happened. We would have eaten lunch, done anything but what we're doing now.

The silence drones on. Eventually his legs stretch out in front of him, he's making himself more comfortable, and I sigh. Something needs to be said, we need to talk, and we need to figure this...

"I'd be honored if you came to Paris with me. In fact I'm ready to demand that you come with me, but I realized after I let those words slip out of my mouth, that I would be asking you to give up more than a vacation in Vegas." His hand continues his slow lazy circles on my back and hip, reminding me that he's there. "You have a life somewhere else, a life that I have no business interfering with and I apologize because I didn't actually ask you the question,"

"No you didn't, you asked me what I would do if you asked me to go to Paris with you."

He sighs. "You're right, I did."

"Then you never gave me a chance to answer your question, rather you drug me to the Eiffel Tower and fucked me senseless, and it hasn't been brought up since."

He shifts slightly, nothing but tenderness in his eyes. "Cotah, will you accompany me to Paris?"

"Ask me later. Right now, the answer is no, I won't. I'm still angry with you."

His eyes close and reopen slowly. "How can I make you less angry with me?"

"Take back your money."

"Is that all?"

"Well, it will make me less angry, but I will still be upset."

"Good point." His eyebrows lift slightly. "But I can't take back the money."

Anger washes over me again. "Why?"

"Because, if you leave me on Sunday morning, I won't be able to take care of you."

"So if I walk away Sunday, that's it? I'll never see you again?" I watch as the reality of what he's said crashes into him and I know that never seeing me again will be just as, if not more painful than it will be for me. Hope sparks.

"I can't promise when I will see you again, but," He brings his finger to my nose, stroking it quickly. "Never say never, Dacotah."

"You can't do that. That's not fair, Derek. You can't just let me walk away to wonder whether or not I will ever see you again. I realize you like control, I understand it, and I enjoy all of your control freak tendencies, but that is something you can't take away from me. I need to know that if I walk out of that door Sunday morning, that you will either come to me again, or that we part our ways for good, never to see each other again. I can't spend every day turning corners wondering if you will be standing right there. If you let me go, let me go, and don't come back."

His arms wrap tighter around me. "Cotah, I don't know if I can let you go," he breathes against my head. He kisses the top of my head and I soak up the tenderness that I'm feeling from him right now. I don't want to let him go, I can't let him go, but I will, I'll have to.

50

Opening Up...

The rest of Friday is spent enjoying each other. At some point in that closet I decided that I needed to enjoy what I have, while I have it. Derek has been nothing but kind to me and today I've been a complete idiot.

We go swimming in the pool, and then he treats me to dinner on the patio after the sun has gone down, in the quiet and the twinkling lights of Vegas. "Is there some place you'd like to go tomorrow?" he asks as Arnold clears our plates. I shake my head. "I've just kept you here this week, your friends have been out seeing the sites and..."

I put my finger over his lips, silencing him, he kisses the pad of my finger. "No, I want to be where you are."

"Have you been to Vegas before?"

"No, and until Rachel sprung this trip on me, I'd never had a desire to come here. If I'd had more notice, then I would have done some research, looking for places to go, but..." I trail off, remembering Jessica showing up at my door, then Jason, and...

"What's wrong?" His voice is soft, curious.

I shake my head, but decide it doesn't matter, and that I can either forget it, or tell him. "I caught my ex with his pants down and his dick shoved into some slut."

"Ouch."

"Oh that's nothing, it's one thing to catch your boyfriend in bed, or a bathroom, as is the case here. But it is a whole other story when you catch him in the bathroom of the restaurant where your very own rehearsal dinner is being held."

I watch as his eyes fixate on me. "Fuck Cotah, I didn't know that." He runs his hand through his hair. "Well now, don't I feel ridiculous?"

"What's that supposed to mean?"

"When did this happen?"

'Uhm, about a month ago."

He stands abruptly, his chair falling back. "That happened to you, and then you agreed to this..." His arm waves around toward the penthouse. "God Dacotah, I'm sorry."

"Stop saying you're sorry. I'm a woman, I'm capable of my own decisions, Derek. I told you, I did this because I wanted to get to know you, because I was intrigued and more than anything, for this week, I've completely forgotten all about Jason and his bullshit, I've forgotten about my pathetic life back in Wisconsin. Yes, I have a house, a ridiculous job, and friends where I live, but I no longer feel like Wisconsin is my home. It hasn't been my home since my grandmother died. Don't you see, I've learned so much this week, not just about you, but about myself, about what I'm capable of. And believe me, I would have never in a million lifetimes learned a tenth of what I have this week had I not come to Vegas." I stand and lean over the railing, looking down on the fountains, my skin flushing as I remember Wednesday night. "Do you want to know what drove me to say yes to Rachel, to coming here?"

"Please?"

I turn, facing him, placing my elbows on the railing. "Jessica."

"Who?" I give him the look. "Oh, how?"

"She showed up at my house." His eyes grow wide. "She showed up to apologize, saying things like Jason lied to her, told her we were over, things like that. But when she showed up, I was almost relieved because of the fact that she proved to me exactly why Jason and I never moved in together, why we never really progressed. I realized that catching them was the best thing that could have ever happened to me, it was the excuse I needed to stop the wedding. But, it was after she told me that she was pregnant," He inhales sharply. "then left again, that I started to really thank my stars. At least until the next knock came." He raises an eyebrow. I nod. "Yup, Jason showed up, begging me to forgive and go back to him."

"What did you do?"

"I yelled, called him names and told him to get off my property. As soon as he was gone, I grabbed my stuff, locked up my house and went to Rachel's. We made Mandy show up and we left."

"And?"

"And what?"

"You look like you want to say something."

"When we pulled out of Rachel's driveway, I said goodbye to my house, deciding that if I never returned, that I'd be okay with that."

"You would have stayed where, Vegas?" He raises a skeptical eyebrow at me.

I shrugged. "Here or Minneapolis."

"But how?"

I sigh. "Believe it or not, I'm not entirely poor, Derek. When my grandmother died, she left me her house, free and clear, and a sizable inheritance" I turn away, leaning on the railing, emotions from talking about my grandmother flood me and I don't want to cry in front of him anymore and the look of sorrow and pity on his face is not helping. "I did some remodeling to the house, hoping to update its sixties decor and for the last year, I've thought about selling it."

"So is that money that you have why you won't accept the winnings?"

I roll my eyes knowing he can't see me. "No." I sigh. "I won't accept that money because, well, to be honest, if I sell the house, I can take care of myself. I wouldn't need to work for a long time."

"What are your dreams, Dacotah?"

I turn to look at him. "What do you mean?"

"Well, I get the sense that a lot of what you do in your life isn't for yourself. That you put others before you, no matter what the personal sacrifice is. So, what are your dreams?"

I lean back on the railing again. "To travel Europe, see more of the U.S., go to college, figure out what it is that I want to spend the rest of my life doing. I'm twenty-six years old and I've held the same dead end job for ten years. It's time for a change."

He smiles at me. "What is it that you would go to college for?"

"I have no idea."

"Well, what are some of the things you like to do?"

"Oh hell Derek, I don't know, I love to read, I love a good story, maybe work for a publishing house, or as an author's assistant, maybe even an editor. I'm good at finding the mistakes in stories."

He smiles. "What about our story?"

My eyes meet his. They're full of wonder and he smiles. "What about our story, Derek? So far it's pretty great and pretty fucked up at the same time."

"What are the high points and low points?"

I snort. "Uhm, there are no low points."

"You sure about that?" His hands slide into his pockets.

"Despite our arguments, no, I don't see them as low points, except for the fact that we have to hit those points before you open up to me." I give him a pointed look.

"Okay, your point received. What would you like to know?"

"What about your parents?"

I see a slow smile spread across his face. "They're both alive, they live up in Portland. My father is a retired Vietnam Veteran and a retired surgeon. My mother is a housewife."

"Are you close?"

"Not really." He has a faraway look in his eyes so of course I'm curious.

"Why not?"

He sighs, then starts to pace in front of me. "It's a rather long story."

He doesn't continue, trying to brush it off, but I won't let him. "I'm all ears, Orion."

He gives me a smirk at my nickname for him, a reaction that I've come to enjoy. "When I was twenty-one and finishing up my senior year of college, my sister passed away." Oh shit. My hand goes to my mouth. "I guess maybe it's not a long story, but once she passed away, my parents withdrew from me, from a lot of things. They say that they're proud of the things I've accomplished, but..." he trails off.

"But since your sister's passing, they don't pay much attention." He stops pacing and looks at me, though it wasn't a question, he nods. "Does that bother you?"

He doesn't hesitate. "Yes and no. Alison was sick for many years, in and out of hospitals, nurses in and out of the house multiple times. When she passed away, my parents had been so convinced that she'd pull through like she had in the past. They didn't take her death well, so I can understand, but in the same I can't. My father gave me fifty thousand dollars after I graduated, I used that as startup capital and I've been building my empire ever since."

"You've done an amazing job at doing just that. Though I still don't know what it is that you do exactly."

He smiles at me. "There isn't much I don't do. I own a series of Vegas casinos, though more as an investor than an active participant. After college I moved here, started working for the Stardust as a dealer, then made my way up the ranks. Within three years of graduation, I was put in charge of a couple of the grand openings around town, and caught the attention of more than a few Vegas big wigs, and we started investing together." He is still pacing the balcony. "By the time I turned twenty-five, I'd made my first million, by twenty-eight I tripled that. Just before my twenty-eight birthday my net worth topped a billion dollars."

"And now?"

He stops, looking at me rather seriously. "I'm not sure you want me to answer that question, Cotah."

"No, I probably don't, but I asked it, and since we're being so open, I'd honestly like to know."

"About fifteen billion dollars."

My head swims. "I'm not even sure how much money that is."

He chuckles softly. "It's more than enough. It is so much that the money you won in that bet means nothing, and I've made about five times that much since then. Like I said in the casino, you're a lucky charm."

I cock my head at him. "How so?"

He smiles. "Since that afternoon, in the Miracle Mile, I've managed to buy and sell three different companies, increasing my business portfolio, and the stock market has been wonderful this week. So, it's been a good week."

"You were irritated the other day, why?"

"Ahh, that. There were a number of reasons for that. One was a phone call from Tristan reminding me about the gala, and him ribbing me about a date."

"Is that when you told him about me?"

He nods. "Though he made me laugh and told me, and I quote, 'get your head out of your ass, if you're this fucking excited about a woman, you need to bring her, and you need to treat her right.' So with his words I realized that I hadn't been very nice to you, or at least treated you in a way you deserved to be treated, which irritated me further."

"What else?"

"It's business related, not sure it is something you'd be interested in hearing about."

"On the contrary, I see how excited you get when you talk about business."

He grins at me. "I do, I love my job, I love what I do, and more than that, despite the fact that I work my ass off when it's necessary; I enjoy the fact that I'm capable of unwinding. At least when you're around." He winks at me.

"So spending afternoons in dungeons or evenings on the patio with someone who isn't 'business', isn't something you indulge in often?"

"No," he says shaking his head. "Cotah, I am usually working about eighteen hours a day, but that is only because I can't turn my brain off and focus on other things, nor do I have other things to focus on." He winks again.

"Ahh, so in other words," I push off the railing and he stops pacing, facing me, a few steps away, "I'm a distraction." I close the distance and wrap my arms around his waist.

He growls, "Yes." I look up at him and my hunter has returned, his eyes are milk chocolate and my desire spikes.

"Is that a good thing?"

His arms come around me. "Yes." He moans and his lips are on mine, hard and fierce. The kiss is all consuming and our conversation is over, for now.

51

One More Day...

Boneless, tired and deliciously sore- that's how I wake up Saturday morning. I hear the shuffling of something, papers I think, and roll over toward the direction of the sound. Sitting up in bed, his back against the headboard, his hair is pulled back, wearing dark rimmed glasses and he is so completely engrossed in whatever he's looking at that he jumps when I reach out to touch his leg. "Sorry."

"Good morning. I didn't wake you, did I?"

"Mmm...no." I stretch, feeling the effects of being tied up yesterday, being taken so roughly, then so deliciously soft and sweet last night. I think I finally fell asleep, staying asleep, around three. "What are you working on?"

"Nothing important. You were sleeping so sweetly that I didn't want to leave you, so I thought I'd get some work done."

"Mmm."

"Not very talkative this morning."

"Nuhuh."

He laughs then leans over, kissing my forehead. "What shall we do today?"

I wrap my arm around his waist, pulling myself closer to him. "Stay in bed, all day."

He quickly snatches up the papers off of his lap, throwing them onto the floor and sliding down into bed. "I like that idea."

He doesn't hesitate in taking me for an early morning, sheet twisting horizontal roll around the bed.

"That was far too quick," I grumble.

He laughs. "It was, but I figured you might need to..." I squirm and pop up out of bed. He's right of course, and I slide into the bathroom.

When I come out he is stretched out on the bed, the sheet is barely covering his hips. One arm tucked behind his head, the other stretched out, waiting for me with a beautiful smile that stretches his lips thin and takes my breath away. I still struggle with why me, but he's proved it time and time again. Right now is no exception as the sheets begin to move and tent at his crotch.

"Will you let me do something?"

"That depends," he says, his eyes growing hooded and full of desire. His erection is now making a full tent out of the thin sheet that's draped over him.

"Oh?"

"On what you want to do."

I walk to the foot of the bed, grab onto the sheet and pull it off of him. His cock bounces into full standing ovation and I lick my lips as I stare at it. It twitches and I smile.

"Come here," he says as his hand grips the base of his cock. I watch him for a moment as he begins to stroke it up and down. The muscles in his thighs tense and release as he continues to pleasure himself. I kneel on the bed then fall to my hands, my breasts sway and his breath catches. I crawl up between his legs, determined to take him into my mouth, to lick and suck him until he explodes down my throat.

I look up at him and bite my lip as I come to within a couple of inches of his cock. "You want it?" A smile playing on his lips, despite the fact that I'm making the move, he is absolutely in control.

"Yes, sir." His breath catches in his throat and he continues stroking along the head of his cock. His fingers are long and wrapped completely around him.

"But this feels..." His back arches. "So good." He groans. His hand slides down his full length and I pounce, seizing my chance, and my mouth wraps around him and I suck, forcing him in my mouth and he hisses. The muscles in his thighs spasm as the sensation radiates. "Fuck," he groans.

His hand comes away from the base of his cock and I'm in control, at least briefly. Then his hand comes to rest on the side of my head. His fingers sliding into my hair, possessing me and he has control again. My sex heats and I can feel the effect as it slides free of my folds and onto my thigh. My own arousal spurs me on, and I begin sucking vigorously on the head of his cock, swirling and sucking my way down his shaft until his cock is in my throat. I pull a breath through my nose, hoping to take more without gagging. I do and he hisses again, his hips thrusting, pushing himself just a little further into my throat and then his hand stills in my hair holding me. His thighs tense and then it's there, the twitch followed by an explosion of his hot seed sliding down my throat. I swallow greedily as he continues to come undone below me.

His eyes are closed, his body trembling as I continue to lick and suck, milking him dry. His hand, the one in my hair tightens and I slow my motions, licking one final time on the underside of his cock and he twitches and groans again. "Shit," he says and then relaxes back into the bed. I lean back on my feet, placing my arms close to my body, close enough to push my breasts together.

Slowly his eyes begin to open and they're hungry and needy and the erection I thought I'd just tamed, springs back to life. He climbs off the bed, cool as a cucumber, like nothing happened and I'm stunned by the action. "On your back, hands on the headboard," he commands and I shiver. My nipples are achingly hard. Desperate for him, I do as he orders. "Don't move," he hisses and exits the room.

I shiver at his orders; my mind is going a million miles a minute at what he plans to do to me.

Within a few minutes he's back, but he doesn't come into the room. "Close your eyes, Dacotah, do not open them, or peek, or I will punish you." I comply and then I can't help rubbing my legs together to help soothe the need he's just sent to my core.

I hear some weird noises, the first thing is the sound of metal clinking on metal and I immediately think of the cuffs, but this is different. "Spread your legs." His tone is harsh and demanding and I shiver. Doing as I'm told, I spread my legs wide, exposing myself to him and I can hear his breath change. I smile. I have this effect on him and I relish it, soaking it up. His long fingers wrap gently around my left ankle, the touch sends a shiver and goose bumps. Then I feel something cool and hard wrapping around my ankle.

The anticipation is killing me and I want to open my eyes. Would a punishment be so bad? Just as I think the thought, his hand comes down onto my thigh, his fingers hitting just on the inside and I jump. As the shock and pain radiate outward, I writhe on the bed as the pain turns to pleasure and consumes me.

Then his hands are on my right ankle, and I feel cool metal wrapping around my ankle. "Try and move," he orders.

When I move my legs, I can't bring them together, but when I tug harder on my left leg, the right one follows. "Open your eyes." I do, and look down the length of my body, past my swollen breasts. I lift my head as best as I can, inhibited by my hands on the iron headboard.

Down around my ankles are two cuffs, one for each ankle and the cuff are attached to a bar, effectively preventing me from bringing my ankles together and I groan, my head flopping back down.

He laughs. "Hmm, cuff your wrists or not?"

Though it isn't really a question, I answer him. "Please, sir."

"That's my girl," he praises and then the bed is dipping to my left and I look up at him. He looks at me, his eyes on fire, and the darkness in them sends another shiver through me as his hands go to work binding me to the headboard. I test my bindings, though I know I won't be able to move. "So beautiful," he breathes and then his mouth is on mine, kissing me, sending the fire of desire running through my veins at lightning speed. His hands begin to roam gently over my body, my sex heats.

All too soon he pulls away and I pout. He smiles. "Close your eyes," he whispers, though not a command, I comply and I feel him shift off of the bed. Then I hear a clicking against glass, I want to open my eyes but the mystery has me more excited than anything, the excitement screws my eyes closed. Then my legs are lifting into the air, the bed dips and I feel him crawling between my legs and up my body.

He lowers my legs behind him and then his body weight is pressing against me and his breath is coming in warm spurts across my face. He doesn't say a word, then suddenly his mouth is on my neck, but instead of heat and warmth his mouth is wet and ice cold. I squirm and moan. He continues licking and kissing down my body, soon the cold starts to warm, when it does, he pulls back. I hear the clink again and understand that it's ice; he's torturing me.

When the cold comes back again, it's not his mouth, but there are drips of burning cold falling down along my chest, my nipples peak and the ice is searing into me and onto my nipple. I squirm, fighting the need to open my eyes and watch. "Watch," he breathes. How does he do that?

I open my eyes, and he is holding the ice cube to my nipple, then he begins circling along the darkened areola of my nipple, goose bumps make my nipples harder. He is trailing the ice into bigger circles until he is circling my entire breast. The ice is getting smaller in his fingers and I know it's coming to an end. He takes the ice away, placing it into his mouth and I sigh. I know what is coming next.

He leans down into my neck, letting the semi-warmed water drip, and then his ice cold tongue is licking along my neck to the underside of my arm that is exposed from being bound to the headboard. As soon as his mouth starts to warm, he pulls back again. Then he pulls another cube from the highball glass that is sitting to my right.

The ice is brought out of the glass, along my right breast and he repeats the motion from before. Now both my nipples are burning with the coldness of the ice and I hear his hiss when my sex warms and leaks. The warmth is spurred on by the sudden flick of his hips against my sex. "Please," I moan.

"Please what, Dacotah?"

"I need you, inside me. Please, sir," I mewl and watch as his eyes grow darker, more sinister, but no less sexy. I see a determination on his face. Though he's determined to torture me with the ice, he also can't resist. His hips pull up and then his cock is pressing gently at the entrance of my sex. "Gah! Please, Orion, I need you." His resolve fades and he slides inside of me, achingly slow but his eyes are alight, happier. Though I didn't use his preferred 'sir', he is satisfied with Orion and I smile as he pushes further into me.

His slowness is excruciating, but he keeps moving the ice along my breast, and soon the ice is nearly gone. Instead of his mouth, he lifts himself up. The action pushes him deeper inside of me and I moan as the fullness starts to consume me. Then, out of nowhere, he deposits the tiny ice cube into my belly button and I writhe, trying to buck it out. His hands are on my hips, stilling me. He says nothing but slowly shakes his head back and forth. The motion stills me. "It's so cold," I whine and he smiles as he comes to a stop inside me, fully sheathed. Doesn't move an inch, just simply sits there. Our bodies have become one, he's buried inside me and I'm so full. He reaches behind himself, lifting the spreader bar, effectively forcing my hips to sink into the bed, the water in my belly button begins to overflow and it is trailing down my sides. The coldness sets me on fire, but I can't move.

The spreader bar is now resting on his shoulders. My legs immobile, unable to move. I feel his cock twitch inside me once, then again, and again, reminding me that he's buried inside of me and I moan. "Please Orion."

He chuckles and shakes his head again. Once the spreader bar is settled, he reaches over for another ice cube and I groan, desperate to move but unable to do so. I watch as he licks the dripping water from his fingers, then the ice cube is on my stomach and I jump, squeaking as the coldness consumes me once again. This time he moves the cube lower and lower toward my sex, and my now throbbing clit. "Oh no, no, no," I groan and just for that he slides the ice between the lips of my sex and the hot and cold mixes and I feel my pussy spasm around his cock. I pull in a sharp breath, hissing through my teeth as the cold water slides down my lips, and my sex, surrounding his cock, buried inside me and his cock jumps at the cool water.

My orgasm is right there, right on the brink of exploding. My legs tremble, rattling the metal and my pussy clenches. Then he and the ice are gone. I'm empty and I groan. But before I can protest too loudly, his mouth on my clit; taking away the cold with his hot tongue and I jump. "Please, sir."

"What?"

"I'm going to cum, can I cum, please sir?" I continue begging as his mouth vibrates against my clit, then I feel cool fingers sliding into my opening.

"Yes," he commands and I explode as his fingers pound into me, their coolness gone, replaced by the warm, wet rush of my pussy and Derek groans as I feel my juices leaking onto the sheet below me. "Fuck yes." He grinds his face into my sex, his fingers pounding in and out of me, building me right back to my orgasm again and I groan. I don't know if I can do this again, but he doesn't care. His tongue continues its circling and licking, then sucking and finally teeth.

As soon as his teeth graze my clit, I explode again. This time I can feel my own juices pushing quickly past his fingers and his mouth is gone, his fingers slamming into me, working that spot and his other hand is slapping against my clit. "God! Fuck!" I am moaning out a string of expletives as I explode harder and faster than I ever have in my entire life. I have no strength and all the tension in my body is gone.

The fingers retreat and the slapping stops. Without understanding what is really happening to me, the next thing I know is Derek is slamming into me, hard and hot. Pounding and grinding against me. His movements are jerky and I realize that he is going to cum and that he slid inside me because he wasn't going to cum without being inside me and I moan. His hand comes to my clit, rubbing furiously and once again my orgasm takes me.

"Dacotah!" he howls as he twitches and explodes inside me. After the cold of the ice, his cum is searing hot and I tremble around him. "Fuck." He continues spurting and my sex tightens around him, milking him dry.

My whole body is limp and I barely notice when the cuffs are gone with the flick of a wrist and he is leaning above me, undoing my bindings. I notice vaguely that while he is doing this, he is still buried inside of me, softening for the first time all morning. I give him a lazy smile and he kisses me. His hands are massaging my body. He's gentle as he slides out of me; the loss of our connection is overwhelming.

I can't think about anything when he rolls me onto my side, covering me with the duvet and spooning behind me. I can't open my eyes and I'm in that stage, right before falling asleep when I hear a whisper, "I love you." Though it is so soft I can't decide if I'm dreaming or not. Then I fall asleep.

52

This is going to hurt...

When I wake up a little while later, Derek is sleeping soundly, his breathing even and steady, but at some point we separated from each other. I feel a little chilly as I remember what he whispered, or at least what I thought I heard. Was he serious? Or was it said in an unguarded moment. Either of which I'm not sure how to process. I know that somewhere along this crazy journey I fell in love with him, only to realize it yesterday when I was so upset with him. But to hear it come from his lips-jeez, what does this mean now?

Before I squirm too many times and wake him up, I slide from the bed, grab one of my bikinis and a robe from the closet. I slip into the hallway to change before I head downstairs, unsure if Arnold is around.

When I climb down the stairs, there are a couple of domes on the table, the plates have been cleared, and we've slept through lunch. My stomach rumbles and I head into the kitchen. Inside the fridge there are two dome covered plates. I pull one out and find a sandwich and some chips inside. I don't hesitate because I need to eat, I'm starving.

Sitting down at the table, I dive in, trying to decide what I feel, and what this changes about our relationship. If he loves me, he won't let me go. Do I want him to let me go? That answer is a little too easy. No, I don't.

But can I walk away from everything I've ever known for a man who still holds secrets, mystery and intrigue? My answer is that I have nothing to lose.

Can I board a plane to Paris with him in the morning? That is the question. I know that I could, very easily. If he wanted me to, but then what? We go to Paris, then where... What happens beyond Paris? There are too many unanswered questions surrounding what lies beyond the time we would spend there. He asked me about my dreams; does that mean he wants to make my dreams come true?

Jeez, there is too much to process.

By the time I finish my sandwich, I'm surprised that Derek hasn't emerged, but decide that he needs his sleep. I grab my Kindle and head out to the patio and the pool, deciding that I will let him sleep, and that when he wakes, we can talk. At least if he is in a talking mood.

I've decided that I can't go to Paris. Though the passport I have and the means are available to me, I can't subject myself to job loss at the expense of not knowing. If it doesn't come up, or we don't discuss it tonight, I can't even begin to board a plane with him. Going with him means that I forfeit everything that is consistent for me. My job, especially. On the other hand, I could forego the job, and the life in Frederic for another what? A week? By then

I'd have lost my job and getting another job in Frederic after abandoning one I've had for years would be impossible.

Also, if I go to Paris with him, spending more time with him means the deeper my emotions will go and the harder it will be when he finally rejects me, kicking me to the curb after Paris and he tires of me.

My visions of the future include nothing but him, but his unwillingness to talk about how he feels openly makes that hard. I've tried to keep myself in check, and I know that it would be easier for me to walk away with my emotions and my tail between my legs if I didn't know that he felt the same. It would have made it easier to lick my own wounds without knowing I was hurting him too. I resolve to wait out the rest of our day together. See what happens as the day progresses and where our conversations go before I make a final decision.

It is nearly four when I go back into the penthouse, ready to shower, wash off the sunscreen and chlorine. When I step across the threshold, I see him just barely touching the bottom step, he's frozen in place, a pair of flannel pants hanging from his hips and I watch as his face visibly relaxes when he sees me. "I thought you left." The silence in the room makes his words travel as if he yelled them.

I smile, trying to comfort him. I shake my head. "I wanted you to sleep."

He comes off of the stairs, coming toward me. We meet in the middle and he wraps his arms around me, his lips kissing the top of my head. "Thank you," he says and I look at him. "For letting me sleep. I didn't realize how much I needed it." He sags into the couch, bringing me with him to sit on his lap. He puts his head back and rubs his eyes with the heels of his palms.

"We can go back to bed."

He shakes his head. 'No, we need to get ready. I just woke up too fast, I panicked when you weren't in bed."

I bring my hands to his cheeks, his hands fall away and his eyes meet mine, sincerity and love looking back at me, his words ringing in my ears from before we fell asleep. "Where are we going?"

He smiles wolfishly at me. "I have a surprise for you."

"I thought we were staying in bed all day."

"Surprise." He grins.

I roll my eyes and he smirks. "What am I wearing?" I ask him.

"Something fun and sexy. We're leaving at six."

"Want me to get dressed down here?"

"No, the dress I'm thinking about is upstairs and so is all of your stuff." He smiles and I squirm as his gaze heats. I move to stand up and his arms go around my waist. "Not yet," he breathes as he pulls me onto his chest, his arms tightening around me, kissing my forehead; my heart feels like it's in a vice, ready to explode at his tenderness. He's different, his demeanor has changed just since we went to sleep and I can't tell if it is because of our impending separation or if it is because of what he said before we fell asleep. But I decide that I need more time to be able to talk about it with him, and if we are leaving in just over an hour, that is hardly enough time. I just snuggle into his chest and his embrace.

We stay like that, saying nothing, snuggling and holding each other for some time. Then finally he starts to release me. "You need to go get ready."

"Join me." His expression grows dark and lust-filled.

"Then we will never leave."

"So let's stay here." He shakes his head at me.

"Nope." Then he laughs. "Remember, sexy and comfortable."

It is a quarter 'til six when I'm finally ready. I found the dress that I think he is referring to and dressed in it. It is purple, with cap sleeves and a square cut neckline. The hem is slightly shorter than what I'm used to, but I don't hesitate to wear a matching garter belt, panties and bra. I forego the matching pumps for more sensible black wedges. I know I can handle these a lot longer than the five inch Louboutins.

Taking one final look in the mirror, my hair is pulled up and super curly, going a thousand different directions in a very messy bun exposing my neck and my tattoo. Though I don't wear my hair up often, I enjoy displaying my ink.

When I come downstairs, I expect to see Derek standing facing the window, but I don't see him anywhere. I take a few steps, trying to decide where he could be hiding then I feel it. The hairs on the back of my neck stand up as he draws nearer to me. Coming up behind me, his arms snake around my waist and his face goes into the crook of my neck and shoulder. He kisses me gently. "Hello, gorgeous." My skin heats and my sex is ablaze with need from just those two words. My eyes close and he holds me to him tighter.

I wrap my hands around my back, seeking to steady myself with his pant legs, only I'm thrown off balance when I feel denim against my fingers and I'm surprised. I pull away from him, desperate to drink in a very casual Derek. He lets me go and I turn around.

My breath hitches when I take in the beautiful man standing before me, clad in a dark pair of boot cut jeans. His slender, yet powerful legs sheathed in the confines of denim that bell at the bottom. But I nearly fall over when I take in the cowboy boots he's wearing and nostalgia rings through me, I miss my cowboy boots.

My eyes travel lazily up his legs, alighting on the slight bulge in his pants, then I take in the belt and the fact that he is wearing a tucked in black dress shirt that is open at the collar, no tie, and a black t-shirt peeking out. My eyes continue roaming northward until our eyes meet. He blushes slightly and I step toward him, taking his cheek in my hand and he softens into it. Then his hand comes around his back and he places a cowboy hat on his head and the look is complete. My breath is gone; I'm unable to breathe as I take him in once again.

53

Cowboys Rule...

"I never pegged you for a cowboy."

"Then it might surprise you more to learn that I rather enjoy country music."

My mouth falls open. "No way."

"Oh but Ms. Miller, my primary home is a ranch that sits in the hills of Tennessee, God's Country."

I pull in a deep breath. The fact that this man has overbearing controlling tendencies, on top of the fact that he owns a ranch, that he's a billionaire and a goddamn CEO, it's all too much. "You never stop surprising me, do you?"

He smiles. "I hope not. Speaking of which, I have something for you." He slides his hat from his head. His hair is pulled back into a low pony tail and there is simply no other word to describe him than fucking yummy.

He takes my hand and escorts me over to the couch. Sitting on top of the coffee table is a rather large box and excitement warms my insides. He ushers me to sit down, then, he picks up the box and turns around, sitting on the table, his legs on either side of mine. His jeans are tight and sexy and I just want to peel them off of him. I can't stop my tongue from licking my lips and he chuckles. "Open it." His eyes are excited, mirroring my own excitement.

I carefully pull the wrapping paper on the sides, controlling the urge to rip into it with every ounce of excitement I have.

When I finally free the box of its silver paper, it's blank, no indication of what's inside. I lift the top of the box, and nestled in tissue paper are a pair of brown with purple accent, cowboy boots. My hand covers my mouth at the shock. They're beautiful. I begin pulling them out, but that is not all that is in the box. I smile as I see a pair of thick socks. He knows well how to work new cowboy boots and the prospect of wearing them is exciting, though I'm not sure about the dress. But I keep digging into the box where I find a pair of artfully faded blue jeans. Pulling them free, I see that they are gorgeous. The pockets are embellished with a little embroidery and some stones that are sparking in the light of the room.

Beyond the jeans there are two more things, a black velvet box, and something purple. I pull the box out, setting it on my lap, then grab the shirt. It is a purple button up that is shaped with the sides coming together and a flare at the bottom. The kind of shirt that is not meant to be tucked in, there is also a purple camisole underneath it.

I put the original big box on the couch next to me and then I turn to the box that is sitting on my lap. I have tears in my eyes for reasons I can't begin to explain. I hesitate long enough that he takes the box from my trembling fingers. He turns it toward me and opens the box. I gasp as the necklace comes into view. It is silver, or knowing him, platinum. But what has my complete attention is what is hanging from the links; an infinity symbol that will lay flat. It is connected to the links by the sides so the infinity creates part of the necklace. "Derek, it's too much, I don't know what to say."

"Say you'll wear it." I look up into his eyes and they're serious but soft and warm. "Say you'll wear all of it, tonight."

I sag. "I'm already dressed."

He shrugs. "So, you can go change."

My face lights up as I pick everything up and take the box from his fingers. I lean forward and kiss him sweetly. "I'll be right back." As I turn to step away, he grabs my wrist, bringing me back for a more urgent and needy kiss.

By the time he pulls back, I'm breathless and my head is spinning. But excitement floods through me and I dart into the bedroom I once used.

I shed the thigh highs and garter, no longer needing them under my jeans. I rid myself of the dress and lay it out along the foot of the bed. I pull on my new jeans, they're a bit snug, but when I catch a glimpse of myself in the mirror, they fit perfectly. Lastly, I throw on the camisole and the shirt, buttoning it up before bending down for the socks and boots. The boots would have looked awesome with my dress, but the casualness in which he dressed made me feel overdressed.

I admire myself in the mirror, eyes wild and excited because he is taking me out on the town. My hand grazes the pendant on my necklace and I bring it to my lips, kiss it, and then remove the necklace. I quickly add the new necklace he's given me and the ensemble is complete. Smiling at the fact that I feel comfortable, more like myself in jeans and excited about our evening, I dash from the room.

My boots are beyond comfortable and a perfect fit. When I come around the corner, he's wearing his hat and his eyes glow with his own excitement. I turn around and he appraises me. "You look..." Words fail him and my heart flutters. "One more thing." He smiles wildly and then picks something up off of the table.

"Derek," I squeal as he hands me my own cowboy hat. "You're going to mess up my hair."

"Hmm," he muses. Then he proceeds to pull the binding from my hair, the curls fall around my face, and he places the hat on my head. "Yes, that's better."

His arms wrap around me, he tilts his head to the side so that we don't bump brims and his lips are on mine, hungry and wanting and my sex heats with need for him. He pulls back. "We're late." He grabs my hand, pulling me toward the open, waiting elevator and we step in, doors closing and we're falling toward the lobby.

"Thank you," I say as I snuggle up to him.

"Absolutely, you look gorgeous."

"What I want to know is how you knew?"

He chuckles, "I took a chance. I figured that in a worst case scenario I might be able to talk you into the boots, but, when I saw your face light up, I knew that I had you." He winks at me.

My heart pounds as the doors open in the lobby and we exit. This time there is no show through the casino, but we walk straight to the doors in front of reception to find a limo out front. The men scramble to open the door for us and Derek ushers me inside. I pull my hat from my head and climb in, sliding over. Derek folds himself inside, the door closes and we're off.

"So are you going to tell me where we're going?"

An evil smirk plays on his lips. "No." He raises his eyebrows at me.

"You're so mean," I huff, crossing my arms, pushing my breasts upward.

"Oh really," he growls, sliding close to me. He removes his hat and then begins pecking kisses along my mouth, to my chin and I burst out laughing.

He joins me in the laughter. He is so carefree and uninhibited by the fact that we have about twelve hours left with each other and my heart sinks. I push it down, fighting not to let the sourness of our impending separation ruin this evening.

Suddenly he starts to poke at my sides. I squirm and he keeps it up, then the next thing I know, I'm flat on my back being tickled by this beautiful man. I'm laughing so hard that he starts to laugh too. I try to fight back and tickle him, but I fail and am overcome by the carefree laughter and the fact that for the first time all week, Derek looks younger, carefree and completely relaxed.

After a couple of minutes of giggles and a few deep settling breaths, we stop and the limo door is opened. "Ready for your surprise?"

I nod with a smile and real excitement. He climbs out and he is met with flashbulbs, though nothing like the gala. I watch as his hat goes up onto his head and then he offers me his hand. I take it and slide out. Standing next to him, the bulbs go crazy and I can't help but smile, giggling when I feel him tickle me. Then his mouth is on me and the bulbs go wild, but I don't care, the only thing that matters is this man.

He pulls away, as breathless as I am, but we're both smiling wildly at each other. "After you," he says and I step up onto the curb, then my peripheral vision captures a sign.

TONIGHT ONLY, Limited Engagement
The sign changes into a face and a name.

"Blake Shelton? You're freakin' taking me to see Blake Shelton?" His face lights up with a big wide smile and I jump into his arms peppering him with kisses and he laughs.

"You act like this, assuming we're just going to a concert. I can't wait to see your reaction when you see the rest of your surprise."

I kiss him a couple more times and he sets me down. "Come on, gorgeous girl." He takes my hand, leading me into the hotel.

54

Best Night Ever...

"Good evening Mr. Hunter, Ms. Miller. They're ready for you." A man at the door informs us.

"Thank you," Derek says and I can still hear the excitement in his voice.

We walk through the doors and immediately Derek presses me against a pillar. We're out of camera sight. His hands cup my cheeks and he is kissing me very tenderly. Though not as passionate as before, it is equally breathtaking. He pulls back. "Ready?" He raises his brows with excitement.

"Hmm, let me think..." I laugh at his expression. "Yes Orion, I'm ready."

I realize as we start walking that my jeans and casual attire have given me some of the confidence that I've been lacking. I guess because I can finally feel like myself and

I'm not overwhelmed by the fact that I'm dressed for the sophisticated.

We walk through a couple of doors. I notice the deeper into the hotel we go, the attire of the men at the doors changes from livery to suits and finally tuxedos as we continue down a hallway. Security, no doubt. Finally we come to a set of double doors, nothing fancy beyond the metal and crash bars, but he stops and turns to me and kisses me a couple of times.

"The anticipation is killing me, Orion!"

"Keep calling me that, and I'll make you wait all night just so I can hear you say it again and again."

I wrap my arms around his neck, pulling him down to my level. "Orion." Kiss, "Orion." Kiss again, "Orion." His mouth crashes into mine and then someone clears their throat.

"Keep that shit up, Hunter and you'll have to get a damn room."

That voice, the southern drawl, I know that voice. I've heard it a million times and I freeze. Not at being busted but because of the man who's busted me. Derek's lips twitch against mine.

"I mean, seriously you two. I don't even kiss my wife like that." The drawl is back and I melt. Derek straightens and he raises his eyebrow at me. I nod.

"Dacotah Miller, it is my pleasure to introduce you to Mr. Blake Shelton." He lets me go, gesturing toward Blake who is standing to my left. I flush, of course, and turn in his direction.

"Pleasure to meet you, Dacotah," he says extending his hand for mine.

"No, Mr. Shelton, the pleasure is mine." He smiles warmly then, without warning, tugs my arm and pulls me into a hug.

"So you're the woman who's finally captured his attention?" I hear Derek snort. Then Blake lets me go. He's quite tall and I barely come up to his chest. "And missy, don't you dare call me Mr. Shelton. Blake or asshole is fine." He laughs and I can't help but join in. "Come on, they're waitin'." Derek steps aside and Blake crashes through the doors.

Then Derek takes my hand and leads me in behind him. "I'm so going to get you for this," I whisper in his ear and he laughs.

"Promise?"

"Oh, absolutely."

In front of us and to the left is a small stage and in front of that are about ten tables, all of which have about eight or so chairs set at them. All except for the one smack in the middle of the stage, there are only two chairs at that table.

Suddenly Blake stops, turning back toward us. "I almost forgot. Come up here."

I look from Blake to Derek and back again, but Derek leads me on and up the steps Blake has just climbed.

"Sweetheart," Blake shouts.

Then there is a bustle of activity back stage and coming from behind the curtain opposite us is none other than Blake's wife Miranda, and I damn near faint.

"Miranda, this is Derek Hunter." I watch her eyes light up, "And the beautiful Dacotah Miller." Her eyes meet mine and she smiles warmly. She walks toward us, she takes Derek's hand first.

"Mr. Hunter, it's a pleasure to finally meet you."

"Derek, please, Ms. Lambert."

She smirks, "Oh no, Miranda, please."

Then she turns to me, her eyes are alight with her own sense of excitement. "Hi Dacotah." She extends her hand to me. "It's a pleasure." She steps back and Blake wraps his arm around her.

"You guys want to come backstage while they let everyone else inside?" Blake asks and Derek looks at me. I nod. "Fine then, come on." We follow them backstage, it's not as spacious as I would have thought but there are a lot of people milling about back here, getting things set up for the show.

The evening starts off perfectly when we enjoy a couple of drinks backstage with Blake, Miranda and a couple of the crew, but I notice that there is no one else back here besides Blake's people and I feel a sense of honor knowing that not many people get this experience and I'm excited all over again.

"Dacotah?"

I smile at Blake. "Yes, sir?" I feel Derek smile at me.

"What would you like to hear tonight?"

I flush. "Uhm…Anything."

Blake laughs and Derek joins in. "I know what I want to hear," Derek says and Blake looks at him, the look is comical in the fact that it is very pointed.

"Then tell her to tell me, because I ain't taking your requests." Then Blake bursts out laughing. "She's prettier than you are."

I flush and they both start laughing, I join them, then finally one comes to mind, but I don't want to say it out loud. I step away from Derek, toward Blake and I can feel Derek's pout.

I lean in to Blake and he offers his ear. I whisper my request and he lights up. "You got it, darlin'."

When I turn back to Derek, he looks crestfallen because I'm keeping something from him.

"Oh for Pete's sake, Hunter." Then both men burst out laughing again.

Someone breezes into the room. "Five minutes."

Blake nods, acknowledging him.

"That's our cue," Derek says.

"Both of you come on back after the show." He smiles, "Especially her. I like her, Hunter."

Derek moves, turning his back, protecting me. "She's mine, Shelton." The tone is serious but then both men are laughing again and I relax.

Derek escorts us to the center of the stage and our table. The rest of the tables are full, but not ours, it is just for the two of us. He pulls my chair out for me and I take a seat. We're served drinks and some hors d'oeuvres.

I take a drink, but food is just too much right this moment. Anticipation and excitement are overwhelming me and I'm enjoying myself immensely. The other guests are at their tables talking amongst themselves. Derek leans over, "Are you enjoying yourself?"

I smile and nod. "Very much. Thank you so much."

"It's my pleasure, Dacotah."

Just then someone steps on to the stage in front of us.

"Good evening, ladies and gentlemen, and welcome to the Wynn and tonight's intimate experience with none other than the amazing Blake Shelton."

Applause erupts as the gentleman gestures toward my right and coming out from the curtains is Blake. We're both clapping with excitement as Blake takes his spot on stage and picks up his guitar, strumming a few chords.

"Hello ladies and gentlemen, thank you so much for coming tonight. It is an honor to be here, and I hope you enjoy tonight's show." He winks in my direction. I smile. "Tonight is dedicated to a couple of good friends who are in the audience tonight. Derek and Dacotah." He nods at us, my face flushes and warmth overcomes me, whether it is Derek or Blake's doing, I don't really care, the gesture is overwhelming. "What do y'all say, should we get this party started?"

The audience erupts into claps and cheers as Blake begins strumming his guitar with the chords of one of my favorite songs, 'Ol' Red', and the audience cheers, and Blake smiles as he starts to sing.

The intimacy of the evening is easily felt by just looking around toward a lot of the couples and how they're leaning into each other. Derek does the same thing with his arm lying across the back of my chair, his hand gently rubbing on my shoulder as Blake continues singing.

A couple more songs into the show, couples start to get up and dance. The space provides a great area to dance with your partner and embarrassment floods through me when Blake begins singing 'Hillbilly Bone' and I realize that Derek is going to make me country dance. Thank god, this is something I really know how to do.

I think I surprise Derek, forcing him to up his game just a little bit as I start to dance circles around him. Then he takes it a few steps further and the next thing I know, I'm spinning over his arm. Breathless, we both laugh and he continues twirling me around the dance floor until the song comes to its end.

"Since everyone seems to want to dance, I'm going to do this now. Dacotah?" I blush beet red and he continues. "This is dedicated to you, from Derek." My mouth falls open and then Derek takes me into his arms as the subtle chords of 'My Eyes' starts to play. A tear streaks down my cheek as Derek begins moving me around the dance floor in some semblance of a quick step.

He is singing along with Blake and no one in this room is here but Derek and I being privately serenaded by Blake Shelton. Throughout the entire dance, Derek's eyes never leave mine. When the chorus sets in, we stop and dance a little more provocatively and I giggle. Derek is being so unbelievably sweet to me and I'm overwhelmed.

Blake continues singing the song and I'm completely lost in Derek and listening to him sing along that I realize that I'm sad when the song ends. Then Blake is back talking into the microphone. "I don't know about you, but I need a cold shower after that."

I roll my eyes then blush. "Dacotah, are you ready for your song?" I look at Blake and nod. "Good. Ladies and gentleman, if you'd please leave the floor, for now, let Dacotah and Derek have it." Everyone begins walking away from the dance floor back to their seats. A few grumble, but I don't care.

Then suddenly the guitar is going, the beat being drummed out by taps against the guitar and I pull Derek into my arms. "No theatrics, just hold me," I say and Derek complies, bringing my into a gentle sway. "Just listen," I urge.

"Okay."

Then Blake starts in with his words. The words of 'Don't Make Me'. Derek's breath hitches as he gently starts to move. I watch him carefully as Blake's lyrics sink into him. The song explains exactly what I'm feeling right now. I can see it in his eyes, each passing word that Blake sings, sinks deeper and deeper into him. His dancing slows some, but we're still moving gently together and we're both looking into each other's eyes.

By the time the song is drawing to a close, I have tears streaking down my cheeks, spurred on by the look in his eyes, and my heart tightens as Blake wraps up the song.

The audience applauds loudly and Derek wipes the tears from my eyes with his thumb. I expect Blake to make a joke but when I look at him, he too wipes something away from his own eye. Rather than speak further, he rolls right into 'Drink On It' and the audience joins us in dancing again. Neither Derek nor I say a word to each other. I think the point I had in choosing that song is sinking in and he's desperate to figure out what to do; at least the many emotions that flit across his eyes tells me that he is warring with himself about what is coming.

"I'm sorry," I breathe, laying my head on his chest, but he releases my hand, and tilts my chin up to look at him.

"What for?"

"The song."

"It's perfect, Cotah. It says a lot more than I'm sure you were ready to say to me." I nod and he kisses me before leading me back to our seats as Blake finishes his song.

The night isn't over when Blake closes out the show with 'God Gave Me You'. The room erupts into applause and Blake takes a few bows, thanks the crowd and the gentleman who announced him comes back to the stage. "Ladies and gentlemen, please do not leave without your bags that are being passed out now, and if you give Mr. Shelton a few minutes, he will come out and join you in the audience for some Q and A, and sign some autographs. Thank you all for coming."

Derek and I get our bags and then we wait for Blake to come on out. Neither Derek nor I seem to have a lot to say to each other as we both take into account that it is nearly nine thirty in the evening and we're a few hours closer to separation. Then there is a commotion and Blake comes through a side door. He waves and everyone claps for him and his amazing show, including Derek and I. Blake stops to chat at the first table and he makes his way along the back row, snapping pictures and signing autographs, talking very animatedly. Finally he's made his way around to our table, but he holds up a hand, indicating that he's going to finish up with the last two tables before coming back to us.

As Blake finishes, the majority of people have left after having had their time with Blake. When he is done, the room is empty except for a couple of stage guys and us.

"Thank you," I tell Blake as soon as he comes over.

He wraps an arm around me. "It was my pleasure. You two sure know how to put on a show." His accent is thick, but he smiles at both of us. Derek and I both smile back.

We exchange some pleasantries and then pose for a few pictures and a stage guy comes over to take one of the three of us with Derek's phone. Then he signs all the goodies in the bags we were given and we chat a little more.

After a while Miranda comes looking for him, telling him that they have to catch a plane back to Nashville. Blake hugs me again. "Take care of yourself, Dacotah. I look forward to seeing you again."

My heart aches to think that likely won't be possible, but I tell him that I'm excited too.

He and Derek exchange thank you's along with back slaps and wishes for a good time. Miranda does the same and they leave. Leaving us alone.

Reality bites. There is no other way around it, but I try again to not dwell on it. Derek and I are quiet on the way back to the hotel. I can feel the distance coming between us and I hate it. I'm desperate to hold him, be near him or to even talk to him, but before I build up the courage to slide across the seat to him, we're back at the Cosmopolitan and climbing out of the limo. The atmosphere shifts between us, growing warmer the closer we get to the elevators for his penthouse. The faster we climb the more things heat up and the coldness thaws.

When the doors open there are no less than a hundred candles lit around the living room, concentrated mostly around the couch and the dining room table which is laid out with our dinner.

"Will you do me the honor of joining me for dinner?" he asks, his voice is soft and I nod, not trusting the emotions in my voice. He leads me to the table, pulling out my chair and I take a seat. He follows suit and we sit in companionable, less uncomfortable silence as we start to eat. I don't have an appetite, but I decide that I need to eat. So I dive in, devouring the salad. Derek seems to have the same mind set because he is eating like I am.

We move onto the main course of filet mignon and vegetables. Delicious, of course, and I eat it all. But then I'm super full. I drink some of the wine, but I'm desperate to keep a clear head with him tonight.

"We need to talk," I finally blurt out.

"Yes, we do."

55

Reality Bites...

"Stay with me?"

"I can't go with you."

We both speak at the same time, but his words ring louder than mine.

"What do you mean you can't go with me?" Fear strikes through his eyes as he picks up on my statement, his question overruling anything I said. He's asked me again, and suddenly I don't know if I can tell him no anymore.

I start with my deepest insecurity about going with him to Paris. "Because I'm afraid that you'll tire of me in Paris and that I will have lost a decent job and tarnish my reputation in the tiny town I live in."

"I'd give you a job, in a heartbeat."

"Be serious, Derek, if you tire of me in Paris, how in the world could we work together?"

"Easy, I have no plans or desire to be rid of you, now, in Paris or any time soon. Cotah, this last week has been beyond my expectations when we started this journey, and I don't know how in the world I can go about my life without you in it."

"What are you saying, Orion?" The question is out there before I can process the question myself, or prepare me for his answer.

"I love you."

Our eyes meet, his fearful and anxious. "So it wasn't a slip."

"So you heard me?" I nod. "Why didn't you say anything?" His anxiety is leaking into his voice.

"Honestly?"

"Always."

A smile plays with my lips. "I figured it was a complete slip on your part, or I was only hearing what I was hoping to hear. Then when you woke up, you were different with me, the dominant that you are was gone. Your heart was on your sleeve and I just figured that at some point you would say it again, if you meant it."

"Believe me, Dacotah, I meant it. Though it hardly covers the way you make me feel to be around you. It has killed me to wake up, get dressed and go to work every day, leaving you to sleep. I have been petrified that when I came back, you'd have run away. That you'd have left."

"We barely know each other."

"So what? That doesn't stop my heart from feeling, or my brain from telling me I was a complete idiot yesterday. When I'm with you, it just all...everything changes when I'm with you."

"You realize that this conversation is completely backward, right?" He looks at me, puzzled. "I'm the one that is supposed to be spouting these things to you and you're supposed to be calling me crazy."

He cocks an eyebrow at me. "So I'm crazy now?" I can see the smile playing on his lips.

"No, Orion, you're not crazy, but how many times is it in life that the man in a relationship is the one jumping head first into something?"

"I only jump in head first when I know it's right."

I can't help but agree with him. "From the moment I saw you, I knew that there was something special about you. When you walked past me in your suit, stared at me from the bar, I knew it wasn't just sex between us, that there was something more."

"The song lyrics...," he pauses, organizing his thoughts. "Why did you choose that one?"

"Because I felt that the lyrics spoke everything I'm not sure I can say."

He ponders it, almost as if he's hearing Blake sing the song again in his head. I don't say anything, not wanting to disrupt his thought process. Then he looks at me, fear and anxiety in his eyes. He stands and I'm left sitting at the table, shocked that he's stood up, unsure of where he's going.

He comes to stand at the credenza near the elevator. His back is to me and I can't tell what he's doing, suddenly there is music filling the room. The clicking guitar of Lee Brice's 'Hard to Love' begins ringing in my ears.

"What are you doing?" I ask him.

"Dance with me." He turns around, looking at me, the fear is gone, but I can still see the anxiety.

"Why?" I say, standing up and walking toward him.

"So I can make you fall in love with me." The vulnerability in his voice makes my eyes prickle with tears.

His arms come around me and he starts to dance, his body close to mine, pressing hard inches into every inch of my soft curves. His eyes never leave mine. The lyrics of his song choice are something else entirely, unsure if this is him singing to me, or if it is the other way around. But I don't care, not right now I don't.

We don't talk, we just dance and when the song draws to an end, he doesn't let me go. I open my mouth to say something when the next song starts. "Shh, just listen."

When the singer starts to sing, I recognize the voice, but not the song. It begins talking about taking it all on faith and about trying. The music moves me emotionally the way that Derek is moving me with his dancing. The lyrics certainly have a double meaning, balancing for both of us. "Who is this?" I whisper.

"Natalie Manes, 'Take It On Faith'."

I nod, soaking up the lyrics realizing how much more this song is about me than him.

He keeps me dancing through John Legend's 'All of Me', Passenger's 'Let Her Go', then the one song that has eluded me since I heard the instrumental version in my headphones upstairs- 'Lying In The Hands of God' by Dave Matthews Band, and then finally stopping on Jason Mraz's 'I Won't Give Up'.

Each of the lyrics in each song giving way to some of what we're both feeling. 'I Won't Give Up' is my undoing and I can't stop the tears from flowing. He is quick to help me wipe them away. But they won't stop, and neither does he, determined to finish our dance.

The song draws to a close and he wraps his arms around me, his lips near my ear, he whispers, "I need you."

My heart melts, my tears flow, and I can't stop the nod.

Our mood appears somber on the surface, but rather than run away from it, he's helping me embrace it. I need him more.

56

Silence is Golden...

There is something extremely powerful about silence. Especially when you're able to communicate with your lover silently. Which is exactly what Derek and I were doing.

He leads me upstairs- no words, no anecdotes, nothing. Just simply him and me. As soon as we cross the threshold of his bedroom, his lips are on mine. The need and powerful emotion behind his kiss makes me dizzy instantly. I try desperately to portray my own emotions back at him, to let him feel a small portion of what I feel for him.

His hands roam, as do mine. I reach the nape of his neck and free his hair from its confines. It falls over his shoulders, framing his face in a way that makes him younger and more vulnerable and I take it upon myself to bring him closer to me by burying my hands in his hair, gripping him tightly and he moans into my mouth.

His long fingers work the buttons of my shirt easily. When he reaches the last button his hands slide hungrily up my body, squeezing and grabbing the higher up he goes. He continues the same motion over my breasts and my back arches into his stomach as he presses me against the door he's closed. My hands come out of his hair, sliding down to take his cheeks in my hands at the same time his hands find mine.

The emotion that passes through our kiss and our touch sends a deep shiver though me, kick starting my heart and sending fire racing through my veins at the need I feel for him. The pain of loss I've yet to feel is almost too much.

I let my hands slide down his neck to the collar of his shirt where I work his buttons as he pushes my shirt off my shoulders. Then the straps of my bra and camisole are sliding down my arms, his hands working to bring my breasts above my bra. He succeeds and my chest is trussed up high and my nipples are burning for his hands, his mouth, his gentle caress. My hands work over his buttons faster, until I reach the button of his jeans. Deciding not to fight pulling his shirts out, I undo the button of his jeans followed by the zipper.

He groans into my mouth, his kisses growing more desperate. I pull his shirt free, neither one of us wanting our hands off of the other long enough to remove our clothes and I'm pinned beneath him and unable to move away to break our kiss, needing skin on skin. Finally my breathing grows so ragged both with lust and frustration at needing him pressed against me. He pulls back, but his hands are still on me, so I force his shirt down his shoulders.

Reluctantly he pulls his hands away long enough to rid himself of both shirts. I do the same. When I reach around for my bra, he presses into me, trapping my hands between my body and the door. I keep working at the clasp as best I can from the bad angle. His eyes stare into me, saying everything he wants to say without speaking a word. I'm lost in the melted milk chocolate of his eyes and I pray my eyes are betraying the flood of love and desire I feel for him right now.

Finally my bra comes loose and I let it fall away from the weight of my breasts, though I'm still trapped by the straps. His eyes light up at my predicament, but the dominant man I've come to know is gone tonight, my hunter is nowhere to be found. Tonight he isn't hunting for prey, no, he is hunting for a lover, his other half, and he knows he's found it. He eases off of me and I lose my bra, finally.

He groans and his hands are on my jeans, unbuckling them, both of us knowing full well that the boots have to come first, but that doesn't stop me from pushing the waist band of his pants further south. His erection springs free of his jeans and I can feel the warm wetness of pre-cum that sends my sex into spasms of pleasure and need. Before he can trap me by lowering my own jeans, I drop to my knees, desperate to taste him, to have him in my mouth.

I don't wait for any acceptance from him. My hand wraps around the base of his cock and I lick the head. The sweet and salty taste that is this beautiful man I love assaults my senses and I'm beyond needy for him. My sex is dripping now, soaking my panties and I'm hating the confines of my jeans, but I keep going, licking, sucking and stroking his cock into my mouth. I'm awarded with another small taste of pre-cum and I moan. The vibrations radiate through him and I watch as his eyes roll back into his head and his hands catch himself against the door, giving me the perfect view of him from between my lashes. His long hair creates a curtain around his beautiful face. His arms are tight muscles and veins as he fights for the strength to keep himself from crashing into the door.

His mouth falls slack as I suck harder and harder against his cock. Then, out of nowhere, he musters the strength to step back from me, one step, then another, faster than I can grip his cock, and he is out of my reach. Looking up at him, he crooks his finger at me, beckoning me to him. I stand and walk toward him. His arms wrap around me, the bare skin of his chest to mine is the warmth I didn't know I needed until the heat causes a shiver to run through me.

Turning me so that my knees are against the bed, he pushes me gently so that I fall onto the bed, but he is right there on top of me, pressing his erection into my sex, through my jeans and I don't need the barrier between us.

My hands trail along his chest to his stomach until I find the waist of my jeans, hooking my thumbs between my skin and the lace panties I'm wearing. He catches on to what I'm doing and he pulls his lips from mine, pulling his body off of me. He slides down my legs until he is kneeling before me, lifting my leg to remove my boot. He tugs and off one comes, followed by the other.

My socks are off and his magic fingers go to work, rubbing my feet that don't really hurt, but with each press against my instep I can feel it down there. The lust turns to pleasure and a desperate need for release.

He knows this because there is a soft smirk playing on his lips and I groan, throwing my head back in frustration at his driving need to make me wait for him to be ready. His need for control is winning out over everything he is doing to me. I sit up suddenly and he drops my foot. I begin using my own feet to rid myself of my jeans. "Stop torturing me and love me," I breathe and without any ceremony of affection, my jeans and panties are gone. He stands, kicking off his boots and pushes me back on the bed.

I slide toward the center of the bed and he is on me, his tongue hot and wet searing into my folds and I moan. His tongue makes circles around my clit, my legs quake with the pressure against my button and the pleasure is too much, I feel my orgasm building quickly as he continues to lick, suck and lap at my juices. His hands begin to roam along my legs, along my thighs as he buries his face deeper into my sex. He lifts my legs, bringing them to rest on his shoulders and he climbs to his knees.

I watch him as his ass comes into view, along with a good portion of his backside. I can't take it anymore and my hand goes into his hair, gripping tightly, holding him to me as I start to grind my hips against his mouth. His circling, flicking and nibbling doesn't stop. Pleasure races through my sex, and I'm so close, I'm right there. We maintain eye contact. The wave of my orgasm is so strong that it closes my eyes, my whole body shudders, and I collapse back onto the bed, mewling and moaning loudly, my whole body succumbs to him.

My grip in his hair loosens, but he doesn't stop. His tongue flicks against me softly. My hand slides along his face, seeking his chin, seeking to pull him up to me. He complies, raising himself from between my legs. His mouth is covered in my juices and the look in his eyes is liquid fire and desire, bursting at the seams. "Take me," I breathe and he slides up my body, licking and sucking his way up my stomach, making my muscles jump and bounce with the soft prickle of his stubble and the bite of his nips along my skin.

My nipples are inches away from his mouth and I can see him zeroing in on one. His eyes dance between my eyes and the tight peak of my breast, pointing toward the heavens, cold and needy. I watch him closely but as soon as his mouth comes into contact, my eyes roll up, and he moans, vibrating my nipple in his mouth.

His hand grips my breast, making it stand up, pressing it toward his mouth. His free hand slides along my body until it reaches my other nipple, gripping, teasing and torturing as the fire sparks again. My hands go into his hair again and I tug gently, again he groans but complies, coming further up my body, up to my mouth.

I take his mouth in one fierce, hot searing kiss. Tasting Derek and me, it's a heady cocktail of sensuality and I lick and suck at his lips, cleaning them of my juices as he lines up the head of his cock with the entrance of my pussy. He presses into me slowly. And it's agony, pure sexual agony. I move my feet up so that I have leverage and I lift my hips, sheathing him inside of me. We both moan at the tight wetness. He doesn't move for a minute, but I can't wait. I begin to grind my hips against his. My clit is rubbing on him, driving my pleasure higher and my orgasm hotter. Finally he starts to move.

He kisses the corner of my mouth, then my jaw, down to my ear where he licks and sucks at my lobe. His thrusts grow more demanding. I relax and let him take the lead.

Rather than lick at my breasts or kiss my lips, he buries his head in my neck, wrapping his arms around me, holding him to me, shifting the angle of his thrusts to accommodate our new position. My hands go around him, under his arms, pulling him onto me.

The sweat from both our bodies is mingling along my stomach and breasts and it is the most exhilarating feeling. I pull him tighter. I need him closer to me, I need us to become one and it is impossible, I can't get him close enough. My orgasm is building deep down. I feel my pussy clench as the first inclination of my orgasm, his pace increases marginally and his breathing is short and ragged in my ear with each thrust. I feel his cock twitch and I tighten around him, my pussy, my arms, and then finally I bring my legs around him, trapping him within my circle.

My orgasm rocks through me, shattering my mind, my body and my soul. As soon as I feel the first squirt of cum inside me, tears spring, and I'm shuddering with sobs. My hands claw at him to pull him closer to me. My legs are a vice around him. I can't breathe, but I don't care. "I love you, Orion."

57

Shattered Dreams...
***** Derek *****

The covers are cold. Why are the covers cold?

My eyes snap open, and the bed is empty. I rub at my eyes as an empty feeling fills me. "Fuck!" I throw the covers off of me, sitting on the side of the bed. Grabbing my bearings, or at least trying to. I know she isn't here. The penthouse is far too quiet and empty. "Shit." I rub my eyes again. Upon opening them, I see something on the table, a note.

Anger washes through me, why did she have to leave with a note?

I pick it up, my eyes trying desperately to focus on her handwriting but they are blurry with tears. Fuck. I try and blink them back long enough to read her note. I notice that there is another envelope underneath it. It's that damn Planet Hollywood envelope with the check in it. Failure washes through me. She needed that, she deserved that.

The anger of having that money returned to me without a chance to argue about it again clears my eyes, and I read her note.

Dearest Orion,
Where do I start? How about Thank You?
Thank you for everything you've done, everything you've given me, and more than anything, thank you for loving me.
I couldn't stay. I couldn't bare the sadness in your eyes as I walked away. We both know it was going to be this way. I meant what I said last night, I love you Orion. You've shown me what it means to really truly love some-one and I can't thank you enough for that, but I'll never be enough for you.
This week started with a proposition, an indecent pro-posal of sorts, and I knew a week ago that I would walk away from this with pain and heartache, because I think I knew even then that I loved you.
Please forgive me, but I couldn't handle saying good-bye.
All my love,
Cotah

Anger washes away, replaced by loneliness and desper-ation. *Get her back.* The voice that has been dominating me this week is back. I've listened to it every step of the way so far, I shouldn't stop now.

I set into motion, finding clothes to go downstairs in; clothes to go searching for her.

Her clothes are still in the closet. My heart sinks, she couldn't even- dammit!

I race downstairs to her bedroom, the emptiness is creeping deeper into my soul and my heart is breaking the closer I get to her room.

She was the light in my darkness, the hope I needed to make me feel alive again. One can only have mindless sex for so long and that's what it had become, until her.

I stumble into the doorway and her dress from last night is laid out on the foot of the bed, with her shoes below it. I race into the bathroom, the last bit of hope washing out of me when I see it's empty. I turn back to go to the closet and my eyes catch on something glinting in the light of the room. A necklace.

My heart sinks further, thinking that she returned the one I gave her. When I pull it from the stand, I realize that it is not my necklace, but her grandmother's. "Fuck."

She forgot. Hope blooms, maybe she isn't gone. I rip open the closet door and freeze; her clothes are all still here too. I take a moment to look. The hunter green sundress she wore last Sunday is gone. I look at the floor. "Dacotah!" I shout in frustration and realization. She's left me, and left everything I gave her, taking back what she came here with. I rush out into the living room, my last hope, but my last flicker is extinguished when I see her phone is gone, along with her e-reader and she isn't on the patio or in the pool.

The elevator chimes, my heart is racing as the doors slide open, only to be met with sheer disappointment when Arnold comes through the door. "How long ago did she leave?"

"Sir?"

"Don't give me that, when did Dacotah leave."

He shakes his head. "I have no idea, sir."

"Damn it. Get my fucking car, have it meet me in front of Hollywood in ten minutes."

I dash between the elevator doors as Arnold goes to the phone; I stab the button repeatedly until the doors finally close.

Why would she do this to me? After what I told her. Then the words of Blake's song come flooding back to me. If I love her, let her go. Dammit, I do love her, like crazy, but I can't let her go. I need her.

Finally the elevator chimes and the doors slide open, I dart out the door. "When did she leave, Andrew?"

"Over an hour ago, sir, said she was going to the airport."

"Fuck!"

I burst through the doors and into reception, running at full tilt toward the casino doors closest to Planet Hollywood. There are people and security yelling after me to slow down, but I don't care. I have to find her. But in order to do that, I need her friends.

I reach the doors, flying through them, I don't think twice as I dart into the road, car tires squealing as they come to a stop inches away from where I was. Thank god, it's early. I cross both sides of Las Vegas Boulevard, darting up the escalator into the Miracle Mile, my heart wrenching as the vision of her standing there in front of the restaurant flits through my mind. The first moment I saw her. I damn near tripped over myself. I'd never seen anything as beautiful as her before. I knew I had to have her, any way I could take her, but I knew she didn't live here. She had that wide eyed look in her eyes like most tourists who've just landed in Vegas.

I run through Hollywood's casino toward the elevators I need for the penthouse I'd given her friends.

Finally when I reach it, I swipe my card, thank god I'd grabbed it. The doors open immediately and I begin the twenty story ascent. I start pacing in the elevator, my heart is about to crash through my chest from running and from losing the one woman who did it all for me.

She was submissive to me; she devoured everything I threw at her. Everything I seemed to want, she took and soaked it up. With one exception. I shake my head. That was the biggest mistake I'd made, ever, and it took everything I had to tie her up again. Her trust in me was so damn important and I blew it, but she gave it right back to me. She was good, very good, and I surprised myself more with each passing day that the need to be in control subsided, at least when it came to her and being in bed.

I'd never made love to a woman until Dacotah, until...the elevator chimes and the doors open slowly. Alejandro is there to meet me. "Where is she?"

"Who, sir?"

"Damn it, Dacotah. Where is she?"

"I'm sorry, sir; I haven't seen her since last Saturday."

"What about Mandy and Rachel, are they here?"

"No sir, they left about an hour ago to catch their flight."

"Fuck! Fuck! Fuck!"

I punch the wall next to the elevator, thankfully nothing breaks. I push the elevator button again and it opens. I duck back inside. "Sir, they took her stuff with them, said they were flying back to Minneapolis."

"Thank you," I groan.

I doubt I can catch her and during the descent in the elevator, the thought that I need to let it go, let her go, courses through me and I curse again. I never swear, but I am so angry right now, angry that I let this happen. She said she loved me and I did nothing. She clawed at me, pulling me closer to her, pulling me into her. I couldn't get enough of her. I couldn't touch her in enough places; I need her inside of me, to be with me. The love I felt for her in that moment was so damn powerful and I didn't say a fucking word!

The elevator opens and I start toward the entrance, toward a car to take me to the airport, but I'm losing steam and hope.

Fifteen minutes later we are pulling into McCarran Airport and I dart into the main terminal. I'd managed to make contact with a few people, and learned that her flight to Minneapolis could only be one of three that would leave around the time frame she left. One of which leaves in ten minutes and I need to slide through security and get to her, or try. The other two flights are already gone.

My cell phone rings. I look at it.

"Hunter."

"She's registered on the Southwest flight. I'm emailing you a boarding pass."

"Thank you, Erik."

My phone chimes with the email, a boarding pass to Boston? Then I look at the gate number, then flip to the email with her gate number and I smile at Erik's thought process.

I dart into the pre-screen line and I am through security in about four minutes flat. If I can get to the gate, I can stop the plane from taking off. Pull her off the plane. I don't care what she says, we need to figure this out, but I'll be damned if she is going away to Wisconsin without me. I start running through the airport, running past C25; of course she'd be at C8.

You ever have that bad dream, the one where you're running but going nowhere? That is exactly what I feel like right now, and no, I am not going the wrong way on a moving walkway. The gates pass me slowly as I dodge between people, jumping over luggage and even a toddler as

I finally draw closer to her gate. One advantage to being tall, I can see over people, the disadvantage is that I can see her rather empty gate. I fight to pick up the pace but the nightmare kicks into full effect and the distance stretches between me and my destination.

As I come to the gate there is an attendant at the podium, but I bust past her, bust past all FAA regulations, I don't fucking care, I need her, I have to get her off of that plane. I screech to a halt at the end of the jet way as the nose of the plane passes me on its way to backing out.

"Sir, what the hell are you doing?" I look at the gate attendant and she cringes away from me. "Sir, the plane has left, with all passengers on board."

"Fuck!" I drop my head. "Can you tell me if someone was on that plane?"

"I'm sorry, sir, I can't do that. But you need to come off of the jet way. You can't be here, and right now, I'm not going to call security, but you've got to get out of here."

I nod and start to walk past her, reaching for my phone. Searching for Jeff, my pilot. When I finally stop long enough to focus, I find it and press send.

"Good Morning, sir."

"Change of plans." I cross the threshold back into the terminal. "We're going to divert to Wisconsin. I need you to…" I stop dead in my tracks, and then fall to my knees. Grief overcomes me and I can barely breathe.

"Mr. Hunter?"

"Never mind," I manage before I drop the phone to the floor.

"Sir, are you alright?" The attendant asks me. I pull in short shaky breaths as I take in the beautiful sight before me.

I slump down, staring at her, staring at the woman who walked out my door with my heart and soul. "I'm perfect." I breathe out, then I watch as the attendant follows my line of sight to Dacotah, who is standing about fifteen feet away from me, her suitcase held in a vice grip in front of her. Tears streaking down her cheeks. She's as beautiful in her hunter green dress today as she was a week ago.

My eyes heat, as I lower my chin and raise my hand. I beckon her to come to me. She swings her suitcase to her side, dropping it onto the floor and she runs to me, crashing into me so hard she knocks me over. Lying on the floor of McCarran airport, my hand goes into her hair, the other against her cheek. I smile at her and her lips crash into mine. I hold her there, letting her lips consume me. My body comes alive and my heart starts to beat again, my soul is on fire for her.

"I'm sorry. I'm so, so sorry," she pleads with me. "It was the stupidest thing I've ever done."

"Shh. Kiss me, Cotah, kiss me, then tell me you love me."

She kisses me, "I" Kisses me again, "Love" And another kiss, "You."

"Never, ever stop saying that," I breathe and roll her over so I'm pressed on top of her, the biggest smile I've ever seen spreads across her face.

"I promise," she breathes.

Then suddenly there are loud cheers of applause, a few flashes of cell phone cameras and no doubt there is video, but I don't care. The woman I love is back in my arms and I will never, ever let her go.

"You forgot something."

Her brows knit together. I reach into my pocket and pull her necklace from my pocket, holding it above her. Her eyes widen then soften. "Keep it, I have a new one."

Her hand goes to my necklace, her delicate fingers stroking along the thin infinity symbol.

"Dacotah?"

"Yes?"

"Will you go to Paris with me?"

She smiles, her arms wrap tighter around me. "I thought you'd never ask me again. Yes. I will go with you wherever you want me to be." I kiss her.

"Good, now can we get off of this airport floor?"

She laughs and nods.

I stand up, bringing her with me to another round of applause and cheers. She wraps her arms around my waist, pulling me to her side and I wrap my arm around her shoulders, holding her to me.

As we pass her suitcase, I bend down, picking it up and carrying it with me as we walk slowly out of McCarran airport and on to Paris.

I jump awake, sending my tablet flying as the plane touches down. Emptiness consumes me. If only it had been that easy, if only she really had been there waiting for me. Instead, I am landing in Paris, alone.

I spent a good portion of the flight sifting through records, looking for anything I could find on Dacotah Miller. Where she lived, where she worked, it didn't matter, I needed to find her. But I needed to deal with the pressing issues in Paris before I can even begin to look for her.

As soon as we're stopped and the door dropped down, I am there, waiting. Erik Parker greets me. Just the man I need to see. "You have twenty-four hours, whether the situation is resolved or not, I'm leaving, got it?"

I give him a look that doesn't give him much choice in the matter.

"Where do we stand?"

Erik starts in on the situation, though I am only half listening to him, too lost in the fact that I'm missing Dacotah and that she should be here with me right now. But she's not, so I do my best to focus on dealing with the impending business problem.

58

Solace in Old Friends...

After hours at the negotiation table, things finally seem to be settling, though they have two more hours before the deadline and if a decision isn't reached, all hell could break loose and the factory is going to strike. For what? More money? I rub my face with my hands as irritation washes over me. Their demands are not at all unreasonable and I can't fully understand why we are having this discussion. If we give them an inch, they will run away with a mile. That's why.

"Give it to 'em," I say, pushing back from the table and standing.

"Sir?"

"This whole thing is ridiculous; give them what they want, with one exception." Fourteen pairs of eyes are now trained on me. "A contractual clause that forbids this type of nonsense threat going forward."

Half of the room nods in agreement, the other half is hesitant as they stare me down. "I will not be taken advantage of going forward, I will give you what you're asking for now, but I'll be damned if we will be right back here a week, a month or even a year from now. If what you've laid out in your contract is what is wanted and warranted, I don't see the need to shut down the factory for a strike that will inevitably lead us right back here to this place in a few days. I don't have time and frankly, it is unnecessary to drag this out beyond a reasonable time frame. Give them what they want, and everything goes back to normal."

I can't take the irritation anymore, there was no need for this fucking trip, it could have been handled over the goddamn phone for fuck's sake, but regardless, I'm here. "Are we good?" I ask the room and fourteen heads nod in agreement. "Good. Then if you'll excuse me?" I say and the room stands. I shake hands, doing my good natured business owner nonsense and take my leave.

No one follows me out, thank god. I grab my phone and call Jeff.

He answers on the second ring. "Good evening, sir."

"Are we good to go?"

"Yes sir, we have a pilot lined up to take us back when you're ready."

"Why aren't you flying?"

"FAA regulations prevent me from flying too many hours in a certain time frame. Don't worry sir; I've flown with Mr. Miller before." Ugh, that fucking name.

"Fine, I'm making a pit stop on my way back to the airport, I should be there within ninety minutes."

"Yes, sir."

The call ends as I step out into the chill of Paris at night and a gentleman opens my door. I tell him where I want to go, he nods and we're off.

Ten minutes later I am in the center of it all, right in the heart that is Paris- the Eiffel Tower. After what happened with Dacotah and me in Vegas, I couldn't resist the urge to go. I've been a dozen times and each time is more breathtaking than the last. This time, it is with a very heavy heart.

As I enter the elevator that will take me to the top, the attendant tells me in broken English that the tower is closing. I nod, slipping him a two hundred Euro note. He smiles wide and nods, the elevator closes and I'm shot toward the top.

My hands and arms feel empty and my heart is somewhere in Frederic, Wisconsin being held by the woman that I love.

My phone begins to vibrate; I pull it out, hope blossoming that it just might be her. I shake my head as Cami's name pops up.

"Hi Cami."

"Derek Hunter, what the hell is wrong with you?"

"Jesus, what the hell did I do?"

"Whoa there, cowboy," she laughs, "I was just kidding."

I fail at laughter, "Sorry, it's been a long day." I rub at my face again.

"Sorry to hear that. Listen, I just called to remind and re-invite you down to Phoenix for Memorial Day weekend, Jaden's party is on Saturday."

"Crap, Cami, I forgot." The elevator doors open and standing in front of me, facing out to the city is a woman with long light colored hair glistening in the light of the moon and the Eiffel Tower. For a brief moment, I wonder if it could be, but then I realize that it isn't the curvy, beautiful girl I'm looking for. Cami brings me back.

"No worries, so will we see you Saturday?"

"What day is it now?"

She laughs. "It's Monday, around one. Hello, earth to Hunter," she chides.

"Sorry, love, I'm in Paris."

"Oh well shit, I'm sorry. What time is it there, like midnight?"

I laugh a little. "Not quite, it's ten."

"Oh, well then I don't feel bad." She laughs again. "I've also been ordered by Tristan to tell you to bring Dacotah with you."

My heart stops beating at the mention of Dacotah's name. "That's a bit complicated."

"What the hell is complicated about it, Derek, you bring her, she has a good time, you woo her socks off and life moves on."

"Uhm."

"So you really are being an ass, aren't you?"

"Yeah, I guess I am."

"What happened, Hunter?"

I sigh, "She fell in love with me, told me as such, and then left me."

I hear her own sigh. "And what about you?"

"What about me?"

"Did you fall in love with her too?"

I step up to the railing, looking out over the sprawling city of Paris. "Yes, I did."

"Did you tell her that?"

"What is this, twenty questions?" I ask.

"No, I just need answers."

Fuck. "Yes Cami, I told her."

"Oh." There is a pause and some shuffling. I can hear Jaden in the background vying for his mother's attention.

"I should let you go, you sound busy."

"No, no, it's okay. What are you going to do?"

"Get her back."

I hear her soft laughter into the phone. "Good, now get on that, and then bring her on Saturday."

I don't need to go into details about the fact that I barely know a thing about her. But I'll be damned if I'm going to let that stop me from finding her. "I am a man of many resources."

"Oh yes, I know. Speaking of which, Mick wants to sit down with you while you're here, so let me know when you'll be coming in and leaving so I can let him know."

"How is he?"

"Better than you are."

I laugh a little. "Everyone is far better than I am right now."

She sighs. "I really like her, Derek." Her voice is soft and understanding and I smile a little.

"Me too."

"Good, now get your ass out of Paris and find her."

I roll my eyes. "Yes, dear," I say playfully and she laughs again.

"Call me if you need anything." The way she said anything alluded to something, but I didn't quite catch it.

"Will do."

We say our good-byes, me telling her to say hi to Tristan and what not, but when I'm alone with myself, the silence and the wind on top of the Eiffel Tower, I close my eyes and all I can see are her beautiful baby blue eyes looking at me, loving me, and mocking me for my own stupidity.

I shove off of the railing, bee lining for the elevator that quickly opens. Descending back to street level seems to take forever. Once I do and the doors open, I take off in a flat out run to the car. I can't run fast enough in my quest to get back to her.

Once on board my plane and in the air, I go into the bedroom, change and try like hell to catch some sleep. But it is met with fits of tossing and turning before sleep finally claims me somewhere over the Atlantic.

59

Can't Stop Now...

Several hours later, we land in Duluth, Minnesota. Jeff told me that it was the closest he could get to Frederic and there is a car waiting for me when we land. I grab the small duffle bag on the plane and pack a couple of things from the closet. When I left Vegas on Sunday morning, I'd only had the clothes on my back which were jeans, a t-shirt and my boots. Now, all I have are suits.

Once inside the car, I realize that the GPS is already programmed for downtown Frederic, but I'd searched on my tablet for some place in Duluth that I could go shopping. Though I love my suits, I'm not sure how easy finding her is going to be and I'd rather not be wandering around in suits.

After a brisk jaunt through Miller Hill Mall, I have a pair of Uggs, a few pairs of jeans and some nice shirts and sleeping pants. I hate shopping and it is not something I've done in a long time, but given that I'm in new territory, I don't have anyone to help me out here. Regardless, the deed is done and I'm on the road.

I look at my watch, thinking about the watch I gave Dacotah, hoping she is still wearing it and knowing that I have her necklace tucked safe inside a small pouch I'd made from one of the pocket squares from a suit.. Thinking about Dacotah always distracts me. It's only nine, according to my watch and my brain scrambles to figure out what time it is, then I look at the car and realize that it's eleven in the morning. We would have been here sooner, but we faced a rather nasty headwind coming back from France and a flight that should have taken about nine hours requested two stops for fuel and more time in the air than normal while I kept cursing the gods for all the obstacles standing in my way.

According to GPS, my erratic driving, and barring no major traffic delays, I should be pulling into town just before one.

I flip through the songs on my phone, having synced it with the car, and find what I'm looking for. Good ol' Blake and listening to her song again and again as the miles slip by under my wheels.

With fifteen minutes to go, according to the GPS, my phone rings, interrupting Blake's 'My Eyes'. I roll mine because I am being interrupted in my misery.

"Hunter," I bark

"Sir, it's Dana. I wanted to let you know that I found what you were looking for."

"Good. Do it," I tell her.

"Yes, sir."

"How long will it take?"

"Provided it's received, it will arrive tomorrow morning."

"Good, thank you."

"And sir?"

"Yes."

"I wouldn't be surprised if she received a phone call when it is completed."

"Good. Anything else? Any luck with finding me an address?"

"No, sir. Nothing is registered in her name. Though-" She pauses. "There was a new real estate listing that went up this morning."

Shit. "Send me the address."

"It's on its way, sir."

"Good, thank you."

"Anything else?"

"No."

We end our call.

Fuck, would she really sell her house? Fuck, that was quick. My phone chimes with an incoming text. I display it on the screen.

Cami: I thought you might want this. (715) 555 - 2682 P.S. It didn't come from me.

Derek: How?

Cami: After lunch at your place. We bonded pretty well. Though I haven't talked to her.

Derek: Why didn't you tell me yesterday?

Cami: I figured you had it, but given your unrest, I figured you didn't.

Derek: Thanks.

Cami: Have you found her?

Derek: Almost to Frederic now. We'll see.

Cami: Good, keep me posted. *Hugs*

Derek: Will do, thanks again.

She didn't reply. I scroll back up, pressing the hyperlink of her phone number, the pop-up asking me if I want to call, I hit "OK"

There is a quick half ring, followed by a few clicks and her voice fills my car.

"Hi, you've reached Cotah, sorry I missed ya, you know what to do." There is another beep followed by the automated voice. "The voicemail box is full, please try again."

"Damn it." I press end on my steering wheel just as I pass a sign on the side of the road.

Welcome to the Village of Frederic Est. 1903

I didn't realize how much weight was on my shoulders until I cross that sign and I suddenly felt lighter. I am closer than ever. Then I was rolling down Main Street and Main Street USA is exactly what I find. Both sides of the street ensconced with old, run-down two-story buildings, their lower levels containing various shops, the local bank, which I'm guessing is Dacotah's. There are several restaurants along with hardware and other needs. There is a small market at the end of one of the sets. I pull into an open spot opposite the market. I need answers and I have questions.

I slide from the car, stretching as the two hour drive has turned my muscles to cold butter. I look around, trying to see where it is that she might work. But I don't see any pizza joints. I frown.

Shutting and locking the car, then rolling my eyes since the big city in me never leaves and I look both ways before crossing the street. There are not too many people milling about, but plenty of cars in front of the shops. I can see more than a few people staring at me, and then I remember I'm still wearing my suit and it makes perfect sense.

I step into the market, which is more like a convenience store and the door chimes. An older woman peers over the wall of candy and she appraises me. "Can I help you?" Her voice is timid.

"Just need a couple of things." It is obvious that this town isn't frequented too much by tourists, so no doubt I look like an idiot. Though there were several cars on the highway with me, they all seemed to pass right through town.

I go for a bottle of water and come back to the counter. "Dollar fifty," she says rather deadpan and I roll my eyes, pulling out two dollars from my wallet.

"Can you tell me if there is a place to stay here in town?"

Her eyes widen in shock at my question, questioning why I'd want to stay here. "There's a motel," She gestures to her right and the direction I was going when I stopped. "Just past downtown. On your left."

"Good, thank you."

She gives me my change and I dump it into the charity or tip jar on the counter. She appraises me again with new eyes, softening slightly. "One more thing, can you tell me where I might find Dacotah Miller?"

Her eyes widen. "What on earth has she done?" She asks me, her eyes scrutinizing me as if I went from nice guy to CIA in a nanosecond. I smile at her sweetly.

"Nothin', ma'am, she's an old friend, I'd like see her while I'm here."

'I ain't seen you round these parts before, not sure how she could be your friend."

I resist the urge to roll my eyes. "She's not in trouble, ma'am, I'd just like to talk to her."

She huffs. "She works at Pete's, just down the road, on the right, past the motel."

I nod, smiling as I realize the woman who's eluding me is within a stone's throw. I smile, and nod. "Thank you, ma'am."

I realize that my prying will not go unnoticed by the locals and I'm curious what the wild rumors will be about the weirdly dressed man asking questions about Dacotah, but I got the impression that while the small town may gossip, they take care of their own too.

As I am crossing back across the street, my eyes alight on a sign, Barker Law Firm, and something about that name rings a bell, but I can't place it.

I slide back into the car, back out, and decide that before I tear up the world by entering into Pete's that I'm stopping at the motel first. Of course it is right where the woman at the market said it would be and it is a run-down four room motel, the open sign in the window is missing the N and there are several letters missing from Vacancy.

60

Confrontations...

After ten minutes, I have rented a room that still requires a manual key to enter and when I do I find it is surprisingly clean, but I still shiver. I haven't slept in something this seedy in probably ten years and when I did, I was
roaming around Europe. Seedy and Europe can be synon-
ymous if you let it. I throw my bag on the bed, deciding
that before I go anywhere else, I need to ditch the suit.

The bathroom is surprisingly cleaner than I expected it
to be. No mildew or mold, and the tile looks relatively new
and I wonder how a motel in this little town can afford to
remodel. I shake my head, needing to get the pretentious
pompous asshole out of my system. I am in a small town,
and I am staying here because I refuse to force myself on
Dacotah, when and if I find her.

I will start with Pete's, then from there I will go to the address that Dana had sent, and if all else fails, I will camp at the bank tomorrow morning, assuming that the small town bank will go ballistic when they receive a wire transfer tomorrow for three hundred thousand dollars for one Dacotah Miller and they'll call her, hoping they have more success than I did at reaching her. Either way, I will find her. I have to, and more than anything, I have to talk to her.

If my leaving her to her life is really what she wants, then I won't stand in her way, but before I can let that happen, she has to hear me out.

The idea of seeing Dacotah again gives me an erection, damn it, of all the times.

I finish washing up; ignoring it, hoping it will disappear, but for as long as my thoughts linger on Dacotah, the harder it throbs and bobs. I need her back.

Pete's is a very typical small town establishment, with red plastic tables, and bench seats that don't move. The tables are decorated with cheese and pepper shakers, and old fashioned napkin holders. The lighting overhead are the old stained glass lampshades and they cast each table into a small circle of light. I grab a seat in a booth at the corner by the window and the wall. It is darker over here and I'd rather not scare her off before she has a chance to approach me.

When some guy comes up to the table instead, my heart sinks, but I'm hungry, so I order a beer and a pizza from the dirty blond haired boy who appears to be too old to be in high school.

"Jason," someone calls from the back and my blood runs cold. The voice isn't Dacotah's, but the name, that name, is a name I'd hoped to never hear again.

He disappears into the back and then I realize that if this is the same Jason, asking questions about Dacotah has just become impossible. I fight the urge to get up, to leave money on the table for the pie I won't eat, and leave. But, being the asshole I am and wanting to size up the dick that hurt her, I stay, seething.

The woman who, I'm assuming, called for Jason is the one who delivers my pizza and beer. "Anything else?"

I smile up at the pudgy older woman. "When does Dacotah come in?" I ask and she stiffens.

"Who...Oh Cotah, um, she doesn't."

"What?"

"She showed up Sunday afternoon to check her schedule, saw him," She jerks her head toward the kitchen, "And she promptly quit, turning around and walking out the door."

So it is him. Fuck. "Thank you. Do you know where I can find her?"

The woman sighs. "She lives in her grandmother's house out on Post Road."

The address from Dana, it's hers. "Thank you."

"Anything else?" She appraises me, silently asking me if I want to ask more questions.

"No, I'm good, but if you see her, please don't mention that I'm looking for her."

The woman winks, nods and returns to the kitchen.

Knowing that I have a destination, I relax a moment, eating some of the pizza. It doesn't taste like cardboard, but after having pizza in exotic places like Italy and locally like New York, nothing compares to that.

I finish my meal, and leave a fifty on the table. I swallow the rest of my beer, ugh PBR, and walk out the door. I'm almost to my car when Jason comes barreling out of Pete's. "What the fuck do you want with Cotah?" His hands are in fists and anger is evident on his face. I smirk. Let's go, boy.

"That's none of your fucking business," I snap at him.

He stops in his tracks. "She's my girl, you fucking stay away from her."

I charge toward him, his big tough man attitude is gone as he takes in the fact that I am a good six inches taller and far leaner. "Your Girl?" I growl. "Your GIRL, how fucking convenient since you couldn't be bothered to remember that when you were sticking it in someone else's snatch."

He stumbles back, my tone and the ferocious look in my eyes has him scared. I roll my head, flex my fingers, and take the two steps between us, crouching down. "If you EVER go near her again, I'll snap your neck. Got me?" His mouth falls open. "I said, got me?"

He nods, clearly shaken by our exchange and a thrill runs through me. I back away, not taking my eyes off of him. From the corner of my eye, I catch the woman standing at the door of the restaurant, watching me, but she smiles and mouths a silent thank you to me. I smirk and climb into my car. I program the Post Road address into my GPS and I speed out of the parking lot, throwing up gravel in my haste and I watch with satisfaction as Jason flinches, covering his face from the spray.

"What the fuck did she ever see in him?" I growl to myself.

So, he's managed to push her to run away to Vegas, now away from her job and my heart sinks- she is selling the house.

I call Dana.

"Mr. Hunter?"

"Dana, I need you to do something for me."

"Yes, sir."

I launch into my plan of action and she quickly agrees, complies and sets about her task.

61

Where...

I drive a few minutes, though the town was sparse enough, this is farm country. I come up on two houses, relatively close together, surrounded by farm land and a barn in the back. There is only one car in front of the house closest to me and nothing at the other house, nothing except a "For Sale" sign. My heart starts racing in my chest and I can barely control my breathing. I pull into the driveway of the second house, the one that matches the address.

I stare up at the cute little two-story A-frame house with a screened in front porch. It's actually a very pretty house. The white color is broken up with green vines climbing up lattices that reach to at least the second story. The green and white are dotted with the bright red of roses. It's very cute, making what I just told Dana to do all the more perfect.

I step out of the car, my boots crunching on the gravel beneath my feet. I take a deep breath of fresh air. The smells of the nearby farmlands makes me nostalgic to go home. I haven't been to my ranch in more than a month. I stifle the nostalgia. If I can get through this, get through talking to Dacotah, then I can bring her there.

I look around, noting that no one is around, and I'm thankful for that. I don't want to make a scene, though I've already done that throughout town.

I step up the couple of steps to the porch and notice that the door just has a handle on it. I open it, stepping inside and noticing the porch swing on one end and two plastic chairs surrounding a table on the other end. I smile at the pretty purple flowers resting in the vase.

I walk up to the door, press the doorbell, and then follow it up with a knock.

Nothing.

After a few heartbeats, I do it again.

Nothing.

The emptiness of the house is radiating over my skin and I know she's not home, even the absence of a vehicle told me that, but sometimes you'd be surprised.

Again I ring and knock and nothing. No sounds coming from inside the house.

I bang my head against the door and it rattles. For curiosity's sake, I try the doorknob, but it is locked. I also notice that there is no realtor lock box. Then I roll my eyes, it's a small town, that kind of thing isn't needed around here.

I decide to settle in and wait for her to come home.

I step out of the porch and down the steps. I'm headed back toward my car when something catches the corner of my eye and I look in its direction.

Some distance away there is someone, a woman, with chocolate brown hair tossing bales of hay around. Rachel?

I squint, but I can't tell. I start walking toward her, maybe, if its her, I can get some answers.

It seems like it takes forever, then she finally sees me, then looks pointedly toward my car then back at me again.

"Hi Derek," she says as I draw closer to her.

"Rachel, I assume?"

"The one and only." She cocks her head. "What are you doing here?"

I give her a half smile and cock my head at her. "What do you think?"

She gives me a sad smile. "She's not here."

"I can tell by the lack of response to my persistent pounding on her door."

"No, I mean she's gone, Derek." My heart sinks. "She left out of here yesterday."

"Where'd she go?" She shrugs. "Come on, Rachel, you're her best friend, how can you not know?"

"Easy, she's a grown woman, capable of making decisions for herself. She doesn't need my permission."

"No, but she put her house on the market, she quit her job, and she doesn't plan on coming back here."

"How'd-? Well the house, yeah, but the job?"

I snort. "I ran into her friend Jason."

"Oh shit." She covers her mouth to stifle her giggle. "How'd that go?"

I smirked back at her. "I don't think you'll be seeing much of him anymore and I get the impression that he's not exactly wanted at Pete's." I raise an eyebrow at her.

"Um, no, he's not. Dacotah made her decision to leave on Sunday after returning from Pete's. She went off about what happened and then she realized that if she stayed here that there would be no escaping him going forward. I respected her decision. When I asked her where she was going to go, she just shrugged. She's been wanting out of this town for years, even before all this bullshit with Jason."

"Where would she go, Rachel?"

She shrugs. "Honestly, she is either in Minneapolis or on a plane on her way to Europe." She gives me a rather pointed stare.

"What did she say, on the plane?"

Rachel's eyes sadden. "She about lost it when we pulled away from the gate. She said she swore she saw you, but then she couldn't get off."

"She did see me. I was there, just...'

"You went after her?" Her voice comes out in a high squeak.

"Yes Rachel, she left me without even a good-bye, I needed to know why, but I couldn't get there fast enough, she had a good head start. I was standing on the jet way as the plane backed away."

"So why has it taken you until now to show up?"

I sigh. "I couldn't avoid the trip to Paris, I had to go, though I didn't actually have to go in the long run and I hate it. Otherwise I would have been here Sunday afternoon."

"Derek, I wish I knew what to tell you. But unless she decides to start calling someone and letting us know where she is, I don't know what to tell you. I've left her several messages, sent texts and nothing."

"I know; her voicemail is full."

She cocks her head at me. "She said you didn't have her number."

I shake my head. "It's not important. I'm staying at the motel."

"Ugh, how's that for you?"

"Awful," I grumble, "But if she'd been here, I wasn't going to force myself on her."

"She loves you. She hates herself for leaving like she did. She thought it was the right idea at the time."

"We left a lot unsaid between us before we fell asleep. I didn't expect her to be gone when I woke up."

"Is that why you're so determined to find her?"

I frown. "That and I have her necklace."

The skies open up and it starts to rain. "Come on, let's go inside," she says pointing toward her house.

I nod, though the rain feels nice. But the sadness washing over me is almost too much to handle.

My phone starts to ring. I pull it from my pocket. It's Dana. "Hunter."

"It's done. They will be sending everything to her via email."

"Great, thank you."

"Her phone is on, sir."

My heart does a million flip flops. "Where?"

"On Highway thirty-five, moving south toward Oklahoma City."

"She's driving?"

"Appears so, sir." I roll my eyes.

"Thanks, Dana."

I end the call without the pleasantries. "Call her." Both Rachel and I say together.

"I can't. Will you call her, find out what the fuck she's doing driving toward Oklahoma City?"

Her eyes widen. "She's driving? How do you know?"

I give her a pointed look. "I am a man of many resources."

"I gather. What do you want me to find out?"

"Where she's going."

She nods. "Alright." She pulls her phone from her pocket.

"But do not tell her that I'm here."

"Why?"

"Because, I want to be able to do this right. I need to go after her and I need to know where it is that she's going in order to do that."

Rachel gives me the puppy dog eyes and I fight the need to roll mine.

She presses some button on her phone. "Speaker," I whisper.

She does and then the front room is filled with a ringing phone.

Ring.

Ring.

Click.

"Hi." Her voice fills the room and I nearly fall over.

"Hi there. What are you doing?"

A snort comes through the phone. "Driving."

"Driving, where to?"

"I'm almost to OKC."

"Why there?"

Laughter fills the room and I become dizzy with the sound. "I'm not staying there."

"Then where are you going?"

62

Torture...

Three days later...

Standing at the door, I can hear commotion on the other side and the sound of feet running down stairs.

The door finally swings open and I'm greeted by Tristan. "About time," I tease him.

"Ha-ha." He takes my hand.

"How was your flight?"

"Private." He snickers.

"How are you?" He shuts the door.

"Overrun by females." He smirks.

"Is she here?"

He nods his answer. "In the living room with Cami and Jaden." He smiles at me.

"Does she know?"

He shakes his head then ushers me up the steps. I step aside, allowing him to go first. "Tristan? Who is it?" I hear Cami ask.

He doesn't answer, just bounds up the steps and I follow after him. Equally as quick, desperate to see my girl. To talk to her. Damn it. Fear races through me as I feel like I'm going to get rejected again.

I round the corner. Fear and excitement balance each other out as I step around the corner.

63

Replete...
***** Dacotah *****

Tristan bounds into the room, scooping Jaden off of the floor and twirls him around the room. Fits of joyful child giggles fill the air and I watch, laughing to myself at the excitement on both of their faces. "Tristan, he just ate," Cami scolds, but Tristan doesn't stop.

I watch them, until the hairs on the back of my neck come to stand on end. A feeling I haven't felt in so long, but I rub at the back of my neck absently. The last time I felt this was when Orion would approach me, but Cami assured me, over and over again, that he wasn't coming. If he was, I don't think I would have agreed to come. I can't bare the idea of seeing him again. It would destroy me. Who am I kidding, I'm already shattered.

My eyes meet Cami's and there is an excitement in them that I hadn't expected to see. My skin prickles again, and then suddenly there is a hand on my shoulder.

I jump, free myself of the chair, and nearly stumble in my haste to turn around.

My knees go weak; my breath leaves me in a wild rush. "Orion," I manage to squeak as I crumble.

"Hello gorgeous," he greets as he catches me and I can feel Tristan and Cami retreat into the kitchen, leaving us alone.

"What...how? Why?" I can't manage anything coherent to say.

His hand comes to my chin, bringing my face up to look at him. My eyes burn with tears. His arm is around me, holding me, comforting me. "What am I doing here?" I nod. "I was invited to a birthday party. How? Easy, I own a plane, remember?" I nod again. "Why? Because..." Words fail him and tears blur my vision of him. His beautiful face, his hair loose around his face, it looks a little shorter, but his eyes are the beautiful milk chocolate that makes my heart melt. "Because I love you."

My heart goes flying into a million mile an hour sprint. My breathing is quick and shallow, my mind is blank. Then without warning, his lips are crushing into mine. Lightning and fire race through my veins, causing shivers to radiate from deep down to race over my body. My hand comes up to cup his cheek, pulling him closer, tighter against me. It's not enough as the fire licks my broken heart, healing it, making it whole once again.

"And," he breathes. Our contact is broken when he moves his hand from my chin, looking for something in his pocket. "You forgot something," He says softly, his breath caressing my heated skin. He hands me a hunter green pocket square. I cock an eyebrow at him. "Open it."

I do, and wrapped up inside is my necklace, my grandmother's necklace, the one I'd left in my haste to leave him nearly a week ago.

His hand comes to finger the necklace I'm currently wearing and I can see his own tears welling up in his eyes. "I've already got one," I breathe and his lips crush into mine.

"I've missed you," he breathes against my lips. "Please, don't run away from me again. I can't take it." His eyes are pleading. The demanding, controlling man is gone, replaced by someone who is sincere and who loves me.

"I won't."

"Good. Dacotah?"

"Yes?"

"Will you go to Paris with me?" His voice is soft and I melt into him.

"I thought you'd never ask me again." I kiss him again, this time a little more chaste as I can see Jaden coming at us at lightning speed. My eyes dart to look at Derek. Derek stands up quickly.

"Jaden," he coos and the toddler jumps into Derek's arms. "How's my buddy?"

Our trance is effectively broken, for now.

My heart swells as I realize the man that I love has gone to great lengths to find me, to track me down, and it sends a thrill of heat, need and overwhelming joy through my heart.

I look at Cami. She's prepared for anger, but I only smile and mouth thank you.

She smiles a wide, overly excited smile.

I look at my hunter as he plays with Jaden and my heart fills to near bursting when I realize that he's come back, come for me, and that he is mine to keep, forever.

He sets Jaden down, who goes running toward his mom, and I walk over to wrap my arms around Orion. He wraps his arm around me, holding me to him. "We're really going to Paris?"

The biggest smile I've ever seen on his face spreads wider still. "Paris, Rome, London, anywhere you want to go, we will go."

"Let's start with Paris, shall we?"

"Paris it is."

Then his lips are on mine, crushing me with love, passion, desire and need. He's back, in my arms, and most importantly- he is ALL mine.

Epilogue

Epic...
An Epilogue
Two Years Later...

Paris was amazing. Derek made good on his promise and took me atop the Eiffel Tower. I thought it was odd that we were the only ones up top, that was until he lifted my skirt and reenacted our Vegas night. Only this time it was far more romantic. It was Paris after all. We spent the next year roaming around Europe in-between jaunts back to the states for business related events. The entire trip put more than thirty stamps into my passport. But my favorite stamp is the one we added in Bora Bora when Derek took me to Tarah with Tristan, Cami and Jaden. The week we spent on a private island with just the five of us, was amazing. That was the weekend that Derek proposed. Of course, I said yes and we were married a few short weeks later on top of the Eiffel Tower in Paris. It was quaint and beautiful and absolutely perfect.

Rachel and Mandy were there, of course. They've been so supportive of my relationship with Derek and the fact that we haven't seen each other too much doesn't seem to bother them. Which is okay, but I do miss them like crazy.

It was two years ago this weekend that Derek propositioned me in Vegas and tonight we're going out to dinner to celebrate. I have my own surprise for him this year.

"Are you ready, love?" I look up into Derek's eyes, and even after two years, the milk chocolate still steals my breath away when I look into them. The depth in those beautiful brown eyes is beyond anything. It's like I can see straight into his soul.

"I am." I take his offered arm. He refused to let me know where we were going tonight, but told me that I needed to dress up.

We're back in Vegas, which seems to be where we always are during this week, and I love that attention to detail. I'm still thrown by the overly romantic and sappy side of a hard CEO. But his ability to separate personal from business is uncanny and it makes me love him more. I'm not even sure that it is possible anymore, but somehow he manages it.

We take the elevator down to the lobby. He then leads me to through the doors and into our favorite stretch Hummer limo.

Once we're settled in, I turn to Orion. "Are you going to tell me where we're going?"

He smirks at me. "No."

I huff. "That's so not fair, you know?"

"I know, but it's fun." We both laugh and he pulls me closer into his side. This is one of my favorite places to be. Well, aside from on top of or under him.

"Cami called me today." It may seem random, but I have a method to my madness.

"She did? How is she?"

I smile. "Pregnant."

He laughs. "Are you serious?"

I giggle a nervous laugh. "Yeah, she said she's about four months."

"It's about time they gave Jaden a little brother or sister." I can tell he's still smiling. Which is good.

"Yea, I thought for sure it would be sooner than this, but, I'm really happy for them. She said Tristan is over the moon."

Orion laughs. "I don't doubt that. He adores Jaden and I imagine them having at least one more after this one."

"Derek?"

He looks down at me, his eyes are bright with excitement. "Yes, love?"

"Do you want kids?"

He frowns slightly, but his eyes are still excited. "Cotah, we've been married for a year and you're just now asking me a question like that?"

My heart sinks a little bit. I shrug. "I never really thought about it, not until now. I always knew that I love kids, but I was neither here nor there when it came to having children."

His hand comes to cup my face, holding me to him. "Of course, I want children. I didn't know that I wanted them until I met you. Everything in my life has changed since we met two years ago."

"Is that a good thing?"

He smiles. "Absolutely. There is nothing about the last two years I wouldn't change, Cotah. I've grown and changed so much since you stepped into my life. Everything has been made better between us by the fact that we get along so unbelievably well. I always knew that what my parents had was special, but I never imagined I'd find that for myself. You support me in everything I do. You're always there for me when I need you, and you know that I will do anything to make sure your dreams come true."

The tears well in my eyes at his speech and knowing that his love is unconditional makes it all the sweeter, and it makes what I'm about to say next that much easier.

"Orion," He smiles at my nickname for him. Something that I call him more than I call him Derek. That look will never grow old for me. "There is nothing I wouldn't do to make you happy. Nothing I wouldn't fight for, and more importantly, the fact that each and every day I'm with you, my impossibly full heart grows fuller. It is to the point of bursting with the love I feel for you, but I know that I will have to find a way to squeeze more love into my life."

He cocks his head at me.

"I'm really glad you want to have a family because..." The tears overwhelm my eyes.

"Cotah?"

"Oh hell, I didn't expect this to be so hard."

He squeezes me tighter to his side. "You know you can tell me anything. There is nothing you can say or do that we can't work through, that we can't survive. My love is forever yours."

I give him a half smile. "Well, I'm going to have to share it because we're pregnant."

I watch him closely, but he sweeps me off the seat, managing to position me on his lap. His arms wrap tightly around me and he buries his face into my hair. "God, I love you," he says against my neck. I wrap my arms around his neck, holding him close to me.

"Orion, you're my life, my everything, my entire world."

We stay in this embrace for several minutes, not moving, just enjoying and loving each other.

I never knew what happily ever after would feel like until this moment. It is amazing, sensual and fulfilling in every way imaginable. I know that every day, for the rest of my life, I will love him and he will love me. No matter what happens between us, we will survive and thrive off of each other. Derek has given me my life and it is more than anything I could have hoped for.

I squeeze him tighter against me and he returns the squeeze. I can feel the silent shakes of his body and the warm wetness against my shoulders. I pull back, looking at him. "What's wrong?"

"Just when I thought I couldn't love you more, I realize that I love you so much more than should be possible. You're my everything, Dacotah." I smile and crush my lips to him. Devouring him in my own happily ever after.

The End!

www.ingramcontent.com/pod-product-compliance
Lightning Source LLC
Chambersburg PA
CBHW051519250626
47156CB00001B/146